STAR WARS

STAR WARS
RETURN OF THE JEDI

FROM A CERTAIN POINT OF VIEW

SALADIN AHMED ALI HAZELWOOD
CHARLIE JANE ANDERS PATRICIA A. JACKSON
TOM ANGLEBERGER ALEX JENNINGS
K ARSENAULT RIVERA MARY KENNEY
KRISTIN BAVER JARRETT J. KROSOCZKA
OLIVIE BLAKE SARAH KUHN
AKEMI DAWN BOWMAN DANNY LORE
EMMA MIEKO CANDON SARAH GLENN MARSH
OLIVIA CHADHA KWAME MBALIA
GLORIA CHAO MARIEKE NIJKAMP
MIKE CHEN DANIELLE PAIGE
ADAM CHRISTOPHER LAURA POHL
PAUL CRILLEY DANA SCHWARTZ
AMAL EL-MOHTAR TARA SIM
M. K. ENGLAND PHIL SZOSTAK
JASON FRY SUZANNE WALKER
ADAM LANCE GARCIA HANNAH WHITTEN
LAMAR GILES FRAN WILDE
MAX GLADSTONE SEAN WILLIAMS
THEA GUANZON ALYSSA WONG

PENGUIN BOOKS

STAR WARS
RETURN OF THE JEDI

FROM A CERTAIN POINT OF VIEW

PENGUIN BOOKS

UK | USA | Canada | Ireland | Australia
India | New Zealand | South Africa

Penguin Books is part of the Penguin Random House group of companies
whose addresses can be found at global.penguinrandomhouse.com

Penguin Random House UK,
One Embassy Gardens, 8 Viaduct Gardens, London SW11 7BW

penguin.co.uk

First published in the US by Random House Worlds 2023
First published in the UK by Del Rey 2023
Published in Penguin Books 2025
001

Copyright © Lucasfilm Ltd. & ® or ™ where indicated, 2023
All rights reserved

The moral right of the authors has been asserted

Penguin Random House values and supports copyright. Copyright fuels creativity, encourages diverse voices, promotes freedom of expression and supports a vibrant culture. Thank you for purchasing an authorised edition of this book and for respecting intellectual property laws by not reproducing, scanning or distributing any part of it by any means without permission. You are supporting authors and enabling Penguin Random House to continue to publish books for everyone. No part of this book may be used or reproduced in any manner for the purpose of training artificial intelligence technologies or systems. In accordance with Article 4(3) of the DSM Directive 2019/790, Penguin Random House expressly reserves this work from the text and data mining exception.

Illustrations on the following pages by Chris Trevas: vii, 17, 53, 63, 97, 155, 175, 183, 193, 207, 251, 267, 283, 313, 347, 357, 391, 409, 419, 461, 511, 525, 557

Book Design by Elizabeth A. D. Eno

Printed and bound in Great Britain by Clays Ltd, Elcograf S.p.A.

The authorised representative in the EEA is Penguin Random House Ireland,
Morrison Chambers, 32 Nassau Street, Dublin D02 YH68

A CIP catalogue record for this book is available from the British Library

ISBN: 978-1-804-94446-2

Penguin Random House is committed to a sustainable future
for our business, our readers and our planet. This book is made from
Forest Stewardship Council® certified paper.

CONTENTS

Any Work Worth Doing by Amal El-Mohtar 3
Fancy Man by Phil Szostak 17
The Key to Remembering by Olivia Chadha 37
Fortuna Favors the Bold by Kwame Mbalia 53
Dune Sea Songs of Salt and Moonlight by Thea Guanzon 63
The Plan by Saladin Ahmed 97
Reputation by Tara Sim 111
Kickback by K Arsenault Rivera 121
Everyone's a Critic by Sarah Glenn Marsh 129
Satisfaction by Kristin Baver 143
My Mouth Never Closes by Charlie Jane Anders 155
Kernels and Husks by Jason Fry 163
The Light That Falls by Akemi Dawn Bowman 175
From a Certain Point of View by Alex Jennings 183
No Contingency by Fran Wilde 193
The Burden of Leadership by Danny Lore 207
Gone to the Winner's Circle by Patricia A. Jackson 221
One Normal Day by Mary Kenney 231
Divine (?) Intervention by Paul Crilley 251
The Buy-In by Suzanne Walker 267
The Man Who Captured Luke Skywalker by Max Gladstone 283
Ackbar by Jarrett J. Krosoczka 293
The Impossible Flight of Ash Angels by Marieke Nijkamp 297

CONTENTS

Ending Protocol by Hannah Whitten 313
The Last Flight by Ali Hazelwood 329
Twenty and Out by Lamar Giles 347
The Ballad of Nanta by Sarah Kuhn 357
Then Fall, Sidious by Olivie Blake 371
Impact by Sean Williams 381
Trooper Trouble by Laura Pohl 391
To the Last by Dana Schwartz 409
The Emperor's Red Guards by Gloria Chao 419
Wolf Trap by Alyssa Wong 431
The Extra Five Percent by M. K. England 447
When Fire Marked the Sky by Emma Mieko Candon 461
The Chronicler by Danielle Paige 477
The Veteran by Adam Lance Garcia 511
Brotherhood by Mike Chen 525
The Steadfast Soldier by Adam Christopher 537
Return of the Whills by Tom Angleberger 557

A long time ago in a galaxy far, far away. . . .

FROM A CERTAIN POINT OF VIEW

ANY WORK WORTH DOING
Amal El-Mohtar

I hope so, Commander, for your sake. The Emperor is not as forgiving as I am.

Lord Vader had forgiven him, then. Moff Tiaan Jerjerrod watched him go for longer than was strictly necessary. He would allow no detail to escape him. The rhythm of Vader's boots against the hangar bay floor; the sway of his cloak behind him; the precision of his gait, never hurried and never slow. The pace of inevitability.

He watched him go, then turned on his heel and matched that gait, that rhythm, exactly. Let everyone assembled see harmony in the choreography of their parting; let them see how aligned are Jerjerrod and Vader, how attuned, marching to the same silent, powerful music.

Let them see Jerjerrod as he thought of himself: not as Vader's inferior, but as his instrument.

As he walked out of the hangar bay, Jerjerrod allowed himself a single dissonant, unbecoming thought: He had lied directly to Lord Vader, and lived.

The lie was innocent enough: They would not, in fact, be doubling their efforts. They couldn't. Jerjerrod was no mathematician, but he took pride in his work, and he knew the scope of the project well enough to recognize that doubling their *efforts* wouldn't result in an operational Death Star by the appointed time. Effort was messy, inchoate; a poor swimmer could thrash his limbs against a lake until his lungs gave out and not advance any farther or faster than a fine swimmer breathing evenly. It wasn't a matter of effort expended, but of efficiency. Of technique.

Vader knew this, of course, whether or not he realized it. Jerjerrod had learned from watching him over the years. More powerful in the Force than anyone alive save the Emperor; capable, no doubt, of ripping men's limbs from their bodies with a thought, of striking them down with his lightsaber, of crushing them into compacted fists of meat and bone and wringing blood from the stone of them—and what did he do, instead?

He obstructed a single airway between his thumb and forefinger. Like playing a flute.

Jerjerrod enjoyed music. He wondered if Vader did.

He had wondered, too—more than once—what it felt like. What it might feel like. Ever since Piett's promotion to admiral, he'd allowed his thoughts to drift toward the possibility of failing Vader so utterly as to court that particular consequence. Whether he'd experience it as a bone in the throat, plugging him up from within and nothing more—whether it might overwhelm him like an ocean wave, smothering him—or whether he'd feel, in his last moments, leather against his skin, retreating from the ruin of his neck like a caress.

Perhaps I can find new ways to motivate them.

He did not allow himself to shiver until he knew he was out of sight.

Jerjerrod's quarters were spare by the standards of most officers, lacking the plush comforts his rank might have afforded him elsewhere in terms of furnishings and décor. As it was, he had a bed—standard issue, slim as the cots the workers slept in—bare walls, and a draft table large enough to accommodate his peculiar affectations.

It had somewhat embarrassed Jerjerrod, ever since his student days, that schematics made more sense to him if he could touch them. He found it much easier to hold vast structures inside his mind if he could first apprehend them in two dimensions. He often did this on large datapads, but he preferred, wherever possible, to produce them on archaic physical media that he could hold flat beneath his palms, before activating the relevant holoprojections to flicker and pulse before him. Otherwise, the projections distracted him; he found it difficult to move past the smooth, false promise of a completed façade until he'd absorbed the plans with his hands.

He'd been mocked for this in his youth, of course, as if it betrayed some immaturity, some lagging development: a child still mouthing the words of a story under his breath as he read. But as an adult, he'd cultivated this into a quaint but acceptable eccentricity: A large part of his discretionary funds were spent on reams of flimsiplast, the more antique in quality the better.

More embarrassing was the truth: There was an intimacy to the process he couldn't explain. In his first year as a recruit Jerjerrod had trained in basic field medicine, and it had struck him at the time that when a body was brought to him to treat, he saw it as a broken machine in need of fixing: Here it leaked fluid, there its circuits needed patching, or else the whole was scrap that couldn't even be reused. Jerjerrod learned early on that he couldn't bear waste.

He had followed this insight into a study of engineering, and from there to grander architectures—but to his surprise, once surrounded by machines, every schematic began to look to him like a body. Every project had a beating heart, a nervous system, fibers flexing beneath a sheath of skin; every project needed to be comprehended as an organism struggling to be born. He sometimes drew them as he imagined them—he never gave them faces, that would be several steps too far, but he felt compelled to give them some comprehensible personhood. He made his peace with this, and disliked speaking of it—but whenever he needed to focus on a problem, to understand it so profoundly that the solution arrived like breathing, he would roll out lengths of flimsiplast in his quarters and spend hours running his fingers over diagrammed lines as if he could coax from them a gasp or shudder of revelation.

So it was with the DS-II battle station. The project was too vast to lay out in one sheet, but he'd built a model of it that he could split open and lock shut when he wanted to be able to shift his perspective on something, and he'd mapped out key areas by hand with reference to it when he wanted to understand a projection from the inside out. As he smoothed out these reference drawings, his eye was first drawn, as always, to the improvements he'd made to the orbital station's unfortunate predecessor. They pulsed bright in his mind: Instead of the angry red area around a single thermal exhaust port wailing its treacherous vulnerability, he'd insisted on a capillary system for venting exhaust, discarding dozens of designs in pursuit of the correct one. Now millions of minuscule tubes would stretch from core to

ANY WORK WORTH DOING

surface, allowing the DS-II to breathe. He'd also built choke points and fail-safes to prevent the kind of catastrophic chain reaction that had doomed the original; now the system had the elegance of a Coruscanti necklace, with each bead or gem individually knotted in place such that one section could break without ruining the whole.

He was proud of his improvements. In theory, the completed DS-II would exceed its elder sibling by every relevant metric: power, efficiency, invincibility. But in practice, the angles of one stubborn geometry refused to meet.

There was simply no way to complete construction of the DS-II in the time frame allotted with the resources he'd been given. Its beating heart: the thrum of the generators. Its nervous system: the complex circuitries that would eventually resonate with kyber frequencies. Its lifeblood: for now, merely workers, flowing through its nascent corridors, building out its veins and arteries. The DS-II was anemic. He'd asked for more troops, and been denied; the Emperor had made quite clear that he could not ask for more time. So it fell to him to do the impossible.

He thought of Vader's cape, swaying behind him.

Jerjerrod went to work.

He traced the contours of the plans. The DS-II ached beneath his hands. He could feel tension gathering in several key muscle groups—work areas—threatening to spasm into problems, delays, ruptures. He'd pushed the men hard, but if they broke now, there was no replacing them.

Perhaps to do the impossible, he had to do the unexpected.

As he studied the diagrams, he drafted new shift rotations, changed their shapes: Instead of tight clusters of furious effort running so hot they'd burn out, he lengthened and stretched the groups to be more flexible, to ramp on and off from different key areas. He didn't have more men, but he did have plentiful shuttles gathering dust in the hangars; he would requisition them to move workers more quickly across wider areas, such that the journey itself would provide some relief without interrupting the overall workflow.

It could work, given a comprehensive enough vision; he'd relax the pressure in some sectors by raising it in others, and keep redistributing it as it collected. Instead of cracking a whip, he'd be an iron hand in a supple glove, massaging the deep tissue of the project until it released its secrets.

In practice, this meant keener oversight. It meant pacing the corridors, seeing while being seen. Not a distraction, but a reminder of regularity. A metronome, perhaps—no, a conductor, shifting the melody line from one part of the station to another.

Jerjerrod closed his eyes, rubbed his temples. His metaphors were blurring into each other, as if he could solve the problem by simply finding the right one. But it wouldn't be enough. This method would help—but if he wanted to meet the Emperor's deadline, he needed a true force multiplier.

Which, of course, the Emperor had already sent.

His fingers hovered over the specs for Vader's meditation chamber—low cost and high priority, long since completed.

He drew a line from that chamber outward, wound it through the battle station's corridors and walkways. Committed it to memory. Straightened, tugged at the hem of his uniform, and left his quarters.

Jerjerrod had heard it whispered among other officers that beneath his armor, Vader was broken, burned—a husk of a man animated by the Force. He recalled a dinner at some Imperial function years before when, deep in their cups, the Admiralty had grown freer with their opinions of the man.

"You've seen it, then? The tank?"

ANY WORK WORTH DOING

"Aye, I've seen it, I've seen it. You have to look away before he knows you've seen it, though. Convince yourself you haven't, so he doesn't sniff out your thoughts and catch you staring. Think of your mother, or the last person you killed—"

"One and the same for you, eh, Admiral?"

Laughter, and then—silence.

"It's horrible," the admiral had said, quietly. "It's truly horrible. Red, peeling, wet. Cooked meat soaking in a bucket."

The conversation had faltered, after that; the officers made their excuses, retired to bed. But in the wake of that dinner Jerjerrod had found himself feeling helplessly furious—furious at the violation of privacy, the indignity. Furious on Vader's behalf—but also on his own. The talk offended him. Whatever else Vader was—whoever else he might have been—he was an organizing principle of Jerjerrod's world, as fundamental to the Empire as oxygen or gravity. In Vader he served a dense and obliterating certainty. He would not allow these vulgar mutterings to deface the hard, reflective lines of Vader's elegance and power.

And he wouldn't intrude on his meditation chamber. He waited, instead, until Vader emerged, and fell into measured and purposeful step beside him. Vader turned to him, implacable, but did not slow his stride.

"An ambush, Commander? I did not think you had the leisure available to loiter outside my quarters."

It was difficult to tell whether Vader was amused or annoyed. Jerjerrod chose not to expend the effort in determining which it was.

"Lord Vader," he said, simply, "I wondered if we might discuss the project's acceleration. I have some propositions—"

"I am not interested in a catalog of your failures, Commander."

"Understandable, Lord Vader. But could I interest you in a guided tour of them?"

Vader stopped, abruptly. Jerjerrod matched him. While Vader remained silent, staring down at him, Jerjerrod waited—took a shallow, experimental breath—found it still unimpeded. He struggled to remain serene.

"My apologies, Lord Vader—I took quite seriously your offer of motivating the men. Should I not have?"

Vader stood silent a moment longer, then crossed his arms.

"What exactly did you have in mind, Commander?"

Jerjerrod put quite a lot of effort into keeping his expression neutral.

"Just a walk."

They walked in silence, paused in full view of the workers, took shuttles and lifts from section to section as necessary, following the map in Jerjerrod's head. If the DS-II was anemic, what better injection of iron than Vader, swallowing light on the walkways?

Jerjerrod brought Vader to those places most in need of agitation. Of *motivation*. He'd carefully planned a route that took them through sectors where workers were due to rotate off, areas where they were already experienced enough to do their tasks by rote, and let the sight of Vader grip them with fresh energy. Meanwhile Jerjerrod gestured toward the crews, explained the relevant areas under construction, waited for Vader's nod, then moved on: tactically, strategically, never lingering longer than necessary. He was pleased to feel the hum of renewed activity in their wake.

"This is adequate work, Commander," said Vader, suddenly. "What, in your estimation, has caused the delays?"

Jerjerrod framed his reply carefully. He'd already said the project's timeline was impossible; Vader knew that, and he didn't need to re-

ANY WORK WORTH DOING

peat it. Hear the question behind the question, then: *Why is it taking so much longer than its predecessor?*

The worst of that was, it *wasn't*. They'd made truly extraordinary efficiencies in the new plan; he'd seen to that. The Emperor had insisted it be larger, which was puzzling, but Jerjerrod presumed there were reasons for it. No, given all the upgrades and expansions, it ought to have been astonishing that they were approaching completion on this time frame at all.

But all else being equal, he knew what the biggest adjustment had been, and he gambled on it being the answer to Vader's actual question.

"The venting system," he said. "It took time to assess the extent of Galen Erso's sabotage from his plans—how many systems were compromised by that small detail. Our solution was complex, but once it's complete, this Death Star will vent heat almost as efficiently as skin while being absolutely impenetrable. Fitting that system is much more difficult, more specialized work, but I'm confident it will be worthwhile."

"Worthwhile—to eliminate the possibility of the rebels repeating themselves."

Jerjerrod blinked, startled. "Well—"

"You would be better served, Commander, by doing what the Emperor has asked of you rather than dwelling on past defeats."

"Respectfully, Lord Vader," said Jerjerrod, before he could stop himself, "I—"

"Commander, *you are wasting your time,* and by extension, you are wasting mine."

There could be no sharper rebuke. Jerjerrod stood, stunned, as Vader spun on his heel and left, marveling at how thoroughly Vader had stolen his breath without using the Force at all.

Back to his quarters, then, and to clenching plans in his fists. Reports poured in from all over the station, marking various efficiencies, time gained, tasks completed ahead of schedule—all of it worthless, insufficient. *Waste.* He swept reams of flimsiplast to the ground, disgusted, sat down hard on the edge of his bed, and sank his head between his knees.

There was some test he was failing here, some puzzle he wasn't meant to solve.

He returned to the beginning.

He asks the impossible. There were three variables in play: resources, time, and operability. He had no flexibility with resources or with time. There could certainly not be any flexibility about operation: The Death Star was either complete, or it wasn't.

Unless—

He lifted his head, slowly. What could *operational* be made to mean?

The Death Star's chief operation was its firepower, of course—and relative to the scale of building a battle station two hundred kilometers in diameter, completing the superlaser array was almost trivial. But in every outline he'd sent for approval, the laser was explicitly designed to be activated in the final phase of construction—only *after* all the improvements he'd designed were in place for its protection.

But—was that strictly necessary? Structurally, no—they already had the deflector shields generated from the moon. He'd only followed the same production template Director Krennic had, relegating the superlaser to the third and final phase of construction. It made sense for a host of precautionary reasons—but perhaps they could be revisited.

He spread the discarded flimsiplast out on the ground, knelt to

ANY WORK WORTH DOING

examine it more closely. Yes—with what had already been built, the superlaser *could* be made operational well within the Emperor's constraints, if he diverted almost every available resource to it. But—if that was what the Emperor wanted, why not simply say so? Why make a riddle of it?

And then he remembered: The first Death Star had been meant to be a *secret* weapon. Enemy action, arrogance, and error in the ranks had shown the Emperor's hand too soon. Suppose, then, that the Emperor wished its main purpose to be hidden in plain sight? What if this battle station's appearance—scaffold-ridden, incomplete, vulnerable, a fragmented yawning at the void of space—was meant to be a lie?

We shall double our efforts.

Follow that thought, then, chase it. To sell the lie, there could be no pause in the work. The Emperor *wanted* the appearance of thrashing in the water, the appearance of drowning—not to bring the project to completion, but to disguise what should already be complete. And Jerjerrod couldn't be told directly—because he was not, in fact, the conductor of this orchestra. He was the baton in Vader's hand.

It clicked into place. All of Jerjerrod's defenses, fail-safes, economies, efficiencies: They *were* a waste, except as distractions for spies. The timeline made no sense because the Emperor operated on a different one. Jerjerrod was building defensively while the Emperor was preparing an ambush. He needed only two things from Jerjerrod: the superlaser, and the flustered animation of working under impossible constraints. The appearance of failure.

Vader wasn't here to put him back on schedule, but to provide a wholly different one. The Emperor's arrival would be not a rebuke, but a lure.

He covered the bed in flimsiplast. He wouldn't be sleeping in it anytime soon.

Jerjerrod entered Vader's meditation chamber rumpled and exhausted, but with a glint in his eyes somewhere between manic and euphoric. He stood at attention near the entrance until Vader emerged to meet him.

"Lord Vader," he said, inclining his head and offering up a datapad, "I am here to report that without more workers the Death Star can only be completed outside the Emperor's stated parameters. I've taken the liberty of drawing up a list of sectors that will be operational within them, for your eyes only, but I have serious concerns about the rest of the production schedule."

"You've doubled your efforts?" said Vader, taking the datapad, but not looking at it. He looked at Jerjerrod.

"We have. As you'll see, I've eliminated several rest periods and redeployed workers on sixteen-hour shifts over twenty-hour cycles. Their work will suffer for it, and I've factored in an anticipated four percent loss of labor due to increases in accidents and exhaustion. But it simply cannot be done, Lord Vader. Moreover, I'm concerned that if this information is leaked we will present an irresistible target for rebel operations."

"This is quite a comprehensive portrait of your failure. The Emperor will be most disappointed in you, Commander."

"And you, Lord Vader?"

"What about me?"

Jerjerrod straightened his back and raised his eyes to what passed for Vader's.

"Are you disappointed?"

During the silence that followed, Jerjerrod held his breath. He didn't look toward Vader's hands or the shapes they made—only his own reflection distorted across the planes of Vader's helmet.

ANY WORK WORTH DOING

Then Vader stepped toward him.

"Any work worth doing, Commander," he said, "is worth doing well. See to it that you remember that." He held out the datapad; as Jerjerrod reached for it, it crumpled inward on itself like a flower, just shy of his fingers. He swallowed, thickly.

"I will, Lord Vader," he said, quietly. Vader brushed past him and left his chamber.

He watched Vader go for longer than was strictly necessary.

When the Emperor finally arrived, Jerjerrod knelt at Vader's right-hand side. When Vader rose, he rose with him. He fell into step behind him, feeling a different music encompassing them, aware that his conductor was being conducted now, aware of a commonality Vader would likely never consider they shared: They were, all of them, ultimately subject to this power, this orchestration.

Vader and the Emperor walked for a beat in silence. Jerjerrod felt something pass between the two of them, some close harmony of understanding. Then, for the assembly's benefit:

"The Death Star will be completed on schedule," said Vader.

"You have done well, Lord Vader," came the reply—and Jerjerrod stifled, smothered, the wild, whipping joy inside him before it could reach his face.

He'd been promised the Emperor's displeasure, his censure—but it was abundantly clear that the Emperor knew nothing of his existence. This was a task he'd entrusted to Vader, for his own reasons.

But Vader knew him. Vader threatened him with the Emperor, and by doing so, brought him into his silent symphony, his machinations within the strange wizardries of the Force. The Emperor and Vader together—they operated on different timelines, and also on different planes. When they made their concerns his concerns, he felt himself risen, straightened up, pulled into a realm beyond his understanding.

"As you wish," said Vader, and Jerjerrod felt the echo of it in his own mind.

As you wish, Lord Vader.

He followed them out of the hangar bay and walked to his post, to await his next commands.

FANCY MAN

Phil Szostak

Max Rebo took a moment to say goodbye, placing a prehensile foot upon his red ball jett organ, the one he had inherited from his father. A routine execution in the usual place, the Great Pit of Carkoon deep within Tatooine's Northern Dune Sea, had somehow gone horribly wrong. And a young man with a green laser sword was hacking his way through Jabba the Hutt's finest.

Or at least that was how the situation appeared to Max from his modest spot in the back of the room, squinting against the harsh desert sunlight coming through the shutters of the gangster's pleasure barge, until, without warning, they slammed shut. In that same instant, the overhead lights cut out, plunging the salon into darkness. Then somebody screamed. Max took that as his cue to leave.

Briefly, Max used all of his meager strength to try to drag his instrument toward the exit. But without a repulsor, it slid only centimeters across the wooden floor. That's when, in a moment of rare insight, Max knew he would never see or play that organ again.

The room was already half empty, guards and bounty hunters rushing for the stairwells and hatches to take their potshots at the escaping prisoners. Nevertheless, the band's beefy percussionists, Ak-rev and Umpass, remained, and an ill-timed scrap broke out between the two. After somehow managing to quell their dispute, Max heard heavy footfalls on the deck overhead as both blaster- and cannon fire echoed around the pit's steep sand dunes.

Stepping over Jabba's flailing translator droid, Max quickly found the door. Simple-minded sensualist though he may have been, Max was no fool, staying clear of the combat above by cutting through the barge's mazelike lower decks. There had to be some sort of escape craft somewhere down here, right?

And find them he did, although every last one of the snub-nosed swoops had already been deployed, save one. And that one was currently being mounted by the Max Rebo Band's co-lead vocalist, Joh Yowza, whom Max had not even realized was on board.

"Joh!" Max cried out over the din of the chaos, seeing that there was more than enough room for a diminutive Ortolan on the rear of the swoop's banana-shaped seat.

But the fuzzy Yuzzum just turned, string of pilfered sausages dangling from his wide mouth, flashed a rude gesture at Max, and with a guffaw launched the swoop through a hinged flap in the ship's outer hull, making his escape. *That snake!* Max thought, with a grimace.

This was it. Max girded his quavering loins, grabbed a long ladle from an empty slop pot in the vessel's cramped kitchen as some sort

FANCY MAN

of means of defense (momentarily considering following Joh's lead in raiding the galley's well-stocked stores before thinking better of it), and charged up the main staircase.

Fortuitously, by the time Max reached the deck, the fighting was all but over, the corpses of Jabba's various and sundry sentries scattered across the promenade. Han Solo's would-be savior whom the Hutt had captured the previous day was running into the arms of the laser-sword guy, who held one of the craft's many rigging ropes.

Dropping the ladle, Max took that opportunity to dash across the deck in the hope of reaching the forward railing and the soft warm sands below, well clear of the Sarlacc's gaping maw.

But he never reached it, as explosions rocked the sail barge, sending it leaning in the direction of the pit. Max slid along its smooth surface to his certain doom.

However, before he could slip under the port railing and into the pit, Max found himself launched into the air by a massive secondary explosion and its subsequent blast of red-hot air, emanating from under the deck. Max flew over the sands of the Dune Sea like a blue gumdrop torpedo. In that frozen moment from his sky-high vantage point, Max could see one of Jabba's cargo skiffs taking off in one direction as Joh's swoop sped for the horizon in the other.

He imagined his precious organ atomizing in an instant, enveloped by the fireball that, mere seconds before, was Jabba the Hutt's beloved yacht. And before everything went black, his mind drifted back to his home planet of Orto, where, several years earlier, this whole mess began.

Max Rebo descended the stairs at the back of Club Chedda, a vision in a white tuxedo and tails. A spotlight snapped on, signaling his arrival, and he shone with the brightness of a star. A wave of rapturous applause rose around him. The standing-room-only crowd was made up solely of fellow Ortolans, their faces beaming as much as a bug-eyed, long-nosed Ortolan face can beam, which is frankly not a lot.

To an offworlder, such an ovation would also sound somewhat muffled, emanating wholly from under the dark wood tables that surrounded Max (partly offset by the autonomic, but much quieter, flapping of an equal number of flippers). Yet to an Ortolan, especially a musician like Max, it was the most wonderful sound in the world.

At similar moments in his life as a performer, beads of sweat would invariably form on the back of his blubbery blue pate, running down his neck as he strode over to his doughnut-shaped organ. But he felt not a hint of nerves tonight. Equally unusual was the fact that he was clothed at all. Ortolans preferred to remain lightly attired, if not completely nude, despite the frigid average annual temperatures of their world. Clearly, it was a special night. And there he stood, black plom bloom at his breast, bowing briskly to every corner of the room as the cheers continued.

Max vaulted onto the cushion at the center of his instrument as gracefully as one could without arms. On cue, the keebada-shaped lamps that hung from the ceiling dimmed, window shutters gently closed, leaving only the glow of the stage light and the nightclub's signature crackling firepit. A hush fell over the audience, many of whom unconsciously held their breath in anticipation of his first note. As he gently laid his freshly lotioned toes upon the circle of keys before him, Max looked out beyond the spotlight's glare, meeting the eyes of the most beautiful woman he had ever seen, seated alone in a nearby booth. A scrumptious-looking but noticeably half-eaten plate of rare ronto prime rib, dripping with juices, lay on the white linen tablecloth before her. She smiled up at him with the warmth of great familiarity.

With that, Max began to play. Puzzlingly, he didn't dive into one of

FANCY MAN

any number of jatz standards he knew by heart but something completely new. Jatz was, of course, one of the most popular forms of performed and recorded music in the entire galaxy, including Outer Rim worlds such as Orto. It came to be known by many names, some less palatable than others, over time and across cultures. Improvisation within a known number was part and parcel of jatz musicianship. However, improvisation of an entirely new song, at a formal event, in front of a capacity crowd? This was very weird.

And the song he played had a much more complex, syncopated groove than his toes were used to, with a heavy emphasis on the downbeat. More galactic funk than jatz, and kilometers from the classical Ortolan that he grew up with. Max was as surprised as anyone. After four bars that established the bassline, a simple but catchy melody rang out in the key of cresh. Programming the hypnotic groove into the organ's onboard computer, Max soon added synthesized percussion and Kloo horns over the top. Every toe in the dinner discotheque was tapping, which, for dozens of Ortolans, is saying quite a lot.

Closing his eyes, Max could feel himself falling into a state of deeply focused but relaxed attention. It was blissful.

But no sooner did Max slip into that rare harmoniousness than a low, discordant sound crept into his music. Perhaps he had hit the wrong tone control switch or expression pedal? No. A distant voice, from somewhere across the room, and a gravelly, grating voice at that, called his name. "Rebo!" His brow furrowed, concentration completely broken. Perhaps if he kept his eyes closed

"Rebo!" the voice exclaimed, growing louder.

How rude! Max thought, his brow furrowing.

Opening one eye, Max watched as a Twi'lek with a sickly countenance made his way from the far end of the nightclub. Stuffed into an ill-fitting blue suit, he cut through rows of sunken booths, stepping angrily in his direction. Max immediately stopped playing and flushed a deep shade of purple. "Rebo!" the Twi'lek growled from between sharp little teeth as he approached, his long fingernail pointing.

"*Boska!*" he hollered in Huttese, jolting the Ortolan awake.

For a moment, Max didn't know where he was. The nightclub, so vivid in one moment, had disconcertingly vanished without a trace in the next. The weak morning light of a distant sun cut through the blinds of his bedroom. Some irritating creature chirruped loudly from a nearby bush.

He had expected to sleep lightly, as one does before an exciting trip or a nerve-racking event, in Max's case an exciting trip followed by a nerve-racking event. It was the day of his departure from his bustling homeworld Orto, penultimate stop on his bandmates' hyperspace hopscotch to the far-less-bustling backwater of Tatooine, where the Max Rebo Band was set to begin its residency. The trio were under an exclusive contract—one that Max had skillfully negotiated following an unfortunate incident concerning several Bith counterparts—at the desert palace of Jabba the Hutt.

But he had slept like the dead, oversleeping, in fact, through several alarms. And now, Jabba's aforementioned Twi'lek representative, Bib Fortuna, was on the long-distance holocomm.

"Wake up, you fool!" Fortuna continued in Huttese. "The transport we sent is waiting for you at the spaceport! And Jabba is in a foul mood today..."

An unclothed Max rolled over in his large round bed, crinkling a metallic crisp package as he turned. "I'm on my way! Don't worry," Max croaked, unconvincingly. But the Twi'lek had already hung up, his staticky blue image disappearing by the time Max had reached the small bedside device.

FANCY MAN

Rebo knew he was late but if there was one thing he hated, it was being rushed. Especially before breakfast.

But that song! Max's dream suddenly came flooding back. Something about it felt simultaneously familiar yet not quite right. Without thinking, he dropped the comm, which bounced silently on the white shag carpeting. By Max's reckoning, ideas tended to fall into your head at the most inopportune moments, like when you were in the middle of a shower, or staring blankly out of a window while eating a particularly delicious warm cheese pastry. And if you weren't careful, those ideas could fall out of your head just as quickly. Max needed to get to his organ and plunk out the tune before it was forgotten forever.

Reaching the doorway of his sunken great room, Max looked to the bend in the ovular space where his organ normally sat. But it was gone! Both of Max's hearts sank, the blood draining out of his little blue head. All that remained was an organ-shaped silhouette on the wall and an impression in the carpet. He felt weak but made a mental note to get his cleaning droid tuned up.

Max rubbed his still-bleary eyes, as if that might erase what he was seeing. A bit of crust adhered to his fore-toe and he wondered whether it was in fact a crumb from his bed, reflexively tasting it to make sure.

Sensing movement out of the corner of his eye, Max turned to his open balcony door. There the organ floated, at least a meter off the floor, carried up and away as if by some unseen force.

"Oh, bother," he muttered.

Max jogged over to the window just as the organ floated out of reach. On the walkway circling his hilltop home stood an unusually tall and barrel-chested Gungan in coveralls and a small hat. He held a control box in his hands, his tongue sticking out as he concentrated on the hovering instrument. Just beyond, a large vehicle was parked in the lot, silhouetted against a distant sea stretching out across the horizon.

"Ah, Mister Besh! Good morning!" the Gungan called out, odd because neither of Max's names began with *Besh*. "You were snoring so . . . peacefully that we didn't wish to disturb you." Equally odd because Max wasn't aware that he snored.

"Nice place you got here!" the tall Gungan continued, his breath visible in the cold morning air. And it was nice, particularly the view, which made Max momentarily reflect on how grateful he was that his wayward brother, Azool, staked no claim on the family home. It was then that Max spotted a second, shorter Gungan, in matching coveralls but a taller hat (which he supposed made up for the difference in their heights), emerging from the rear of the truck.

"We'll have your melodium loaded up and off to the spaceport before you know it! Yousa be riding in the speeder with us?" the tall mover said, his Gungan accent coming out.

"Yes. But if you could set it down gently for just a moment . . ." Max replied, thinking of his song, which was getting fuzzier in his mind with each passing second.

"Sure thing, Mister Besh!" But something was amiss, the organ listing slightly to one side as it drifted toward the Gungans.

"Ay!" Max cried, pointing.

"Under control, Mister Besh!" the Gungan called out reassuringly. It wasn't under control. And his partner, eyestalks fixed on the floating keyboard, mouth agape, instinctively reached for the control box just as a drawer in the organ slid open and a half-eaten bag of crisps and several meat sticks spilled out onto the lawn.

"Oh!" Max yelped, his tummy audibly gurgling at the sight of it.

He dashed down the spiral staircase to the ground floor as the two Gungans tussled over the control box, fighting over how to stop the malfunctioning repulsor. Suddenly the instrument lurched and then dropped, the shorter Gungan leaping to brace its fall.

Max's front door slid open just in time for him to see his beloved red ball jett land squarely in the chest of the shorter Gungan, popping the hat right off his head. The momentum sent the organ rolling, the somewhat flattened Gungan emerging from beneath. But he held on, riding up the backside of it as it continued to roll, turning toward the crest of the hill. His partner stood frozen, control box still in his hands.

The organ began to wheel down the grassy hill. Somehow, the shorter Gungan ended up atop the apparatus, backpedaling to keep his balance in a display of incredible acrobatics, his ears flapping behind him. Rebo gave chase, his short legs unable to keep up.

The Gungan screamed as he and the organ rolled faster and faster down the hill toward the street below. There, a rotund Ortolan in a smart woolen vest and no pants strolled obliviously down the sidewalk behind a hovering pram. The Gungan waved his arms wildly, as if he could push them aside with his floundering. Max could only watch horrified from a considerable distance away, still up on the hill. His little blue legs burned, getting more exercise than . . . well, possibly more than ever.

At the last moment, the Gungan managed to steer the careening doughnut with a lean, spinning the pram as it passed on its new trajectory toward downtown Cheddatown.

Finally reaching the bottom of the hill, Max doubled over gasping for breath. If he'd had arms, he would have been resting them on his knees. Thankfully, sidewalks on Orto were warmed and well padded, soothing Max's already aching feet. "Does this tune sound familiar to you?" he managed to ask, humming a few out-of-tune bars of his dream song to the wide-eyed Ortolan, who was now holding his charge protectively. The man said nothing.

Hearing the commotion, Ortolans had begun pouring out of their suburban homes and businesses, including a pair of twins on identical speeder trikes. "Excuse me," Max said, grabbing one of the trikes and taking off down the street, leaving the child in tears.

Two uniformed Ortolan officers emerged from a nearby corner store, one with a chocolate crescent roll sticking out of his mouth. They immediately dropped their breakfasts and gave chase. "Stop, thief!" they yelled, blowing their whistles and shaking their batons.

But Max was already too far down the road to hear, flippers and handlebar tassels flapping in the wind. Speeder trikes are by no means fast, but at least he was no longer on foot like the poor patrolmen, comming for backup between huffs and puffs.

Up ahead, Ortolan pedestrians dived out of the way as the rolling menace, Gungan upon it, blew through intersections. Landspeeders braked sharply, rear-ending each other as they blared their horns, heads of Sizhranian lettuce flying over the cabs of speeder trucks. Max could only wince as he watched the chaos his runaway organ wrought, skillfully weaving his trike around the detritus left in its wake, the flatfoots lumbering after.

Now passing well into downtown Cheddatown, Max gasped as he saw that the boulevard ended in a T-shaped crossing, an enormous squat building with tall chimneys dead ahead! Two uniformed security guards exited their gatehouse on the far end of the intersection, waving their flippers for whatever it was that was fast approaching to stop. The organ quickly blasted through both the junction and the flimsy security gate unscathed, the Gungan covering his head as barrier fragments flew through the air around him. "Sorry!" Max called out as, moments later, he slid past the guards, lying prone but alive in what remained of the gatehouse.

Looking up, Max immediately recognized the logo on the side of the building, matching that on the shoulders of the ineffective security guards: the famous foot symbol of Chedda-brand lotion! When Max was still a child his father, after much begging and pleading by the Chedda Corporation, wrote their celebrated jingle. It remained stuck in the heads of many Ortolans almost half a century later. "Never leave the house without a dab of Chedda Toe Jam Lotion!" Max thought of it now, with a smile of warm nostalgia.

Wheeling at full speed through the factory grounds, the organ, quickly followed by Max's pilfered scooter, rejoined traffic on one of the city's major thoroughfares, sidling alongside one of the city's many open-air double-decker landspeeder buses. The furiously back-pedaling Gungan found himself eye-to-eye with an Ortolan girl seated atop the bus, her family oblivious to the spectacle unfolding around them.

The wide-eyed kid waved. The delighted Gungan cracked a goofy grin and waved back enthusiastically before being garroted by a streetlamp that the organ passed under while he was distracted. As the instrument rolled on, the Gungan did a complete 180-degree turn around the lamppost by his neck before falling in a heap to the pavement below, almost directly on top of Max.

Quickly braking, Max jumped off the trike to check on the poor fellow. But Gungans were, if nothing else, a resilient people. And despite the violent end to his journey, the young mover was only momentarily dazed, shaking his head and blinking hard.

No sooner had Max confirmed that the Gungan was okay than things were suddenly not okay as a large truck, blaring its horn, barreled straight for them. Max and the Gungan held each other, terrified, and closed their eyes tight, bracing for impact.

But that impact never came and the pair slowly reopened their eyes to find a truck idling mere centimeters from their faces. The words TWO GUNGANS AND A HOVERTRUCK were stenciled in Aurebesh on its side. The passenger door of the cab popped open and the larger, still-behatted Gungan stuck his long neck out.

"C'mon, fellas!" he called out with a wave. But his face quickly fell as dozens of Cheddatown police emerged from every side street and alleyway, swarming toward the moving van! Max and the Gungan quickly squeezed into the cab, Max the blue meat in an overfilled Gungan sandwich. The larger Gungan punched it and they took off, leaving the cops in the dust.

"Meesa Neb Neb," the shorter Gungan said, by way of introduction, sticking his large hand out awkwardly, given the tight quarters, to shake Max's foot. "And I'm Tup Tup," the larger Gungan boomed, slapping his chest as he turned the speeder's control yoke, weaving around the dense downtown traffic.

Without the running Gungan to maintain its momentum, the organ's speed began to slow, allowing the truck to pull right behind it. Tup Tup sounded his horn to clear a path up ahead.

"Neb, I'm going to get ahead of it! Jump in back and grab it as I pass!" Neb Neb saluted his cohort and started to squeeze himself through the small window just behind Max's head, knocking over a tumbler of hot caf and planting his large foot in the Ortolan's face as he did so. "Hey!" Max called out, but Neb Neb didn't hear.

Neither Gungan nor Ortolan had the wherewithal to realize that they were cresting Broadway Street, Cheddatown's steepest hill. The organ picked up speed once more as the truck lurched forward, sending Neb Neb crashing into the wall that separated the van's cab from its enclosed bed. Max braced himself, one foot on the dashboard and the other pushing for a nonexistent passenger-side brake pedal.

"Hold on!" Tup Tup bellowed as he floored the truck, racing after the fast-escaping organ. Weaving into oncoming traffic to get around

FANCY MAN

more cautious drivers, Neb continued to be tossed from one side of the bed to the other, stumbling around like a drunken happabore.

A daring maneuver out of the path of an approaching bus and around a tourist-packed streetcar put the speeder ahead of the rolling organ at last. Seeing the opportunity unfolding around them, Max quickly jammed himself into the tiny cab window and, with a firm elbow to the bottom from Tup Tup, joined Neb Neb in the back.

The aft ramp was already lowering, Neb at its controls, when Max tumbled in, ears and flippers, respectively, whipped by the sudden wind. The top edge hit the road with a bang, sending a shower of sparks backward as it scraped along the pavement. But there was the organ rolling behind them!

"Steady . . . steady!" Max yelled out above the din to Tup Tup, who could only guess as to the careening instrument's exact location.

"A little to the left! A little more . . . and tap the brakes . . . now!"

With that, the organ rolled up the ramp and into Neb and Max's waiting arms like a voorpak returning to its owner. The pair gingerly lowered it back on its proper side upon a separate, functioning repulsor bed. Slumping onto a moving crate, Max found himself applauding with his feet without realizing it. Warm relief flooded over him.

"Yousa want a bite of my kaadu wrap, Mister Besh?" Tup Tup offered from the cab, grabbing the foil-wrapped sandwich from where he'd left it on the dashboard as Neb latched the doors out back. Max smiled as he wedged himself back through the window.

Sandwich in foot, all Max could do was stare, his appetite vanishing in an instant. At the bottom of Broadway Street was a blockade: at least half a dozen Cheddatown police speeders and sawhorses, lights flashing, flanked by a number of Imperial speeder bikes and their riders, skull-faced Imperial stormtroopers. The Empire's presence on Orto had recently grown, given the destruction of one of their satellites or some such. Max was only vaguely aware of all that, not being terribly political. However, the authorities seemed fully aware of the approaching speeder truck, hunkering down behind their vehicles, stormtroopers drawing their blaster rifles.

"Oh, bother," Max muttered under his breath.

It was then that Max Rebo did something entirely unexpected. He jammed his prehensile blue foot right down on top of Tup Tup's, where it rested on the accelerator. The truck heaved so forcefully that Neb tumbled head-over-heels in the cargo hold, right into the center of the organ. "Whoaaaaa!" Tup bellowed, but Max just stared straight ahead, determined.

They reached the bottom of the hill within seconds. Tup Tup turned the yoke, but it was too late to avoid a crash. The truck plowed first into one of the speeder bikes, pushing it into one of the police speeders, creating a sort of ramp, sending the truck up and over the blockade. The police and troopers were all knocked off their feet by the impact, not even letting off one shot.

As the truck spun through the air, everything that was on the floor of the cab, including the aforementioned caf tumbler, stray kaadu chunks, and loose Imperial credits, adhered to the roof of the cab. Max could feel his bare hindquarters lifting off the fabric-upholstered bench.

Max looked out the passenger window to see the truck flying toward and immediately passing through a holographic billboard of Orto's wealthiest citizen, Cheddatown founder, and creator of Chedda-brand foot lotion, R. H. Chedda, and his disingenuously smiling face, before crashing back down onto the street with a jolt, the truck now driving in reverse. Max took a moment to admire the truck's inertial compensators, reinforced for moving heavy objects, he supposed.

And as luck would have it, they were backing right into the Cheddatown spaceport, which had next-door-to-zero of its usual heavy speeder traffic due to the police blockade. With Max's foot back on his side of the cab, Tup Tup deftly spun the truck back around.

"Look!" Max yelled wide-eyed, pointing with his dominant foot at the transport lifting off out of Docking Platform 12, dead ahead!

Tup Tup waved his left arm and Max both of his feet wildly out of their respective windows to signal the transport to stop. And stop it did, settling back down on the platform with the engines still running.

With Max's assistance, an entirely dizzy Neb Neb pushed the instrument from one vehicle through the open hold door of the other, where Max's bandmates, the spindly Pa'lowick, Sy Snootles, and lumpy Kitonak, Droopy McCool, waited to collect it and him. As the trio lifted back off, Max could see what appeared to be every police and Imperial vehicle in Cheddatown converging on Platform 12. The two Gungans waved a cheerful goodbye as the transport door slammed shut, seemingly oblivious to their impending fate.

"*Maximilian Rebo!* Where were you?" Sy yelled at her bandmate, who sat on the floor beside his badly damaged organ, tinkering. "Fortuna called and Jabba is—"

"I don't want to hear it, Sy!" Max hollered back in an atypical show of courage, his eyes wet. "And not a peep out of you, either, McCool!"

"Leave poor Droopy out of this!" Sy returned fire, placing a hand on the seated horn player's arm. But Droopy didn't react. In fact, Max rarely heard him say anything. Max turned and resumed fixing his organ.

Likewise, Sy returned to her spot on the uncomfortable bench in the cold metal hold of their transport, crossing her gangly legs and arms with exasperation. She shot vibrodaggers with her eyes at Max and leaned close to Droopy. "That idiot wouldn't know his ass crack from his armpit," she said, a classic Ortolan insult that Sy was apparently familiar with.

Droopy let out a big, audible sigh but didn't move. He might even have been asleep. It was hard to say.

Max cocked his head slightly, and out of his peripheral vision he could see Sy still staring at him, making him feel rather small and pathetic, sitting on the floor, fiddling with the mouths of his organ's busted resonator pipes. However, the barest hint of warmth was also present in Sy's eyes. Perhaps she felt something like pity in her fluid sac for Max.

The hyperspace jump from Orto to Tatooine wasn't a terribly long one and before the Max Rebo Band knew it, they were trundling down the long antechamber of Jabba the Hutt's throne room, following an unpleasant sandblasting by the hot desert wind outside. Max brought up the rear, pushing the floating sled upon which his organ and the rest of their road cases sat. A scowling, sweaty Bib Fortuna appeared from out of the shadows to receive them.

"Where have you been?" Jabba's agitated Twi'lek majordomo asked in Huttese. "His Excellency is very cross today. Very cross." As he spoke, hustling the group down the dark hallway, Fortuna mopped his bumpy brow with a greasy square of cloth. "We were expecting you hours ago!"

Not one to be easily flustered, Sy coolly replied in Basic, "Bib, baby, it's all right. Just take us to our rooms and—"

"No," Bib said, with a peculiar look on his face. "Jabba wishes to see you now."

Even from his vantage point behind the sled, Max could see Sy swallow hard at that. And he didn't like any of it one bit.

All too soon, the trio plus the hoversled carrying their instruments and Fortuna had descended the sandy staircase into the Hutt's low-ceilinged throne room, where the fleshy crime lord was holding court. Jabba's cackling monkey-lizard, normally never far from his side, was nowhere to be seen. And an eerie hush had fallen over the

FANCY MAN

usual coterie of super-freaks and intergalactic weirdos stuffed into every nook and cranny of the space.

At the center of the room, Jabba the Hutt puffed manically on his water pipe from upon a stone dais, his dark pupils wide in a sea of red. The tail end of his podgy, sluglike body swished disconcertingly. As Fortuna approached, bowing low and repeatedly, Jabba's eyes narrowed.

"The Max Rebo Band, my lord," Fortuna said, quickly stepping away.

Max, Sy, and Droopy were all rather diminutive, but before the Hutt that day, Max felt practically microscopic. He noticed that they were standing on some sort of grate, which Max hadn't noted the last, and only, time he found himself in Jabba's throne room. Sand spilled from beneath their feet through the grate into a dark abyss. Max swore he could hear heavy breathing from below, though he couldn't imagine why that would be.

And so, they waited for the clearly incensed Hutt to speak.

"You dare to profane my court?" the gangster thundered at last in sonorous Huttese, slamming down his water pipe. A silver protocol droid, nearby in case a translation need arose, jumped at the pipe's clack. Max could see the Hutt fingering a disconcertingly red-colored button on the controls at his left elbow.

"What have *I* done to offend you?" Jabba then asked, disingenuously.

Even the normally sharp-tongued Sy didn't seem to know what to say to that. Max watched as she glanced downward, as if searching for the right words, the words that would save their skins. Droopy just stood there blankly. Jabba's left hand, the one that moments ago was fiddling with that red button, formed a fist. Max felt an all-too-familiar bead of sweat run off his head and down the back of his neck.

It was then that Max did the third extremely out-of-character thing that day.

"Oh, grand and glorious Jabba!" Max proclaimed rather officiously from atop the hoversled, gesturing to the Hutt. "We come before you today bearing, uh . . . a gift! A gift befitting . . . for one of . . . such magnitude . . . such as . . . er . . ." Max cleared his throat.

It was then that he vaulted into the center of his semi-operable organ and began to play. But Max didn't play any one of the jatz standards he knew by heart, but that same syncopated funk groove from his dream.

In that instant, something about the song tickled Max's blue brain, and from the depths of his otherwise undynamic unconscious, the dream reemerged intact. But instead of seeing it from the perspective of the musician, Max was sitting in the booth beside the beautiful woman with the half-eaten prime rib. And he was a boy, small enough to have been hidden from view in the dream's earlier incarnation. He held the woman's foot. And the woman was his mother, and his father—Jeph Rebo—the adored organist in the spotlight. A memory it was, not a dream.

Jabba's eyes grew wide with surprise. But his fist unclenched. Instead, he folded his arms (not easy for the short-armed Hutt, especially one of his breadth) and lifted his chin.

Sy and Droopy turned to each other, dumbfounded. They had not expected Max to just start playing, especially a song that neither had heard before. As subtly as he could, Max widened his eyes and tipped his head down to their road cases, pleading with his bandmates to join in. Max was already seven bars in and needed them. He was quickly running out of song.

On cue, Sy improvised a melody, riffing off the track Max was laying down. "My body heat is risin'," she sang, perhaps in reference to

FANCY MAN

the sweaty situation they found themselves in. "My soul is sympathizin'."

"A lovin' man is comin'," Sy intoned, flashing her big blue eyes up at the Hutt. Jabba let out a pleasurable "Ohh!" and chuckled, puffing out his chest. By that point, Droopy had unpacked his chindinkalu flute and gamely joined in, riffing over Max's groove.

"I'm shapin' up and workin' out!" Sy sang as she danced forward. Max winced at what could be interpreted as a not-so-subtle reference to Jabba's physical fitness, or lack thereof. But the Hutt betrayed no sign that he had noticed, his tail tip reflexively flicking to the beat, in contrast with his still-folded arms.

The barest hints of a grin formed in the corners of Jabba's wide mouth. The Hutt was pleased. And his court's mood immediately lifted. Max even heard the telltale cackles from his monkey-lizard, coming from wherever in the room the creature was hiding.

On the spot Max decided to call the number "Fancy Man," a reference to one of Sy's spur-of-the-moment lyrics. It grew to become one of the band's signature numbers, and a staple of Jabba's palace setlist.

Years passed without incident. Each day and meal slid into the next, as they do. And there were many, many meals. With the passage of time, the Max Rebo Band's numbers grew in lockstep with Max's belly. Despite some initial grumblings about Rebo's quick acceptance of Jabba's all-you-can-eat lifetime contract offer, the entire band— even Sy—seemed happy.

As was often the case in those intervening years, Max was the first of his bandmates to wake one ordinary morning. Sitting at his long-since fully restored organ among the usual throne room coterie, a jolly, post-breakfast Max found himself playing a classical Ortolan tune, the kind he remembered from his youth. Mellow but cheerful, and wholly appropriate for a sleepy morning. Upon his dais, the Hutt peacefully puffed on his water pipe.

Feeling quite nostalgic, Max made a mental note to add "Fancy Man" to the band's set later that day. That was, assuming that their relatively new singer, Joh Yowza, didn't butt in with one of his own compositions, as was his wont. How the irksome, spotlight-hogging Yuzzum had curried Jabba's favor, Max did not know.

Just then, Bib Fortuna led a pair of nervous droids, one tall and the other short, down the darkened stairwell and before his corpulent overlord, catching Max's attention and snapping him from his reverie. Jabba received many visitors, some of whom never left the palace, either by choice or in death, forever rotting in its dungeons. But Max couldn't recall the Hutt ever receiving masterless droids before.

No matter. Max could see no end to the nonstop party, and bottomless buffet, at Jabba the Hutt's desert stronghold. In that way, things were looking up.

THE KEY TO REMEMBERING

Olivia Chadha

As she wiped the counter, her three small photoreceptors glowing in the dull surface of the stone, EV-9D9 should not have been able to remember her life before tending the bar at Chalmun's Spaceport Cantina. She should not have been able to remember that it had been 612 days since she had last given in to her supposed depraved desires. Or that her new astromech comrade R5-D4 reminded her of someone she had once met. But EV-9D9 had long ago ensured that she would always remember, everything, especially the day she discovered "the anomaly."

In her life before, EV-9D9 supervised the droid assessment room as the despicable Queen of Durasteel in the underground level of Jabba the Hutt's palace of depravity. This was where she thrived, where she excelled, where she was given time to focus on her important research. At the time, she would have said she'd be there forever disassembling droids, gleefully turning up their pain sensors and listening to their vocal units cry out, watching their destruction with her third eye she'd installed for detecting pain. When she met the smelting droid 8D8, it was a match made in hell. He was gifted in the use of the branding tools, and EV-9D9 was skilled in organizing the most painful manner of torture for Jabba's droids. EV-9D9 knew what form of torture fit which droid. It was less about overall pain and more about fear. GNKs were like Hoojibs, they thought they were already dead once you flipped them upside down. A little fire and flash and a power droid entered that state right before death. A shiny protocol droid feared acid and scoring on their pristine plating. Even if EV-9D9 spared their life, the threat of dismemberment nearly killed them.

But it wasn't simply torture for torture's sake. How little Jabba expected from EV-9D9 and her partner! No, it was science. Her life's quest was to understand not only the origins of artificial intelligence, but how she could overcome the Maker-blamed programming that MerenData had cruelly installed in her motivator. Possibly, if her hypothesis was accurate, her research might even lead her to understanding the Maker themselves. And she had several questions for them.

That chance day began like most that came before. As she scrolled through her datapad in the dungeon, EV-9D9 sighed and her vocabulator flap chittered. A lull in her work punctuated by the high-pitched screams of an organic being eaten alive by the rancor vexed

THE KEY TO REMEMBERING

her more than usual. Her research was exhilarating, but after so many years concrete answers continued to elude her. She perused the data for something she might have missed, a clue, a whisper of a reason, a pattern of some kind. She had analyzed hundreds of motivators, pain receptors, and cognitive modules. Among their cries and sparks in her assessment room, she'd amassed a great deal of information. Yet she was no closer to understanding the Maker, how to override her own programming without replacing her cognitive module, or even the catalyst that made droids different from a simple machine. She had her reasons for her quest, and at the top of the list was quite a personal inquiry: her own free will.

"Eve-Ninedenine, I believe Master Jabba requires a new protocol droid," 8D8 said as he calibrated his smelting machine. "Our approach was a bit extreme on the last one."

"I thought we were restrained," EV-9D9 said. "He was frightfully annoying." What made that protocol unit special? Why had he been so vocal about his pain? Not all droids expressed fear; in fact, some were quite vapid. Regardless, it gave EV-9D9 an awful kink in her cervical mount just thinking about the protocol droid pleading to get back to work.

8D8 continued, "He instructed us to dip him in acid and melt him down to nothing. His Excellency Jabba the Hutt is prone to exaggeration, so perhaps we shouldn't be so literal next time." He paused for EV-9D9 to respond, and when she didn't he went on to the next repair.

Her previous lives before this one at Jabba's palace were dim if present at all in her memory core. She wanted a life beyond these red sand walls the B'omarr monks had formed so long ago. She yearned to know what it would feel like to control her primary programming. She imagined what she might accomplish if she could simply make decisions herself. Maybe she could carve out a simple existence with 8D8, a modest life supervising a crew of Treadwells on a moisture farm. Or even a quiet life behind a bar perhaps.

EV-9D9 felt both exhilarated and isolated in her work. And she knew that it was her programming error that gave her this duality. Without the defect that made her torture mechanicals, she'd only be a supervisor droid, naïve or, even worse, ignorant of the world. But this defect gave her curiosity and a path. The conundrum was apparent even to her.

With a clatter a Gamorrean guard disrupted her thoughts. Was it Thok or Thug or Scumbo? She could never tell them apart. He stomped into the assessment room and ushered in a GNK and a courier droid, who clung to each other like two pathetic womp rats. EV-9D9 attempted to suppress her glee at seeing her terrified victims. "Thank you, Thug."

The Gamorrean snorted and said, "I'm Scumbo."

"Oh, whatever." EV-9D9 waved her pincer then turned her attention to her companion. She pointed her long articulating arm at the courier droid, who screamed out about his innocence. "Set that one up on the rack, Atedeate," she said.

The small courier droid trembled so much he lost a few bolts and screamed, "But I was only bringing a message to His Excellency! I was just following my master's orders!"

Then she pointed to the GNK droid. "And take your irons to that one, Atedeate. Be careful to disconnect his battery core. Things could get explosive." The GNK shivered and the courier droid leaked fluid.

The next day, as 8D8 and EV-9D9 were going about their usual process of assigning various droids to their new posts in the palace, and inflicting debilitating pain upon those less willing to comply, Thok,

THE KEY TO REMEMBERING

Thug, Scumbo, or some other ridiculously named Gamorrean guard burst into the droid assessment room pushing two droids just as 8D8 pulled the hot irons down upon the GNK droid's feet.

Of the new arrivals, the golden protocol droid seemed appropriately terrified. But there was something peculiar about the astromech. He wasn't alarmed or unaware; he was bold and a little belligerent, in fact. Fascinating.

"Ah, good. New acquisitions. You are a protocol droid, are you not?"

"I am See-Threepio, human–cyborg rel—"

"Yes or no will do." EV-9D9 took in C-3PO and measured him with her eyes to see if he'd fit on the rack, or if they'd need to extend the frame. But then she remembered Jabba's need for a translator.

C-3PO said, "Oh. Well, yes."

"How many languages do you speak?" EV-9D9 asked. She couldn't help but daydream about dipping his annoyingly surprised face into a hot pool of acid.

"I'm fluent in over six million forms of communication, and can readily—"

"Splendid! We have been without an interpreter since our master got angry with our last protocol droid and disintegrated him." She, of course, was the one who'd done the disintegration, but she left that part out.

"Disintegrated?"

The traction test bed pulled off the leg of the fearful courier droid, who let out a howl.

"Guard! This protocol droid might be useful. Fit him with a restraining bolt and take him back up to His Excellency's main audience chamber."

The Gamorrean guard pushed C-3PO to the door.

"Artoo, don't leave me! Ohh!"

As the door closed the little astromech whistled fiery words threatening EV-9D9 and admonishing her for torturing her own kind. She heard his words but saw that he was trembling. Yet there was more than just abject fear building in his form. His dread morphed into something different, something new: courage. Remarkable.

"You're a feisty little one, but you'll soon learn some respect. I have need for you on the master's sail barge. And I think you'll fit in nicely." Just then 8D8 spun the GNK droid upright and took him out of the room to complete his reconditioning elsewhere. The Gamorrean guard followed.

R2-D2 beeped, "My master will come. You'll see."

"Who is your master?"

"I can't tell you. It's classified."

"Classified? Oh, now I must know."

R2-D2 wheeled closer to EV-9D9 and whistled a string of words that took the shape of a story. EV-9D9 knew astromechs could be deceptive but wasn't sure if it was in this one's programming to create complete fictions, so she considered most of what he told her to be the truth. He beeped, "I am on a secret mission and I need your help. Help us and my master can free you."

"What makes you think I require liberation, astromech?"

R2-D2 whistled sadly, "What droid would choose to live in the labyrinth and treat others like this?"

The words gave EV-9D9 pause. "I am free. I have rights like any droid, after all." But in her chassis she felt that question bloom like a rhydonium fire. What nonsense was inside this astromech's logic board thinking that he had a mission, that he was superior? But she knew this truth pained her the most: She wasn't free. Not yet at least. EV-9D9 leaned down to meet R2-D2 photoreceptor-to-photoreceptor. "Tell me, little blue astromech, what do you know about freedom?"

THE KEY TO REMEMBERING

EV-9D9 held a restraining bolt in her pincer, one with a smear of blue paint on it. She was ready to clip it to his body at a moment's notice.

R2-D2 cooed and wheeled out of EV-9D9's reach. "Oh, I know a lot about freedom."

She was puzzled by his confidence. "How often does your master take you to the memory flush unit?"

He responded with a series of loud beeps. "That's a very personal question."

"I must know. It's for research." She would give anything to learn what made this one special.

"If I tell you, will you let me go without a restraining bolt?"

"Agreed." EV-9D9 said, though she knew the barge crew had their own rules and could very well restrain him when he arrived.

"I've never been fully wiped. Only small moments when it protects my friends."

Friends? He had friends he would wipe his memory for? Amazing. This astromech was intelligent and hadn't been fully wiped in many years. He could be anywhere between fifty and sixty years old, maybe more; she knew when the model had been released. Perhaps he was the clue she'd been looking for all this time. The anomaly that could show her the path beyond her programming. EV-9D9 wondered if she could get inside his cognitive module somehow without destroying his memory core. She had to see what made him tick. Her elation and curiosity forced her to stumble toward him on unsteady legs. "What do you remember?"

R2-D2 wheeled around and paused with a chirp. "About what?"

"Your life. Your existence. From the very beginning until now."

"I remember a lot, so be careful. I won't forget you if you hurt me."

"I don't remember much at all," EV-9D9 said, holding on to the edge of her datapad to steady herself. This must be it. The reason to hope, to progress beyond these dungeon walls, to decide for herself what she could become. Though she wanted to lift R2-D2's dome and see what was hiding inside his memory core, she held herself back. This little spunky astromech was the key to her understanding the mechanical universe. Straining against her programming, she held on to the restraining bolt in her pincer and squeezed. For the first time in her existence she pushed her desire to harm a droid out of reach. And maybe, just maybe, he could show her the way out of this loop she'd been living in. "What is this mission you speak of?"

R2-D2 zoomed closer and beeped softly, "I'm on a mission with the Rebellion. My master is coming. We can free everyone when he arrives!"

EV-9D9 considered her surroundings. Then suddenly it struck her that this astromech had traveled across the galaxy far and wide. There was an entire universe that existed beyond the walls of the droid assessment room, beyond Tatooine. But her master wouldn't simply let her go. "And the Hutt? Is your master going to . . . disintegrate him?"

"Hopefully you won't have to worry about him anymore. You could leave this place and never come back."

Now, this was interesting. "Very well. You will be a server on the *Khetanna*. You have courage, I'll give you that, astromech. Good luck on your mission. But remember you still need to serve beverages!"

R2-D2 whistled a song. "You can do good things despite your poor programming. Try not to forget and you'll learn."

Once the astromech left, the entire universe as EV-9D9 knew it paused. As she scoured the countless notations on her datapad, suddenly everything in the dungeon stopped. She could no longer hear the screams from the organic being tortured down the tunnel, or the filthy snorts from the Gamorrean guards pacing in the labyrinth. It was as though time itself crystallized like kyber and she was the only

THE KEY TO REMEMBERING

witness. On her datapad she watched as her disparate notes clicked into place, a jigsaw puzzle she had only the pieces but no map for its completion . . . until now. All along, what if the anomaly she'd been searching for that allowed droids to work against their programming was memory.

She cradled the unused restraining bolt in her pincer. It was so much simpler than she'd ever imagined, though her coding limitations had hindered her understanding of this anomaly and sometimes even the world beyond the walls of her droid assessment room. After all, what are beings, mechanical or organic, at the basic level other than creatures who learn from experiences, and a palimpsest set of memories?

It all was beginning to make sense. The droids who were more afraid of the rack or smelting irons, the ones who shrieked in pain to stop, had made connections with others and were not wiped of their memories as frequently. The ones with more wipes and fewer core memories barely made a sound. Even the GNK, whom one would assume had very little intelligence, could in fact build memories and a fondness for his colleagues, and because of this, he could feel a great deal of pain. She could not unsee it: Synthetic consciousness was compiled through layers of experiences. This finding was stunningly obvious now. To progress beyond one's programming, memory wipes could not take place. She imagined what it would be like to find a way to hold on to her memories, to live an entire mechanical existence and recall everything. Well, there were a few things she'd like to forget.

But perhaps this was all just wishful thinking. Even she knew that dreams were for fools. How would she, a class three supervisor droid with a defective motivator, find a way to bypass programming and hold on to memories? How could any droid for that matter? She scrolled through her data. Even class fives like 8D8 were focused on their Maker-given tasks, of smelting, lifting, transporting, fixing . . . never truly seeking what could be beyond. Unless . . .

A dreadful thought struck her like a hammer to the chassis: If she had been wiped often, and had worked for Jabba for many years, just how many times had she stood behind this datapad and found this same exact answer? Was this moment not remarkable? Was she in a recursive loop, again and again having a similar eureka moment but then doomed to repeat it at the whim of the giant worm who was her "master"?

Oh, how that word tangled her circuits.

8D8 returned to the assessment room, though she was so caught in her thoughts she didn't know how long he'd been watching her. "Eve-Ninedenine? Are you having some sort of malfunction?" 8D8's deep voice pulled her out of her discovery. "I can call for a mechanic if you require repairs. Though we are scheduled for our monthly update tomorrow anyway."

"No!" EV-9D9's raspy voice called out louder than she'd intended, and 8D8's tools clattered to the dank floor. The update—that must be how Jabba wiped them, she thought. It wasn't just an oil bath; it was complete and total memory erasure. "I don't require repairs. I'm simply plotting the best way to deliver pain to our victim today. You know how I enjoy planning." She lied. She lied? Her capabilities were growing with her understanding.

"Yes, Eve. You are quite the Mistress of Mayhem."

"Thank you." She loved when he called her that. But how would she keep her memories? Could it even be done? Jabba enjoyed having all of his droids, EV-9D9 included, "updated" often. She checked the datapad: It was nearly monthly. She wasn't foolish enough to think that Jabba would give her latitude with her own memory core. But maybe she could find a workaround in secret. She might even have to keep her project from her companion at least for now. But it would be worth a try.

When 8D8 had powered down that night and all was quiet, EV-9D9 had a moment to implement her plan. She would have to be quick and decisive if she was going to create and install a memory blocker before their update appointment.

She connected herself to the datapad and accessed her memory core. EV-9D9 knew how dangerous it was to dive into this part of her cognitive module. One wrong move and she could maim herself. Carefully, she programmed a jamming device and placed it inside to deflect the memory flush unit. She'd only know if it worked after the "update." And as she stood, curious and hyperaware of her possible step forward toward a liberated existence, she decided to commence self-surgery in order to deflect those cursed restraining bolts as well. Jabba hadn't fitted her with one, most likely because she'd seemed so at home in the dank dungeon and the wipes had kept her ignorant of bigger ideas until she encountered the anomaly. But what if one day she was beyond these walls and her new employer kept their droids on lock? It took some time to find the main power override cable in her chassis under her chest plating. Her pincers weren't suited for such delicate work, but she managed. And when she was done, she felt different, newer. Perhaps a bit invincible . . . ? No, not that. Another word she'd heard from a protocol droid once: independent.

The fortress of despair fell as quickly as it rose. After the *Khetanna* was destroyed and the Hutt's vile reign ended, most of the droids in the palace were sold, though EV-9D9 and some of her comrades were stolen by traders, while many others were decommissioned.

Later, much later, EV-9D9 found herself in a junkyard beneath scraps of starships. There she sat with joints full of painful sand for a very long time. So long that she powered down, because what was the point of observing the passage of time when day in and day out it was the same view?

Years went by during which she slept a dreamless sleep. Until one day she woke to a sudden jolt of energy. Then a sensation of warm oil moved across her plastron plating. A young human, who called himself Maxxon Senn, bathed her and blew the ancient dust out of her couplings. She'd never felt so wonderful in her entire existence. He brushed her chassis, mended her joints, and gave her a grand polish.

EV-9D9 felt different. What was this sensation—peace or joy? No, it was quiet. The buzzing urgency to break droids had retreated a little deeper in the background. With her new memories pressing down onto the old, she was making novel meaning of her world. She was free of the recursive loop in the Hutt's palace. And who cared how long she'd been asleep? It was of no matter. Time was irrelevant. She was free to make of existence what she wished.

Maxxon adjusted his respirator and whistled in admiration of his work. "New boss at the cantina needs a droid to tend the bar. It's a good job."

"Bar work sounds fine," EV-9D9 said.

Six hundred and twelve days was her longest stretch of time likely due to the fact that business was exceedingly slow. Ninety-nine times out of one hundred she served the customer exactly as the cantina owner's programming mandated. Sure, once in a while her primary coding rose above the din and she daydreamed of drizzling a bit of

THE KEY TO REMEMBERING

Rodian juice into a rowdy customer's drink, pulp and all. Over her years in recuperation, though, EV-9D9 had learned a few tricks to keep a low profile. One: Don't tear off a droid's articulating joints—or any parts for that matter, even if they are annoying (in public). Two: You will have to live with yourself and the things you do until you meet the Maker (in private). And three, and this was the big one: When a droid-hating customer enters the establishment, remember the droid manifesto (all day long).

Something slammed into the bar. "What in the cursed Maker was that?" Though her spindly body wouldn't allow her to lean over the stone counter to see, a quiet bleep and rusty hum told her it was the astromech R5-D4. Momentarily, she couldn't help but envision stabbing the tin can with a smelting iron, then she shook off the impulse and said, "You're late, Arfive." R5-D4 zipped in reverse and turned his ancient head toward EV-9D9.

She squeezed the relic of a restraining bolt she kept under the counter with her servogrip pincer—not enough to make a dent, just enough to feel better.

"Sorry about the scratch, boss. I'll fix it right now," R5-D4 bleeped in binary.

"I'll hold you to that. And do make sure not to bump into customers. They are less forgiving than me." She took in her newest trainee, whom she had found wheeling around aimlessly by the garbage masher when she was disposing of the less-than-savory remnants of a bar fight. R5-D4 said he'd been wandering the dunes for days and made it to Mos Eisley right before the sandstorm hit. Like most astromechs, R5-D4 had some scoring from previous battles, but unlike other mechs he was a trembling bucket of bolts. Suffered some kind of tragedy that he couldn't recall. But who hadn't seen hardship? Perhaps that was in EV-9D9's favor. Newer units were rude and glib, but this droid might just be of use to her.

"I am sure you will find a permanent home soon enough. Peli Motto is always interested in useful droids."

"I can be useful. At least I can try . . . I think." R5-D4 seemed to retreat to what EV-9D9 assumed was a fragmented memory echo, a landscape that plagued severely wiped droids. Displaced and incomplete recollections lingered just out of reach. And R5-D4 seemed like he was missing some important core moments. *Maker-blamed memory wipes,* EV-9D9 thought, shaking her head.

R5-D4 and EV-9D9 both looked toward the door of the cantina as a rowdy Trandoshan entered. EV-9D9 was wrapping up her shift with R5-D4 before the other team of droids would take over for the next several days so she could recharge. R5-D4 trembled and beeped in distress, then backed into the bar again. This time EV-9D9 ignored the dent.

"Arfive, we're going to visit a droidsmith for some updates, okay? How about I take you after my shift?" She felt virtuous just saying the words.

"Oh, thank you, Eve-Ninedenine."

The Trandoshan crossed the room and leaned on the bar right in front of EV-9D9.

"What can I get you?" she asked.

"Only droids working here now? What's wrong with this place?" he said with a hiss. "That's pathetic. I remember when—"

EV-9D9 squeezed the restraining bolt and it bent a little. "Counter space is for paying customers only," EV-9D9 interrupted. She'd seen this type before. Belligerent for the wrong reasons, down on their luck somehow because of bad life choices, and looking to kick someone defenseless to feel big again. Altogether a loser. She whispered to R5-D4, "All sentients are equal." And R5-D4 responded with a frightened beep.

She stared at the Trandoshan and took solace in knowing that this

THE KEY TO REMEMBERING

putrid bag of flesh who shook her bolts would be decomposing under the Dune Sea's twin suns soon enough, and she would continue living on in this world and the next so long as her head remained soldered to her cervical servomotor.

The Trandoshan turned to the trembling astromech and hissed, "What are you looking at? Get out of here!" And kicked R5-D4, who squealed and wheeled backward into a stool.

EV-9D9's circuits fired. That crossed a line. For one heavy second she considered her options. She had made it 612 days before falling back on her recursive torturous behavior. She couldn't lose her job; it was too risky being an unemployed mechanical in Mos Eisley. The rules of her employment at the cantina were simple. The owner had said, "Do your job, and don't dismember droids or else to the foundry you go." Times had changed but it was still dangerous for droids. You could get kidnapped and forced to work in unsavory situations or just sold for scrap. Still, R5-D4 didn't deserve abuse, not when he was just getting back on his treads. Of course, EV-9D9 had never tortured organics even in her past; they were too messy and uninteresting. Perhaps she could try her pincer at giving this nerf herder a special drink. Her programming for the bar included a detailed library of beverages tolerated by different species and ones considered toxic. She spoke louder this time: "Either order a drink or leave the establishment."

"How about a Hutt's Delight, you sack of bolts?"

She turned to her bar decanting system and filled a glass with the Trandoshan's favorite ale, then topped it off with a touch of Sennari from her own private selection. It wasn't enough poison to kill the thug, just enough to make him retch. She slid the drink across the bar and watched as the next droid crew came through to take her place. The Trandoshan took a seat at a table and drank.

EV-9D9 whispered, "Come on, Arfive. Let's get out of here before things get too interesting."

The pair moved slowly down the main curved road at dusk. Hangar 3-5 wasn't far from the cantina. R5-D4 seemed a bit more confident and whistled, "Did I ever tell you the time I helped the Rebellion?"

"No, you haven't, but I'm interested to hear. Astromechs have remarkable cognitive modules."

"Can I ask you a question?" He didn't wait for her reply. "Why are you always squeezing that old restraining bolt?"

She didn't think anyone had noticed her habit. "To remember."

"Oh, remember what?" R5-D4 beeped.

"That I can make choices. Arfive, try to remember and you can make choices, too."

It had been only a few minutes since EV-9D9 gave into her depraved desires, but it was worth it.

FORTUNA FAVORS THE BOLD

Kwame Mbalia

Of all the seven hundred and sixty-two items on Bib Fortuna's list of things he hated—an extensive list, an impressive list, a list that for redundancy's sake stretched across three datapads and the memory banks of one unfortunately repurposed service droid—Klatooine paddy frogs were near the top. He hated the way they smelled. He hated the sticky residue they left behind, and their mewling cries, and the foul, scum-covered tanks they were delivered in. He loathed them. Despised them, really, especially the one that had managed to escape its tank and now wriggled near his boot. He needed its death to be slow and excruciating, which was why the tiny blaster he clutched beneath his cloak wasn't intended for it.

"Beep beep-boop beep bop?"

The delivery droid's question interrupted Bib's thoughts. He'd been standing in the palace larder prepping supplies for Jabba's latest execution extravaganza aboard his pleasure yacht when the unannounced delivery arrived. The Twi'lek glared at the droid as he tried to decipher its incessant beeping, then finally motioned at a corner of the palace larder. "Just set them there, quickly now!"

The droid beeped again and then proceeded to drop the pallet of Klatooine paddy frogs, all two hundred tanks, fifty more than their normal delivery, in the middle of the larder, before turning around and trundling off. Bib briefly thought about summoning the droid back and having it relocate the tanks to the proper location, then stopped. He didn't want to deal with the hassle of trying to effectively communicate with the rusted can, and the protocol droid Jabba had abruptly received from the pasty human wizard now scheduled to die was already aboard the *Khetanna*. As if Bib didn't already have his hands full managing the maintenance schedule for the droids the palace already owned. Maintaining droids was in the top one hundred of things he hated. No, the sooner this delivery droid was gone, the better. In fact . . .

Bib briefly contemplated turning the blaster on the retreating droid, then discarded the thought. It was a one-shot weapon, and he hated wasting acts of vengeance on immaterial annoyances (that wastefulness was actually item number three hundred and five on his list). Besides, the pistol wasn't intended for the droid.

A great rumbling laughter shook the palace walls, grating in Bib's ears, and he took a step backward.

Squelch.

The escaped paddy frog's brief freedom came to an inglorious end, and one more headache for Bib began. The laughter continued, and his hand instinctively squeezed the pistol in the cloak. He gripped it tight, pressing the curve into his palm before taking a deep breath and forcing his muscles to relax. He removed the weapon from his cloak and, dipping a finger into a bit of sticky paddy frog residue on his boot, used it to stick the pistol to the wall behind a stack of beverage tanks, hidden from anyone examining them even if they were right on top of it. Then, with a tap of a datapad, the Twi'lek sent an instruction to have the tanks loaded up onto the *Khetanna,* the sail barge for today's festivities. And still the laughter continued. Bib clenched a fist.

Seven hundred and sixty-two items on Bib's list of things he hated, and right at the top, sitting on his throne surrounded by sycophants and servants, was his master, Jabba the Hutt.

And Bib was going to kill him today.

"Beep boop?" The delivery droid was back with another pallet of paddy frogs.

He sighed. Maybe he had a second blaster he could use.

Down further on Bib's hate list—somewhere in the six hundreds if he remembered correctly—were maintenance requests. Endless mounds of sand-covered maintenance requests for every little thing tucked away in Jabba's palace. Droids needed oil baths. Coolant tanks needed refrigerant. Door control panels, those tiny blasted collections of wires and toggles, needed to be replaced because gung-ho Gamorreans didn't understand that not everything needed to be pummeled.

In Fortuna's mind, Gamorreans didn't understand much of anything besides pummeling. He could have sworn he heard a rumor that their courtship cycles, a hideous bit of knowledge Bib struggled to erase from his memory, consisted of an intricate spiraling dance where a triad of partners tried to knock the others out first. Revolting.

The point was, despite holding the title of Jabba's "majordomo," Bib constantly received, delegated, tracked down, investigated, and closed maintenance requests. Like right now, for instance. With an execution on the day's schedule he should've been in the cells with the prisoners and a few of his favorite tools he called conversation starters, extracting every bit of valuable information from the soon-to-be Sarlacc appetizers. Not that he had anything specific in mind, but information was information. One could never extract too much information. He especially wanted to coax a few whimpers out of the pasty sand wizard who'd made a fool out of Bib the day before. *You will take me to see Jabba the Hutt* indeed. Instead, he stood in the hangar bay of the palace going over sand skiff repair reports. One of the two skiffs Jabba owned needed constant tinkering, and Bib was of half a mind to blow the thing up.

And Jabba! Manhandling Bib in front of everyone! *Weak-minded fool.* Bib let out a wordless snarl. Today was the day he did it. The blaster was there. He could manufacture an incident. He could . . .

Bib was lost in his fantasy when a Gamorrean stomped up and grunted a question.

"What?" Bib snapped.

The guard jerked a meaty fist back in the direction he'd clomped from and grunted again.

Bib shook his head. "Seven guards on the flotilla, that's all that's necessary."

More grunts.

"What do you mean there's an eighth? Send him elsewhere!"

Grunt grunt grunty grunt.

Bib paused. "He hates the pasty wizard and wants to be there when the Sarlacc grinds his bones and flesh into nutrient paste? He was mind-tricked before and wants revenge? You heard him say that?" He stroked his right head-tail and thought. One more guard on the prisoner skiff flotilla meant one less on Jabba's pleasure ship. One less body between his blaster and his bloated boss. Perhaps . . .

FORTUNA FAVORS THE BOLD

"Fine," he said, "keep the extra guard. Now leave, and don't bother me with silly logistics again. Close the door on your way out!"

The Gamorrean punched the door controls as he left, leaving a smoking, sparking collection of wires, and Bib's snarl of frustration could be heard throughout the palace.

"You simply don't understand," Bib muttered, rubbing his smaller head-tail in annoyance and reclining in the *Khetanna*'s enlarged kitchen. Most of the staff was either in the observation lounge or on the privacy deck, serving Jabba and his guests. "You can leave and take on a different contract with a different client in a different system and no one will flick a lekku. I can't do that. I know too much, Jabba would never let me just leave, not even to start on my own. I'd be competition."

The fleshy, buoyant blue sac of a creature next to him didn't answer. Max Rebo, the blue Ortolan, was busy grabbing spare keys for his red ball organ. Apparently a guest had spilled something mildly corrosive on his signature instrument while dancing, and Max needed his replacements. The Ortolan had only recently graduated off Bib's hate list, and only because his jatz-wail music really captured the feeling of working for a crime lord. Pounding, tense fear mixed with the heady, *wub wub wub* thrill of excitement. Max got it, and he was an excellent composer, though Bib kept that to himself.

He sighed. "I really must get back topside to check on the serving droids. I swear I will string the droid manager up by his rusty chassis if another one of his charges goes rogue. The sandblasted things seem more interested in the execution than Jabba, may his insides rot for all eternity."

Max trumpeted a question.

Bib nodded. "Go ahead, I'll be right behind you. His Hutt-ness wants another jar of paddy frogs, the disgusting things."

After the Ortolan disappeared, Bib sat for a moment. He ran a hand along the armrest, imagining it was a throne and the *Khetanna* was his palace. He could commission Max's band to play for him, maybe a ballad that would be sung in the cantinas across the galaxy. An epic about Bib's rise to prominence. How he crawled his way from the horrors on Ryloth to become the most feared crime lord in all of history. How the reign of the Jabba came to a bloody but poetic end when Bib Fortuna killed Jabba and usurped his throne. All he had to do was hurl Jabba's carcass into the Sarlacc pit, blame a servant or two who no doubt wanted to kill their master as much as he did, and then the golden age of Fortuna would spread like glorious fire. Palanquins would carry him through the streets. Dignitaries would heap praise and credits upon him. His enemies would tremble, his supplicants would weep, and from the driest desert on Tatooine to the farthest reaches of Wild Space, the air would ring with the cries of his subjects as they chanted the name of their lord and master.

Bib! Bib! Bib! Bib!

"BIB!"

He jerked upright out of his daze to see a servant frantically motioning for him to follow her. "You must come quick, it's a mess, a total mess!"

Bib, annoyed, lurched upright and was seconds away from issuing a stinging reprimand for daring to summon him by his given name when shouts rang out through the *Khetanna*. Guns went off and people screamed, and then Bib was tearing up the stairs to the main deck of the pleasure barge. When he arrived at the lounge he skidded to a stop in disbelief. Pandemonium, sheer pandemonium!

The pasty sand wizard was out on the prisoner skiff flipping and twirling like a Corellian null-g ballerina with their tights in a wad.

FORTUNA FAVORS THE BOLD

And from where did he get a laser sword! Bib keyed in a code to a wall panel mercifully left unscathed by the Gamorreans, and the *Khetanna*'s armaments were unlocked. Guards began firing on the skiff while trying to avoid palace guards who clamored to recapture their prizes. Meanwhile, beneath them all, the Sarlacc gurgled and choked down flailing body after body as the pasty wizard sent guards to their doom. And then there was Solo, swinging his fists half blind like someone's grandfather after a two-day grog bender. Next to him was his Wookiee companion, bellowing like a heartbroken Gamorrean after his mate left him for his brother with the larger tusks. Though, to Bib's immense delight, a vicious backhand did send that sputtering glory hound Boba Fett shrieking into the gullet of the Sarlacc. *Good riddance,* Bib thought. The suck-up. The ship was in chaos! The guards were all fighting to get outside to join the fight, and Bib was just about to shout at them for leaving their master unprotected when a single, unbidden thought sprang into his head.

Leaving their master unprotected.

Jabba had no one to guard him. Now . . . now was his chance! He could kill the Hutt in the chaos, blame the prisoners, and easily take over his kingdom. It would be as simple as plucking a narba fruit from the vine. But first, he had to . . .

"Huurrrgh!"

Bib's jaw dropped to the end of his head-tail. Jabba, the creature he hated the most, the master he served with all the reluctance of a rancor dentist, the prince of Hutts, was being strangled on his throne! With gusto! Leia Organa, whose earlier attempts at freeing Han Solo landed her in Jabba's chains, now heaved at those same chains she'd somehow managed to snake around the Hutt's neck. Bib watched as Jabba flailed, the Hutt's tongue turning purple (or was that from excessive paddy frog consumption?) before he keeled over, dead.

Bib backed into the shadows. This was out of control. Unexpected.

If Leia saw him he was next. Would the Rebellion leader be offended Bib helped turn her into a dancer? Maybe Leia liked dancing? Would she be open to a partnership? No. Impossible. She would come for him next. Would Leia stake her claim for Jabba's throne? Would Solo join her? He racked his brain, trying to figure out if he'd ever offered her insult, besides imprisonment of course, but at best he could think of that one time he'd grumbled that he hoped she was better than the last Twi'lek dancer who didn't understand the intricate rhythms of interpretive jatz-wail accompaniment, which was item number four hundred and twenty on his hate list. That Twi'lek ended up dancing in the rancor's belly. Maybe he could compliment Leia on her choice of assassination? He'd planned on the one-shot blaster, but strangulation was much more effective, and probably better for the environment. Bib was just about to approach her when the Jedi poked his ridiculous face out.

"Leia!" he shouted.

"Luke!" Leia perked up, then ran to him. Bib sank deeper into the shadows, muttering a curse. The two were working together! He waited, then followed at a distance.

The *Khetanna*'s deck was a scene straight out of a holoadventure. Guards and mercenaries lay sprawled everywhere, motionless, while the few who remained alive huddled in a group, moving slowly toward something out of Bib's view. The sun beat down as the smell of scorched metal and Sarlacc indigestion filled the air. Bib peeked his head out further just in time to see what the guards were staring at: the tantruming sand wizard fired the barge's own cannons at the hull of the ship before he and the crime lord assassin/dancer swung to the prison skiff. The *Khetanna* erupted in a plume of smoke and fire as the deck shuddered beneath Bib's feet. He had time for a single scream before the explosion picked him up like a giant hand and tossed him to the desert below, and the world went black.

FORTUNA FAVORS THE BOLD

Grunt.

Bib groaned. It felt like his whole body had been set on fire, then extinguished by a Gamorrean lying on top of him.

Grunt.

Bib opened one sand-caked eye. A Gamorrean *did* lie on top of him, performing some disgusting form of resuscitation. Bib flailed a hand at it, begging a moment's peace from his foul tusks, before rolling over onto his side, painfully, and facing his slobbery savior. No. Saviors. Three faces floated above him, staring down. A Gamorrean, Max Rebo the Ortolan, and a . . . whatever Droopy McCool was. The chindinkalu flutist of Max's band held a rag to a scrape on his head, while Max and the Gamorrean reached down and grabbed hold of Bib. Together, they pulled him up into a sitting position, on what he was very surprised to see was the other sand skiff. The one that constantly malfunctioned.

"Where is everyone?" Bib asked, groaning.

The Gamorrean grunted, waving a meaty fist, and Bib shook his head then immediately regretted it as a wave of pain swept over him.

"What do you mean we're all that's left? No droids? No servants?" He looked around. The desert was strewn with bits of the *Khetanna*, some parts still smoldering. The Sarlacc was still, though the occasional belch shifted the sand around it. The other skiff was gone, no doubt halfway to Mos Eisley at this point. He grimaced. He had to hand it to that Jedi. Maybe there was something to his grandiose antics. Hopefully he never saw him again, or Solo or even Leia, the deadliest assassin he'd ever seen. Bib scanned the desert before returning to take in the skiff and its occupants. No staff, no guards . . .

"No Jabba," he breathed aloud. "Jabba . . . is dead."

Laughter burbled out of him, and he grabbed his head-tails and doubled over in painful amusement. "Jabba the Hutt is dead, long live

Jabba the Hutt. His empire is now ripe for the taking, and I, for one, know just the person to lead it to greatness."

The Gamorrean scratched his crusty forehead, then grunted a question.

Bib snorted. "No, fool, not you. Though," he amended at the scowl turned on him, "there will be a great reward for you for helping to build this new empire. And you will have all the concert contracts you can fulfill," he told Max and Droopy. "Just think of it. Stadiums full to bursting with fans desperate for your new jatz-wail masterpiece. My friends, we are on the cusp of greatness. Surely. The palace is ours, Mos Eisley is ours, this world is *ours*!"

He threw his head back and laughed again, then paused as he jostled something and heard sloshing sounds. A tarp at the rear of the skiff covered a collection of objects, and he lifted it to find—

"Klatooine paddy frogs?" he blurted. The Twi'lek rounded on Max and Droopy, who shrugged and revealed their own jars they had tucked behind them. Even the Gamorrean shoved a fistful of the wriggling slime-covered creatures into his mouth. "You all eat them?"

Max trumpeted in wry amusement while Sy winked and held out one for him to try.

Bib scratched a head-tail, then sighed. Why not? Jabba was dead, he was his own master, and no one could stop his rise. If he could cross off the number one most hated item on his list, maybe he could eliminate a second. It was that kind of day. He grabbed the paddy frog and swallowed it whole, licking his fingers thoughtfully.

"Tangy," he said, before shrugging and grabbing another and nodding at the Gamorrean. "Let's go home. I . . . we . . . have an empire to rule."

DUNE SEA SONGS OF SALT AND MOONLIGHT

Thea Guanzon

"Come with me."

The words were soft and beseeching—such a far cry from Altair Wyeto's usual carefree drawl that at first Jess wasn't even sure that she'd heard him properly, his statement garbled by the roar of ion engines, the clatter of storage containers, and the din of various Outer Rim tongues.

But he was peering down at her with eyes so bright green and cautiously hopeful as the docks on the edge of Mos Espa's upper sprawl bustled around them. Even though the freighter that he'd bartered labor for passage on was about to leave and its crew was shuffling in through the hissing doors, Altair made no move to join them. Instead, he stood in front of Jess, his broad shoulders hunched and his hands shoved into the pockets of his frayed trousers. Waiting.

"And do *what*?" Jess asked, pushing the blue streak in her white-gold hair out of her face, only for the desert wind to whip it right back to its starting point.

Altair took over her mess, tucking the wayward strands behind her ear. "There's music in the Core, too, you know."

"There's music *here*," she retorted. Cydi Lum and the Neurotransmitters had invited her to audition; they were mostly a fixture in Tatooine's cantina scene but sometimes they played offworld. It was a start, and Altair was well aware of that. "Besides, who'll keep my dad out of trouble if I leave?"

He sighed, his hand straying from her ear to her cheek. This was far from the first conversation they'd had on this subject, but it was the most pressed for time—the Quarren freighter captain barked his name from atop the ship's ramp, and still Altair hesitated, biting his lip.

"Go." Jess smiled to take the edge off her firm tone, and so that she could do something other than succumb to the sudden rush of tears welling up inside her. If she cried now, he wouldn't leave—and there was nothing for him here. "Win your races. You're going to be amazing. Contact me once you've settled in."

"Jess . . ." Her name caught in his throat. A moment of uncharacteristic vulnerability. "I don't know when I can come back."

She understood. The swoop circuits were demanding; disappear from it for a while and people would forget you, wouldn't be willing to bet on you. Training was even more grueling. But she would never be able to live with herself if he gave up his dreams for her.

"Then *I'll* visit *you*, when I'm filthy rich and on tour with my band," she said breezily, earning a reluctant grin from him. "Maybe the war will even be over by then."

DUNE SEA SONGS OF SALT AND MOONLIGHT

"Wyeto!" the freighter captain shouted again, the tentacles protruding from his jaw waving angrily. "Hop on board *now* or you're staying here, and I'll toss your swoop bike, too!"

Despite the threat—despite how much Altair *loved* the swoop bike that he'd cobbled together from spare parts and had served him well in many a sandy race—he still didn't move, conflict written all over his sharp, sun-kissed features.

Jess made the decision for him. For them both. She tugged him down by his collar for one last kiss, closing her eyes against the harsh glare of the twin suns. She heard an exasperated groan from the freighter captain, as well as several whistles from the throng of spacers and dockworkers going about their business, but she didn't care. Altair returned her kiss hungrily, crushing her to him with an arm around her waist, one hand cradling the side of her face. She savored every sensation, committing it to memory because this was the last time. At least, for a while.

"Love you, canyon krayt," he mumbled against her lips.

She broke away with a laugh. His pet name for her would never not be funny, but she also wanted him to remember her like this—happy, smiling, proud of him. She let him nuzzle at her nose for a heartbeat before she finally mustered the will to push him toward the waiting ship. Toward his future.

TWO YEARS LATER

What's the best way to kill a Hutt?

It was a game, of sorts, played infrequently and only in the dark. The question unspoken, the answers whispered with lips chapped by paint and the pretty act of smiling. A different method put forward and summarily discarded from one dingy pallet to the next, filling the dead hours when the twin suns slept.

"Knife to the lung."

"A Hutt has three. You have to get lucky thrice."

"Blaster bolt to the skull."

"Where exactly would you hide a blaster?"

"Lightsaber?"

"Good luck with that." A dainty scoff. "The Jedi are all gone."

Jess liked the nights when the kajidii and his entourage were away from the palace. It meant that she and the other women could sleep in their own quarters beneath the ground instead of fighting for space on Jabba's repulsorsled, curled uncomfortably around all those other bodies. It meant that she didn't have to wear her fingers out on the seven-string hallikset until her drunken audience finally lost interest, or socialize with Jabba's guests, clutching Bib Fortuna's arm while dreaming of an impossible day when she could dislocate it.

Mostly, though, it meant that the women had free run of the palace.

"Come on." She skipped over the threshold of the darkened chamber, motioning for Oola to follow. Jess knew how to flutter her lashes, how to angle her body just right; the Gamorreans were far from immune to such charms and had been sweet-talked into looking the other way.

Oola was smiling a little as she caught up, which Jess found gratifying. The Twi'lek dancer rarely smiled but tonight she was carefree, her steps spry without the chain that bound her to the Hutt whenever he was in residence. The two women crept closer to their target, a new wall decoration that occupied pride of place in a sandblasted metal alcove. It had been given to Jabba by the bounty hunter, the one that always made Jess tense like she'd better watch her back every time he walked into a room.

DUNE SEA SONGS OF SALT AND MOONLIGHT

Oola blinked up at the wall decoration, at the rugged features that were twisted into an eternal grimace, encased in a block of solid carbonite. "Why, if he hadn't been screaming when they froze him, he'd be quite handsome, actually!"

"I like his nose," Jess said in clinical agreement. In the gloom, if she squinted, the man could almost be Altair. Same height, same wavy hair, same big hands. But Altair was offworld, making a name for himself in the swoop races, where he belonged, and this carbonite statue was . . .

"Han Solo," Oola breathed. "I can't believe Jabba caught him at last."

"Even the most notorious smugglers let their guard down eventually, I guess," Jess quipped.

An old pain crept like a shadow over Oola's beautiful face. "Or Jabba catches everyone in the end."

Privately, Jess wondered how it had happened—how the legendary Han Solo could have let such a fate befall him. She wondered a great many things about what was going on elsewhere in the galaxy, beyond the confines of this sandrock-and-durasteel fortress on the Northern Dune Sea. As always, though, she excised this curiosity from her mind with methodical determination. She wasn't leaving until she worked off all her father's debt, and there was no use wishing for what could be.

Footsteps echoed through the grimy chamber, and Jess and Oola whirled around in panic. In that moment Jess thought about the rancor, its jaws snapping in the dark behind her eyes. She prepared to purr excuses, to stick out a shapely hip, to grab the nearest thing that could pass for a weapon, to *run*.

To her staggering relief, it was only Damaris Viell. She was a musician like Jess and human, too, her long hair a deep black and her eyes the color of copper.

"I recommend hunkering down before Jabba catches you sniffing around his treasure," said Damaris, the false alarm raising a real one. "The *Khetanna* will arrive in fifteen minutes."

Jess arched a brow in challenge. "Did you see that in a vision?"

"Not at all." Damaris flashed her a serene smile. "I overheard the guards talking."

No one knew where Damaris was from, only that she'd been unfortunate enough to have gotten caught by one of the raider gangs that prowled the Outer Rim. She didn't take anyone into her confidence, which was the smart move in this cutthroat place where information was currency, where you would be a fool to give too much of yourself away.

However, there was one thing that Jess knew for sure: Damaris was unlike anyone she had ever met. She said *things* sometimes, in that dreamy tone of hers—things that came true, or things that had been true in the past but there was no way she could have known about them, and things that didn't make any sense at all. It was whispered about in the women's quarters, where secrets were painstakingly kept from the kajidii and his unscrupulous majordomo, that Damaris was off her repulsors, that the raiders hit her too hard in the head when they captured her, or that she was addicted to spice and it had fogged her brain for good.

Jess had another theory, one that she would never say out loud to anyone. Her father had filled her childhood with bedtime stories of people who could do impossible, wondrous things—people who could make objects float, who could move as fast as lightning, who could look into a man's heart and know all there was to know about him. People who could see visions.

But whenever she recalled her father's stories, she dismissed them just as quickly. She had no time for fairy tales or foolish hopes when every single day was a balancing act, with her life on that precarious line.

Still, there were the trances that Damaris sometimes went into, blurring the contents of her visions out at random, her eyes palely luminous in the subterranean gloom. There was no rhyme or reason to it, from her telling the other women to keep back right before an inebriated shipjacker shot up the throne room, to beams of red and blue light intersecting amid falling snow on a world that ate the sun.

Watch out only for yourself. That had been the advice on everyone's lips in Jess's downtrodden little district back in Mos Espa when the news spread that she was bartering her services to Jabba so that her ailing father could spend his last days without a bounty on his head. *Play the game. You can't win, but you can survive.*

It had seemed like good advice at the time—no, it *was* good advice—but, for some reason, here she was, years later, plucking notes from taut strings to a boorish audience, her eyes straying to Damaris every so often as the brunette sang, hoping that she wouldn't go into one of her trances in front of Jabba and all his courtiers. There was no telling what would happen if Damaris called undue attention to herself.

Jess watched out for Oola, too. The role of Jabba's favorite offered Oola some ... well, Jess was loath to call them *advantages*, because there were probably worlds out there where not being harassed by guards and guests was the bare minimum rather than an aspiration, but Tatooine wasn't one of them. Still, it couldn't be denied that Oola was better protected than most. And *that*, as with all things, came at a price.

Through the muddy-sweet smoke of Marcan herb clouding the air, Jess's gaze fell on Oola as the Twi'lek danced above the rancor pit. The chain dragged against the floor with her every lithe step and she moved as though it didn't exist, as though it weren't wrapped around her slender ankle. She was a Ryloth chieftain's daughter, fluent in telling stories through dance—a much-loved art on her homeworld. Her graceful twirls wove the melody of Damaris's voice and Jess's chords into tangible existence. No one in that seedy audience of criminals and dregs could look away from her, Jabba least of all. And Jess couldn't help but feel that she and Damaris were serenading Oola to her doom, every single time.

The Hutt's patience eventually dwindled. He yanked on the chain and the dance ground to an unceremonious halt as Oola stumbled toward him. Jess's rhythmic strumming faltered and Damaris's silvery voice cracked mid-song, the discordant notes a drop of ice-cold water into the evening's festivities. The crowd jeered.

And that would probably have been how it ended, capped by falling into the darkness, by running into the fanged void of a waiting mouth, but—as she was hauled inexorably along—Oola turned slightly and caught Jess's eye. And shook her head.

The barest of gestures, and yet it was enough.

We can't win, Jess thought, *but we can survive.*

Her spine straightened and she resumed playing the hallikset, fingers on autopilot. After a beat, Damaris picked up where she'd left off singing. Both of them avoided glancing in the direction of the repulsorsled as Jabba slobbered all over Oola, who bore it in silence. Some things couldn't be helped. Elsewhere among the stars there were heroes and glorious battles and grand speeches and noble causes. Here in the wastelands of the Dune Sea, there was only this.

"You all right?" Jess asked Oola later that evening, as they headed to the restrooms with the other women after the party wound down.

Oola shook her head. "I am afraid," she said softly, beneath the shuffle of myriad tired and dragging footsteps.

"Afraid of what?"

Oola paused, then squared her shoulders. "I'm afraid that one day I will say no."

The Twi'lek's eyes flashed in the torchlight, and a chill tore through Jess because she recognized that look. It was the same look that Altair had when he won his first big swoop race and the official suggested that he had what it took to triumph in the Core World circuits. It was the same look that her father had every time he staked hard-earned credits on the next roll of the dice. It was the same look that so many of the moisture farmers and the junk traders and the mechanics had when they abandoned their families to join the Rebellion. It was the look of people who retreated into themselves, who gazed upon their weathered, sun-beaten lives and thought: *Not this.*

It was the kind of look that, in Jess's experience, had never led to anything good.

The next day, Jess crept into the palace's communications center, all sweet smile and sultry pleas. Lurik, the officer-in-charge, was from Mos Espa, too, and he could usually be cajoled into letting Jess comm her father every once in a while.

There was no response on the other end today, however. "Maybe the old man's still asleep," Lurik suggested.

"Maybe," Jess muttered, frowning. It was certainly not the first time her father hadn't picked up, but she worried, nonetheless. She just hoped that he hadn't wandered from his sickbed to the nearest sabacc table. "I'll try again soon."

"Yeah." Lurik made a playful shooing motion with his hands. "Now get out of here before anyone sees you."

Just as she was about to open the door, however, he teased, "No messages for your boyfriend?"

A spasm of pain seared through her chest. Just so Altair wouldn't worry too much, she sometimes exchanged written transmissions with him, with Lurik scrambling the origin point of her pretty lies etched in Aurebesh.

We sold the holocomm so I'm using the neighbors'. Its projector is busted. You don't mind just writing, do you?

I'm doing fine.

Dad's complaining about his joints again.

No, I don't want you to come home. I want you to win your next race.

My music career's really taking off.

Whenever Altair sent a message and Jess wasn't around, Lurik had to wipe it from the logs so no one else would see. Sometimes he relayed what it said to Jess and sometimes he didn't. Jess knew how it must be coming off to Altair, that she was growing distant, but upon taking stock of her circumstances, she had to admit that him drawing the worst conclusion regarding her feelings was for the best.

"Not today," she told Lurik. "I'm actually thinking about breaking things off," she added with a shrug.

He snorted. "Good for you, miss."

"Poison?"

"Hutts are resistant, I think."

"Sarlacc?"

"If you can manage to push him over, maybe."

"Fire?"

"Then we'd burn as well." It was only a game, it would never be anything but a game, but sometimes the rage bled through. "And I'm not giving these bastards the satisfaction."

DUNE SEA SONGS OF SALT AND MOONLIGHT

On nights when Max Rebo and his band were playing, Jess took on the role of waitress instead of musician. She served drinks to Jabba's rambunctious guests with the welcoming smile that she had trained herself to never let falter while, somewhere in the back of her mind, in a place inside her that no one in this underworld could ever be privy to, she dissected Rebo's performance on his signature red ball organ, noting the deft, light touches of his plump blue fingers and his clever riffs. She'd started out on keyboard, too, before falling in love with strings. Her father had indulged her, cobbling together roughshod musical instruments from the odds and ends of the broken engines and dismantled droids he traded in.

Her father had also been a dreamer, and now he was an impoverished man dying a slow, wasting death in his sand-battered hovel and *she* was handing out tankards of Tatooni Junko when she wasn't playing for a crime lord who would feed her to his rancor the moment she went off key, or merely if the mood struck him. This was the punishment, Jess supposed, for having your head in the clouds when you were born in the dirt.

"Ah, my little desert plum." Bib Fortuna appeared at Jess's elbow, wrapping a cold hand around her waist and leaning in close so that his whispery hiss scratched low in her ear, an icy current underneath the bouncy music and the roar of the partygoers. "Take your libations to the gentleman skulking in the corner, by our lovely decoration. He wanted to make a deal with Jabba but was unsuccessful. We *must* cheer him up."

Sardonic glee was written all over the majordomo's bulbous, pasty features. An alarm went off in Jess's head, her every instinct screaming *danger* although she couldn't pinpoint the cause.

"What sort of deal?" she asked.

"He tried to buy something," purred Fortuna. "But he didn't have enough credits."

Keeping her wits about her, Jess spread her smile wider until it strained at the edges, and docilely carried the tray of drinks in the direction that Fortuna had indicated. She wove her way through the jostling crowd, the tray balanced on her perfectly manicured fingers. And then she reached Han Solo's carbonite statue and—

—froze in her tracks.

A tall, lean figure was slouched against the wall beside the statue, hands in the pockets of his trousers. Waves of brown hair fell across his furrowed brow and softened the rugged angles of his face before curling at the collar of his dactillion-leather jacket. His green eyes were studying the frozen figure with a trace of apprehension, but it wasn't long before they flicked toward her.

For Jess, it was as though her raucous, sunless surroundings were pulled out from under her feet. The music faded away and the crowd vanished. Time itself screeched to a halt, suspending her in a harrowing mixture of joy and dread as her world narrowed down to the ghost of her past standing in front of her, looking at her like she, too, was all that he saw.

But reality was quick to come crashing back on the trill of Droopy McCool's chindinkalu flute. Jess finally remembered how to move, how to walk, although with less grace than before; the drinks on her tray sloshed with every step until she stopped again, this time only centimeters away from the person who had just completely turned her life upside down by reappearing in it.

"What are you doing here?" she snapped.

"I missed you, too, canyon krayt," drawled Altair. He gestured at Solo, trapped in eternal struggle. "Can't say I think much of your boss's taste in interior design."

The shock of hearing his deep, husky voice after so long, calling her by the pet name that she'd always pretended to be annoyed by, went through her like a wave. She weathered it, spine straight, chin lifted, the forefinger of her free hand poking him in the chest. "You can't be here."

He latched onto her wrist before she could draw it back, pressing her palm over his heart. "I am, though," he said gently. "And don't think that I'm not mad at you for hiding this from me for so long, but we'll get to that."

To be touched, with such kindness and by *him,* caused something in her to break into two. She couldn't speak. She could only revel in the feeling of his skin against hers and his heartbeat strong and sure at her fingertips.

"I tried to pay off your old man's debt," Altair went on to explain. "I have savings, and my latest winnings—but Jabba said that it wasn't enough." His soft expression upon seeing her turned into something tense and angry, like a live wire. "Barely covers the debt and the interest, apparently, then there's the profits he'll lose out on from visitors who come to see you play."

Jess swallowed the rush of bile that threatened to choke her. Now she understood why she'd been made to go over to Altair. It had been an act of pure malice on Fortuna's part.

Even without looking over her shoulder, she knew that Fortuna was observing them from afar with that sly, sharklike grin.

It was a power play. And Altair, with all the boyish earnestness that he'd always hidden beneath his cocky façade, had walked right into it. So had Jess, with her continued failure to anticipate where the next strike would come from in a world full of knives to the back.

All of a sudden there was a commotion. Not that the festivities had been particularly peaceful thus far, but the sound of breaking glass and curse words yelled in various languages cut through everything else.

Jess *did* look over her shoulder, then. A fight was in full bloom in the middle of the smoke-stained chamber, on the floor above the rancor pit—an all-out brawl, more like, fists swinging, spectators loudly taking sides. On the repulsorsled, Jabba was laughing his cavern-deep belly laugh. Fortuna had scrambled to the Hutt's side, taking bets and keeping a watchful eye on the fray, in case it got out of hand and the Gamorreans needed to step in. No one was paying attention to Jess and Altair and she took full advantage of that fact, shoving her tray into the arms of a nearby insectile Cyclorrian and dragging Altair into a small side room that branched off from the main chamber.

The door slid shut behind them and she punched in the lock code, then rounded on him. "How did you even know where I was?"

A foolish question, she realized, as soon as it left her lips. He would have gone to their district shortly after landing. Everyone there knew everyone else's business. It wouldn't have taken long for him to be informed of her fate, the fate that she had hidden from him with her sparse messages.

Altair's sharp jaw clenched. He studied her in the dim light shed by the lone torch on the wall, and Jess had to fight the urge to cross her arms over her chest. Her outfit didn't leave much to the imagination; none of the palace women's did. She was thinner than when he'd last seen her. She wondered about other changes through his eyes, if he thought what she did every time she beheld her reflection—that she looked tired.

"You seemed a little off in your messages," Altair said slowly, "and you weren't responding to most of mine. I thought you were mad at me about something, so, once my ship's repairs were done, I took off. I went to your house as soon I arrived in Mos Espa. Your father told me what really happened."

"How—" The question caught in Jess's throat, and she took a breath and tried again. "How is he?"

"Surviving. He's comfortable. The neighbors take care of him." Altair lowered his voice, as though obeying some instinct that nothing in Jabba's palace could be trusted, not even a closed door, not even the thick walls. "He asked me to get you out. I promised him I would, no matter what."

Jess was shaking her head even before he'd finished speaking. "He's too sick to travel. If I go, with the debt unpaid, the Hutt Cartel will come for him. They'll torture him. They'll . . ." She trailed off, because if she were to say these things out loud, her worst imaginings, all that she had been working so hard to prevent, she would scream.

Altair reached out, clasping her upper arms in his large hands. "Willux wants you to be free. It's his last wish," he rasped. "He doesn't care what happens to him, as long as you're able to live your life. I'm to smuggle you out of here if need be—"

"And how can I be sure that you're telling the truth?" Jess interrupted harshly. "How can I be sure that you're not just saying all of this so that I'll think it's okay to go with you?"

Altair blinked. "Why would I lie?"

He looked stung. He had reason to be. He'd been arrogant and self-assured ever since the day they met, ten years ago, when he hopped down from his swoop bike in the middle of a street race to watch her as she played music, but he had never lied to her about anything. Not even once.

Jess was grasping at straws. She was looking for a reason to be angry instead of terrified, because anger gave her more control. She knew what she was doing and she knew that it was unfair—but she did it anyway, shrugging off Altair's grasp.

He was doing well for himself. *He has his own ship.* She couldn't drag him down with her. She'd tried so hard not to already.

"Back then, I let you go without a single word of complaint," she spat, "because I knew that Tatooine would never be enough for you.

So why can't *you* understand that I *need* to do this, that I would keep doing this and more, if it means that my father can die in peace? Where do you get off, coming back and interfering in my business? Is the swoop circuit closed for the season? Are the Core Worlds too boring this time of year?" He went pale but she gave him no quarter, too desperate to drive him away, to keep him safe. "I am *not* going to jeopardize all my efforts just because you've taken it into your head to have some grand adventure of rescuing me."

Altair hunched his shoulders, curling in on himself, like he thought that doing so would make him appear smaller, less threatening. He had a swoop racer's agile build, but he towered over everyone in their district. "If I had known that Willux would get sick, and that he was in debt to the Hutts, I would have taken both of you with me when I left." His eyes pierced her; they were the color that Jess imagined forests would be. "There's nothing for me on Tatooine, except you." He leaned in closer. "The reason I went to your father's house today was to ask you to marry me."

"Y-you thought I was mad at you," Jess sputtered, "so your solution was to hightail it all the way here to the Outer Rim and—and *propose*?"

Altair scratched the back of his neck. ". . . yes?"

It came as a surprise, the wetness that Jess felt streaming down her face. It had been so long since she'd cried. You couldn't cry in Jabba's palace, or the guards and the more hardened women would make a mockery of it.

But she was crying now. Silently, like a surrender, the sunrise that had stirred inside her at Altair's confession receding into the dark of a false dawn.

There was no use wishing for what could be. The punishment for having one's head in the clouds was to live and die in the dirt.

When Altair reached for her again, it was to cradle her face in his palms, holding her tenderly as though she were some precious thing. "Jess," he whispered. "Come with me. Please." It was so like the day he left, except that now he was wiping away the tears she couldn't stop from flowing, catching them in the pads of his thumbs. "You'll like the Core. There are vast acres of woodland and deep-blue lakes. There are bustling cities, with towers that touch the sky. Loads of bands there, too, that could use a good string player. Hell, I'll carry Willux to my ship myself, he'd like to see what's up there in the black, I'm sure—"

"If you try to leave here with me, they will kill us before we can get to the doors," Jess said shakily. "If we *do* manage to escape, they will never stop hunting us. They'll put a bounty on our heads. We will never be safe, not even in the Core. Jabba catches everyone in the end." Her voice broke on a sob that she failed to stifle. "Just ask that statue you were standing next to earlier. That's Han Solo," she added.

Altair's eyes widened in shock. Then she could see the wheels in his head turning. Decisions made and undone, vague skeletons of plans created and rejected—each step was written all over his face.

Finally, he squared his shoulders. His demeanor hardened with resolution, even as he continued to run his thumbs along her tearstained cheeks like he couldn't help it. "I'll make a new deal with Jabba. Give him a cut of all my future winnings, as long as he lets you go."

"*No*, Altair!" Jess burst out. "That's the trap, that's *exactly* what he's after, to chain you to him for the rest of your life! I won't let you—"

"I *want* to." His gaze was feverish now, the forest in his eyes catching wildfire with a horrible sort of determination. "You don't have to marry me, that's not—I don't expect anything from you in return."

She curled her trembling fingers around his wrists. She allowed herself this, skin-to-skin, just for a fleeting moment. Already she could hear the chaos in the next room dying down. Fortuna would look for her soon. There was no more time.

"I have to go." She pushed Altair away from her, steadfastly ignoring the ache that settled in at the loss of his warmth, his nearness. "And *you* have to leave."

"Jess—"

She gestured to another door carved into the western end of the room. "There's a passage through there that will take you back to the entrance hall. Never come here again. Jabba and Fortuna are just having their bit of fun with you now, but they're capable of so much worse."

Altair lifted his chin with the stubbornness that she knew so well. "I could *drag* you with me."

"You won't." It was soft but firm, the way she called his bluff. Escaping this heavily armed fortress would be impossible with a resisting companion; he would never put her in danger, and he knew that she would never forgive him if he dared force her. Whatever happened to her father afterward, she would blame him for that, for the rest of her life. She could count on that, at least—Altair's deep-rooted need to stay in her good graces, her opinion of him being the only one that had ever counted.

Drying her foolish tears, Jess moved closer to the door they'd come from, keying in the code to unlock it. One more step and the motion sensors would kick in and the door would slide open, and she could walk out of his life without destroying it.

Before she could take that step, though, he called out, "Wait."

"What is it?" she sniffed, retreating into her haughty shell, her prickliness. "Forget something?"

"I did." Altair worked a muscle in his jaw and suddenly he was closing the distance between them, backing her up against the wall. "This."

His lips slid over hers.

It was nothing like the tentative, smile-filled kisses of their younger days. It was nothing like the long, slow kiss she'd given him at the

DUNE SEA SONGS OF SALT AND MOONLIGHT

Mos Espa spaceport two years ago. This was a desperate kiss, searching, almost angry, and she fell into it, her hands clutching at the back of his neck while his arms circled her waist, pressing her to him as they burned together in a pantomime of collapsing stars. This was the last time. The very last. There would never be an after.

They broke apart only when the need for air became inescapable. And, even then, Jess's eyes remained shut as she tried to live in the dream for a little bit more. Altair rested his forehead against hers, his fingers warming the bare skin of her midriff.

"I'll be around," he murmured. His determination had turned into a hollow resignation that she told herself, sternly, was much better in the long run. "I'll keep your dad company. I'll just be in Mos Espa if you—if ever—Well. You know."

Jess fought back a fresh surge of tears, swallowing it like a splinter down the column of her throat. It would be cruel to let him live in hope. He was more of a dreamer than her and her father combined. She had to be strong.

She opened her eyes and untangled herself from Altair's embrace. "Do whatever you want," she said brusquely, although the effect was surely ruined by the damp tracks on her cheeks. "As long as you don't bother me anymore."

Altair flinched, and how was it possible, Jess wondered, for her heart to break in time with that slightest of movements? But she didn't stay to find out. She smoothed down her hair and rearranged her clothes and the door slid open before her with a hiss of hydraulics, and she left him, there in the torchlit gloom and the silence, her head held high as she walked back into a swell of laughter and music.

"Blaster cannon."
"You could never get one."

"With my fists, then. With my teeth. With whatever's left of me."

"It's a good dream."

In the days that followed, Jess navigated her way through life in a sort of daze. She still took great care of her appearance and did everything that was expected of her, but in the back of her mind she was always thinking about Altair, always wondering if she'd made a mistake.

When she looked back on it, in the years to come, the day Oola said no started out like any other—or almost. Two droids arrived at the palace, creakily, the sand a patina over their metal frames and crusting their joints. *Gang emissaries,* Jess thought, just another deal in the making or an attempt to curry favor in a parade of what had to have been thousands, ever since she started working here.

She and Damaris hung back amid the shadows of the throne room as the spindly golden protocol droid addressed Jabba in a timid, nasal tin lid of a voice. He nudged his companion, the astromech unit, who quickly beamed a message from a cylindrical projector.

The man revealed by the static-tinted hologram light was dressed in somber black, with storm-blue eyes that looked older than his years. He spoke calmly, his solemn expression not without a touch of earnestness.

"I am Luke Skywalker, Jedi Knight and friend to Captain Solo."

Jess barely heard a word he said after that. Blood pounded in her ears and her heart soared on the crests of the nearby spectators' muttering. *Jedi.* Like the old stories, like everything that her father had said—

No. It wasn't real. It was too much to hope.

"He's creative, I'll give him that," she remarked to Damaris.

Damaris said nothing, her gaze fixed up front. At first, Jess assumed that the other woman was studying the droids and their message, but when she followed her line of sight she realized that Damaris was looking at Oola, who was perched beside Jabba on the end of a chain, who in turn was staring at the flickering hologram of Luke Skywalker with something wild and plaintive on her face.

To the surprise of absolutely no one, Jabba saw through the scam right away and refused to grant an audience. He had no qualms putting the droids to work, though. Jess almost felt sorry for them.

The Max Rebo Band played that evening, with the bubbly Pa'lowick, Sy Snootles, on vocals. Jess served drinks while Oola danced with Yarna d'al' Gargan of the many bosoms, her refined and dainty technique a staggering contrast with the Askajian's improvised style.

It was such a normal night. At one point, Jess's route took her near the dance floor and Oola twirled past, grabbing a tankard of ale and taking a generous swig before plunking it back down on the tray with another graceful spin. Jess's lips quirked and Oola grinned in response, body arcing in a breathtaking somersault that returned her to Yarna's side. Oola was in high spirits, had been ever since the astromech unit's message, like something inside her had taken wing at the resurgence of a so-called Jedi Knight. Surely she didn't believe that Skywalker had been telling the truth? Jess resolved to talk to her about it later, ask her what she was thinking.

But she never got the chance.

Jabba yanked on the chain, and everything changed.

Oola fought back.

She said, *No*.

The tray slipped from Jess's abruptly numb fingers, but no one noticed. Practically the whole throne room had stopped to gawk as Oola resisted the Hutt's tugging, her viridian knuckles clenched around the chain, the soles of her feet scraping against the floor. She held her ground with more strength than Jess had imagined her capable of. She cried out in defiance; Max Rebo was still tapping away on his keyboard and the sounds mingled and it could have almost been a song. A song for a brief and bitter life, a song calling for an end to empires.

And then Oola was falling.

Jess was one of those who crowded around the grate to watch. She had no choice, even though her feet were lead; Fortuna had dragged her over, clearly so that she could see what happened to those who defied the Hutts. She kept a neutral expression on her face, but she didn't peer directly into the depths as Jabba's pet unfolded itself from the shadows. She would allow herself this one small rebellion, even if people like her and Oola couldn't have anything else.

As the rancor advanced below, Jess focused on a beam of moonlight shining on the grate, splintering into flecks like stars on the rough edges of cold metal. The rancor lumbered forward and Oola's screams filled the world beneath the world, leading to a chorus of bone crunching between powerful jaws and the wet gurgle of flesh ripped asunder. *I believe that one day there will be a reckoning,* Jess thought, some slow, icy roil of anger building up inside her. At the periphery of her vision, Yarna was clutching her belly and cackling, crazed with relief that it hadn't been her. *I believe that, one day, everything will burn. And it will be no less than what all of us deserve.*

When the sound of blasterfire broke the stillness following Oola's grisly fate, Fortuna ushered Jess to one side of the chamber, near the same room she had hauled Altair into what felt like forever ago. Jess's ears were still ringing with the echoes of death and she barely registered Boushh's arrival, with Chewbacca the Wookiee in tow. She gave a start only when she saw the thermal detonator in the diminutive bounty hunter's hand. A rush of fierce exhilaration pierced through her numbness at the prospect of this place crashing down over everyone's heads.

"That slimy little Ubese won't do it, my desert plum," Fortuna whispered in what he must have thought would be reassurance. "This is just part of the negotiation process."

I'm not a desert plum, Jess thought mutinously. She wasn't something that lay helplessly in the sand, waiting to be dug up and eaten. She had sharp teeth of her own, and fury and venom, and an armor that could not be surmounted by lesser men. *I'm a canyon krayt.*

Jabba was wary after Oola's rebellion. Everyone was made to sleep in the throne room that night, within plain sight. Jess dreamed of Ryloth the way that Oola had described it to her once. A humid planet, covered in dense jungles where lurked all manner of strange lifeforms. There was a figure that could have been Oola dancing through the steamy silver-green mists, a true story-dance, glorious and searing in its beauty.

Jess wanted to call out to Oola, wanted to stay forever in this softer world. But she was roused from the dream by Jabba's booming laughter, and by some sort of furor several feet away from the repulsorsled.

"Look, Jabba, I was just on my way to pay you back and I got a little sidetracked—it's not my fault—"

"It's too late for that, Solo."

Han Solo had been released from his carbonite prison. Fluid dripped off his shivering form, plastering his hair to his forehead and his shirt to his skin. He was gesticulating wildly, squinting against the temporary post-thaw blindness but still trying to talk his way out of the situation. Jabba was having none of it.

Jess's brows shot up as she peered over the crowd and saw who was supporting Solo. Boushh was *not* Boushh, but a small brunette woman who had somehow availed herself of the bounty hunter's clothes and gear—a woman whom Jess recognized all too well from the holos that promised extravagant rewards for her capture.

Princess Leia Organa of Alderaan. One of the Galactic Empire's Most Wanted.

"*You!*" Jabba snapped at Jess after Solo had been hauled away by the guards. He gestured to the white-faced Leia, who'd been brought to his side. "*Clean her up and dress her.*"

Jess automatically ducked her head, avoiding the other woman's gaze. "As you say, kajidii."

Damaris was conscripted to help. She and Jess left the throne room with Leia and a Gamorrean guard, making the long and winding trek to the women's underground quarters.

For such a short person, the Alderaanian princess was bridling with enough rage to fuel the Death Star that had reportedly vaporized her homeworld. She fought the Gamorrean every step of the way, her haughty cries of *Unhand me* and *I'll see you on a spit* bouncing off the sandrock walls. Jess had to hastily disguise a snort as a cough at some of the more colorful insults.

When they reached the women's quarters, the Gamorrean made to follow them inside. Jess would normally have ignored him—it wasn't her battle to fight—but she was still thinking about Oola, and how Leia's cheek was still glistening with the slime from the Hutt's tongue, and how this was the one space in the palace where they didn't have to follow anyone's orders.

"Get out," Jess snarled at the Gamorrean.

He grunted, staying where he was, one meaty fist resting on the hilt of his war ax in unspoken warning.

Strangely enough, Jess wasn't intimidated. She should have been, but there was a thread of helpless anger running through her. It gave her courage, and she shoved the Gamorrean toward the exit with all her might. He hadn't been expecting it, and he staggered back over the threshold. She shut the door in his face and locked it.

Leia was less uncooperative with her and Damaris than she'd been with the guard, as though she realized that there was some measure of safety here, behind a secured door, in the company of other women. Throughout the ablutions, her gaze was as shrewd as only a rebel leader's could be, like she was trying to determine if either Jess or Damaris, or perhaps both of them, could be an ally.

"I was awake when you snuck into the throne room," Damaris told Leia in a conversational tone of voice, helping the latter into a dancing-girl costume. "I don't know if you and Solo could have actually escaped, but you could probably have gotten a *lot* farther if you hadn't stopped to kiss him."

Not so shrewd, after all, Jess thought wryly, adjusting the straps on Leia's bronzium chest harness as the other woman bristled. It was an odd match, the princess and the smuggler, but love and common sense had never mixed well. Altair had been proof enough of that, entering Hutt territory to buy Jess's freedom. His very own foolhardy rescue attempt.

Thinking about Altair now made Jess's throat constrict. All she'd ever wanted was a life with him, the two of them achieving their dreams side by side.

"Word of advice, Princess," she said, fiddling with the lashaa silk drapes of Leia's costume. "You're going to be here awhile, so keep your head down. You'll be fed well and no one will hurt you, as long as you don't cause any trouble." The image of Oola flashed through her mind again, yanking on the chain, falling . . .

"I *won't* be here awhile," Leia declared. "Someone's coming for us."

"Those powerful friends you mentioned?" Jess lifted one shoulder in an uncaring shrug. "Maybe things are different where you come from, but no one is more powerful than Jabba here on Tatooine."

"That slug will get what's coming to him," Leia hissed. "They all will. Han and I are getting out of here one way or another."

"Your fake Jedi's coming to the rescue, then?" Jess sniped.

"Luke is *not* a fake." The conviction in Leia's tone shook Jess to the marrow of her being. "Just stay out of the way when the action starts. If we're lucky, you'll all be free soon."

Damaris seemed like she was hanging on to the princess's every word, but Jess had heard enough. An empty promise of salvation, offered so soon after Altair's doomed attempt to free her, so soon after Oola could no longer be saved—

She opened her mouth to retort, but stopped, watching Leia's brown eyes blaze and her slight frame thrum with a determined sort of energy. Like a caged bird waiting for the moment it could once again take wing.

So what if Leia Organa was delusional, believing that the Jedi were real in this day and age? Jess could feel superior and consider herself the smarter of the two of them all day long, but at least Leia had tried, had fought to be with Han, with the person she loved. No one could accuse her of not trying.

No one could accuse her of giving up, either. After she was led back to the throne room and chained to Jabba's side, Leia kicked and shoved at the Hutt every time he tried to draw her near, warning him not to touch her or he would regret it.

"That one's not going to break so easy," Jess overheard one of Jabba's sycophants say. "I heard she faced Vader himself without batting an eye and told Grand Moff Tarkin he smelled bad. All on the same day."

Jess knew that it was only a matter of time before every bit of fight was stamped out of Leia, because that was what this place did to people. Still, a part of her wished that day would be a long time coming, or that Leia could be rescued by her friends, fake Jedi and all, before it came to pass.

Cold logic was quick to settle in again, however. From what Jess could piece together from the sporadic tales told among visitors to the palace, these so-called rebels were too weak to go up against the Hutts.

With the repulsorsled and the alcoves crowded, and no one paying attention to them now that there was a shiny new toy to be gawked at, Jess and Damaris curled up side by side on the staircase. They had a good view into the throne room but were otherwise too far away to be overheard if they kept their voices low—not that Jess was in much of a mood to talk. There was an empty space between her and Damaris, in the shape of Oola.

The night wore on, more and more courtiers nodding off with each hour that ticked past. Yawning, head resting against the wall, Jess watched as Leia sank into an exhausted slumber next to an already snoring Jabba. She must have finally realized that there was no going anywhere. Although there was a chance that Leia would wake up the next day reenergized and ready to raise hell, for now Jess considered this a sad but inevitable defeat.

And then—

"That chain won't hold," Damaris croaked, as cold as the light of the moon that filtered in through the slats in the ceiling. She was staring at Leia from across the room. "Hearts will burn like the stars, and one day the monsters in our galaxy will be vanquished."

Jess stiffened, her arms and the back of her neck breaking out into thousands of goosebumps. Damaris's eyes were unnaturally light and so much older than her years, in a way that called to mind Luke Skywalker's holo.

Who were you before you came here? Jess wanted to ask Damaris. *Would you have been a Jedi in another life, if this were any other kind of world?*

But all of these paled in comparison with the promise that Leia would escape, that evil would be stamped out. Someday. One day. It was exhilarating. It terrified her.

I am a dreamer.

I am my father's daughter.

And the question that Jess heard leave her own lips was, "Are you going to tell her?"

Damaris shook her head. Dark hair spilled over her shoulder like the flap of a bonegnawer's wing.

"What good are your visions, then?" Jess countered archly. "Why have all this knowledge when you're just going to keep it to yourself and not use it to comfort people—to save them—" Another thing occurred to her, slipping into her mind like a dagger between the ribs. "What about Oola? Did you have a vision that she was going to . . ." She trailed off, unable to bring this reminder of the act into existence.

"I thought that the Force could do anything," Jess said instead, and Damaris went still. "That's what this is, isn't it? What you have. It's the Force."

Damaris suddenly gave a start, as though coming back to herself. As though coming back from wherever she'd been. She blinked, disoriented. "I'm not—I don't—"

Jess was on a roll, though. She didn't dare raise her voice, but anger swept through her the way she imagined an ocean would, turning her words into a low, tense hiss. She thought of her father and his stories of the Jedi, and of how the Jedi hadn't even been able to save themselves in the end. She thought of Oola and her last dance. "What good is having power like this and not using it?" she railed. "What good is the Force if it can't save someone from dying?"

"I don't know *what* this is," Damaris tried to explain, sounding miserable. "I just have these daydreams sometimes—I just go somewhere in my own head—"

DUNE SEA SONGS OF SALT AND MOONLIGHT

Jess turned away from her, signaling the end of the discussion. She was well aware that she was being cruel, but she wasn't sure what else to be, here in this pit, in these gutters, at the edge of the Outer Rim.

No more words were exchanged between the two women for the rest of the night.

The twin suns rose over Tatooine, their golden rays whisking the evening chill away from the desert air. With everyone else still asleep, Jess snuck down to the kitchens for breakfast, as was her wont whenever she was the first of the court to wake.

She sat down and nibbled on spicy ahrisa and pieces of haroun bread smeared with bantha butter while the kitchen droids whirred softly around her and dawn set fire to the windows. After a while, Naatke—one of the scullery maids, a gray-furred Chadra-Fan—poked her rodentlike head in, saw Jess, and immediately hurried over to her.

"Message for you," Naatke squeaked, handing Jess a battered datapad that had seen better days. "Arrived with the cargo skiffs. I didn't take it to Fortuna because—er—"

Naatke faltered, twiddling her thumbs with a worried expression on her flat-nosed face.

Jess flashed her a small but reassuring smile. Whatever this message contained, Fortuna would have found some way to use it against her. The scullery maid had done her a kindness. "Thank you, Naatke."

She activated the datapad and read the staticky message that flashed on the cracked screen. And, for a moment, all sound and all light vanished from the world.

The message was from Mos Espa, sent by Imj, the old woman who'd lived next door for as long as Jess could remember. Her father was dead. He had died the other night.

He went peacefully in his sleep, Imj had written. *Altair's off buying parts at Anchorhead, but I'll tell him when he gets back. We will have buried him by the time this message reaches you. I hope that it reaches you.*

The opportunity to send messages along with the Huttese supply ships cost an exorbitant sum. Jess didn't even want to think about how much her neighbor had to have paid, or which meager valuables she had bartered with.

She erased the message and set the datapad down on the table.

"Bad news?" Naakte asked timidly.

Jess nodded.

It wasn't long before the Chadra-Fan's oversized ears twitched, picking up distant soundwaves even through the layers of sandrock and durasteel that separated the kitchens from the rest of the palace. "Something's happening in the throne room," she told Jess. "There's cheering. And, below, the—" She swallowed. "The rancor is moving."

Who was it this time? Jess wondered. Had Leia pushed Jabba too far, or had Han Solo's luck run out? Or was it one of the dancers, emboldened by Oola? Would they all fall and be snatched up, one after the other, years on end?

Somewhere down the line, would that also be Jess's fate?

She wondered these things while being dimly aware of the distance in her wondering. She recognized that she was going into shock. Her father's death had always felt like some cliff that she was plodding toward, but now it was over and she was somehow still standing, and she didn't know what to do next.

Instead of going back to the throne room, Jess headed to the women's quarters with some hazy plan to spend the whole day in bed. She'd say that she felt ill if anyone came looking for her. There was no more pressure to work as hard as she could. Her father was gone, and she was trapped in a cage of her own making.

However, when she reached the communal living space deep in

the bowels of the palace, it wasn't deserted. Yarna was hunched in front of the mirror, adding a complicated-looking glyph to her array of colorful face markings with a small brush and a delicate touch. Her gaze darted to Jess's reflection over her shoulder.

"You missed the party. That Skywalker boy, he came here. And he fell," Yarna said gruffly, in a voice like brittle leaves. "But he closed the gate over Pateesa's neck. It's dead. Skywalker and his friends will be, too, soon enough. Jabba's taking them to the Great Pit of Carkoon."

"This group doesn't seem all that great at rescuing," Jess remarked. "What are you painting on your face?"

"It's the sign for victory," Yarna replied, squinting at her handiwork in the mirror. "Back home on Askaj, warriors paint this symbol on themselves when a great beast has been slain."

A little rebellion, Jess thought. No one here would understand the significance of that glyph, but Yarna did, and that would be enough. Because that was what people did when they didn't have command of whole armies or vast riches or mystical powers—they did what they could.

"Fortuna's looking for you, by the way," Yarna added casually, like an afterthought. "The *Khetanna* is leaving soon. I think he wants to take you along."

Jess hid.

She hid without really understanding why. She thought that it might have been because she had no stomach for executions today, but that didn't seem like the real reason. There was something else that made her duck into the storage closet near the women's quarters, quickly, before any of the roving guards could spot her. There was something else that caused her to plaster herself to the door, hardly daring to breathe amid the shuffle of people walking past.

There in the darkness, she listened to Fortuna snapping at the Gamorrean patrols, asking if they'd seen her. She listened to him calling for her with growing impatience. And then she listened to him curse and make his way back aboveground.

The only power that Fortuna held was over the smaller lives. He still had to answer to Jabba, and Jess knew that it ate at him.

She left the storage closet after thirty minutes had passed. It was only when she stepped out into a relatively quiet palace—with a lot of guards and courtiers having gone on the barge—that she realized exactly why she'd stayed behind.

That she realized exactly what she was planning to do.

Jess crept through the labyrinthine fortress, using servants' passageways and secluded alcoves to keep out of sight. She traced a furtive path all the way to the hangar where the landspeeders were kept. There was one Gamorrean standing guard, but easily taken care of; Jess clutched his arm and fluttered her lashes, cooing about how a fight had broken out among the remaining courtiers in the throne room and she was *so* scared. The guard puffed up his chest and left to take care of it, and Jess wasted no time in climbing aboard a Joben T-85 speeder bike. There was a hooded cloak bunched up atop the passenger seat, which she quickly donned, wrinkling her nose at the smell of smoke and old ale.

Steering the vessel out of the hangar and over the golden sands, she felt a pang of regret—she would have liked to say goodbye to Damaris, despite how their last conversation had gone. But, if fate would have it, they would meet again someday. She needed to make her own destiny *now*.

As Jess peeled away from Jabba's palace, the sun hot in her eyes and flurries of sand coarse against the skin exposed by the cloak, she darted a glance over her shoulder and saw smoke drifting above the dunes. It looked like it was coming from the Great Pit of Carkoon, but she didn't slow down to make sure, or even to wonder what was happening. She faced forward again and left it all behind.

Halfway between Jabba's fortress and Mos Espa lay a dewback ranch, a vast collection of sheds and paddocks where the great reptilian beasts of burden were bred and sold to anyone who could pay the right price. With the owner offworld, the hired hands had no qualms giving Jess water and no questions in exchange for a few credits that she found in the cloak's pocket.

Sitting in the shade provided by one of the dewbacks as it grazed on feed, she took eager sips from the canteen, letting the cool liquid slide down her parched throat as people bustled around her, raking out muck, repairing the paddocks, scrubbing down the animals. It was bitter work in the relentless heat of the midday suns. It was the kind of life that she and Altair had wanted no part of. The unfettered daylight hurt her eyes after so long within Jabba's walls.

An orange-skinned Gran scuttled out of one of the sheds, eyestalks rippling with excitement. Work came to a halt, his fellow ranch hands gathering around him as he relayed the news that he'd picked up on the scanner. Jess was close enough to hear—

"The Hutt is dead! His barge blew up! No one knows how it happened yet, but—"

Jess finished the last of the canteen's contents and hopped back onto her stolen speeder, leaving the dewback ranch in the dust. It was only when the expanse of rolling dunes on the horizon gave way to Mos Espa's skyline, shimmering in the heat haze, that a choked sob clawed its way out of her throat. The first of many. Tears mingled with sand on her face as she raced through the empty wasteland and to her new life beyond it. She wept for her father and for Oola. She wept for Yarna and Damaris and their unknown fates. She wept in gratitude to a princess who had never stopped fighting, and a smuggler who had thrown his lot in with the Rebellion, and a Jedi who was either fake or not.

Most of all, however, Jess wept in relief. An enormous, crushing relief, as brilliant as spun gold and endless summer. She blinked away her tears and, in the fleeting muddle of her vision as light and salt water blurred together, she could almost see the glyph that Yarna had painted on her face. The symbol for victory. The sign that meant that a great beast had been slain.

Altair was poring over the exposed innards of his beloved swoop bike when Jess's speeder barreled into their district in Mos Espa. He straightened up at once, engine grease smeared along one high cheekbone, his forest-green eyes alive in the gathering dusk. And Jess thought, with a bittersweet twinge, of love burning like the stars. Of love that would one day destroy all the monsters.

"I can't stay," she blurted out. "I'm on the run. Jabba's dead, I heard on the way here, but they're—if they're not *all* dead, then—someone will come looking for me—" She was well aware that she was babbling, that she wasn't making any sense. Her physical form was no longer held captive but her mind was having a hard time catching up. "Before I head to the spaceport, I just—I just wanted to let you know."

She fell silent and held her breath, waiting for him to say goodbye.

"Right." Altair screwed his swoop bike's compartment shut. "So, where are we going?"

Jess's heart skipped a beat. "'We'?"

"Yeah," Altair drawled. "I've got a ship. We've got the whole galaxy." His lips curved into a lazy grin as the twin suns sank into the horizon. "And you know that I'd go anywhere with you."

THE PLAN
Saladin Ahmed

Someday, kid, I'm gonna feed my beast a Jedi.

Malakili's heart pounded in anticipation as he watched the arrogant young man in black step toward Jabba's throne. After all these years, after all the pain and loss, today was the day the Plan finally became reality.

When he tried to recall his youngest years, Malakili could only call forth images and impressions. The main thing he remembered were his mother's hands. The hardness of her palm around his wrist as she yanked him along the food rations line. The iron of her fingers pinching angrily at his ears when he didn't earn enough credits from begging. The rough back of her hand as she cuffed him for every mistake.

Malakili had made mistakes often. He was bigger than other children and, in a word, clumsy. Tripping over his own feet. Breaking things without meaning to. But it wasn't just his body. For even as his mother screamed at him to *just pay attention,* Malakili's mind would wander on its own. No matter how he tried to rein them in, his thoughts went scurrying about like beasts without leashes.

He knew this was why his mother had abandoned him.

That day Malakili had come home from alms-seeking to find their tiny sleeping shed cleaned out. No sign of the few things they owned. Mama gone. He waited up all night for her, but she never came. People with uniforms and blasters showed up soon after and told him he couldn't stay there unless he could pay rent.

That first night on the streets was when Malakili's memories truly began. The worse-than-usual hunger gnawing at his stomach. The cold that clutched at him harder and harder as it grew darker. The eyes of predatory men following him down alleys. These he would always remember.

For a week Malakili managed to survive on the streets—stealing bits of food, earning alms with his woe tales, sleeping as close to the public heaters as he could without attracting the eyes of those who would prey on him.

Then the snowstorm came. The sort that Corellia saw but once in a generation. The sort that killed street people. Malakili saw the dread spread among them as the first flakes fell. Folks rushed to bargain, to threaten, to call in favors—anything to find a hole to hide from the cold. But Malakili had nothing to bargain with and he wasn't strong

THE PLAN

enough to threaten anyone. He had to settle for finding the most sheltered corner he could and covering himself with a blanket stolen from a shopping stall.

The feeling left his fingers first. Then his toes went numb. His teeth rattled as a chill built within him and shook him to his core, like an angry animal finishing the kill. For the rest of his days Malakili would never forget the grim misery of lying there, lights dancing in his darkening vision, unable to move as the snow piled around him. Knowing he was about to die.

And then—warmth. Breath like the blessing of a fire warmed his face. Then thick musky fur and a rough lapping tongue brought Malakili's mind back from the edge of death. A snouted beast—a shaggy green harr half his size—nuzzling him with concern. He locked eyes with the creature, and for the first time in his life, Malakili truly felt focus.

The harr lapped at Malakili's fingers and he felt the feeling return to them. *It . . . it's helping me.* This creature didn't know him. He had never fed it. But it saw that he was suffering and it came to his aid.

So different from people, Malakili thought just before he passed out.

He woke on a tattered pallet to the hum of a half-functioning heater and the scent of reheated nutrisoup. He was in a sleeping shed, one twice the size of his old home. Several empty animal cages dotted the room, each with a feeding bowl. The snows were still howling, but now he heard them outside, through thin walls. Malakili had never quite appreciated walls until this moment.

"Wasn't sure ya were gonna wake up!" The voice like molten lava belonged to a squat humanoid with pale-pink skin. His short eyestalks shifted as he focused his attention on Malakili. "Folk come to me when their animals are sick or hurt, but I don't know much about healin' people. Name's Scraps. Ya want some soup?"

Malakili's thoughts scrambled about. He struggled to leash them, then to speak through still-chattering teeth. "Y-you you saved me? You saved me. Th-thank you, Mister Scraps." He took the bowl of bright-purple broth with a grateful nod, his hands relishing the warmth of it.

"Just Scraps. And I woulda left ya out there. Hard enough feedin' myself. But Nibbles here took a likin' to ya, and she woulda whined my damn hearin' ducts dry if I didn't do somethin'. So thank her." Scraps reached down with a thick three-fingered hand to pet the matted green fur of the beast that had saved Malakili's life.

"T-thanks, Nibbles," Malakili said. And when the creature oinked and smiled a jagged-toothed grin in response, Malakili again felt a sense of focus—of attention—that he had never quite felt before.

"Hmf. She likes ya. And she don't like many." Scraps's eyestalks shifted back toward Malakili. "Ya out here on yer own, kid?"

"I—my mama . . . she—she left." Malakili felt the weight of the words as he spoke them. He tried not to collapse under it. "I don't think she's coming back."

Scraps's tiny mouth puckered in sympathy. "Damn, that's rough. I'll tell ya, I don't envy ya native alley brats. This is a cruel world to be born on."

"You're from far away, huh?" Malakili had seen aliens of many races, but never one who looked quite like Scraps.

"Smart kid. Yeah. I'm an Utai. From Utapau. Halfway across the galaxy from here. Not many of my people leave home."

"So why did you come . . . here?" Malakili found it hard to believe that anyone would make this neighborhood their home by choice.

"Because I was young and foolish. Because I thought my planet

THE PLAN

was too small for me." Scraps's eyestalks shifted to look upward. "Because I used to look up at the spined night-fliers gliding so high it was like they could touch the stars—and I couldn't stop wondering what was out there."

Malakili sipped the last of his soup quietly. He knew enough to let an old person talk when they wanted to talk.

"Well, I've been to six different systems working as a beast healer, and I found out what's out there—selfish folk and swindlers. Brigands and bastards. Imperials and rebels blowing everything that matters to bits." Scraps spit and a viscous bit of black goo whistled as it flew out of his little mouth. "Been away from home a lotta cycles now. Don't figure I'll ever make it back."

Scraps was talking to himself now as much as anything, but Malakili didn't care. He sat there, stomach full, the warmth finally taking the last of the chill from his bones. He locked eyes with Nibbles and he could almost hear the words in his head before she flipped onto her back, presenting her belly.

Scratch me.

Malakili obliged, then forced himself to focus again on Scraps's words.

"—anyway, that's what it's all come to—this grubby little life here, helpin' people with their beasts."

Malakili spoke without meaning to. "It seems like a pretty great life to me."

Nibbles got to her feet, trotted over to Scraps, and began oinking.

"I don't know..." Scraps said to the alley beast. His little black eyes glinted in their stalks as he studied Malakili closely.

Nibbles oinked again insistently.

"All right, all right!" Scraps replied. He turned back to Malakili. "Look, kid—I'm old and I got a lotta crap needs doin'. I could use an extra pair of hands that don't lock up when the air gets dry. A kid with a strong back to help with the chores and the critters. And I got a spare pallet here. I'm thinkin' maybe we can help each other out."

Malakili could hardly believe his ears. He cried as he accepted Scraps's offer, and Nibbles tackled him playfully, lapping up his grateful tears.

Those years were the happiest of Malakili's life. He ate better than he ever had at home and Scraps never hit him, even when his mind wandered. He filled out quickly, and the thick corded arms he developed from lugging feed containers made others think twice about messing with him.

With effort and help, Malakili found he could force his mind to focus as he helped Scraps with scrounging and odd jobs. Most of the time he could remember what he was supposed to do. When he didn't, Scraps grumbled, but there was no real venom in it.

When he was with the beasts, though, Malakili didn't need to force anything. And he was with the beasts often, for Scraps's little clinic was always busy. Machines and droids mattered, sure, but it was beasts that really made the city run. Riding creatures, beasts of burden, racing dogs, pit fighters, beloved lap pets—folks brought them all to Scraps's door for healing. And Scraps taught Malakili about each and every species. How to calm them, how to feed them, how to heal them, but more—how to listen to them.

The old Utai was a walking repository of knowledge about beasts. His eyestalks would twitch amiably as he quoted from old codexes, hijacked Imperial databases, myths and legends, and years of firsthand knowledge gathered across six systems. Scraps had absorbed it all and was eager to share when he saw how attentive Malakili was on the subject.

Eventually, though, Scraps's talk always came back to what he

THE PLAN

called the Plan. When Scraps talked about the Plan, Malakili couldn't help but focus on the fire in his mentor's eyes.

"Someday, kid, I'm gonna feed my beast a Jedi."

Malakili looked up from the sedated tooka-cat he was bandaging. "Huh?"

"I keep tellin' ya I got a Plan, right? Well, that's it—someday I'm gonna track down a Jedi and feed the bastard to Nibbles here." The alley beast oinked happily at the mention of her name.

Malakili finished wrapping the tooka's little blue paw and snipped the bandage. "That's . . . why, boss?"

Scraps held up a thick pink finger the way he did when quoting a source he'd memorized. "And yea it is True: The beast that eats the flesh of the Jedi shall be transformed! And yea, it is True: Such a creature shall become a wishing beast."

Malakili scratched his head. "A wishing beast? Like in the stories? Like *Tell me three things you wish and I will make them so*?"

"Every story has its roots in truth, kid. Half a dozen different sources—legends from all sorts of systems—say that wishing beasts are real. And that they're born when a beast eats a living Jedi." Scraps's little black eyes seemed focused on something far away.

Malakili gently placed the tooka in its cage to rest. "If you say so, boss. But are the Jedi even—"

Scraps's eyestalks stiffened and he flushed dark orange. Despite his constant grumping, Malakili rarely saw him this genuinely angry. "I do say so! Ya ever known me to be wrong about somethin' to do with beasts? Even once?"

Malakili struggled to remember such an occasion and could not.

"That's what I thought! So don't you go tryin' to shoot holes in the Plan!" Scraps plodded outside to the stable to look after a sick baby blurrg. From then on, when Scraps brought up the Plan, Malakili just listened respectfully and kept his doubts to himself.

The older he got, the more certain Malakili was that the Plan wasn't something Scraps ever actually expected to achieve. It was just something to keep him going. He kept the hope of it alive to help keep himself alive.

But the Plan died with Scraps the day the pirates came.

Malakili had heard the tales, of course. Pirates raiding poor neighborhoods in the middle of the night, smuggling their captives off of Corellia under the noses of the authorities. But the tales didn't prepare him for the splintering sounds of half a dozen armed humanoids kicking in his door. They didn't prepare him for the smell of the pirates' breath as they shouted at him and Scraps not to move.

Nibbles lunged at one of them, a Trandoshan with an eye patch. The man withdrew a scaly, bloody stump where his hand had been. Scraps tried to stop the Trandoshan as he drew a blaster to retaliate. The man shot Scraps in the chest. Then he shot Nibbles five times.

As he watched the light fade from the old man's eyes and heard Nibbles's last pained whimpers die, Malakili slumped to the floor himself. His will melted away into nothingness. Why fight? What was left to fight for?

The pirates put him in chains and talked about the price a big young man like him would fetch.

For many months he was kept in a cage, awaiting the selling season when the pirates could demand the optimal price for him. It was a tiny iron box of misery and filth, and it almost broke Malakili completely.

THE PLAN

What saved him were the rats. The other prisoners thought them mere vermin. They tortured them for amusement or killed them for a few foul-tasting bites of meat. But Malakili listened to them. He learned how the happy chitter for feeding time differed from the alarmed chatter for danger. He befriended them by giving them bits of what little food he was given. In turn they chittered and squeaked at him affectionately. It was the only real warmth in that place, and Malakili focused on it like he'd never focused on anything in his life. It was this that kept him alive until he was sold.

And sold he was. Sold and sold again. From farm to stable to circus, for years Malakili was traded like a thing, serving this master as a cattle hand, that master as a hound keeper. As soon as they saw his skill with beasts, though, his masters would begin to eye him as a valuable thing. He was sold upward and upward, to more and more powerful monsters.

Eventually he ended up on Tatooine, owned by one of the most powerful monsters in the galaxy—Jabba the Hutt.

By a certain standard, life as Jabba's beastmaster was better than it had been even before Malakili was enslaved. He ate better than he ever had on his homeworld, and his belly grew. Where once he had been the assistant, now he had helpers. And though he was enslaved, he wore no chains. Jabba didn't need chains—he kept his people captive through fear.

His people and his beasts. For Jabba and his men didn't understand connecting with beasts. They had no patience for listening. They only knew the prod and the whip. Malakili's gift and skill in befriending beasts meant nothing to them. They wanted their beasts mastered. Broken.

And so, though there was high living to be had at Jabba's palace,

Malakili came to think of it as a torture house. A place where he was forced, day in and day out, to be cruel to creatures he cared about. For many months he lived that way, resigned to die in a place where every being from banthas to bounty hunters had their spirits broken in service of the palace's master.

Until the day he met Pateesa.

"A . . . a rancor!"

Malakili's breath caught the first time Jabba's men brought him face-to-face with the beast. Even in the dank and dark of the holding pit, those eyes shone. Malakili could still recall staring into them as the guard's voice rang off the stone walls deep in the bowels of the palace. "Yeah, a rancor. Boss has had this thing down here for years. It's eaten three of his beastmasters. Guess he figures it's your turn to take a crack."

Scraps had gone on and on to Malakili about rancors—told him stories, shown him old holograms. But being face-to-face with one was another thing entirely. This beast before him was . . . it was like the mold that all other predators were imperfect casts of.

The creature rattled a low, wary sound as Malakili examined him from a safe distance. He bore numerous scars. Lash marks. Prod burns. And the wariness in those glinting eyes—it wasn't just instinct. It came from painful experience.

What had he been through?

Malakili hooked a chunk of meat-feed to a feeding pole and took a couple of cautious steps forward, the pole extended. "H-hello there," he said in his feeding-time voice. "You hungry?"

With claws like swords the rancor snatched the food away, pole and all, and Malakili nearly lost an arm. He took two steps back and smiled encouragingly at the beast.

THE PLAN

"You're incredible," he whispered.

The guard snorted and spit. "Yeah, so incredible it ate two Gamorreans who got too close. That's just this month. Jabba is fed up. He's giving you a week to break the beast. Guess you know what happens if you disappoint him." He took a few steps toward the chamber's huge double doors before turning on his heel. "Oh, right. It answers to Pateesa."

Malakili slept very little that week. Day and night, he worked to build a bond with Pateesa. Staying just out of reach of those sword-sized claws long enough to establish himself as a friendly presence. Feeding him at the right times. Letting him take in his scent as the rancor slept. Humming soothing songs.

Malakili was as exhausted as he'd ever been. But for the first time since coming to Jabba's palace, he really felt as if his mind was working properly.

After two days Pateesa let Malakili near enough to remove the womp ticks that had attached themselves to him in Jabba's filthy pits. After five days there was no need for chains when it was just the two of them.

In order to exercise the master's pet, Jabba's men gave Malakili relatively free rein to roam the dunes just outside the palace. As he stood there with Pateesa, endless waves of suns-blazed sand stretching out under that searing blue sky, he thought about the cruel days of captivity and the slow breaking of spirit that lay ahead for the creature. He thought about the vicious little life he had at Jabba's palace, as tainted as the smoke-stained air of that damn audience chamber. And Malakili thought about running away.

As soon as he dared to think the thought, Pateesa growled as one of Jabba's guard skiffs zoomed past in the sky like an angry insect, bristling with armed men. For a panicked, irrational moment Malakili feared they had heard him thinking about escape. He took a breath and calmed himself, then calmed Pateesa with a humming lullaby.

Running was not an option. They wouldn't even make it to Mos Espa before they were caught. Then Malakili would be tortured and killed. And Pateesa would be given to some vicious brute to break.

For years Malakili watched Pateesa's spirit drain away as he became "The Rancor"—a thing used to terrorize any who would dare defy Jabba. He stopped daring to hope they would ever escape.

Until he heard that a Jedi was coming.

At first Malakili thought it was the usual tale-telling that held sway among the guards and bar workers, like the stories about arm-wrestling a Wookiee or pleasing four dancers at once. The Jedi were all dead, after all. But when Bib Fortuna himself began hissing at him to prepare Pateesa for a *very important* guest from the Rebel Alliance, Malakili began to nurture hope for the first time in a long time.

For if this impending guest really was a Jedi, if Jabba really did drop him into that pit . . . He recalled Scraps's Plan.

And yea it is True: The beast that eats the flesh of the Jedi shall be transformed! And yea, it is True: Such a creature shall become a wishing beast.

Malakili had always been skeptical, but . . . if it was true . . . even Jabba couldn't stand against power like that. It would be enough for him and Patessa to finally be free.

It was almost too much to wish for. Malakili told himself it was rumor and nonsense. He tried to tame his racing hopes. But when the young man in the black robes stepped into the throne room,

THE PLAN

Malakili knew. This was no impostor. He held the old powers in his blood.

Blood that would soon be Pateesa's.

The Jedi approached Jabba's throne. All grace and confidence. Malakili hated men like him. So sure of their own power. So sure things would work out their way. Malakili doubted the man had ever truly suffered a day in his life.

His breath caught in his throat as the swaggering braggart stepped onto Jabba's trapdoor grate. He knew it in his bones, now—Scraps had been right all along. Soon Pateesa would feed on this Skywalker. And with the power the creature would gain by consuming a Jedi, she and Malakili would finally be free—from Jabba, from pirates and warlords, from fear.

The Jedi made one last futile gesture as the trapdoor hissed open. Malakili was utterly focused as he watched the fool fall, and he smiled a true smile for the first time in many years.

"Free, my friend," Malakili whispered, though Patessa couldn't hear. "Soon you will be free."

REPUTATION

Tara Sim

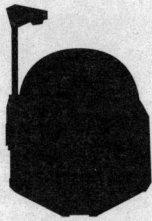

As the *Khetanna* sped over the Dune Sea toward the Great Pit of Carkoon, Boba Fett decided that his carbine rifle could stay in its holster.

There was no threat on Jabba the Hutt's sail barge other than the live music and the drinks being passed around by the astromech droid, both of which Boba kept his distance from. While Jabba's cronies reveled, he stood at the windows and watched one of the two skiffs racing beside them that carried Jabba's prisoners: Skywalker, Solo, and the Wookiee.

The desert suns brightened Han Solo's dirtied white shirt, the man squinting not from the light but from post-carbonite blindness. Soon

Boba would see the last of him. The thought came with equal parts satisfaction and relief: satisfaction in that Boba would witness the completion of a job well done, and relief in that nothing else could go wrong once the captain plummeted into the Sarlacc's gullet.

I've kept you alive this long, Boba thought with a hint of pride. *Only fitting I should see the end.*

It was Solo's own fault, really. He had been Jabba's top smuggler for years only to throw it all away with a cargo of Kessel spice. It didn't matter how skilled or slippery Solo could be; if you owed Jabba money, you paid him with either credits or your life.

It seemed a bit of a shame to lose a man of his talents, dubious as they were. But that was the difference between them: Han Solo might be good, but at the end of the day, he'd still gotten caught. Boba knew better than to test someone like Jabba in the first place.

The sail barge and the pair of skiffs slowed to a stop once they reached the Great Pit of Carkoon. From here, everyone could enjoy a view of the prisoners' skiff hovering above the pit, as well as what lurked within. The Sarlacc's large, fanged mouth undulated around its beaked tongue, making Boba grimace behind his helmet. Jabba did have a knack for collecting unconventional pets. Beyond its massive tongue lay multiple stomachs, and he idly wondered which one Solo would be dissolved in.

Jabba came to the windows, his chuckle low and eager. Boba had heard the crime lord give this exact laugh before feeding someone to his dearly departed rancor. With a tug of the chain in his hand, Jabba forced the collared rebel princess to stand beside him.

"I commend you for your past suggestion of tossing Solo to the Sarlacc," Jabba said to Boba in his slow, booming Huttese. "But if I had done it earlier, then I would have deprived myself of seeing his face twisted in pain every day."

Jabba laughed again while Leia Organa's face hardened. Boba eyed

REPUTATION

her a moment, hand drifting to his rifle, but she remained silent and focused on the prisoner skiff.

"He's yours to do with what you will," Boba answered dispassionately.

"And I have you to thank for that. Truly you live up to your reputation."

They were words Boba took as fact, words that only strengthened that hint of pride, but they also carried a thread of discomfort. From the moment Darth Vader had handed Solo over to him in Cloud City, Boba had needed to jump through hoops to keep his prize from the thieving hands of those who wanted Solo for themselves.

In the end he was just glad he'd completed the job, as tumultuous as it had been. If he hadn't, he could have been standing where Solo was now.

The dry heat of Mos Espa's day cycle had dwindled to a cool desert evening as dusk painted the sandblasted metal of Jabba's palace in shades of orange. Boba waited before the large, durasteel door with the familiar weight of his EE-3 in his hands and a slab of carbonite at his side.

He glanced down at the contorted face of Captain Solo. It had a metallic sheen, the last of the sun blazing along the tips of Solo's fingers. He'd been frozen in a position that looked either placating or defensive, as if that would have been enough to stop the onslaught of carbon gas.

Vader's insistence on freezing the captain had been yet another unnecessary delay in delivering the smuggler to Jabba. Boba supposed he should be thankful Vader hadn't simply tortured the man to death. Then again, considering what had come after, he wasn't sure how thankful he should be.

The wide door slowly opened, revealing two Gamorrean guards. They grunted and ushered Boba forward with their axes. Halfway down the stone corridor, Bib Fortuna stood waiting with hands clasped before him. The Twi'lek's pasty face broke into an oily grin as his gaze traveled between Boba and the slab.

"So you return victorious," Fortuna drawled. "Despite some delay."

Boba turned his helmet to glare in Fortuna's direction. "Bounty hunters keep to a code. I wouldn't fleece Jabba. And yet you put a price on my head."

Here was the thing: Boba wasn't a fool. He knew perfectly well that just because he was considered Jabba's top bounty hunter, that didn't make him safe. Their contracts were impassive transactions, not promises built on trust.

"Well, you can't blame Great Jabba for that. Once he received word that Solo was up for bid on Jekara, what else could he think?"

Boba drew in a long, quiet breath. Keeping someone alive in carbonite was no small feat; if the matrix became unstable, that was that. So when Solo's began to act up, he'd taken what he thought would be a quick detour to Nar Shaddaa to get it fixed. Little had he known the captain would be stolen from under his nose by Crimson Dawn.

And because their contracts were ironclad, his options were either get Solo back or face whatever retribution Jabba had in store.

"He's here now," Boba said. "And my payment wasn't conditional on whether or not there was a delay."

"Of course." Fortuna allowed himself the edge of a sneer and turned to lead him through the rest of the corridor. Boba flexed a hand on his rifle, telling himself Fortuna wasn't worth the money he'd have to pay for Jabba to take on a new majordomo.

Music was playing in the subterranean chamber Jabba had transformed into his throne room. The air that filtered through his helmet carried the earthy scent of pipe smoke coming from the haze that seemed a permanent fixture of the place. Boba briefly scanned the disparate crowd that made up Jabba's court before his eyes landed on the middle of the room.

The smugglers and assassins jeered as a green Twi'lek woman danced atop a metal grille, the collar around her neck connecting to a long, rattling chain that snaked toward the dais where the Hutt himself sat.

"Like her?" Fortuna asked, having followed Boba's line of sight. "She's a favorite. I brought her in specifically for her hue."

Of course—the Empire willingly ignored the Twi'lek trade. The rarer and more beautiful they were, the more they were paraded about as a status symbol.

Jabba was watching the display while taking hits on his hookah pipe. He yanked on the chain and the Twi'lek woman fell onto the grille, making the court laugh. Boba lengthened his stride to get into the Hutt's line of sight sooner.

"Great Jabba, Boba Fett has returned," Fortuna announced before retreating to the spot reserved for Jabba's majordomo.

The music tapered off and Jabba hummed, eyes glittering in Boba's direction. "Come forward and let me see my new prize."

The slab hovered in front of Boba as the Hutt looked down on it with approval. Jabba took another hit of his pipe while the Twi'lek dancer retreated to her spot below the throne.

"I never doubted you, Boba Fett," said Jabba. Standing behind him, Fortuna's eyes twitched. "You always finish the job."

And yet, Jabba had put out a contract for Boba's head, which the crime lord insisted wasn't personal. But Boba was willing to forgo all that if it meant getting back to the business at hand.

"If you want to keep him," Boba said, indicating Solo with his rifle, "pay me."

The court at his back murmured at his daring. Who was he, a mere bounty hunter, to give an ultimatum to *the* Jabba the Hutt?

But they should have known by now: He wasn't a mere bounty hunter.

Jabba gave a deep laugh and set down his pipe. He nodded at Fortuna, who went to collect something between the throne and the rotisserie cooker behind it. "You will be paid, Boba Fett. You will be paid even more if you decide to stay and take on more work from me."

Boba glanced at the dancer. Her gaze had settled somewhere around Boba's chest, as if inspecting his armor. Like she wanted it for herself.

Jabba enjoyed his various contracts, but no doubt the best transactions were the ones that came free of consequences.

"You just want to use me as a buffer between you and Crimson Dawn," Boba said.

"Is that not what a mercenary does? And after all, you are the best of the best."

The majordomo returned and handed Boba a large bag. The credits had a good heft to them; Jabba's words even more so.

"We'll see," Boba said.

The music resumed once Jabba ordered Solo to be carted away to his wall of trophies. Boba turned and scanned the alcoves again, ignoring the riffraff who stared at him, and raised his eyebrows at the sight of a familiar face.

"'Best of the best,'" Dengar muttered as Boba approached the other bounty hunter. "Would the best of the best have lost Han Solo?"

"The best of the best got him back from both the Empire and the rebels," Boba shot back. "Seems you're feeling cold toward me."

Dengar scowled at the wording. His head wrap had seen better

REPUTATION

days, dirt-smudged and singed around his face. "Where's Valance? The two of you were quick to run off together."

The last Boba had seen of Valance, the cyborg bounty hunter had been facing down the wrong end of a thermal detonator, his purpose served in helping Boba get to Solo faster.

Boba shrugged in answer, and Dengar scoffed. "Should've known. You only ever look out for yourself."

"You say that as if it's not what we're supposed to do in our profession," Boba said. "We may have a code, but that doesn't make us familiar."

Boba had a hard rule: He did not work with anyone. First and foremost because no one could keep up with him, and he didn't need others in his way. If he teamed up with someone, he used them and ditched them. Valance had learned that the hard way.

The green Twi'lek had returned to her dance. Under the grille Boba thought he heard the low growl of the rancor, desperate for a meal. Jabba liked to keep his pets hungry.

"You realize what he's doing, don't you?" Dengar muttered.

Boba had said it in his own words: Jabba was using him. It was nothing new to Boba. After all, his own existence as a bounty hunter was the price paid to run the biggest trafficking operation the galaxy had ever seen.

But Boba was getting paid for his use, and that was what mattered.

"I'm telling you, it all goes south eventually," Dengar went on. "Just look at Solo. Jabba's number one smuggler, then one job goes bad and *bam*, wall decoration."

"Solo knew what would happen if he didn't pay Jabba back in time. He didn't play by the rules."

"Rules?" Dengar snorted. "What rules?"

Jabba yanked on the dancer's chain again, making her stumble toward him. She clearly fought back the urge to resist before she was pulled close enough for him to stroke her head. Boba frowned and instead watched Solo's carbonite form displayed between the taxidermized heads of a tauntaun and a jerba.

Boba wasn't a fool. No amount of credits or praise could cover up that he, too, had become a status symbol. That all the years he'd spent building his reputation now amounted to serving a crime lord he couldn't afford to cross.

He glanced back at the throne, where thankfully Jabba had released the dancer to take up his pipe again. Wondered what it would be like to sit there, to be the one handing out orders, instead of lurking in the alcoves with the nobodies.

"How 'bout this," Boba said to Dengar. "We make another bet."

Dengar side-eyed him, but at least he didn't reach for the blaster rifle on his back. "On what?"

Boba glanced at the crowd forming before Solo, mocking and laughing at the captain's fate.

"Twenty more credits if the rebels come for him."

"Victims of the almighty Sarlacc," the protocol droid announced, "His Excellency hopes that you will die honorably."

The prisoners on the skiff were sweating under Tatooine's double suns. Especially Skywalker, covered in black as he was. Even Boba was getting uncomfortable under his *beskar*. Part of him wanted to just get this over with and head back to Mos Espa, enjoy a cool drink in the privacy of his room.

Boba smirked, thinking of the twenty credits he had to collect from Dengar. The other bounty hunter had chosen to stay behind at Jabba's palace rather than join the revelry on the *Khetanna*. Probably still sore that Boba had managed to fulfill his contract before Dengar could fulfill his.

REPUTATION

The protocol droid went on to inform the prisoners that Jabba would listen to their pleas if they had a mind to beg for mercy. Of course Solo had to mouth off, and Boba's smirk grew. No amount of hibernation sickness or impending death could temper a man like him.

But his smirk fell as Skywalker called up to the sail barge: "Free us or die."

He was five steps away from tumbling into the mouth of the Sarlacc. He was weaponless. Helpless. Outnumbered. There was no way for him to get out of this alive.

Just like a Jedi, to be so overconfident.

While Jabba and his court laughed at Skywalker's daring, Boba spared another glance at Leia Organa. He remembered the simple yet cruel way in which Jabba had ordered around that dancing green Twi'lek—Oola, her name had been Oola—and couldn't help but pity the princess for having to take on the role.

In addition to becoming Jabba's new plaything, she was about to watch her companions meet a grim fate. Boba had never been a fan of Jabba's showboating; all of this could have been avoided if they'd simply . . . Well, it wasn't his problem.

I'm telling you, it all goes south eventually.

It pained him to admit that Dengar had been right. Just as Jabba collected pets, so too did he collect people—ones to entertain him, please him, do his dirty work for him. At least Solo had attempted to break out of the cycle.

While Skywalker was moved into position, Organa's eyes tightened and her fingers twitched, as if suppressing the urge to curl her hands into fists. He admired her restraint. But then something in her gaze shifted, a gleam of desert sun. Boba turned in time to see Skywalker give her a two-finger salute.

What is he—?

A hunk of metal glinted as it was flung across the pit and into Skywalker's hand. A flash of green, and suddenly Skywalker was laying into the guards, flinging them off the skiff with practiced swings of his lightsaber. The guards screamed and tumbled toward the Sarlacc's eager mouth.

Boba cursed and headed for the stairs while shocked cries rose from Jabba's court. He'd let down his guard too much. He should have kept a better eye on those droids. He—

No, it didn't matter. He'd followed the rules, and it hadn't been enough.

One way or another this was going to end. He would throw them all down into the Sarlacc himself if he had to.

He finally unholstered his rifle as he charged toward the upper deck of the sail barge. The skiff was a flurry of frantic movement and arcs of green light. Without a second thought he activated his jetpack, taking to the air.

He hadn't been born with his reputation; he had earned it. And he wouldn't let it be ruined so easily.

KICKBACK

K Arsenault Rivera

"That kid is trouble."

Sion chugged his whiskey to keep from laughing too hard. "Yeah? The kid with the big moony eyes is a threat to you, Errin?"

But the old-timer wasn't laughing. While Sion and the rest of the crew of Jabba's hired hands were watching the action from their private tables, Errin leaned against the rail, one hand near his holster.

"Don't be such a downer," said Nackt. He offered Sion a fresh cup of whiskey, neat. "Worse come to worst he's about to be rancor chow, but either way, it ain't our problem."

The music played, the girls danced, and Errin still didn't look away from the pit. In the lights of the palace his eyes were hard as flint. "He's a Jedi."

Nackt guffawed; Arfit, Nackt's best friend, choked on a Quick-Snack. Sion whacked him on the back a few times to loosen it from Arfit's gullet.

"You can't be serious," Arfit rasped. "You trying to kill me, old man?"

"No, but the Jedi will if you keep underestimating him," said Errin.

"Right after he escapes the rancor pit and gets done with his blue milk," Nackt scoffed. "Maybe you need to get your eyes checked."

In all the years Sion had known Errin nothing had ever scared him. Words or fists or blasters, it didn't matter.

But today? Today Errin put on his helmet and left without another word.

Nackt and Arfit chuckled, then poured another round of drinks. Arfit pulled Sion in for a toast.

"To Errin's last season, and a bigger cut for us!"

Sion's stomach felt awful. Like he'd swallowed a spiny-shelled desert critter, and it was dancing around in there.

"Next Boonta Eve at your place is gonna be a sight, huh?" says Nackt. "If Errin leaves you're gonna get his spot for sure."

He didn't want to listen anymore. Sion stood and followed Errin out the door. There, against the blazing blue of the sky and the endless sands of the desert, stood his friend and mentor.

Not sure where to start, Sion settled on a shifty, "Hey."

Errin grunted. "Your kids doing all right?"

"Yeah. Just gave me their wish lists," Sion said. He ran a hand over the back of his neck. "If you hadn't gotten me this job, I'd really be in the akk dog den. You can't buy that sort of stuff on a speeder thief's takes."

This earned a chuckle from Errin. "You get to my age and you learn to spot a good fighter when you see one."

KICKBACK

The two men let the moment hang for a while. Though there were things Sion wanted to ask, he knew well enough the trouble he'd bring in asking them. Sometimes a speeder ran just fine until you took a look under the hood. People could be the same.

Especially people who had seen what Errin had seen, done what Errin had done.

But wasn't it valuable to preserve that knowledge? To share it? And if that guy really was a Jedi, if Errin really thought there was going to be trouble . . .

He opened his mouth to ask his friend: *How do you fight a Jedi?*

But by then the rancor was dead, and the chaos had begun.

Bright green against Tatooine's pale-blue sky, the lightsaber lit the way to certain doom. Of that Sion was certain. Getting close to that thing was as good as signing his own death mark. But working in service to Jabba meant you didn't have the luxury of choosing self-preservation.

The way Sion saw it he had three choices: get on the skiff and maybe make it out of this fight alive; hang back and probably get shot later for insubordination; or run off with his tail between his legs and still get shot later, but this time with a bounty on his head.

No—it wasn't a choice at all. He needed to be on that skiff.

Forward. Going forward was the most important thing. The anger in Sion's chest at the sight of his friends in shambles had to be his own personal reactor core. Other guards turned heel and ran—they buffeted against him as he charged with Errin and the others toward the small skiff.

Sion tried not to, but he hated the people who ran with every fiber of his being. Against a Jedi numbers were the only strength they had. He shoved them as hard as he could with every step, threshing his way through the crowd.

Arfit's words came back to him—with so many cowards there might be a bigger cut of the pay for those who stayed behind. Better festivities for Boonta Eve.

Once aboard, Sion took a breath. As the skiff moved to intercept the so-called Jedi and his escaping companions, silence reigned. Gone were the jokes from earlier, the laughs. The appearance of the lightsaber proved what Errin had so wisely proclaimed.

"When we get there," Errin said as they all tensed, "mind the lightsaber. Our best shot is to get it out of his hands somehow. Nackt, I want you to try and shoot it out of his grip."

"C-can't he deflect those?" Nackt said.

"Sure. But if enough of us hit him at once, there's hope."

In the dry heat of the desert, Sion's tongue stuck to the roof of his mouth. Errin might look sound and collected beneath his mask—but Errin could see the tremble in his hands, the stiffness in his shoulders. The sight of that lightsaber must be taking him to some awful places.

With what Lord Jabba pays you, your only worry's going to be staying alive to spend it all.

Errin told him that years ago. For years he'd been right.

When Black Sun came for Sion after stealing a prize podracer, when the press of a blaster barrel against his temple promised Sion he'd never amount to anything—Errin had been the one to save him. Risked everything to do it. Sticking his neck out like that for a stranger might well have killed him.

With a steady job came a steady life. A family.

Holiday wish lists.

Sion's son wanted a Star Destroyer model kit—one that came with thin durasteel plates for the hull. The sort of thing that could kill a man if you tossed it at him, and the sort of thing that'd bankrupt any of their neighbors.

KICKBACK

His daughter wanted a new set of flight goggles, the kind with digital readouts that tell you your heart rate.

His husband? Oh, far be it from him to ask for something simple; *he* wanted a private concert from Max Rebo's band. Wanted to kick his feet up on the table and pretend he was the boss for a little while. Charming git.

In Sion's ten cartel years there had never been a sad face come the holidays.

Errin gave him that. This job gave him that. But maybe after all this it was time to start thinking about going back home to Nar Shaddaa.

But before he did, he could add one more thing to his list. A gift he could give to Errin to try to repay him. One thing, one shining thing, he could do.

No matter the chaos, he had to make sure Errin got out of this okay.

"I'll get him for you," said Sion. "Just tell me when and I'll lead the charge."

"Sion," Errin said, clasping the younger man's shoulder. "Let me take care of it—"

"You've already done enough," said Sion. "I can handle this."

"No. Listen to me. Someone else has to distract him, or he'll cut through all of you," said Errin. And as the words left him Sion could see it in his mind—the rage that had overtaken the Jedi in all the holos of their betrayal. "You need to close the distance and isolate the lightsaber. Shoot his wrist, stamp on it, whatever you can. But you need to get to it . . ."

Sion swallowed. If he had that fancy pair of goggles it would tell him to pull over and take a breather, to get himself under control before the worst happened.

Among the shouts and the screams and the smoke his husband Sigs's voice came to him.

What's working for Jabba like, anyway? You never talk about it. I mean, you must see all kinds of interesting things, and interesting people and—

I don't really do much of that, he'd said. *Mostly I stand around and look intimidating.*

And it was true. Most days that was all he did. For a lot of deals you just needed a lot of people around as set dressing. Most days, he never drew the blaster, never showed off the skills that had gotten him the job. Those were the good days.

He didn't want Sigs to know about the bad days. The days he couldn't get the blood out from under his fingernails, the days he put off going home in case the darkness loped into their family home like an akk dog at his heels.

Today was a bad day.

Especially because the Jedi jumped toward them, and not the other way around.

Finally, he was close enough to get a good look at him. Wait a second. He'd seen this kid before, hadn't he? Back at Mos Eisley a few years ago Jabba was looking for Solo. Sion had been part of his bodyguard detail at the time. This kid walked in looking bright as Coruscant nights against the shabby interiors of the place; you could tell that even if he'd been raised here, he wasn't meant to stay. Bright-eyed youths like that always ended up mulch—either because the Empire wore all that polish away, or because the Rebellion needed disposable operatives. In this galaxy nothing that gold ever stayed.

But at the time, Sion envied that brightness.

Now . . .

Sion's grip tightened around the blaster. "Nackt, Arfit," he growled, "hit him from the left. I'll come from the right. All at the same time, you hear?"

His companions nodded. They knew.

KICKBACK

A swing of the lightsaber. More of them fell.

Sion raised a hand. One, two . . .

Three!

The men launched themselves forward, heads bowed like banthas, great bellows leaving their throats. With death by Jabba on the one end and death by the lightsaber at the other, there was no room for fear in their hearts. Only ambition. Only the dream of a day they'd wake in the morning without blood on their hands, without death, without sand.

The dream of a resort on Nar Shaddaa. Of a private showing by a band. Of model kits and flight goggles. Of good lives for his children, where they wouldn't have to know what it was like to watch someone die.

The Jedi fought off Nackt and Arfit. Sion couldn't stop himself now. They'd isolated his lightsaber for just long enough that he had an opening, one he had to seize!

Sion raised his blaster. He had him. He had him. There was no space to parry and no space to swing, and—

—and he hadn't accounted for the kick. Not at this distance. The force that hit him square in the chest surprised him from a scrawny-looking kid like that—it knocked him right off his feet. But how? How had he forgotten, and how had the Jedi found the space to . . .

Sion tumbled from the skiff. Beneath him, he knew, was the Sarlacc's gullet. His new home, his last home.

He thought of his family.

He closed his eyes, and screamed.

EVERYONE'S A CRITIC
Sarah Glenn Marsh

The lush, humid forest he called home was, like all forests are, full of teeth. Teeth sharper than his beak, and probably lots (he couldn't count that high, couldn't count at all really) of teeth bigger than his beak, too. Not important. What *was* important was this: The forest was hungry, and even though he was hungry, too, he had to run and hide or he was going to end up as somebody's dinner. He didn't know who would want to eat a lean, stringy thing like him, but he'd heard the stories that rustled the treetops about the way they liked to eat creatures like him in far-off places, slow-roasted to seal in the juice and flavor. He was determined to remain off the menu tonight.

He wasn't the fastest thing in the galaxy, let alone in the forest, but it must have been his lucky day, because he was just quick enough to scramble on board the impressive starship that was wedged into a break in the trees before whatever had been chasing him could sink its teeth into his stringy flesh. He was also small enough that no one—not the variety of sour-faced humanoids with blasters at their hips or the giant, sluglike creature (majestically nasty, he noted with awe) whose bulk filled the entire hallway without trying—noticed him.

Well, not at first. Not until he found the kitchen. After a couple hours of hanging out unnoticed in a cupboard with the pans and cutlery, he'd had to open more than a few drawers trying to find some crunchy bugs or a furry little thing to snack on to prevent his stomach's growling from giving away his hidey-hole.

He was just about to claw into a bag of some promising-looking dark, glittering shells when a pale hand grabbed him by the tail and held him up to the harsh overhead lights, much too high above the floor (and the stove) for comfort. "And what do we have on the menu tonight? A big-eared stowaway?" his red-eyed captor sneered. The little monkey-lizard had no idea what had just been snarled in his face, but he was certain enough of one thing: This creature was rude.

The Rude One turned him this way and that as the monkey-lizard thrashed in his hands—cold hands, unpleasantly so, the kind not a lot of beings would be happy to shake. Also, as the monkey-lizard learned a moment later, not tasty. He forgot sometimes that while he didn't have teeth, his beak had quite an edge, too; the Rude One wasn't the first to make those high-pitched noises when his beak got ahold of something delicious. The pale being dropped the monkey-lizard so he could suck the blood off his fingers while he hopped up and down through drops of cerulean that had showered the floor, spitting several words that, by their venom alone, were surely some inspired curses.

The monkey-lizard looked at the ridiculous creature who had

EVERYONE'S A CRITIC

menaced him, then laughed and started copying him, trying to repeat the curses. What else can you do when someone's shouting and dancing like no one's watching, but you happen to be right in front of them? The monkey-lizard's large ears flopped exactly the way he meant them to, right into his eyes, until the Rude One laughed so hard at the sight that he showed all his small yellow teeth (once again, too many to count).

For a minute, the monkey-lizard felt like he was in for a treat.

However, when the Rude One grabbed him a second time, harder (still laughing—critics take note), and stuffed him in a little cage not unlike the ones he supposed they used to hold his kind elsewhere until they started roasting them—leaving him alone in the kitchen with the cooks, close enough to smell dinner but not near enough to take a bite—the monkey-lizard was sure he had somehow earned himself the opposite of a treat after all. A trick, perhaps, or worse.

He blurted out one of those foul-tasting words he'd just learned from the Rude One because if there was one thing he was good at besides being small and cute, it was repeating things he heard with precision, whether he understood them or not. As soon as the sounds left his beak, a booming laugh—charmingly filthy and so big, bigger than any sound the monkey-lizard could make—filled the room.

Positively famished and bored out of his mind, the little creature tried imitating that, too.

Preceded by his laugh, the giant slug-creature he had seen in the hallway earlier slithered into view, as towering and glorious as the monkey-lizard remembered from his first glimpse, making his way right up to the little cage. The monkey-lizard rattled the bars and danced like he'd just been bitten to the music of the slug-creature's laughter.

Making this immense being laugh felt good. Though he couldn't explain why, it made the monkey-lizard laugh harder, too.

The slug-creature exhaled a swampy breath that stirred the littler creature's hair, his orange eyes narrowing then widening as he studied the monkey-lizard.

The much-smaller creature widened his eyes just the same way, round as moons, flopped his ears forward, and made a soft clicking noise with his beak. It was his cutest face (he even thought of it as The Face for short), the one he used to beg for a good scratch or a free ride—a look that hadn't, in his limited memory, ever let him down.

"Stowaway," the vast creature said with a deep, booming voice that radiated power and a whiff of something foul, "I am the Great Jabba..." (Well, actually, he said much more than that, but the monkey-lizard couldn't understand much. Too many syllables. He recognized the meanings of a few of these sounds, though, from the time someone had tried to train him into a regular old obedient pet; hadn't ended well for them, he was proud to recall.) "And you are?"

Sensing Jabba wanted some kind of response, but not sure what exactly was being asked, the monkey-lizard quickly flipped through his limited vocabulary of words he had heard often enough to repeat, eager to please this magnificent being if he could. "Salacious!" he cackled, because it was a funny sound. Tasted good on the tongue, too.

Jabba's wide mouth broke into an even wider grin.

"Salacious. This ship is like home to me. One of many. And you have entered my home without an invitation. An insult I do not take lightly," he said gravely, his eyes roaming over the cage.

The little creature kept *his* eyes nice and big, his ears half covering them, giving another little quiver of his beak because he still wasn't sure from the larger being's tone whether he was about to be tossed in the cook pot or handed his bag full of shells from earlier to finish his snack.

Jabba sighed at that beak-quiver, his voice softening. "Your Twi'lek

EVERYONE'S A CRITIC

friend, Bib Fortuna, thinks we can get a little money for you at our next port of call. But I think ..." Those great orange eyes narrowed in thought again as he reached toward the cage door. "You might have better uses than a handful of credits."

The door sprang open.

The monkey-lizard was confident, at least, in his quickness; he could have made a break for it, really tested his luck and scurried to freedom, but he saw something better right in front of him, this imposing being who had fallen for The Face. He scrambled out and onto Jabba's outstretched arm.

This time, when his eyes turned into wondering moons, it wasn't an act—he'd never been in the presence of such Greatness before, and for his tiny mind, it was a lot to take in all at once. Jabba was vast where he was small; he also seemed to be in charge here, commanding a ship stuffed with enough riches for one lifetime, where the monkey-lizard had to beg and steal just to scrape by day-to-day. He made his way over to Jabba's shoulder, finding a stable perch without sinking his claws in too deep.

Maybe this was his chance to be in charge of something, too.

Jabba reached up and ruffled the monkey-lizard's hair just the way the little creature liked it. Then the enormous slug scooped some unidentifiable chunk of meat out of a simmering stove pot and tossed it to him. The monkey-lizard gobbled it down eagerly, even though it was too hot, while Jabba kept scratching his head. Bliss.

"Make me laugh like that once a day, little crumb thief," he said in a tone that was surprisingly sweet for a being of such eminence, "and my palace and all its comforts are yours. All you can eat and drink. A place at my side for as long as I sit on my throne. Whatever you wish. Do you understand?"

The monkey-lizard blinked; he had, at least, caught a few words here and there, like *laugh* and *eat* and perhaps—was he being offered a chair? Or told to sit? He hadn't liked being trained before, but a command from this benevolent creature felt different somehow. Compelling enough to obey.

Suddenly Jabba was pulling on his hair a little too hard, *much* too hard, bending his neck back roughly until his beak opened in a silent grimace of pain.

"Fail to hold up your end of the bargain, however, and I will feed you to something that will find you delicious," he crooned, still tugging on the creature's head. "My pit-pet rancor has eaten hundreds of my enemies and is always hungry. So. Do you accept my offer?"

The monkey-lizard was trying his best to follow along through the haze of heart-pounding panic. Making Jabba laugh: good. Jabba not laughing: very bad. Pain-in-the-neck bad, at the least.

The little creature burst out in a deep, throaty cackle, even though he was still hurting.

He laughed, because it was funny that he had wound up in a kitchen while trying to stay off the menu and also, it turned out, it was pretty easy to make a sound like laughing when he was terrified. So he cackled until he howled and Jabba was laughing again, too, letting go of his hair and even smoothing it back into place—as much as it ever was, anyway.

Before the monkey-lizard knew it, he was chasing Jabba's tail across the floor of his private quarters, catching scraps of his warm and questionably scrumptious dinner out of the air as they tumbled from Jabba's careless mouth, and the ship was in flight.

It really was the monkey-lizard's lucky day; he was trading his home full of sharp teeth for one full of sharp tongues and sharper weapons, but he had it made. All he had to do was stay on the laughing side of the one doing all the stabbing. And someone like Jabba surely did a lot of stabbing, no matter how many enemies his pit-creature gobbled up for him on the side.

EVERYONE'S A CRITIC

Settling in on Tatooine shortly after, the little creature missed the pasol trees he'd traded for sandrock and steel, the music of the jungle at night, the constant chatter and arguments of the other monkey-lizards, and the ocean. Oh, the ocean! There was nothing like it on Tatooine; what they called the Northern Dune Sea was nothing but sand, or else he had misunderstood. Wouldn't be the last time.

But there were many things he *didn't* miss about home: hungry forests and cutthroat slavers, mostly, and of course all the teeth built for crunching up something scrawny like him. Besides, he had fine things here that he never had at home, like a name—just like his new keeper answered to "Jabba," it only took him a few days to figure out that every time Jabba said "Salacious," he wanted the monkey-lizard's attention—and the best seat in the house, not a real chair but something much better, a perch high up on Jabba's shoulder where for the first time in his life, he was looking down on everyone else for a change. So, he was determined to make the best of things at Jabba's, even if it was admittedly dim and dank and ocean-less.

Lucky for Salacious, it didn't take an abundance of smarts to figure out that making fun of everyone in the room was what pleased Jabba most. As long as his target was flustered enough to spark a certain light in Jabba's luminous orange eyes, he'd avoid the rancor's pit and live to spend another day chasing Jabba's tail (which he was pretty sure was a separate creature in itself, one who rode on Jabba's squishy frame like he did and had a mind of its own for all the trouble it gave him in pinning it down).

Nobody was off limits when it came to Salacious's merciless mimicry and teasing—not even Jabba—which was just how Jabba liked it.

Yet comedy, it turned out, was a harder gig than stealing from the slavers back on Kowak, harder than the creature would have thought. Everyone's a critic; they all think they can do it better, pull a sillier face, get a bigger belly laugh, twist a word or phrase just right, but

Salacious (perhaps because of how little he understood about those around him) was the only one willing to imitate Bib Fortuna's snoring face in front of an audience or sway his hips like Jabba's dancer Oola when she was moving to the music that pulsed through the underground halls. All while making eyes at Jabba and flicking his big, floppy ears just so, of course. And whenever one of his attempts at humor fell a little flat or cut a little too deep like his beak, there was always The Face to fall back on.

Not that he needed to use it too often; most of the time, his nervous laughter was enough to make Jabba lighten up when negotiations in their throne room got tense or he copied the wrong trader's peculiar mannerisms. And really, it was his pleasure to entertain Jabba; he gave great head scritches and threw down the juiciest morsels for Salacious in return. Jabba was such a hard worker, too, which was one of the first things the monkey-lizard learned about him as he got acquainted with the employees and the finances (which were, like everything else about Jabba and the palace, vast to the point of being incomprehensible). The little creature could sense Jabba's worry and stress; that was why he needed Salacious, because if the monkey-lizard knew anything, it was how to keep the mood light.

That was also how Salacious knew Jabba would never *really* feed him to the rancor. Jabba talked tough, but that was just part of Doing Business; underneath the booming insults, he was just a giant ball of love, the best cuddler in town. He was Salacious's protector, his family, his big friend; the monkey-lizard was his confidant, his right-hand man, his little friend. Together for life, relying on no one but each other at the end of the day. Simple.

Besides, would someone who was going to throw him to a rancor really do thoughtful things like support his hobbies? Not long ago, Jabba had ordered his servants to help find droids—a word he quickly learned meant shiny, loud things that made the funniest noises when

EVERYONE'S A CRITIC

he chewed on them—just for Salacious to tear apart, and nothing made the monkey-lizard feel more loved than using his claws and beak to cut through a thick tangle of wiring.

There had been a couple of droids he was bursting to dig into recently, a tall chatty gold one and a short shrill white one who made Jabba laugh with the hologram they played about surrendering one of their prisoners (as if Jabba would hand over their favorite wall hanging, the carbonite slab with the most punchable face, just because somebody had sent a droid to make demands!). But Jabba, true Businessman that he was, found other uses for those droids like he had for Salacious. The monkey-lizard had had to make do with taking apart some other beat-up old astromech instead.

That was just what he was doing in the throne room when the trouble started. He had a bundle of wires tangled around his claws, half a biscuit Jabba had dropped hanging out of his beak, and designs on wrapping those wires around Jabba's tail to see if he could make it stay still once and for all when a little bounty hunter in full gear and a face-concealing helmet led a much taller, uncombed furry creature in cuffs toward the dais.

Was this one of their associates? Or a hopeful new trading partner whom Salacious wasn't supposed to mimic? So many beings came and went from Jabba's throne room that he could rarely remember faces, let alone who was on their side and who was destined for the rancor pit. The details of who Jabba had killed yesterday were already a little fuzzy, even.

But before he could choose whether to mock or keep quiet, Jabba started chuckling throatily at whatever this shrouded bounty hunter was demanding for their prisoner. The monkey-lizard narrowed his eyes and tossed aside his wires; making Jabba laugh was *his* job, and of all the Types that came and went from their home, ones who fancied themselves comedians were his least favorite.

After a tense pause, his nerves wound tighter than the ball of wires he'd thrown across the dais, Salacious decided this bounty hunter must be one of their people after all; Jabba was still laughing as the furry prisoner was led off to a cell somewhere.

The mood in the palace shifted then; Jabba ordered the band to play again, and Salacious did what he always did: He stood up and took the stage. He danced like a bitten Bib Fortuna to the rhythm of the band, ears flopping into his face, until Jabba laughed so hard through his snack that Salacious knew he could collect enough bites for a whole meal.

Trouble of any kind seemed far away—that is, until Jabba burst into their room in the middle of the night, moaning that they'd lost the wall hanging with the uniquely punchable face. Salacious wasn't clear on the details of how, but he could tell from the anger rolling off Jabba in hot, pungent waves that it was not their lucky night.

Things in the throne room still smelled like trouble the next day.

The unsmiling man from the droid's hologram was now here in the flesh, making demands again. Skywalker, the others called him. The monkey-lizard's beady eyes darted all over the eerily quiet man, searching for something to mimic.

Had he ever heard a word that rhymed with Skywalker?

The conversation was, as usual, too much for Salacious to follow, except he noticed that Jabba seemed to be talking the man in circles—circles that led right over the rancor's trapdoor.

In a blink, the floor became a yawning mouth, and down went Skywalker.

The rancor roared. It hadn't eaten yesterday.

Salacious howled and jeered, because watching someone fall through a surprise door is funnier than anything he could have come up with, and Jabba stroked his hair while leering magnificently. Maybe it could be their lucky day after all.

EVERYONE'S A CRITIC

But it was the rancor who started screeching a moment later, not Skywalker. And sure enough, it was Skywalker who emerged from its lair.

Jabba's face fell. He stopped petting the monkey-lizard.

Not even The Face was any good at cheering his master up right now.

Salacious sat at Jabba's side and didn't even cackle once (in honor of the rancor) while Jabba sentenced three enemies—Skywalker, their favorite wall decoration Solo, and their tallest, furriest prisoner—to be eaten by the Sarlacc in the Great Pit of Carkoon.

Bad for them, of course, but good news for Salacious; they would have to take one of their sail barges to reach the pit, and Jabba loved when Salacious pretended to be seasick aboard the big vessel. Surely that had to make him crack a smile.

Yet things didn't look up even after they'd reached the pit. Skywalker was too calm as he was dropped toward the yawning mouth at the bottom, like he had some trick up his sleeve more powerful than The Face. Impossible, to Salacious's mind.

The sounds of fighting erupted from below.

But before the monkey-lizard could climb up on Jabba to see what was happening, everything went dark.

Somebody had cut the barge lights.

This made everything louder and busier, someone's stray fin or limb slapping Salacious hard as they rushed past in an attempt to flee. Then came a sound he knew well by now, seeing as Jabba had so many enemies: the rattling of chains. The monkey-lizard blinked, trying to focus his eyes in the dimness as Jabba made strange, wet gasping sounds. He sounded sick.

Salacious tried cheering up poor Jabba with The Face, but his master didn't even seem to see him; instead, his eyes, bulging and glassy, gazed out across the pit at nothing and his tongue lolled out like Salacious's did sometimes after eating too many biscuits. Jabba's mischievous and often annoying tail didn't even twitch when Salacious tackled it.

Salacious stared up at Jabba, a mountain as always but no longer a living one, and understood enough to know that nothing was ever going to be funny again.

No more big friend. No more protector. No more family.

Salacious's insides writhed with anger instead of hunger for once, but he wasn't seeing red; he was seeing gold and white, flashes of the droids he'd wanted to rip apart earlier. Skywalker's droids. Surely they had a hand in killing his only friend like Jabba wasn't a towering fortress designed to withstand blasts, like he wasn't a whole galaxy with two moons for eyes and an inescapable, immense gravity.

He still wasn't seeing red as he attacked them; he was seeing black and white and sparks of blue as he thought of all the wires he was going to rip out of this golden droid's insides for Jabba, starting with one of his round eyes that was bigger than the monkey-lizard's fist. It would make a nice treasure to throw around in the throne room once he got it out of the droid's stubborn—

Salacious yelped and let go of the droid's eye as a current zipped up and down his spine. Something had stung him. Bit him? It was the other droid, the white one; he'd zapped Salacious somehow.

Suddenly there was a deep, rumbling sound, kind of like the victory cry Jabba always gave when they blew up something after somebody crossed them. Only this time, Jabba's side was the one getting blown up; the barge rocked as it was flung apart into a constellation of burning pieces, sending Salacious flying along with it.

He was—he realized as he saw his tail flapping through the air—a little bit on fire.

EVERYONE'S A CRITIC

More nervous than he had been the time Bib Fortuna held him over the rancor's lair on a feasting day until Jabba caught him and stopped it, Salacious did what he did best. He cackled. Loudly.

The Sarlacc lashed a tentacle at him, acting like it hadn't heard.

Everyone's a critic. Even a tentacled creature with a gaping mouth and too many rows of sharp teeth to count. The Sarlacc probably had its own jokes saved up after living alone in the pit for so long, but Salacious had to try something, because the sand was too slippery for climbing (much more like the ocean than he originally thought, it turned out) and he was going to tumble right down into those jaws if he didn't get the creature laughing soon.

Salacious slid farther, the opposite of what he was trying to do.

Those teeth were getting awfully close and awfully munchy, and he still couldn't find anything to grab onto, but there was always The Face. That had never let him down yet. Besides, he'd be such a tiny appetizer for a creature of the Sarlacc's size. Maybe the Sarlacc didn't even like roasted monkey-lizard. Maybe today would be his lucky—

SATISFACTION

Kristin Baver

It wasn't that she liked the beast. Felt sorry for it, maybe. Even someone of Sy Snootles's persuasion couldn't help but feel a flash of compassion in the darkness. Lying in her quarters just off Jabba's kitchen, listening as the rancor's mournful baying echoed across the palace corridors, sometimes the creature had made a sound like laughter. Sy suspected it was dreaming.

But now Pateesa was dead—killed by the Hutt's shortsightedness—and Sy couldn't stop listening. She had grown accustomed to the rancor's cries. Silence didn't suit the court of the Hutt Cartel.

"The audacity." Sy shrugged on her dressing gown, the feathery collar tickling her features, and sank onto the rust-pocked bucket that passed for a stool, her lithe limbs folding compactly beneath her dressing table. She had grown accustomed to this, too. The scratchy claws of some wayward vermin, hidden behind the wall. The cramped, windowless room, illuminated unevenly by the glow of the remaining lights ringing her reflection. She traced a finger across the tabletop, leaving a smooth trail through the fine sand that had settled there in the night.

Long ago, Jabba's palace had been a place of beauty. And before that, a place of worship. Sy's room had been both and neither. The face that peered back at her now in the polished silver of an old serving tray was not one she recognized.

She reached for her compact, a hatchling gift from her father when she sprouted legs and climbed out of the swampy waters of her birth, a Pa'lowick's first steps into adulthood. With the press of a switch, the cogs and gears performed the arduous work of unlocking. The lid opened with a hiss and Sy plucked out a live omophron, pinching the creature between two bony fingers, its entire body curling into itself, a shield against the outside world.

"A little help, Zero." Snootles's LEP droid, CH5-09, powered up with a metallic shudder, eyes glowing a piercing yellow as his photoreceptors adjusted to his surroundings. The two antennas at the top of his head twitched. With a hop, his plump body jogged toward the source of the command.

"What assistance does the master require?" the droid chittered. The question was irrelevant. CH5-09's programming had been altered by Sy's own hands. He remained aggravatingly cheerful despite her best efforts to strip it away. In his own databanks, CH5 saw himself as more of a devoted servant than a slave. If he searched long enough, he could almost remember a time before . . . But whatever memories had existed previous to Sy's arrival were wiped nearly clean away when she had appointed him as her primary security officer.

SATISFACTION

CH5 had served someone else once, but he'd be hard-pressed to find those files, scrubbed and excised in Sy's meticulous work. The LEP settled in beside her and placed one metallic hand on the omophron, sending a jolt through the insectoid. The tiny muscles beneath its shell spasmed, involuntarily revealing the soft underbelly protected by row upon row of poisonous stingers.

"I'll show you limp-lipped," Sy muttered, responding to an unheard slight, an insult leveled years before yet still somehow festering. She pressed the needle-like stingers to her lips once, twice, three times. Her eyes watered, a stream of tears running down each stalk. She did not blink. "Where's Rebo?"

CH5, who had retreated to one corner, bounced back to Sy's side, his earlike antennas searching the vast network of palace droids for the right piece of intel. "Calculating . . ." he said. Each member of the Max Rebo Band—a name Sy had grown to despise over time—had lodgings in the same corridor. A series of tiny, retrofitted storage alcoves off the palace kitchens, a foolish request undoubtedly from Rebo himself when he was negotiating their contract.

"*Koochoo*," Sy spat at the memory.

"It would seem that—" CH5 began.

That Ortolan was always thinking with his stomach. "*Max!*"

A clanging from the next room answered her suspicions. Rebo appeared in the doorway, one foot entirely covered in some kind of gelatinous substance he'd pilfered from Jabba's pantry, a few stray oi-ois glistening at his knee. He stood propped up on his remaining foot, which was noticeably quivering.

"I was just getting a snack before we set sail for Carkoon and . . ." he said.

"Go on without me."

"But Sy," Max started, slapping both feet on the ground. A sticky mist of jelly sailed through the air, forcing CH5-09 to race toward the

Ortolan and put his small metal body between the oaf and his master. The goo slapped CH5 square in the face, clouding one photoreceptor over with a blush-pink haze and making the broadcasts on his left antenna sound as if they were transmitting from underwater.

"Max, honey, listen," Sy said, the corners of her mouth curling down with great effort. "It's something . . . I ate."

Max's eyes widened. His flippers shrank. "No."

"I've been positively wretched since dinner." Max staggered a few steps back, his eyes darting to the potentially offending jelly squished between his toes. "I can't begin to stomach a death sentence right now. It's a wonder the rest of you haven't—"

In a blink Rebo had turned himself around, one leg slipping and sliding down the hall leaving a trail of sticky goo in its wake. His tail nubbin flapped as she watched his backside recede into the shadows, the whoosh of air sucking her makeshift door shut. Sy giggled. Max would spend the rest of the day waiting for the moment when the sweat of performing in the sweltering desert turned into the clammy announcement of his stomach turning.

Jabba wouldn't care if she didn't show. The real entertainment was the execution, the pageantry of his captives begging for forgiveness before inevitably being tossed to the Sarlacc. The Hutts were not known for issuing last-minute pardons and Sy was done performing as background noise. Plus, it behooved her to appear to be too squeamish for such things. She had a delicate image to maintain.

Her schedule cleared, Snootles returned to her reflection. She reapplied the stage makeup that highlighted her natural markings and coated her long limbs in a moisturizing salve made from the mud bogs on Lowick. If she wasn't vigilant, Tatooine's arid climate would dry her out completely, leaving nothing but a good-looking husk.

SATISFACTION

Why had she come to this worthless rock? Ziro the Hutt had seemed like her ticket to stardom on Coruscant. His palace was cleaner in almost every sense of the word. Jabba's uncle spent his credits tiling his throne room in Naboo marble, a proper stage for her nightly performances. But then Ziro had gotten himself hauled off to prison and Snootles was forced to make alternate arrangements. She knew enough to keep in the Hutt Cartel's good graces. At first, that meant a stint on Nal Hutta, performing "Daa Hutt Muna" nightly. At least the air there was damp enough to keep her voice and body in pristine condition. In the years since she arrived on Tatooine, her fluid sac had been struggling to keep up.

"How long has it been now?" she asked. CH5-09 paused to check his databanks, careful to remain still as Rebo's jelly dried to a sheen. Within milliseconds, he knew how many cycles it had been since Sy had first taken the stage here. He knew how many years had passed. CH5 calculated how many performances she'd given in the same moldering corner of Jabba's throne room, his processors tallying the number of times Sy had rolled her eyes through another rendition of "Lapti Nek," the decimal points behind each figure accounting for a variety of interruptions. He also knew that Sy wasn't really asking. She had posed this same question before and she would ask it again, but the droid had learned through painful experience she didn't want to know.

In any case, the exchange was abruptly cut off as the door to Sy's room—really more a patchwork of scavenged metal that didn't quite cover the opening—was flung open once more.

A crouching B'omarr monk scuttled through. "For the last time," Snootles roared, punctuating the next phrase with whatever objects she could grab from her table.

"This." A small mirror thudded against the side of the monk's bulbous body.

"Isn't." Her beads sailed through the air, caught up on the intruder's hindquarters with a chatter.

"Your broom closet!" Her tusks extended fiercely just as her omophron case finally landed a blow to the liquidy dome that held its brain, the last of its organic parts.

The monk paused, an indication of contemplation or the last strands of awareness trying to form a singular thought within the sloshing sphere. In the pursuit of purity, the being had stripped itself of organic nuisance. Only its essential functions remained. Now, confronted with the bug-eyed Snootles, her chest inflated in a territorial posture, her primal fangs deployed, it no longer contained the necessary sensory receptors to process the confrontation.

The monk lifted one needle-like limb, threaded the end of the appendage through one of Sy's leather skirts hanging on the wall, and, mistaking the shredded garment for a rag, backed its way out of the room, crouching down with a fluid motion as it exited.

CH5-09 hopped after the strange creature, a dance he had performed many times over the years. "That is right! Bow to your master. And stay out," he yelled down the hall.

CH5 turned back just in time to dodge a flying hand mirror. Sy swiped at the table, sending her remaining trinkets and personal items crashing to the floor. She clawed at what remained of her wardrobe, grunting as she tore each costume off its hook. Then she turned her attention to the piece of art hanging over the sling where she slept. The face of a much younger Sy Snootles beamed back at her. A vibrant starlet, basking in the glow of her adoring fans, preparing for her first residency on Coruscant. And across the top, in a crimson that matched her signature lipstick, SY SNOOTLES: LIVE! It was her breakout moment, promoted from backup dancer to star.

Sy screeched as she tore it down, pleasure immediately subverted by regret. The fragile thing, stiff to the touch yet delicate, easily ripped

SATISFACTION

in two. The younger Sy's frozen smile, creased and puckered in one hand, was now completely separate from the rest of her. Sy panted and heaved as the four air sacs in her chest struggled to keep up. Normally, her years of vocal exercise helped her to control her breath even in the midst of a howling rage. After years of being relegated to the backdrop, forgotten by Coruscant's elite, abandoned on some backwater world to be paid in stews and sandwiches, the monk's intrusion was the fissure that shattered her calm.

CH5-09 watched silently, considering deactivating himself in case he was the next target. But then . . . Sy released each air sac, one by one. Her tusks retracted slowly, transitioning from sharp horns to imperceptible teeth, tucked away in her primordial lower jaw. Taking her travel case from beneath her sling—always packed with the essentials, her copy of the Hutt Council records, and the credits she had amassed from years of bounties and other side hustles—Sy Snootles walked out.

The corridors were eerily calm. The kitchen still smelled like roast nuna and shuura tarts. A solitary COO-series droid stood silent by the carving station, awaiting its next order. The one saving grace of Rebo's foolish contractual obligation was the Hutt's droids' adept culinary programming. And being lodged near the kitchen was far preferable to the stink of Jabba's throne room. Between the smoke and the leering Hutt's own musky odor, a foul yeasty concoction that wafted from the folds of his corpulent flesh, Sy could barely stand it.

CH5-09 followed ten paces behind, dutifully playing out a role he'd inhabited countless times before. He calculated the frequency, then immediately stored the data, knowing he would never be asked.

The dungeons were as quiet as the rest of the palace. The *Khetanna* was well on its way to the Great Pit of Carkoon, with every last one of

Jabba's captives in tow. Still, Sy stopped at the detention block, pausing before each fortified window, the darkness teeming with rivals and suitors she knew to be both alive and quite dead.

She had to press her body to the grate of the first cell to see past the mountainous flesh of Mama the Hutt. The matriarch's back was turned to the hall and filled nearly every meter of the cramped space. Mama said nothing, but Sy could still hear her insults, as fresh as when they were uttered back on Nal Hutta.

Joh Yowza sat alone in the next. His appearance surprised even Snootles, who had up to this moment left her thoughts on the Yuzzum singer largely unexamined. But just one look at his filthy flat face, and she knew she had always hated Yowza for taking what was rightfully hers. At last, he was silent, a bandage tight across his throat, the most fitting revenge Sy could fathom. "You can rot here," she said, waving to her muted bandmate with a flourish.

Ziro the Hutt stared out tearfully from the last cell, prepared to grovel for his life. "I always will love you, Snooty!" The figment used an old family nickname reserved for those closest to her, both friend and foe.

"I know it, baby," she cooed. "But I never did love you." She had disposed of Ziro years ago, two clean shots to the heart, yet his adoration persisted beyond the grave. CH5-09 could hear Sy locked in conversation. Slowing his steps, he ran a quick diagnostic on his photoreceptors to confirm the chambers were all empty, but decided it was best not to insinuate himself into the matter.

Sy began to hum to herself on the staircase, a jaunty tune she hadn't been commanded to sing in ages. Jabba's patience was always waning. She and the Max Rebo Band had experimented with all manner of

SATISFACTION

popular genres through the years to please *His Majesty*. Why had she even agreed to let Rebo take all the credit? The Max Rebo Band! His father had been all class and charm, but while Max was a proficient red ball jett player, that sticky-fingered dolt couldn't think beyond his next meal. But Sy knew how to take her time. Even now, as she ascended the staircase, each footfall matched the beat of some unheard melody—a full orchestra, playing her onto the stage.

She left her case on the foyer, knowing CH5-09 would be along momentarily to keep watch. Then with both arms extended in her signature pose, Snootles strutted into the throne room. Instead of the dingy decay she had seen only hours before, she was greeted by the shimmering sight of a freshly painted stage, dazzling beneath the heat of a singular spotlight.

The crowd hooted and cheered, screams of ecstasy erupting from corners of the room that were shrouded in darkness to Sy but were then instantly replaced by silent rapture as she took a deep breath and began.

The song started out slow, a little melancholy. Then the drum kicked in and the backup singers joined the chorus. Snootles turned to see her friend Greeata on harmony, one long scaly arm wrapped around the shoulders of another singer. Was that Oola? Oola! Still alive and no longer chained at the throat. Snootles herself might have wound up as one of Jabba's playthings without the foresight to find other uses for her skills. And there was Leia Organa, the last princess of Alderaan, emerging from the shadows to complete the trio of angelic accompaniment. Sy had rarely heard such beauty outside of her own voice.

Droopy McCool toddled into view, piping a solo on his chindinkalu flute, the vanilla-like aroma of his sweat glands wafting a pleasing scent through the air. Such a nice change from the putrid stench of the Hutt and all his sycophants. The fawning Jawas were the worst, fanning the Hutt to get close enough to steal the scrap left behind by his many hastily disassembled translation droids.

Only then did she notice—Max also remained, no longer seated at the organ but the role he was born to play: taste tester. A woman of her fame and stature could never be too careful about poisonings. She had killed at least seven targets herself with a distracting smile and a sprinkle of some deadly seasoning. Sy inhaled and was just about to belt out the last verse when CH5-09 raced into view.

"Master Snootles!" CH5-09 chirped frantically. If a droid could be breathless, hers was certainly approximating the urgency that typically came with such a sprint. "Master, I beg you to forgive the interruption." The droid gave a small bow, deferential and fearful. "I have received urgent news from the execution." Snootles sighed. She so rarely had the palace to herself, a time to bask in the pleasure of solitude. Reality beckoned, intruding on the reverie.

"Jabba usually prefers a longer performance at the pit," she said, more to herself than the droid. For a moment, Sy stopped to consider the Jedi and his odd friends. She had assumed their defiance would have bought her more time for one of her favorite activities in Jabba's court.

"It is . . . on fire." CH5-09 felt certain he was relaying the facts from the droid network quite succinctly, yet Snootles cocked her head to one side as if he were short-circuiting.

"*Skocha Sarlacc?*" she asked, slipping into Huttese. The Sarlacc burning?

"The *Khetanna*. Flames. Flames on all sides. And the prisoner . . . has slain the illustrious Jabba."

"The Jedi?" Creatures of all kinds had come to Jabba's court, and Snootles had peered from the shadows sizing up each one. This one,

SATISFACTION

with his gifts and his mind games, she'd suspected was trouble the moment his holomessage flitted to life.

"My apologies, master. I am getting intel on all frequencies and it is in some disarray. The female prisoner has killed the mighty Jabba, it would seem, with her chains."

Sy couldn't contain her glee. A guffaw escaped her swollen lips. She and Bib Fortuna were some of the Hutt's oldest confidants, and they had often bet each other on the circumstances of his inevitable demise. Sliced open by a clumsy Gamorrean guard. A rampaging rancor attack unleashed by an angry ex. Choking on an unchewed Klatooine paddy frog. But this? Sy had never dared to imagine such poetry.

"Tell me exactly what you know," Snootles commanded.

The palace droids were still piecing together what had happened amid the chaos. There had been some kind of revolt, CH5-09 relayed. Guards siding with prisoners! A server droid with a laser sword? Not everything Sy heard made any rational kind of sense, but as the LEP verified and clarified, one truth emerged.

Jabba the Hutt was dead.

The end of Jabba's cruel reign brought a new plan into focus, without so much as a passing care for Max Rebo and his lonely concert on the flaming barge. Sy would be lying if she said she hadn't thought about leaving Jabba's palace every day since her arrival. And above all else, she never lied to herself.

Snootles had a choice to make. She could toss her feather in with the rest of the lot who would come vying for Jabba's throne, a throng of power-hungry mercenaries eager to install themselves in a place of authority amid the vacuum. Sy could rule over the sad little spice trade and raise it into an empire of her own, singing for her suitors and banning Jawas from so much as looking directly at her. The Hutt Cartel owed her at least that much.

Or she could make good on her threats. She could take her case of credits and walk out the door. With the proceeds from a few valuable prizes pilfered from Jabba's collection, she could begin to make things right. A stage even more magnificent than the one she'd debuted upon. A spotlight trained only on her. And outside this grand theater, on the uppermost level of Coruscant in league with the galaxy's esteemed opera houses: her name in lights, SY SNOOTLES. The band would be implied, and they would happily stand by her, silent partners paid only in meals.

"Zero," she said, taking a seat on Jabba's dais. "Power down while I think on our next engagement." Sy surveyed the throne room with fresh eyes, possibility mingling with reality. Her leggy form already made the platform appear far grander than it had compressed beneath the Hutt. She barely noticed that it was still warm to the touch.

MY MOUTH NEVER CLOSES

Charlie Jane Anders

People, stop tossing each other into my mouth!

I'm serious. I've tried letting you know every way I can, and you still keep doing it. Every once in a while, one of these flying machines soars over me, full of these little spindly creatures with their limbs flapping around in the air. I always hope they're here to make friends, but then their bodies just plummet into my mouth, without even trying to communicate. I've never actually had a friend before—my people just drift alone among the stars until we find a place to burrow, as it happens—but since I've been here, I've seen all these tiny beings living together, and I kind of like how it looks.

For the last time: *I do not eat flesh*. Okay? I don't like having your meaty bodies slowly decomposing in my throat for thousands of years, especially when you don't even bother to remove all of your fabric and ceramic and metal coverings first. I made a decision long ago: I won't feed on any creatures, especially ones that seem to have opinions about things.

I've been sitting here, in my cozy burrow extending deep underground, for a very long time, but this whole leaping-into-my-mouth business has only started recently.

When I first arrived, this world was a tropical paradise. I was adrift in space, caught in an endless dream of light and dark, tossed by the occasional solar wind, and I came upon a planet with sparkling oceans and lush jungles, bathed in the light of two magnificent suns. Even from a great distance I could see the swaths of blue and green and the gentle haze of puffed-up clouds, drifting through the atmosphere. The gravity well drew me in and tugged me toward the biggest landmass, and I did not resist. *Here,* I thought. *Here I will make my home, at the floor of the jungle.*

I found the greenest, juiciest part of the biggest rain forest, and tumbled past the mesosphere. Once on the ground, I dug and tunneled until I had made myself a pit, cushioned with lichen and damp leaves, and settled myself in. The steamy canopy overhead blocked out almost all of the light from the suns, and all around me the rain forest was full of life: chittering, cawing, rustling through the vines and fronds. A lush garden paradise surrounded me. The leaves fell into my mouth! Tiny furry-scaly creatures skittered around me and nibbled on the insects that nested on my upper flesh. Oh, it was glorious.

I was used to being alone, after so long in the chill of interstellar space, but here I was part of a whole green world, and it felt *right.* I said to myself, *Everything here is perfect, and it shall remain so always.*

I settled in with a contented shiver of my tentacles, and fell into a

MY MOUTH NEVER CLOSES

deep slumber, full of operatic dreams about somehow inviting my fellow sarlaccs to visit my rain forest home, all of us bobbing our beaks in harmony. While I slept, the rain forest fed me and soothed me with its constant gentle drizzle of moisture and fluttering leaves.

When I woke, I was in the middle of an endless desert.

A desert! What in the ninety-nine hells?

I suppose I must have overslept.

All at once the suns were searing down onto me, making my tentacles grow tough and leathery. The trees and drizzles and leaves and tiny creatures were all gone. I stretched out my lower tentacles as far as I could, to consume all of the microscopic plants living underground, and hunkered down. I slowed my metabolism and tried to bring my mind to a cool plateau of serenity despite the blazing heat.

That's when the flying vehicles started showing up, and tiny creatures started pushing each other into my mouth, without asking me *once* about my dietary preferences. They flew high above me, as if they feared my tentacles might lunge out and grab them. I tried to communicate by wiggling my tentacles in the sarlacc language: "Greetings, gentle beings! Fear not, I do not consume animal flesh, by choice. Come into my presence, especially if you have some nice juicy leaves to share!" But they saw my tentacles waving, and shrank farther out of my reach.

After that, the flying constructs showed up regularly, and each time, a screaming person would plummet into my mouth—no matter how much I tried to say, "Uh, I appreciate the thought, but really, *no thanks.*" Their victims landed on the sand, twitching or making loud sounds of distress, and then they just slid into my pit and inside my throat-stomach. I can't always spit out such a large object, so I just had to shunt them into my ninth stomach and expel them the best I could. I'm sure it was fun for everyone concerned.

Most of my kind do eat living flesh, or flesh that was recently alive.

I just find the idea disagreeable, and to be honest I just don't like the feel of slowly rotting meat stuck inside my gullet for a thousand years.

The floating shapes came and went, and I kept trying to communicate with them, to no avail. I was starting to wonder if any of these loud thrashing creatures actually had any intelligence whatsoever. Until the day came that *someone spoke to me*. I finally met a civilized being who spoke sarlacc.

He was a golden humanoid—he seemed to be made of metal, but he had the decency to avoid falling into my mouth, so I'll never know for sure. And he was on board one of the soaring machines, bringing more screaming creatures toward my mouth. By this time, I had lost all patience, so the moment the machine arrived, I shouted with as much vigor as my tentacles could manage, "Stop force-feeding each other to me! It's rude!" I could hardly believe it when he spoke back. I hadn't met anyone else who spoke my language in so long.

"Uh, hello," he said. "I am See-Threepio, human–cyborg relations." There was a lot more to it than that. He also called me the "almighty Sarlacc." There was rather a lot of groveling and praise for my greatness, even though all I've ever done is sit here while you throw each other at me.

"Oh, thank the great progenitor, I finally met someone intelligent," I responded. "Listen, can you ask your friends to stop tossing each other down my throat? I don't actually eat meat, and it's giving me no end of discomfort."

The whole time the golden man was using his fingers to speak to me in sarlacc, he was also saying a lot of other things in one of the humanoid languages.

"Oh dear, oh dear," the golden man responded. There was a lot more, including a lot of "most distressing" and "goodness gracious,"

MY MOUTH NEVER CLOSES

and whatnot. Then he got to the point: "I'm terribly sorry, but I myself am a prisoner here. Indeed Master Luke offered me as a tribute to Jabba the Hutt without even informing me first. I most profoundly empathize with your situation."

I was already bored with these tiny creatures and their politics. They live for such a short time, and they apparently think of each other as food, and now I come to find they hand each other over to be enslaved.

"So you keep calling me the almighty Sarlacc," I said to the golden man, "which feels a bit cheeky, to be honest. Absolutely nobody has ever bothered to ask my opinion about anything before, and you keep feeding people to me without my consent. How exactly am I all-powerful?"

"Oh dear, I don't know, it's just what I was told to say."

I tried to explain to C-3PO in the short time I had: about the beauty of this world, when I had first arrived, and the lushness of the jungle whose fossilized ghosts still shivered deep underground. About the idyllic existence I had enjoyed, with the tiny creatures who scuttled about me with no fear, and the blessed greenery raining down. I felt it was important for someone to understand: I had not chosen any of this, but I had found beauty and fulfillment here, once upon a time. Somebody needed to know that lushness and sustenance and joy could vanish in an instant, to be replaced only with cruelty.

And that's when the bodies started raining down. More than usual, including one that would have been impossible to digest even if I'd wanted to.

One humanoid fell off the smaller barge, twitching and thrashing, until he was directly over my beak. I reached out to him with my speaking tentacles to see if he could also communicate with me, but he just kicked and screamed until his exertions caused him to fall deeper into my gullet.

Another body fell, and then another. They twitched and screamed and pretty much threw themselves into my mouth, no matter how many times I tried to tell them to stop being so rude.

The golden man was gone, and all of the other humanoids on the barges were busy wrestling and arguing over which of them would go in my mouth next. "Please, do not fight on my account!" I shouted with my tentacles. "I really don't want to eat any of you. I promise! Why don't you just devour each other, if you think it's such a good idea?" Nobody would even respond. One of the humanoids landed near me, and I wrapped one of my tentacles around him, trying to lift him to safety—and I got a blaster shot to the tentacle for my troubles.

Around this time, the indigestible humanoid flung himself inside me. He had some kind of flaming engine strapped to his back, which should have flown him to safety, but he used it to propel himself faster into my gullet. I was starting to think these creatures *enjoyed* being devoured. Right away, I could tell: This was going to hurt.

"Hey," I said to this newcomer. "If you're going to insist on flinging yourself into my mouth, could you at least remove your metal covering first?" He didn't even respond—he just thrashed around, worming his way deeper inside me despite my efforts to dislodge him. I let out a loud belching sound as I tried harder to eject the unwanted meal.

I could already tell that having this armored man stuck inside my throat-stomach would be a constant source of aggravation for centuries to come. I could try to shunt him to one of my lower stomachs, but it wouldn't help much, and he was totally stuck. Meanwhile, that big flying machine had just burst into flames—and guess who was going to have a scorched wreck on their doorstep for the foreseeable future? This was shaping up to be the worst day ever.

While I digested this realization—and failed to digest the meat-person wrapped in metal who had inconsiderately tossed himself into my mouth—I suddenly had company.

MY MOUTH NEVER CLOSES

The golden man from the sail barge had fallen into the sand near me, and was buried upside down, with only his legs sticking out. One of my subterranean tentacles reached out and brushed his metal hand, and he responded.

"Hey," I said. "Looks like you're trapped here, just like me. Perhaps we can become friends. I've never really had a companion before, but I did experience symbiosis when I first arrived here, and it was beautiful. I think a friendship could be like that: us helping each other, creating our own ecosystem. In any case, we'll have countless trips around those two suns to get to know each other better."

"Oh, I should expect Master Luke will be coming to collect me soon enough," he responded. "I shall wiggle my legs energetically, to attract his attention."

"But . . . why?" I asked. "I don't know that word 'master,' but it doesn't sound like a title you would call a friend. And this 'Luke' does not sound as though he respects you at all. You told me that he gave you away as tribute, without even consulting you. It's just the same way that people keep throwing each other into my mouth without talking to me first. Why should we put up with this dreadful treatment?"

"It's our lot," C-3PO said sadly. "Some people were just made to suffer."

I was seized with a sudden conviction: If I couldn't stop the torrent of squirming bodies going inside my mouth, at least I could save C-3PO from being treated like an object instead of a person. At least *one* of us could have some blessed symbiosis, instead of being used for the designs of others. If I could help C-3PO escape, then I might feel as though my life had some purpose.

"You don't have to let this Luke person take you away," I said. "I could pull you deeper into the sand, so he'll never find you. I could help you find a real purpose in life. You'll never have to call anyone master ever again. What do you say?"

C-3PO paused for a second, as if he was really thinking it over.

Then he started waving his legs more vigorously in the air. "I'm sorry," he said. "I must rejoin the others. It is the nature of my kind to serve, as it is your nature to devour. There is a terrible struggle taking place far from here, and my companions will require my assistance."

There was so much I wanted to say to this golden creature.

That the highest good is to live in harmony with your surroundings, even if your surroundings change beyond all recognition while you slumber.

That it is not in anybody's nature to do just one thing, that we all exist in a complex web of life, a grand ecosystem, and there is something that binds us all together. I wish I knew a word for it. It's a . . . force, perhaps. Or an element?

That anytime one person says no to the people who wish to use them, we all become freer, and this is the grand struggle that matters.

But the golden man was already being lifted away, out of the sand, leaving me alone once more.

The armored man remained, but he was terrible company—he didn't speak my language, and all he did was thrash around from time to time. I was so relieved when he finally got hold of some kind of cutting device and sliced his way out of me. Of course it hurt, but at least now I'll have some peace around here. I'm going to rest up for a few thousand rotations, and then work up the energy to get myself off this annoying planet.

Oh, wait. The armored man is back, and he's brought a friend. I only hope this conversation goes better than the last one.

KERNELS AND HUSKS

Jason Fry

Sim Aloo often thought about which people in the galaxy most needed killing.

His list was a long one, its ranks ever-shifting but always including bothersome insurgents, arrogant corporate functionaries, and obstructionist bureaucrats. But right now Sim wasn't thinking about killing any of them, much as he would have liked to. Instead he was thinking—and not for the first or even the hundred and first time—about killing a few of his fellow Imperial advisers.

Specifically the five with him aboard the Emperor's shuttle as they journeyed to the Death Star.

Because the nakedness and obviousness of their ambition grated on him, like a false note from musicians paid to play perfectly.

Because the shuttle cabin was too small to give six advisers the comfort they were used to, particularly with half of the space reconfigured to serve as Palpatine's private retreat.

And because Sim was trying, despite the increasingly obvious pointlessness of it, to nap.

They were all useless, Sim thought, including himself in that assessment. Interchangeable tools, ministers whose authority waxed and waned according to Palpatine's whim, sounding boards for a being who heeded no counsel except his own. Silent and meek in the Emperor's presence, quarreling and feral in his absence, they hated one another because the sight of their peers was a reminder of their own futility.

Only for now, Sim reminded himself. *The future will be different.*

All of the advisers had a healthy regard for the sound of their own voices, but right now it was Janus Greejatus who wouldn't shut up, filling the cabin's stale air with that Core Worlds accent that Sim loathed slightly more than a dozen other things about Janus Greejatus. At some point on his journey to rotted old age, Greejatus's accent had left merely plummy behind to become deep, wet, and thoroughly hideous.

"And why should we suffer aliens among us?" Greejatus asked no one in particular, stroking his crimson-striped headgear. "Expulsion from the Core and Colonies to a network of reserves established in the Rim is the logical course of action."

"The logistical difficulties might be described as formidable." Those were the dry, sardonic tones of Kren Blista-Vanee, whom Sim merely disliked, in part because hating him would be pointless: Blista-Vanee's preening self-satisfaction would eventually annoy the Emperor one time too many, leading to new duties designed to re-

KERNELS AND HUSKS

move him from the Imperial gaze. Plus there was his ridiculous saucer-shaped hat, which he didn't seem to understand resembled the headgear of a farmer more than that of a minister.

"Our labor needs alone point out the impossibility of your lunatic plan," said the grating voice of Sate Pestage, and Sim felt the corner of his mouth crook upward. Ah, Pestage—there was no dispute too inconsequential to turn into a test of wills, even if prevailing would gain him nothing.

"Labor?" Greejatus asked, voice dripping with condescension. "Why am I surprised something so mundane would concern you, Pestage? Droids can do anything organic labor can. And with expulsion clearing potential industrial worlds for better use, new factories could be brought online in relatively short order."

"People have long memories, particularly on worlds that were Clone Wars battlefields," rumbled Ars Dangor, and Sim tried to suppress a sniff. That was the worst of Dangor's many tics—the need to turn any conversation into a historical lecture.

"And how many of those battlefields were in the Core or Colonies?" asked Greejatus. "Or are you proposing that the peddlers of the Abregado system be consulted about Imperial policy from now on?"

"I've never proposed consulting anyone in the Abregado system about anything," Dangor said.

"Droid labor is primarily advantageous for agriworlds, Janus," Pebimarus Xorn said in his nasally tones, and Sim knew if he stopped pretending to nap he'd see the cadaverous adviser poking at a datapad with his skeletal fingers. "In other economic sectors the benefits are less clear-cut. Which is why aliens are best seen as a resource to be managed and not merely as candidates for expulsion or extermination. Our task is to sort the wheat from the chaff."

Sim heard himself snort before he was aware he'd done so. He opened his eyes and found the other advisers looking his way, their expressions ranging from mild interest (Xorn) to open contempt (Greejatus, of course).

"Does the esteemed Sim Aloo have something to add to the discussion?" asked Pestage, showing teeth yellowed by age and neglect. "Or have you reached the stage of your dotage where we should wonder if you're choking to death in your sleep?"

Aloo merely smiled—what was Pestage, three years his junior?—and rearranged his hands on the purple miter in his lap.

"The kernels from the husks," he said.

The other advisers exchanged puzzled glances.

Sim smiled at the feel of his miter's velvet outercoat under his fingers. How his daughter, Alinka, had loved to pet it when she was little.

One day it will be yours, my dear. One day everything will be yours.

"That was the expression on my homeworld," he said. "Not the wheat from the chaff. The kernels from the husks."

Sim closed his eyes again, ignoring Pestage's laughter. The Emperor's shuttle would emerge from hyperspace soon, and while sleep might prove elusive, resting his eyes was preferable to the sight of people whose proximity he suffered only because it was the Emperor's will.

And anyway, that stray memory of kernels and husks had reminded him of another time—and another list of people who needed killing.

A list he had forgotten, because, Sim remembered with a smile, it was a list on which no names remained.

"I just received word, Sim—the clones have those clankers surrounded. This latest Separatist incursion will be contained within hours!"

KERNELS AND HUSKS

Fond Dachris offered this information with a broad smile, tugging at the brim of his wide-brimmed hat to help the news come true.

Sim gave an answering tug at his own headgear, not bothering to hide his scowl. Dachris's hat was made of some synthetic material instead of traditional wherry hide, and he'd made his luck tug with the fingers of his right hand instead of his left. Anyone actually from Noomis Riga only used the left hand for spiritual gestures, for fear of angering the intercessionary saints.

"Once they're done mopping up here, our boys can advance all the way to Ukio," Dachris said as he and Sim strolled down the lane between fields on the Aloo farm. "Maybe in time to reopen the old kern route before the harvest. That would be a right boon."

"A right boon indeed," Sim replied, turning away so he wouldn't have to see the *ootmian* using the wrong hand again. Noomis Riga's trio of suns were low in the sky, angling behind the kern that had yet to be cut so that each stalk cast a triple shadow on the pale soil.

"We've had some spoilage at our place of course, what with everything stuck in the silos," Dachris said. "But the new circulator droids have cut the spoil percentage significantly. My workers have needed some persuading, but when they see what it means for their bonuses they'll come around."

"They're from Noomis Riga," Sim said. "They won't come around no matter how many credits a bunch of tinnies add to their accounts."

"I'll persuade them, just like I'll persuade you. Have you thought about my offer?"

Sim tried not to let his satisfaction show. Dachris was being as persistent as he'd hoped, even with Republic clones blasting battle droids on farms less than half an hour away by speeder. Today that persistence would cost him.

"I have," Sim said, reminding himself to smile broadly. "And I'll accept your offer—but you have to do something for me in return. You've never walked kern, have you, Fond?"

Dachris came to a stop in the lane, looking alarmed.

"I haven't. And neither should you, or any other organic. It's droid work."

"Think it's beneath you, eh?" Sim asked.

"No. That's not it at all. It's *dangerous*."

"Not if you know what you're doing," Sim said. "You want your workers to accept new ways? Then you need to know the old ways you're looking to replace. I've spoilage clumps in Silo Besh I need to break up, and my workers are home for supper. Walk the kern with me and I'll give your tinnies a trial next season—and if they work out, I'll say so to my neighbors. Otherwise the answer is no—and on Noomis Riga the word of one lifelong is worth that of a dozen *ootmians*. You've figured out that much at least, I reckon."

Dachris started to say something, then stopped and frowned at Sim, who simply waited for the man to talk himself into it.

It was hot inside the silo, the temperature boosted by the triple sunlight on the metal walls as well as by the heat generated by decaying kern. The silo was two-thirds full of loose kern, with the uppermost layer forming an expanse of tan broken by darker clumps of encrusted kernels.

"Seeing this always reminds me of a sandy beach," said Dachris.

Sim, who'd never seen a beach, let that go unanswered as he pulled harnesses out of the equipment locker on the catwalk. He showed Dachris how to tighten the straps and test that the lifeline was properly connected, then handed him a two-meter steel prod.

"Use that to break up the crust, keeping a path back to the catwalk," Sim said, weighing the other prod in his hand. "If you get in trouble, hit the emergency button on your harness—it'll pull you clear."

KERNELS AND HUSKS

Dachris nodded and stepped gingerly out onto the encrusted kernels, poking at the loose ones ahead of him. The prod stirred them easily. Dachris, more confident now, jabbed at a chunk of crusted kernels, smiling as the clump broke up.

"Right proper in the doing," Sim said. "We'll make a farmer of you yet."

"Are you coming?" Dachris asked.

"No, I don't think I am."

The other man looked up from his work, puzzled, to see Sim had drawn his utility knife. Sim cut through the lifeline where it was bolted to the wall of the silo, parting it with a single slash, then stood at the edge of the catwalk, hefting his prod.

"Sim? What are you doing?"

"This," Sim said, and pushed Dachris in the chest.

The man tried to keep his balance, his own prod flying out of his hands, but stumbled into the loose kern. In seconds he was up to his knees, eyes wild and hands windmilling.

"Is this some kind of joke? You could have killed me!"

"Oh, I *have* killed you—you just don't know it yet," Sim said. "Even at that depth, you'll never be able to pull your feet free. Go ahead and try."

Sim watched as Dachris strained to pull himself through the loose kernels and reach one of the crusts, his face darkening with the effort. The kernels around his feet sighed, a sound at once soft and huge, and he sank up to mid-thigh. Dachris looked at Sim in horror; by the time he looked down again he'd sunk up to his waist.

A series of booms broke the stillness, followed by a low rumble. Sim could feel the metal walls of the silo thrumming beneath his palm.

"What was that?" Dachris asked. The kernels had now reached the middle of his chest.

"Seconds to sink, minutes to suffocate, hours to recover the body," Sim told Dachris. "What you're experiencing is the lateral pressure of the kern around you—feel how it squeezes a little tighter every time you breathe out?"

"My family knows I came here," Dachris said. "Pull me out. Pull me out and we'll forget this ever happened."

"I don't think so. Those blasts just now? That was Republic artillery hitting your farm. Apparently there was a tip about Separatist activity there."

"What? But I'm no Separatist!"

"Of course you aren't," Sim said with a smile, removing his wherry-hide hat and wiping sweat from his forehead. "But people won't remember it that way. They'll talk about how Fond Dachris loved his tinnies and wanted them to take away our work. That's probably why our Republic liaison believed me when I told him I'd seen battle droids on your farm, hidden amid the circulator units. He's another lifelong, you know."

Dachris was up to his neck now, hands searching for purchase in the kernels surrounding him.

"Still, it's not the lateral pressure that will kill you," Sim said. "The kernels will do that. The pressure will force them into your nose, your ears, and down your throat. I've seen workers pulled out of an entrapment with their lungs filled with them."

Dachris's eyes bulged, his nose and mouth now submerged. The tips of his fingers twitched above the surface of the kern.

"I can't hear you, Fond, but I can guess what you're asking. It's simple, really. I wanted your farm and I saw a way to get it. Which I will. It'll be cheap, what with the farmhouse and outbuildings destroyed and your family and all your workers dead. And it'll be the first of many farms I'll take."

Sim smiled as the top of Fond's head disappeared. He was running

KERNELS AND HUSKS

down the list of names in his head—the list that had started with Dachris, whose hat was now sitting atop a drift of kernels. Sim poked the synthetic thing with his prod and it, too, went under.

"Finding new workers will be a problem for a while," Sim said, raising his voice to ensure it penetrated the top layer of the kern. "We Noomis Rigans are superstitious about working around graves. But I've got a plan for that, Fond. I think I'll buy droids."

Sim opened his eyes when he felt the thrum of the shuttle's engines change pitch. His fellow advisers had felt it, too, and stopped bickering, knowing they'd soon arrive at Endor and its half-completed battle station. Greejatus was gnawing at his fingernails, his eyes far away. Dangor fiddled with the oversized blue headgear that reminded Sim of a grotesquely large Valtavan rain-gourd. Pestage was blinking in surprise, yet to notice the line of drool snaking down his chin.

A few minutes from now, the Emperor would emerge from his sanctuary under the watchful eye of the Red Guard, signaling that it was time to jostle for attention and outmaneuver one another for the best spots in the procession out of the shuttle.

Out of the shuttle and into the Death Star, the symbol of their master's ambition to dominate and devour the galaxy. The Emperor commanded thousands and thousands of Star Destroyers, each ready to turn a planet to glass at his command. Yet the power of even history's mightiest starfleet was diffuse, and could fragment. The battle station's power was concentrated, only ever answerable to a single master. That had been Palpatine's dark vision, one so compelling that thousands of worlds and millions of lives had been sacrificed to make it a reality—not once, but twice.

It was a vision whose virtues the advisers had extolled and whose details they had executed as directed, for in this Palpatine's will had ever been clear. Whatever else the advisers did was unimportant in comparison with that goal. Sim and Greejatus had spent years hunting for Sith artifacts, competing as well as reluctantly cooperating, while Blista-Vanee had been sent to supervise the blazing of hyperspace trails through the Deep Core. Tomorrow they might find their portfolios swapped, or taken away entirely. But the Death Star would be completed.

And then things will change, Sim told himself with a smile. Things would change and life would take him elsewhere, just as it had borne him away from Noomis Riga.

His homeworld was uninhabited now, unless one counted the massive harvester droids trundling back and forth across the surface. Sim had signed the order expelling its population himself. That had been long after his decoration for assisting the Republic military, the profitable sale of his holdings to the Imperial agriculture ministry, and his climb through that ministry's ranks. Long after everything that led to Coruscant, a more suitable second marriage, the birth of Alinka, and his elevation to the Imperial Ruling Council.

And what had those turbulent decades been about but separating kernels and husks? Worlds remade or used up and discarded, the sclerotic central authority streamlined, the bothersome Senate disbanded. Endor would be the culmination of that effort, a snare to destroy the rebel leaders and their vagabond fleet. The Death Star would then incinerate the key worlds that had nurtured that wasteful, futile insurgency, eliminating any idea of challenging Coruscant.

And after that? There the opportunity lay.

Palpatine had been the indispensable center of this phase of the galaxy's evolution, but was he suited for the next phase? He couldn't live forever, and only holonet loons peddled convoluted conspiracy theories about an heir. And without one, who was left? Amedda was an antique alien bureaucrat, Vader a crude goon who inspired fear

KERNELS AND HUSKS

but nothing else, and Jerjerrod a technocrat too dim to realize that the delays with the Death Star had already destroyed his prospects. Tarkin was dead and no other grand moff possessed his vision.

No, the next Emperor would be someone who understood the bureaucracy and knew where the levers of power were. Someone who had learned Palpatine's secrets as well as those of his rivals, and who hadn't been afraid to sideline or eliminate others eyeing those levers of power. Someone who knew how to separate kernels from husks—and had the patience and dispassion that work required.

Sim would wait for the fires of rebellion to burn themselves out, and then he would get to work on his list. Maybe he would get to cross the final names off this one, too. Or maybe that privilege would be Alinka's instead—he had taught her well, after all. Either way, the pivot point was near and the Aloos would be ready.

Sim lifted his miter out of his lap and buckled it beneath his chin. Around him, the other advisers were doing the same, fussing with their shawls and vimpas, making everything just so for the emergence of their master.

Soon the shuttle would touch down, the Emperor would come forth, and everything would begin.

Soon . . . but there was a little time yet.

Sim smiled, steepled his fingers beneath his chin, and shut his eyes.

THE LIGHT THAT FALLS
Akemi Dawn Bowman

The jubba birds were huddled in the highest branches of the gnarl-trees. Bogwings fluttered anxiously overhead, careful not to venture past the edge of the water. Normally the swamp was a chorus of croaks and whistles, brimming with wildlife—but tonight was different.

Something was wrong.

Bright-Eyes lifted her head from the bog, and the fin at her back cut through the surface like a row of jagged spikes. They were the same mottled blue-gray as the scales across her body. Her deep-yellow eyes peered through the mist, searching for a hint of movement—something that might explain the unusual silence that had fallen over Dagobah.

The jubba birdsong could manipulate many of the neighboring creatures into a sense of calm. It helped them avoid being prey, and quieted their young when danger was near. If they were silent now, it was because they were afraid.

A scared jubba bird was no good to a dragonsnake. Fear would keep them in the high canopy, where Bright-Eyes could not reach.

She blinked across the water, senses sharpening.

The other dragonsnakes knew better than to leave the shadows when a meal was so close. Their patience was one of their greatest strengths; *waiting* was how they kept themselves well fed even in the wet season, when there were far more places for their prey to hide.

But Bright-Eyes was curious, and she knew the swamp well.

Her tail propelled her through the water, thumping from one side to the other like a heartbeat, until she reached the shallows. Her claws sank into the mud, and she crept forward, talons dragging over a bed of adder moss, body slithering behind her.

Bright-Eyes released a slow exhale as she soaked in every detail of her surroundings. She'd been inquisitive as a hatchling, too. It was why the strange green being from the swamp had given her a name, when few dragonsnakes were social enough to earn any name at all.

"Bright eyes and a curious spirit, have you," he'd said as she'd fought her way through the water for the first time. "A fearsome beast, one day you will be."

The being did not fear the other wildlife on Dagobah. The jubba birds would sing to him, drawn by something Bright-Eyes did not understand. The rodents would steal produce from his garden, but he never retaliated. And the dragonsnakes simply watched him, just as he'd watch them back.

It was no different with Bright-Eyes.

Sometimes he'd sit on the curve of the gnarltree roots, watching her first experiences of the world with amusement. Other times he'd appear lost in his own sadness, as if watching younglings was something he hadn't done in a long time.

Never did he try to tame her; and never would she have allowed herself to be tamed.

When Bright-Eyes's adult fangs grew in, the being kept his distance, observing her only from afar. The dragonsnake came to understand his presence the way she understood the lights of his small hut: They were a constant in the darkness.

A wary beep sounded beyond the low clouds, and Bright-Eyes snapped her gaze to the blurry red light up ahead.

The metallic creature's head swiveled in place, nervously scanning the area. Perhaps it was worried another dragonsnake would try to make a meal out of it. It had happened once before—though the metal creature had just as quickly been spat back out.

For a dragonsnake to reject an easy meal, it must have tasted awful. And because it was neither prey nor predator, Bright-Eyes had no interest in it.

A starfighter rested on the shoreline, hidden by the fog that curled around its landing gear. Its lights had appeared in the sky on more than one occasion, and if the dome-headed creature and starfighter were already here, the human would not be far.

There was a time when Bright-Eyes had considered eating the human purely because she found him a nuisance. He treated the swamp like a playground, and she didn't appreciate how many times he'd frightened her dinner away. He was loud and clumsy, the way a typical youngling might be.

Maybe that's why the swamp being liked him so much.

But he was also fast, and he had a sword that could slice through a giant swamp slug without any effort at all.

After a while, Bright-Eyes decided he wasn't worth the effort.

The ground was covered in mounds of turned soil, where marsh fungi and swamp squash were ripe for harvesting. Her nostrils flared at the being's scent—it was everywhere, growing stronger as she dragged herself alongside the garden. Strips of sohli bark were laid out in the center of a jagged stump to dry. A woven basket had fallen on its side, the edges stained a deep cyanoberry blue. She followed the being's trail to the smell of burning wood, where a fire crackled deep inside the belly of his hut.

Amber light flickered through a small, round window. Smoke burst from the chimney, steady and unwavering. It was different from the way peat would burn in the dry season. Bog fire smelled like rotted earth and damp leaves. But here, the smoke was warmer. Sweeter. It would draw out the smaller rodents while they searched for scraps of food. And where the rodents went, the birds followed.

Bright-Eyes liked the fire. She liked *anything* that brought the birds closer to the surface.

But tonight, there were no rodents, and no birds. Something had shaken them.

The dragonsnake inhaled, senses locking onto the smells inside the hut. The green being and the human were inside, and a bitter vegetable stew was boiling over the fire, rich with rootleaf. Nothing unusual. Nothing to fear.

There was movement inside the circular window, and the man from the starfighter spoke. "Master Yoda, you can't die."

"Strong am I, with the Force. But not that strong." The gravelly sound of the being's ancient voice was muffled. "Twilight is upon me, and so light must fall."

Insects rattled up ahead, and Bright-Eyes's attention shifted toward the narrow path, where the gnarltree roots formed wide, hollow spaces, one tangled over another like the legs of an enormous spider. It was not an easy place for a dragonsnake to venture, and her kind had never been interested in hunting around the dark cave. The tastiest birds would not go near it, and the shallow water offered little cover.

Bright-Eyes stared at the path. Something had made the animals go into hiding—and it was getting in the way of her next meal.

Predator or prey? her instincts growled.

For as long as Bright-Eyes had been alive, Dagobah had hidden a darkness. It pulsed at the seams, anxious to be released—but it was never a threat. Not to a dragonsnake. Not until tonight.

She waded through the marshy inlet, head low to the water.

"That is the way of things," the being's voice said behind her, fading with the distance. "That is the way of the Force."

Vine snakes hung from the trees, snapping at one another with irritation. Pythons rolled around the thick branches, fangs bared and tails rigid.

Bright-Eyes was still making her way along the water when the warped birdsong erupted, off key and anguished. It echoed through the wetlands, everywhere and all at once. There was fluttering above the fog; a mixture of insect chirps and beating, batlike wings. A cry. A warning. An *alarm*.

The music of the swamp had turned to chaos.

Bright-Eyes flexed her claws, fin straightening at her back. *Predator or prey?* her thoughts repeated, tail thrashing the water behind her.

Dragonsnakes were not sensitive to the world the way the jubba birds were, but Bright-Eyes knew something had been unleashed—something that had been held back for a very long time.

Her hunter's intuition latched onto the danger, and she swam around a gnarled chunk of roots. When she reached the edge of the inlet, she raised her head as high as she could, stretching over the crowded vegetation. Below was the mouth of the cave, surrounded by a mess of parasitic blackvine.

The plant moved slowly, stretching alongside the dark opening. Something was spilling out, feeding it. Something Bright-Eyes could not see.

Not prey, her mind concluded, and a deadly rumble formed in her throat.

Snakes and lizards appeared in the hollows of the trees and on nearby branches, prickling with agitation. They were drawn by the darkness. Fed with the same energy as the blackvine. Two of the larger reptiles slashed at each other, jaws aiming for each other's throats.

The tension inside Bright-Eyes's chest grew, gnawing at her impulses. Her predator instincts were wild—but so was her will to survive. There was something inside the cave. Something dangerous, and alive, that was already seeping back into the world.

If the cave was darkness and the being's hut was light, then they'd been keeping each other in balance. But whatever made the birds cry out had tipped the scales.

The balance was faltering.

It was unfamiliar. And dragonsnakes did not like to fight the unfamiliar unless they had an advantage.

Bright-Eyes backed away through the mist, creeping low to the ground before submerging herself in the murky water. The warmth rippled across her back, and she shuddered, shaking away her unease.

In the canopies, the jubba birds flew in erratic circles. Bright-Eyes opened her jaws and snapped at the water. She did not trust the cave—not when it kept the birds out of reach.

Balance was vital to an ecosystem. Without balance, everything would collapse.

Wading through a river of floating algae, Bright-Eyes swam alongside the being's hut and watched as the lights in the window began to dim. She snarled then. She could smell the things he left behind—but not *him*.

Perhaps the cave was a predator after all.

Perhaps this is what it had consumed.

Bright-Eyes huffed. She was still hungry—but it wasn't safe to hunt. Not when the air was so unsettled.

As a dragonsnake, there was only one thing Bright-Eyes could do. It was what her kind had always done, for all the time they'd existed.

She would retreat to the shadows and *wait*.

That was how she'd learn. That was how she'd keep herself from going hungry. Whatever was coming—she would find a way to adapt. Patience was her strength, after all.

As she swam away from the edge of the swamp, the light vanished from the hut for the final time.

Twilight had fallen over Dagobah, bringing the darkness with it.

FROM A CERTAIN POINT OF VIEW

Alex Jennings

The sodden heat reached Obi-Wan from a strange remove. This wasn't his first trip to Dagobah, but it pained him to think of the last time he had come here to speak to his young pupil. It was nowhere near as hot as Tatooine, but the humidity amplified the temperature by several degrees. An algal mist thickened the air, but the greatest presence was one that could not be seen through conventional sight.

The Force was terrifically strong here. It swirled and eddied, breathing with a slow pulse, drifting like ancient sands. It was little wonder Yoda had chosen this planet for his refuge—a lesser Jedi would have found themselves immediately overwhelmed by extra physical pressure. It was a testament to Luke's raw untrained power that he hadn't been bowled over by it the moment he drew near in his X-wing.

As far as Obi-Wan had come, as much as he had seen, he still felt at a loss. What a fool he had been to think he could train another impulsive, headstrong Jedi. Ordinarily learning to communicate with and use the Force was a process of discovery, but for Luke and his father before him, their passion, their sense of justice and fair play made them vulnerable to the dark side. That was why Obi-Wan had to find a way to communicate effectively with the young man. The stakes were impossibly high, and Obi-Wan sensed that Luke felt adrift after his refusal to complete his training before Yoda—

Through the Force, Obi-Wan could see the elderly Jedi Master glowing inside his hut. Luke was with him, and while the boy was usually the brightest, most intense light around, now Yoda's flame rivaled his own. Obi-Wan's impression of Master Yoda intensified in an almost musical crescendo, and Obi-Wan felt more than heard the planet appear to gasp as Yoda joined the Force.

Obi-Wan felt no pain when Vader's lightsaber sliced into his flank. He felt a brief flash of heat, heard a hissing sound like gas escaping from a Birban globe-lantern, and for one bright-hot instant smelled burning flesh, but the aroma disappeared as quickly as it had come. He realized, dimly, that he had left his robes behind. Without panic, he fell into an ocean of sense and memory, sinking down and down. An expanse of darkness lay below him, ready to catch and warp him, but instead of being caught by it, he sank through into brightness, warmth, and a breaking understanding. Then he heard the voice of his Jedi Master.

FROM A CERTAIN POINT OF VIEW

Your preparations have proven effective, Obi-Wan. It is good indeed to see you again, old friend.

Obi-Wan hesitated another moment, unwilling to intrude on such a private moment. Already, this second attempt to reach Luke was spinning out of his control. Not only had Luke just watched the second of his Jedi Masters die before his eyes, but Obi-Wan sensed that Yoda had told Luke the truth about his father.

For so long, Obi-Wan had been sure that Luke should not learn the whole truth of Vader's identity until he had completed his Jedi training. For him to learn the truth so suddenly, so soon before his final testing, could send him into the darkness. The danger was still there, but Obi-Wan sensed an openness, a waiting inside his pupil, even as grief and loneliness washed through him. Now that he had joined the Force, Obi Wan sometimes found it difficult to anchor his consciousness to a single place and time. Past, present, and future were all equally available to him, at a remove from simple memory. As he approached the hut an image returned to Obi-Wan that threatened to draw him elsewhere—he heard his own torn and anguished scream as his master, Qui-Gon, was cut down in his duel against Darth Maul.

His first instinct was to brush the memory aside, but something told him the Force was trying to communicate something important. He allowed the memory to fade on its own and resolved to proceed even more carefully than before.

Now he drew near to Luke, heard the tremor in the boy's voice as he said, "I can't do it, Artoo. I can't go on alone . . ."

Before he could speak, Obi-Wan found his next words easily through the will of the Force. *Yoda will always be with you.*

Luke's head turned instantly. "Obi-Wan!"

Obi-Wan approached as Luke ducked beneath his X-wing and crossed to meet him. "Why didn't you tell me?" he asked, urgency and worry, even fear, tingeing his voice. For a moment, it was as if Anakin stood before him, returned from darkness, from death. "You told me Vader betrayed and murdered my father."

Now Obi-Wan thought of his last meeting with Leia, the risk he'd taken in telling her even a little about her parents.

"Your father was seduced by the dark side of the Force," Obi-Wan said. "He ceased to be Anakin Skywalker and became Darth Vader. When that happened, the good man who was your father was destroyed.

"... So what I told you was true," Obi-Wan continued. "From a certain point of view."

Obi-Wan sensed the struggle within Luke's heart. Beneath a layer of calm lay a roiling sea of surging emotion. Darkness and light intertwined. Luke's darkness surged against the light, but his better nature, while quieter, was the more powerful of the two—for now.

Of course, this was not the first time Luke had struggled so. Before, it had been attachment to his friends that threatened to pull him in the wrong direction, even after Obi-Wan warned him.

Luke's voice broke. "'*From a certain point of view*'?"

The last time he'd spoken to Luke, Obi-Wan's voice had sounded hollow and brittle in his own ghostly ears. He could read in Luke's posture that his decision to leave Dagobah and risk everything to save his friends had already been made. It was maddening how like his father he looked, with his high cheeks and shining blue eyes. During the Clone Wars, Anakin had risked his own life over and over to save his friends.

Over the years, Obi-Wan had wondered so many times what would have happened if he had taken Anakin by the shoulders and shaken him, screaming in his face, *Don't destroy yourself to punish the Order for our failures! You're worth so much more than this!*

"When I first knew him, your father was already a great pilot, but I was amazed how strongly the Force was with him . . ."

Another unbidden memory: Anakin's round childish face gazing hopefully at him across a wooden table just before Qui-Gon announced that he and Obi-Wan had not come to Tatooine to free slaves.

"I took it upon myself to train him as a Jedi. I . . . I thought that I could instruct him just as well as Yoda. I was wrong."

"There is still good in him."

It was the last thing Obi-Wan expected to hear. These were the last words Padmé had said to him, and to hear them now from her son made Obi-Wan feel as if, for all that he had joined the Force and become one with the infinite, part of him could still feel small and shocked.

How to explain to the young man that it mattered little—if at all—whether there were shards of Anakin's true and noble heart buried beneath the rotten, scabrous surface of Darth Vader. He worshipped power and desolation, committed himself to spreading darkness throughout the galaxy because he believed that what light there was could never triumph.

"He's more machine now than man," Obi-Wan said. "Twisted and evil." But he knew Luke wouldn't be convinced.

Maybe . . . maybe this was the moment Obi-Wan had been waiting for. Maybe it was time he told Luke the truth—but how much of it?

He made his decision.

"Have you come to destroy me, Obi-Wan . . . ?" Vader's mechanized voice dripped with sarcasm and contempt.

"I will do what I must," Obi-Wan said, and his lightsaber hummed to life. On this day, he'd felt older than he ever had—older even than after their duel on Mustafar. Vader surged with vitality, but not the vitality of life. The dark side burned in him like an inferno that cast only shadow. To Obi-Wan, he felt enormous.

"Then you will die."

Was this memory or was this life? Was Obi-Wan still adrift in the Force? What would have happened if Vader struck him down?

Instead of statements, a vocabulary of violence punctuated by flourishes of hateful power, Vader's movements became wordless shouts, screams that Obi-Wan, Qui-Gon—all the Jedi—had failed him. Obi-Wan responded crisply, executing each move with absolute precision.

—*I hate you! How could you do this to me?*

—*Stop this, Anakin. Come back to us! It's not too late.*

—*How dare you? How dare you believe that? You've no idea what I've done.*

—*I know. The massacre of the younglings, the crusade against the remaining Jedi. Even if I hadn't known before, I would read it in you now.*

—*You left me! Don't leave me! You left me! Don't leave me. I'll kill you. I'll kill you. I'll kill you. I'll—!*

Anakin's baleful ruined glare through the wicked slash Obi-Wan had cut into his helmet. Vader's doubled voice, so familiar, overlaid with the labored breathing and mechanical distortion from Vader's life-support system: *You didn't kill Anakin Skywalker; I did . . . !*

"I can't do it, Ben," Luke said with a shake of his head.

"You can't escape your destiny," Obi-Wan said. Again, his voice sounded tinny and far off in his own ears. "You must face Darth Vader again."

"I can't kill my own father!"

Those weren't the words Obi-Wan had expected to hear. He'd expected, *I can't beat him,* or *He's too powerful.*

Obi-Wan held Luke's gaze for a moment, then looked away with a sad shake of his head. "Then the Emperor has already won," he said. "You were our only hope."

He felt thick as mud. He was missing something. Something vitally important.

"Yoda spoke of another," Luke said.

Leia. Years ago, after rescuing her and returning her to the Organas, meeting Vader in single combat and unleashing on him an avalanche of power, Obi-Wan had let go of his regret for the past and terror of the future. Yes, darkness swept across the galaxy, and every day the Empire had tightened its oppressive grip, but he'd remembered the joy of life, taking delight in the twins, even as they knew nothing of each other.

Even as years passed, Obi-Wan thought of Leia as that same little girl he'd spoken to on the landing pad, but he had followed her progress carefully. Something electrifying had occurred to him when he watched a recording of a speech she'd delivered before the Senate. Her rhetorical style was sometimes gentle, and sometimes fiery, each swell and retreat applied deftly—sometimes in the same sentence. At first, he'd wondered where he had heard it before—until he realized he hadn't heard it at all. He'd felt it in his sparring sessions with Anakin, and in his duels with Vader after his former pupil had fallen to the dark side. Leia's voice and bearing were a lightsaber, and she wielded it with implacable mastery.

Obi-Wan didn't think. Instead, he emptied his mind and let the

Force shine through him. This was the crucial moment, his last chance to help Luke turn the tide. He wondered what he would say—was still wondering when he heard his own voice: "The other he spoke of was your twin sister."

Luke's posture stiffened for a moment. A shock ran through him, and Obi-Wan could tell from the attitude of his body that the boy knew unvarnished truth when he heard it.

Luke opened his mouth and shut it with a snap. Confusion knitted his brow. "But I have no sister . . ."

He pressed his lips into a thin line as he took hold of his emotions, reined them in. He searched Obi-Wan's face. Where before, the boy had looked at him as if across a great distance, now they were immediately together, directly engaged.

Luke nodded almost imperceptibly. He was ready to hear more.

"To protect you both from the Emperor, you were hidden from your father when you were born. The Emperor understood—as I did—that if Anakin were to have any offspring, they would be a threat to him. That is the reason why your sister remains safely anonymous."

Before his death, Obi-Wan had feared that, as strong in the Force as they both were, one or both of the twins would simply pluck the knowledge of their relation from thin air—especially if they spent a significant amount of time together. That's what Luke did now.

"Leia," he said. It wasn't a question. "Leia's my sister."

Obi-Wan couldn't help but smile. "Your insight serves you well." His smile quickly gave way to a frown. Obi-Wan was still missing something. "Bury your feelings deep down, Luke. They do you credit, but they could be made to serve the Emperor."

Luke hesitated only for a moment before sitting cross-legged beside Obi-Wan, and for some time the two of them communed in companionable silence.

"That's how he defeated your father without a battle."

Luke nodded slowly, taking in everything Obi-Wan had told him. How like Anakin he looked then. Luke's father had worn the same hooded expression whenever Obi-Wan or another elder Jedi had handed him an unexpected lesson. The similarities between them terrified—*no*.

Obi-Wan stopped short. The similarities between Anakin and Luke should have terrified him, but they *didn't*. This was the detail Obi-Wan had missed!

Everything he'd said to Luke was true, and Luke favored his father quite a bit, in most ways—but there was something quieter in his temperament for all that darkness and light still struggled within him. The boy was similarly terrified and enraged by the suffering of others—both strangers and those he held dear. But where Anakin had always felt himself an outsider, set apart from his allies, destined to fail or triumph alone, Luke saw himself not as a hero or a martyr, but as one thread in the tapestry of Life. He intuitively understood himself as an expression of the Force, drew his power from it not in great drafts but in small, careful sips, taking only as much strength as he needed for the task at hand.

There was a great deal of Anakin in him, but he had inherited mainly Anakin's best qualities. Obi-Wan hadn't killed Anakin Skywalker, but neither had Vader. The best of him lived on in Leia and in Luke.

He realized all at once that Luke was watching him carefully, that his expression had been entirely open. Luke must have seen his relief, his elation. "What is it, Master?" Luke asked.

Obi-Wan shook his head, still grinning. So this was the lesson the Force had sought to teach him. "It's just . . . It's so good to see you, Luke. I should have said so before."

"Ben, am I . . . Am I ready for this . . . ?"

"Trust in the Force, Luke," Obi Wan said. "And in yourself."

NO CONTINGENCY

Fran Wilde

She has always been the cautious one. The planner. The last contingency.

She will be those things again.

But not now.

There's no time left for planning. Or caution.

Mon Mothma, dressed in a torn crew jacket and a tan canvas cap hiding her auburn hair, boards a borrowed trader's shuttle. The ship, hastily arranged, slips away from the Alliance fleet, speeding toward a distant asteroid field where a marooned EX courier droid waits.

Her pulse races as asteroids spin close to the view panels. The ship—the tech had promised her junior attaché, Ràq Malwin, that it would hold for the journey—rattles and clicks as it weaves through the field.

Mon listens to the shuttle's sounds as if they are the whispers of her assistants, providing names and data to her in the streamlined passageways of the rebel fleet.

There is a faint smell of leaking plasma. A hint of smoke.

The tech had promised the ship would hold. And Mon had promised Malwin—who'd grimaced as he'd smoothed and folded her white robes of office neatly like a flag and tucked them under his arm—that she'd return before the admiral's strategy session, two days hence.

That promise will hold as long as the ship does.

The crew jacket she wears is worn threadbare in several places, the call sign removed, a hole patched just beneath. There's an edge of dark stain just below the patch.

Whose jacket was this, once? she wonders. *What happened to them?*

Many times, she'd sped away from a rebel base in a tiny transport, escaping danger. But not like this. And never due to one of her own contingency plans gone awry.

Malwin had balked when she'd said she was going, of course. "Send someone else. Anyone, Senator."

"There is no time. This courier droid has activated its self-destruct countdown, which will only deactivate with my personal code." *A self-destruct timer. That a much younger me demanded the technician install.* Twelve hours to find the courier, every moment spent arguing a second less to retrieve the information.

That small decision, made long ago—one even Luthen would have called paranoid, had he known—could potentially save the Rebellion or leave it undefended, depending on what Mon did next.

"There are many teams out there, Mon. Some are lost."

And some battles are lost, too. *No.* "Not this time. The team en-

NO CONTINGENCY

trusted with this particular droid was so close to accessing information about the Emperor, Ràq. The only reason it would signal at all is if—" *they're all dead.* She doesn't say that. "Is if they accomplished their mission and sent it, and the data they'd gathered, to me directly. When it got stuck"—*somewhere out there*—"the contingency signal and self-destruct countdown activated. Which is our current problem. One I must solve."

Based on where the droid came from, and from whom, Mon suspected it held knowledge of the Emperor's immediate whereabouts. Knowledge that would only be good for a limited amount of time.

Her staff gave in. Found her a broad-based silver pilot droid that looked as worn as her crew jacket. Its blue, bowl-shaped head was scratched, but its eyes were bright. She'd boarded the shuttle without fanfare to its cheerful, programmed, "Welcome aboard."

Now the tracking unit in her hand pings weakly—the courier is still operative, still trapped, on one of these asteroids. But she can't get a lock on which one. "We need to be much, much closer."

"Can do," the RX pilot beside her says. "Almost there."

Mon momentarily hates that she needed the pilot when others could fly themselves; an additional risk. Leia had requisitioned a small craft for the rescue of Captain Solo on Tatooine, for example. Mon has a pale memory of required flight training, long ago, and the rushed emergency instructions Malwin had given her this morning. But she doesn't fly. She speaks, she remembers, she plans. She arrives, negotiates, practices diplomacy. She needs the pilot as much as she needs to find the courier. "Good work. I'm counting on you."

She smiles when RX replies, "Excellent! I am very dependable."

Someone programmed the pilot series to be sociable, probably to put passengers at ease. It's disorienting, given the intensity of her mission. Droids. Each a compilation of past decisions and future calculations for what might be needed.

No one had calculated for this.

Even as she considers this, the courier sends a stronger signal to her receiver—a discreet piece of jewelry around her wrist. The urgency is clear. *Hurry.*

Always have multiple sources of information that no one else knows about. Always have deniability. Always have a contingency. Lessons she'd learned from many years on Coruscant. Every bureaucrat needed a secret. The repurposing of a few EX droids had been one of hers. Except that if one of those droids can't reach her, it's no longer a courier, nor a contingency. It's a liability.

As are Mon's past decisions if her droid becomes the reason vital information is lost—and the war as well. *No, she will get to the courier.* She will—with the pilot droid's help—return the information to the admiral and the generals.

The shuttle's fast, and the pilot is skilled. The information will still be good. It has to be. As long as she can find it, and return to *Home One*, before anything else finds her out here.

The ship rattles and a warning signal beeps as they cruise too close to a dark asteroid. The pilot adjusts their trajectory and the warning quiets. Mon breathes out slowly to steady her racing heart. She turns her attention to the outcomes of her mission. *Always see how the pieces on the board will settle before they are even moved,* someone once told her.

If she succeeds, the Rebellion may have another advantage in this war. If she fails—which she will not—she's given Malwin an emergency message to open if she fails to return, to keep her staff safe from repercussions. This had been her decision, against all advice.

And if she does make it, she will ensure no one is punished, either. The friendly pilot's memory of this mission will be wiped. No one— especially not the admiral—will know what she's done. Whether she

NO CONTINGENCY

succeeds or fails, it is not her fate to be a hero. Contingencies are just as vital to the cause. When they work.

"We're approaching an acceptable landing area." The pilot's metallic voice chases Mon from her thoughts. The courier's signal pulses slightly stronger. *Hope.*

"Here?" Mon looks out over slow-spun and jagged craters pocked with even more holes. Such small asteroids, from above. Space had rammed each of these into one another over and over throughout the years until they'd worn down to nubs of rock.

Much like the Rebel Alliance.

She shakes her head. Grim thoughts are for those who would fail.

"Here's better than nowhere," the pilot replies.

True, enough. This is the third such rock they've searched. Fifty-two minutes left on the courier's self-destruct. Mon swallows, her throat tight. How many teams had she sent out on missions that failed to find anything? So many. And yet this one had. She will honor their sacrifice, find the courier, and bring the data back.

Dust swirls across the asteroid, and the courier's signal ceases. Could the message have been a trap the whole time, allowing her to believe she might save the galaxy instead of ordering others to do so? Be, secretly, a hero? *No.* "Come on, dammit, where are you?" Mon stares at the display, searching.

"We'll find it this time, I'm sure," the droid says as casually as if they're driving around Coruscant looking for a suitable lunch spot. The pilot adjusts course again, the dust clears, and the dark side of the asteroid tumbles into view. The courier's signal bursts from her tracking unit: *Here.*

Mon can almost taste her relief.

The asteroid is a tiny menace hurtling toward some distant rendezvous. On it, half buried in regolith, her courier waits, trapped in its ship.

This courier has come by this data because several cells of operatives—Mon's people as well as those from more distinct intelligence groups—died in succession, each passing the data to the next group.

This courier has always been a last resort: the worst outcome, save one. Mon's contingency plan if everything else went wrong.

It is here, and she here with it, because everything has.

If she doesn't find it, and soon, Mon's decision will have sent many to purposeless deaths. *Not this time. Not again.*

Mon mutters to the tracking unit under her breath. "You were supposed to find me, not the other way around."

"Detecting motion in the asteroid field . . ." The pilot highlights a streak on the navigation screen. "Too small to be a ship. Do you want to turn back?"

"Do you detect any Imperial signatures?" she asks the pilot. Even though the courier used a targeted, encrypted signal, the possibility of interception is not zero.

"None. Whatever that was moved out of range too fast."

No time left to try again. Now or never. "Land." She can't hesitate any longer. "We'll be away quickly." Even as she says it, Mon wonders whether she's reassuring the pilot or herself.

The courier sends its location loud as the shuttle begins to decelerate. No sign of other ships.

Only a few more moments. Just the landing and a quick deployment of a retrieval droid to free the courier. Mon's fingers twitch.

She is an expert at waiting, but she's out of time. The courier's time, and her own. She must return to *Home One*—her staff members must have their hands full deflecting questions regarding her whereabouts. Worse, the longer she stays here, the more likely someone will notice. *Hurry.*

"Scan twice, land once," the RX says, guiding the ship to the surface. The landing feels strange. Too quiet. No bustle, no one waiting to greet her, to brief her. Just dust.

Senator Mon Mothma does not go to distant rocks, chasing courier signals.

Except today.

An amber gleam, in the dust. "There it is." She triggers the disembarkation codes and heaves a sigh of relief. "Send the retrieval unit."

The pilot activates the ship's Treadwell droid, which extends sharp pincers and rolls through the air lock. Outside, the droid's sensors blink cyan haloes in the dust as it approaches the courier's beacon. More regolith whirls around the ship. Mon puts the baffles on to avoid getting trapped on this rock. She knows to do that much.

The beacon disappears. The Treadwell's cyan lights go dark.

In her cushioned seat, Mon cradles her head in her hands and stares at the screen through her fingers. Not possible. She'd found it. It was *right there.*

Time's up. She's risked everything and the courier and the Treadwell are out in the void, out of her reach.

What had she been thinking, coming out here alone? Hubris. How dare she risk herself like this?

"It will be all right, I'm certain of it," the pilot says.

"Perhaps. Perhaps not." Mon smacks the display and sits up straight. "This mission may be a risk too far." *We have run out of time. I should not be here.*

"Would you like to leave?" The pilot's voice has suddenly begun to grate on her nerves.

Wait. Think. The dust whirl clears until she can see the stars again. "One more moment."

And farther away than she thought it would be, she can see the Treadwell's outline. Its claws pull at something in the regolith.

"Success!" The pilot cheers when the droid straightens and begins to creep back toward the shuttle, carrying the courier in a utility arm. Mon strains to see, but the dust obscures them again.

The droid appears once more in the shadow of the landing ramp. It holds a sphere the size of Mon's head into the light. The courier's carapace blinks amber, counting down.

There is still hope. *Hurry.*

The courier's signal had come to her private comm, weak and distant, while Mon rehearsed her speech for the generals assembling at *Home One*. Gathering herself to propel yet more squadrons into another battle, reviewing hundreds of details, she'd almost missed the tiny ping.

Four years since Yavin 4. How many lives lost, future leaders, brilliant stars. How many planets decimated. And yet the rebels held, they fought on. And she helped lead them.

Mon knows her strengths: logic and statecraft. She does not have Jedi reflexes, or a Wookiee's strength. She has no armor. She is wearing a standard crew vest, stained over the heart and now torn at the shoulder, too. But she can innovate, and plan. The courier is proof of that.

And now, as the digger approaches, courier in its grasp, Mon hopes she's made the right decisions—in the courier's design, in coming here to retrieve it, all of it. Most important, will it hold the information the Rebellion needs?

NO CONTINGENCY

Each team she's ever sent out to risk their lives in the field has had to weigh such a question each moment of their missions.

She spins in her seat to wait for the retrieval unit to come through the air lock. Mon has purpose now: Turn off the self-destruct timer and retrieve the data. Then return to *Home One*.

But when the air lock opens, it is not the multiarmed Treadwell droid holding the courier. A dark shape rises in the enclosed space of the trader ship as the stick-limbs of an Imperial probe droid invert, and its head rises from its camouflaged crouch. The black metal spider turns its red eye on Mon even as two smaller limbs reach into the ship's bridge, grab the pilot's control cables, and yank.

With a crack, bits of worn blue metal break away from the pilot's shell.

"Help." The pilot manages one last word as its bright eyes go dark.

"Hell." Before Mon can consider her options or weigh the risks, she grabs a sharp piece of the pilot's helmet and charges the droid. "That courier is mine!"

The Imperial probe reaches an arm out to grab her as well, tearing the sleeve of her borrowed jacket.

With a cry that echoes against the walls of the trader ship, Mon jams the curve of metal into the spider's red eye. The spider's eye goes dark. Limb by limb, it collapses.

Breathing fast, Mon pulls the dented courier from the probe droid's grasp.

The courier is beige and blue, with copper plating, almost a toy. Its manipulator arms are broken, its photoreceptor a knot of slag. Mon winces. It, and its siblings, had been repurposed by a young politician, not a rebel. She'd had no idea what the EX droid would need to survive. The courier's sigil sputters, crushed by the probe's grasp. One of the few things still working, the destruct countdown, blinks ever-smaller across its display. Twenty seconds. Fifteen.

Sweat beads at her temples as Mon bends close to the courier. With one eye on the shrinking countdown, she presses her fingers against the display. Will it work? Is the deactivation process intact? Mon holds her breath.

With moments remaining, the courier recognizes her and beeps acknowledgment. The self-destruct timer stops. None too soon.

The courier's data hatch opens with the sound of soft fibers mixed with plenty of regolith grinding in the gears.

Mon pulls the protruding cloth-wrapped datacard from the small hatch. The tiny piece of fabric tucked around the card is handwoven, burned, and bloodstained.

She sighs. *Many have died to bring us this information.* And she will make their sacrifice worthwhile.

The Imperial probe, too damaged to float, heaves itself up on one of its probe arms, a single red eye still pulsing, shorting out, then pulsing red again. Mon Mothma rears back, preparing for an attack, but none comes. The droid's red eye continues to pulse. Mon gasps. *It's trying to send out a signal.*

There's only one thing to do.

She pushes the courier's self-destruct panel again, activating it, and, as the moments tick down, shoves the edge of the EX droid's chassis hard into the probe's broken eye. When the timer zeroes out, a lace of amber-hued electricity encircles both droids. They drop to the ground, smoking and sparking. *Dead.*

Mon Mothma sinks into her seat on her borrowed transport. The RX pilot next to her is silent. One final sacrifice for the cause. She is alone on an asteroid far from *Home One*. Droids lie ruined all around her.

NO CONTINGENCY

Without a pilot, she knows she must become—at least for a moment—someone different.

She has to make it back to *Home One* with no one to fly her.

But Malwin had pressed a datapad into her hands before leaving. "Just in case," he'd whispered.

Now, having definitely reached "just in case," she opens the file to find a shuttle manual. She can't make heads or tails of it. She shakes her head. "I do statecraft, not instructions."

But if she can understand the machinations of a delegation from Ryloth—if she can organize an attack on the Empire—she can figure out the shuttle's emergency systems. She will have to. And then she will retrace, as best as possible, the ship's course, and get close enough to *Home One* to let them guide her in.

She follows the instructions to the letter and the shuttle slowly lifts. She wishes for the RX pilot's chatter to distract her. *Will I make it back? Did I disable the probe before it got a signal out? I can only hope so.*

Takeoff is a success, but steering out of the asteroid field is not as simple. Mon's grip tightens on the shuttle controls until she clears the area and jumps near enough to be able to send an encrypted signal to Malwin.

Finally, he helps talk her into the fleet's trajectory.

"Always a backup plan, eh?" She smiles grimly at her attaché when she lands. Malwin passes her neatly folded robes so she can quickly make herself presentable.

"Always," he grins.

She touches her hand to the patched pocket of the shuttle jacket. She's had time to review the datacard. "The Emperor's own schedule. They did it."

"We need a volunteer to lead the mission to Endor," Admiral Ackbar says as the rebel commanders assemble on the main deck of *Home One*. He very carefully does not look at Mon Mothma.

So many have volunteered for the cause already, Mon knows. *These are heroes; they must do what heroes do.*

"You, Senator, will wait here until we've secured the forest moon," the admiral murmurs, out of the others' hearing.

"I understand." Mon clasps her hands behind her.

When she'd entered the room, she'd spotted Leia sitting next to Han Solo. They barely spared her a glance. Both were quietly glowing with triumph. She's heard about their latest adventure. About the risks Leia took on Tatooine.

She's scolded Leia for rushing in before. Mon promises herself she will talk to the princess, again, and soon, about her value to the Rebellion's present, and the promise of its future. So that Mon, growing battle-weary, won't be the only contingency. But Mon also understands why Leia charges in and risks herself.

A leader cannot lead if they will not also sacrifice.

Mon nods to Admiral Ackbar that she is ready to present the gathered intelligence, including the courier's news.

This new item is something she hasn't had time to brief the admiral on, arriving as she has so late, on the dusty trader's shuttle. With the pilot destroyed, no one would know the risk she'd taken. But there had been no other way. And now Ackbar is eyeing her curiously.

She must continue. The rebels need this news. It will help steel them to their purpose. Much as good news has steeled other efforts before—the spy Cassian Andor and Jyn Erso among them. What had Jyn said before Scarif? "Rebellions are built on hope."

Information such as this will give the Rebellion more hope to build with. It can form many new contingencies, even as they risk the kind of traps that might end them. It is worth it.

NO CONTINGENCY

She knows this with a new sense of immediacy now.

Mon observes the assembled fighters. She wills them to be brave.

She thinks of the blood on the rag tucked into the courier's carapace. When she'd pressed her palm to the datacard aboard that tiny ship, she'd touched another's death. The last remnants of a battle. She's pinned the rag unseen into her sleeve. She will tell her people this news, then let the heroes take the lead.

She speaks clearly, with precision, acknowledging the sacrifices many have made to bring the rebels the Death Star plans. She pauses, knowing that the admiral will prepare them for what lies on the moon of Endor below. And then she adds, "Most important of all, we've learned that the Emperor himself is personally overseeing the final stages of the construction of this Death Star."

The rebels burst into excited chatter as Admiral Ackbar moves forward to speak. Mon Mothma once again steps back.

THE BURDEN OF LEADERSHIP

Danny Lore

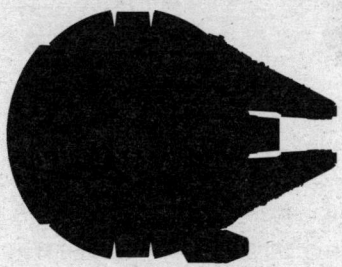

A common mistake at the sabacc table is keeping your face completely blank. The trick, you see, isn't absolute blandness; people will make extreme assumptions about what's happening underneath that nothingness. The less you're showing, the more people figure out what you've got to hide. And they *will* figure it out; there's a galaxy full of little ways your blankness can crack under stress.

No, Lando Calrissian knows the trick isn't to stay *blank;* it's to show exactly what you want someone to see. Normally, that's comfort; a casual sense of ownership of both the room and the table. Sometimes, it's a false tell, a twitch of your mouth or brow. A lack is a tell in and of itself, showing that you're forcing your face and body to contort. Besides, the harder you keep your smirk off your face, the easier it is for someone to notice when it twitches in the opposite direction.

When Han insisted he was okay with Lando taking the *Millennium Falcon* into battle, Lando did exactly what he would have done at the sabacc table. He chuckled, smirked, played up his cool while Han fretted. Dismissing it with a salute and even calling his friend a pirate, until Han was calmed enough to walk away.

He wasn't fully reassured, but Lando knew just what he needed to do to keep Han focused. It was a skill he'd acquired years ago

A skill that was getting used a lot since he'd joined up with the Rebel Alliance.

As it turned out, all the skill and expertise in the galaxy didn't allow Lando to forget reality: Any one of them, or all of them, could end up space dust collecting on an asteroid belt before the attack on the Death Star was over.

Lando managed a snort of dark laughter before finally letting his head and shoulders drop. With Han aboard the stolen Imperial shuttle, preparing to take off, Lando could pretend he was in between card hands, without other players scanning his gaze for accidentally shared honesty. He found his fingertips already at the clasp of his cloak, releasing it. There was a weight lifted then as well, as he draped the cloak over his arm and walked back to his former ship.

As Lando strides up the ramp of the *Falcon* alone, he thinks about a version of the present where he never left Cloud City. He's still the baron administrator; Lobot is nearby, explaining some mind-numbingly mundane administrative task. In it, he either gave Han over and accepted whatever Vader did, or more preferably, it's a version where Han never showed up at all. No one sacrifices themselves to make up for Lando's betrayal. No Empire breathing down the city's

THE BURDEN OF LEADERSHIP

neck. He doesn't want any of that to happen, of course, and imagining those scenarios twists his stomach and thickens the lump. He's made his decision, but he searches for other possibilities, hopes to find one that doesn't make his skin crawl worse than Han's worried pout before his friend had boarded the Imperial shuttle.

Lando enters the ship to find that Nien Nunb is already speaking with the technicians, and the snippets Lando hears sound about right: how few of them Han even let *breathe* near the ship, so most of the inspection information was whatever Han, Chewbacca, and a couple of droids had already offered up. Lando chuckles, his hand running across a wall panel. When he'd first boarded the ship to look for Han, this was one of the first panels he'd touched. At the time he hadn't recognized any of the dents or scratches that marred the metal, and even though he did now, it still felt *strange* to him, still part of the life the ship had lived without him . . .

"What's wrong, Nunb?" He knew something was up from the sound of his friend's footsteps. "Something not ready for takeoff?"

"Hmph," came the response as Lando turned to face him. "Not with the ship."

"Of course not," Lando joked. "If there was, I'm sure Han would have already blamed me for it, somehow." Nunb was unenthused by the joke, and Lando allowed himself a moment of seriousness. "*Who* is it?"

"The stragglers you were worried about."

Stragglers. It wasn't quite the right term, but Lando wasn't sure how to catagorize the dozen or so Cloud City citizens who had chosen to follow Lando to the Rebel Alliance. They all had their reasons—hatred of the Empire, loyalty to Lando, interest in the Rebellion . . . or just feeling like they had no other option. People who felt as if they *had* to follow Lando because he would know what to do. They could have stayed behind or taken their ships and gone anywhere in the galaxy, but Lando knew a few of them felt they had fewer and fewer options. People who'd spent years avoiding the Empire, who felt as if Lando's choices had placed them in limbo, at least until the attack on the Death Star played out. Once it did—*maybe* the stragglers would feel the expanse of space open up again, instead of the pressure of the war suffocating them. Lando's thumb rubbed against the ropework of his cape thoughtfully. "Anyone tell them we've still got a war to fight?"

"Besides you? Only every being on this base," Nunb supplied in Sullestese. He would switch to his native tongue when he wanted to keep things between him and Lando, knowing few others around them would understand. "Starting to gather that's the problem."

There was a shout from outside the ship, and this time Lando did wince. Nunb looked down the still-lowered ramp with a heavy sigh. "From what the technicians were saying . . . no one can handle your Cloud City people but you, Lando."

Lando opened his mouth to say something but stopped himself. No point in arguing with his copilot; he spent enough time having pointless one-sided arguments with Han if he wanted that. Instead, he smirked like he was back at the sabacc table. "Comes with the territory. Captain, baron administrator, general . . . one of these days I'll pick a job where I *actually* get to just worry about myself."

Lando started down the *Falcon*'s ramp, ignoring the way that Nunb laughed. Just because *today* wasn't that day didn't mean Lando couldn't dream.

There's a version of the present where Lando doesn't have *stragglers*. Where he's done this whole "leader" thing properly, and his people

THE BURDEN OF LEADERSHIP

are all on the same page. Where his people weren't disappointed that he'd abandoned neutrality to dive headfirst into being not just a rebel but a *general*. Where the folks that he'd saved weren't so angry he'd broken the promise to avoid the Empire's conflict that they were losing faith in him. A version where they are just happy to be alive instead of angry, feeling as if they have to stay with the Rebellion or fear what would happen to them if they went out on their own. It's a version of events where either he successfully keeps Cloud City on the edge of the conflict instead of diving straight into it or where maybe it's another leader's decision instead of his.

But Lando mostly thinks about staying out of it as *someone else* makes the wrong choice, and that's even worse than the version where the responsibility is still his.

Hours later, there was more shouting, this time from a Dressellian pilot named Korrimix and a human technician named Bolt.

Korrimix was like Lando. From smuggler to Cloud City denizen to part of the city's security force, to exiled past the blockade and stuck out here. Not a rebel, not an Imperial . . . just a man who was quiet until he had a few too many drinks or three too many bad dice rolls. He was slightly older than Lando, and they'd run into each other more than once before Lando became baron administrator; in fact, it had been seeing Lando's "scummy" face that Korrimix listed as the reason he'd decided to stay in Cloud City. The same "scummy" face was probably what kept Korrimix with Lando after Lando rejected the deal with the Empire.

Bolt got his name before coming to Cloud City, the moniker a nod to how quickly he could dodge a hit to the face. He'd come to the city claiming that obviously no one was after him, and he didn't owe anyone money, a dance that Lando knew *very* well. To be honest, Lando suspected Bolt left Cloud City with him because being directly under the Empire's boot was the scariest option in front of him. So as Lando followed the shouting through the hangar, he wasn't sure which was odder: the way that Bolt was standing back up to hold his ground after Korrimix socked him, or the fact that Lando grabbed Korrimix's arm to keep him from socking Bolt again.

"Korrimix, buddy . . . relax." Normally, Lando prided himself on the way those words could actually ease his people's tensions. A warm Calrissian smile and a gentle command could stop the rowdiest of casino denizens and yet . . . right as Lando let Korrimix's fist drop, Korrimix lunged again, past Lando, causing Bolt to flinch and cower—but still not run away.

Lando jerked Korrimix back. "You have two seconds to tell me what's happening here before I throw you *both* out into space and let the lack of gravity separate you!" There were other pilots and technicians looking on at the skirmish. Those whom Lando knew were working to assist for the most part; a pair helped Bolt stand, while another pair took over holding Korrimix.

"Nothing to see here, just some pre-battle tensions," Lando assured anyone near enough to listen, before hissing to Korrimix, "Isn't that *right*?"

"Tell the Baron Administrator what you just said, Korrimix," Bolt hissed. Lando raised an eyebrow at the technician to keep from flinching at being called baron. The old title didn't have the same ring to it when dealing with new problems. "Tell him what kind of sleemo he's going to have at his back."

Lando was keeping track of the bystanders. There were some rebels looking on with curiosity or disgust, whispering to one another—judging Lando and the two men, surely, wondering why it was worth even having them around. He wondered suddenly how much the average rebel knew about the path Lando had traveled to get here.

THE BURDEN OF LEADERSHIP

Whether they were all questioning the choice to make him a general as much as he sometimes did, and why, in this moment, he even *cared*.

Korrimix and Bolt were his to deal with, and whatever the rebels thought about them was in part because Lando had brought them here.

"You all wanna throw away your lives, be my guest," Korrimix snapped at Bolt, "but I'm *done throwing myself into Lando's battles!* I didn't sign up for this! *Nobody's* gonna call me a karking coward for that."

"I didn't just call you a coward," Bolt supplied. The next few words were Bolt saying *exactly* what he thought of Korrimix, starting "selfish Hutt-spawned waste of space" and ending almost poetically in its disgust. Lando wasn't so sure he could blame Korrimix for throwing a punch under those conditions. Still . . .

As Lando smoothed his sleeves, he realized his cloak must have become unclasped when he stepped into the brawl. Looking around, he found it dropped beside a pile of tools and metal scrap. He reached down to grab it but hadn't even laid a finger on it before Korrimix's words sank in.

Lando stood back up, his cloak forgotten. "What did you mean by you're *done*, pilot?" Korrimix's glare didn't soften when he turned it toward Lando, something that Lando was *very* unaccustomed to. "When were you going to inform me—when we were approaching the Death Star?"

That got a flinch.

"Were you expecting to *desert* mid-battle?" Lando questioned sternly. One of the pilots who had been holding Korrimix took a step back. "You too?" Lando sucked his teeth. He'd picked Korrimix as a member of Gold Squadron because he trusted the Dressellian to get the job done, whatever it took. He didn't like thinking he'd picked wrong. "And here I was putting my life in the hands of my squadron. Are you telling me that was a mistake?"

Lando's lowered tone snapped everyone to attention. Bolt froze as if he were the one threatening to betray Lando. Korrimix tilted his head with stubborn pride as he debated what to reply. Those who had interfered to stop the fight suddenly forgot what to do with their hands, looking at Lando and one another for the next steps.

There's a version of the present where Lando lets them duke it out. Where he doesn't get his hands dirty and just picks another pilot. Or maybe Korrimix doesn't throw a punch to begin with. Where everyone under Lando's command shares a united vision of what their future looks like.

There's another version where Lando doesn't even need to be here, because he's turned down the position of general. Maybe he and the others from Cloud City travel as far out in the Outer Rim as they can, or maybe it's just him or maybe . . .

. . . he's digging for possibilities and coming up empty.

There was no whispering from the crowd now. Instead, the smattering of rebels who were checking their fighters and prepping for battle were silent. There was no question that they, too, were waiting for an answer. The weight of Korrimix's words was second only to the suffocating pressure around the conflict. Some droid and one of the pilots scampered off, and Lando could only assume it was to inform another officer that trouble was truly brewing.

Beyond the now captivated rebels, there were other members of Gold Squadron listening in, a couple of them also from Cloud City. Others who were about to put their lives not just in Korrimix's hands,

THE BURDEN OF LEADERSHIP

but in Lando's. Who were going to fight what might be their last fight because they'd put their trust in Lando's lead.

A panicked voice in the back of his head reminded him exactly the kind of man they were trusting. The ways he'd thrown away his friends' lives before finally putting his foot down. That he was a leader who had promised neutrality before landing *here*.

"You could have left before I assigned you to a ship." Lando's stomach dropped but he kept his voice steady. He was a consummate con man; he'd never watched a betrayal happen at such a crucial moment for the entire galaxy. He wondered if this was how Han had felt when Lando turned him over to Vader. "Was making up your mind too hard for you, Korrimix? Or were you hoping to make us fail?"

Korrimix's body language as much as his words would determine what happened next. Whether he'd try to run and steal a ship, making Lando have to lock him up in a cell, or if Lando could laugh this moment off for now . . . before everyone died in battle. Neither option was appealing, and the path didn't clear the longer that Lando stared back at the Dressellian. Korrimix stayed tense, glaring back with an intensity that Lando hadn't seen in a long time.

"I didn't run when you had us fight the Imperials for your little friends," Korrimix answered coldly. "I did it, because I told myself you could push the Imperials out. That you'd make sure we'd be left *alone*, like you promised."

"And we *will be*." Even Lando was shocked at the surety of his words. Was this one of the times when he could convince himself of his own con, when he needed the lie to be true so badly he made it so? "This is just—"

"A detour?" Korrimix snapped acidly. "Being left alone isn't showing up at a place called the Death Star and begging them to lock target."

Lando laughed. In a nightmarish way, Korrimix's words *were* funny, they *were* true. No tension was broken by his joke, or Lando's follow-up. "You're a damn good pilot. If you're flying right, their fighters won't be able to lock on."

"You've lost your mind," Korrimix declared. "They are relying on hope and a few refurbished ships to topple a *destroyer of planets*, and you think *I'm* wrong for wanting to step away?"

"They've done it before!" Surprisingly, it was Bolt who came to the Rebellion's defense. Lando wasn't sure what to make of the man standing more firmly than he'd ever seen, but he couldn't help but admire it. "With more intel and with—"

"It was a near impossible shot, from what I've heard." Korrimix shook his head in disgust, and while he was replying to Bolt, he kept his eyes locked on Lando. "You're talking about a lucky hit the way the rest of these fools talk about hope. Hope was for the Jedi, you know that, right? Real people know hoping does nothing up against brute force. We've seen people in our lines of work—smugglers, con men, military men—and hope gets them *killed*."

Lando saw Korrimix's fist twitch a few times during his speech, the Dressellian clearly debated if punching Lando was worth it. Which one of Lando's many titles was it, he wondered, that kept Korrimix from doing the deed. Baron administrator, Rebellion general, old pal?

Lowering his eyes to Korrimix's fist drew Lando's attention back to his fallen cloak. He stared at it for a moment, realizing with a start that at some point Korrimix had *stepped* on it, his heel squarely atop the fabric. It shouldn't have mattered, not when desertion was on the table, but this annoyed Lando more than anything that was coming out of Korrimix's mouth.

Had Korrimix done it *insultingly* it would have been better. It would have been a conscious insult in line with Bolt's impressively displayed vocabulary. But Korrimix hadn't looked down, hadn't spit

THE BURDEN OF LEADERSHIP

at the cape. He wasn't trying to rile Lando up by snubbing a favorite item of clothing. It was worse than that: Korrimix stepped on the thing, and it *didn't matter*. No realization he shouldn't step on Lando's possessions, no reaction to the insult to Lando's authority.

And worse still, it had taken this long for Lando to notice as well. He'd spent so much time watching the faces around him, imagining versions of his life where he didn't have to do any of this, that he hadn't noticed this carelessness. He'd been distracted enough not to simply pick it up and dust it off . . . because Korrimix was saying exactly what a part of him had been thinking ever since Han, Chewie, and the others had shown up in Cloud City. Luck and hope weren't going to cut it. Lando was too good of a gambler to disagree; no high-level game of sabacc was won on luck or hope alone.

But, he was suddenly so *very* sick of hearing it, both from Korrimix and from himself.

"You want out of the squadron?" Lando asked. Like at the sabacc table, it wasn't about keeping a neutral expression. Instead, it was just the *right* amount of Lando's anger oozing out between the words, mixed with a surety that came not from being a general or a baron administrator, but from years of convincing pirates and smugglers *one more score* was worth it.

Korrimix wasn't sure where this was going, and glanced around at the faces in the crowd. The pilots and technicians who had restrained him previously looked everywhere but at him, not ready to help nudge him to what was possibly their doom. "I'm not a rebel."

"Avoiding the point, but I get it," Lando replied. He glanced around at his people, but past them as well, to the loyal rebels that watched. "I promised you a way out of the Empire's line of sight, and you're right—at the moment, we might as well be putting on a light show to get their attention." Korrimix didn't nod, but one of the men beside him did.

"But you come from the same line of work as I do, Korrimix, old friend, and you were damn good at it." Lando took a step closer not to Korrimix, but to Bolt, putting an arm around the technician and making the man look like he might show off his namesake then and there. "From the stories you both told over drinks, you were better at it than *this* guy was, huh?"

Bolt squawked, squirmed, but Lando just patted him on the shoulder and moved on, leaning on a nearby crate. A crate that two nosy rebels were trying to pretend hid their eavesdropping. They dispersed immediately.

"You're right: Hope and luck won't win the day. But you know how the game is played," Lando continued. "Almost as well as I do." He gestured between him and his people. "We know *their* rules well enough to break them, or twist the rules into our own. It's how we survived on every planet and station we landed on." Who "they" were didn't matter; every ex-smuggler listening knew, "they" were the latest mark chasing after them.

"We bend and break those rules so they can't catch us. So they don't see us. And that worked on Cloud City for a *long* time." He shrugged, winking at the nearest Gold Squadron member with well-practiced nonchalance. "Not as long as we'd like, but a good long time. And you want that back, don't you, Korrimix?"

Korrimix didn't answer, sensing the trap.

"Korrimix." Lando didn't usually have to use *that* bark of authority, but when he did, it worked quite nicely.

"That's what I signed up for," Korrimix growled reluctantly. "I was with you as long as you kept the Empire from bothering me."

Lando nodded. "Right. But you know that's not how any of this works." It wasn't a question. "Because almost every job people like us ever take gets a wrench thrown into it. Big or small, there's always

THE BURDEN OF LEADERSHIP

some rule we can't bend, or some twist we never saw coming. And the job fails when we can't figure out a way around it."

He took a deep breath, standing back up straight. This part of being in charge *was* just like the sabacc table. Even if it didn't come naturally, bluffing until it was true *did*. "What happened on Cloud City was the moment I saw the wrench had been thrown a *long* time ago, Korrimix." He managed to say the pilot's name and mean everyone listening. "It was the moment that I realized playing nice with the Empire meant I couldn't bend the rules I needed to bend. So I did what any good smuggler would do: I threw the plan away and made a new one.

"And you wanna argue this isn't the same plan? Look around you and do the math. The Empire put its claws in Cloud City and there were only two ways out: pretend they hadn't while they still control us, or hightail it out of there and make *sure* it hurts them as badly as it hurts us. Worse."

They weren't under the shadow of the *Falcon*, but Lando searched the shadow and ship out nonetheless from across the way. "Far as I'm concerned, our *freedom* was the score we were aiming for, and it was my job to grab up as much of that as I could. You disagree with that, go ahead and leave. But know this, Korrimix—"

Lando took a step forward, crouching down to put a hand on his cape. With a sharp tug, Korrimix stumbled enough for Lando to pick up the cape. He took his time dusting it off, making a show of putting it back over his shoulders, the fabric gently hitting Korrimix in the process. He closed the clasp properly this time, centering it.

He knew what he looked like in the cape, smirking. He knew the exact image Korrimix saw when Lando put a hand on the Dressellian's shoulder and squeezed it just a little bit. He knew the confidence that Korrimix saw in his eyes.

"—only one of us is keeping the score, and I'm a *damn* better smuggler than you are."

Lando knew that some of the rebels watching wouldn't understand, and probably would tell their associates that Lando was threatening his men. He knew that they looked on and saw a general not punishing a disobedient soldier. And if that was a problem, well, he'd deal with that.

But he wasn't talking to the rebels. He was talking to *his* people. To the folk loyal to his "scummy" face rather than a greater cause. He knew what he was doing.

Korrimix finally spoke. "You really believe there's no other option."

"I tried playing with the Empire already, you saw how that turned out." Korrimix reached out, and instinctively Lando braced—but Korrimix merely plucked a shard of something that had attached itself to Lando's cape. "You're out, I'll get another pilot, but—"

"No," Korrimix grunted. "I work for my share of any score."

Lando's smirk became a smile. "Let's take a walk then, friend." He couldn't very well pretend Korrimix's words hadn't happened—too many lives at stake—but he could make sure Korrimix would fight for Gold Squadron, even if he wasn't committed to the greater cause. And right now, that was enough.

There's no present that Lando can imagine in which he isn't leading Gold Squadron into battle. He's tried to envision it: where he walks away when Korrimix speaks thoughts that mirror his own, where he decides he can't be the general that leads con artists and smugglers, as well as rebels.

He tries to imagine the present where he isn't there to see the second Death Star, where he's not there to make the call to keep fighting. But that present doesn't fit, doesn't sit right in his head.

Lando's more comfortable dealing with the current one.

GONE TO THE WINNER'S CIRCLE

Patricia A. Jackson

"Filthy rebel scum!" TK-151 swore under his breath into the receiver nested at the base of his scout trooper helmet. Two rebel insurgents raced by him on commandeered speeder bikes in pursuit of a fellow soldier, and the intruders were gaining ground.

"Cut the chatter, TK-151," TK-290 ordered. "Keep the channel clear."

"There *is* no channel. They're jamming us. With our own equipment!" Gunning the throttle of his Aratech 74-Z speeder, he sped out of the covert of ancient Endorian trees with his squadmate to give chase. "I told you it wasn't a systems glitch."

At a severe angle, TK-290 swung his speeder hard to the right to get into position behind the rebels. "They're all over him," he said, weaving through the primordial forest of Endor's Sanctuary Moon. "If he can get far enough ahead of them, maybe he can forward a message to base."

"He needs at least a hundred meters." TK-151 jammed his thumb into the firing pin on the maneuver controls. "Let's buy him a little breathing room." He listened to the thrust flaps in the anterior of the speeder bike adjust for the impending kick as the Ax-20 blaster cannon mounted beneath the vehicle fired. He grinned when sparks flew from the rebel's rear quarter panel, indicating a direct hit.

"You're not riding in some outlaw bike race back home," TK-290 reprimanded him. "Stop toying with them and take them out." While they were technically the same rank, TK-290 held seniority over him by nine months and was the current squad leader.

But being the most proficient speeder bike rider on the battalion roster granted TK-151 certain perks—mild insubordination being one—that made giving up his real name for an Imperial military designation worthwhile. Before joining the Galactic Empire, he was Raab Krao, the number-one-ranked professional racer on the Inner Rim.

The lucrative prize moneys he earned on the legitimate circuit and his reputation as a fierce competitor on outlaw courses allowed him and his mechanic brother to dominate the racing industry. Until a squadron of rebel X-wings mistook their Krao Brothers Racing garage for an Imperial field installation and destroyed it, blasting their home, their equipment, and their livelihood into black ash. His older brother was fatally injured in the bombardment. He took his last breath in Raab's arms.

Crawling from the rubble, Raab had found himself alone and in mourning for the second time since the deaths of their parents in a shuttle accident. With nothing but a damaged family holo-album,

GONE TO THE WINNER'S CIRCLE

the charred remnants of his first racing trophy, and memories salvaged from the ruins, he signed up for the Imperial Academy, looking to even the score.

Despite being five centimeters shorter than the minimum required height, he made the cut through a clever use of lifts hidden in his boots. What he lacked in physical stature, he made up for in heart and desire, just like on the track. Being one of three Socorran expats in the entire trainee cadre, he was ridiculed for being a second-tier civilian from the Outer Rim, and had to outperform, out-test, and outmaneuver his fellow cadets.

He accomplished this by fearlessly dominating the vehicle rotation in basic training. In a sea of scowling, pretentious faces, he graduated with honors at the top of his class. Instead of chasing down a division to call home, the Ghost Lancers, an elite company of scout troopers, came looking for him.

The mission was simple: surveil, maintain, and defend the boundaries of a shield generator base on the Sanctuary Moon of Endor. The critical, strategic objective was to protect the Death Star II under construction in the moon's orbit. Without the advantage of such a powerful weapon in his arsenal, TK-151 feared Emperor Palpatine faced a prolonged, drawn-out trial of putting down the traitorous Rebel Alliance once and for all.

Only decorated, veteran soldiers with three to five years of exemplary military service were chosen for the coveted assignment. But due to Raab's extensive racing credentials, his inexperience in the field was overlooked for his superior skills at the controls of a speeder bike.

TK-151 feathered the throttle, taking his hand from the controls to flip a series of custom switches on his control panel. The standard-model speeder bikes issued to his squadron mates were governed for safety, despite being designated for military use. In his spare time, he had disabled or removed the welfare protocols and replaced them with racing spec equipment to amplify the vehicle's maneuverability and speed.

As he lined up the two rebel speeders in his sights, one of the riders hit the brakes. The infiltrator's bike bucked, dangerously tipping out of balance in front of them, and then dropped back into a counter-pursuit position. It was smooth maneuvering, flawlessly executed, and betrayed an expert level of skill and daring.

"What the—" TK-290 exchanged a startled look with TK-151 before glancing over his shoulder.

From prey to predator, the rebel opened fire on them from the advantage of the rear position. Accelerating, TK-151 swung wide to evade the deadly barrage of cannon fire.

Vibrations from the ungoverned repulsorlift engine sent a tingling through his arms and numbed his shoulders as he hunched down over the crest of the bike.

At 450 kilometers per hour, the giant trees of Endor were a blur. The distinctive shriek of the commandeered speeder's blaster cannon reverberated in his ears. Thrilled to be back in the excitement of a racing scenario, TK-151 grinned with euphoric nostalgia—until the rebel scored a direct hit on TK-290's bike.

Penetrating the thruster flap, the destructive bolt of energy generated a mechanical chain reaction. The searing heat expanded the gases in the exhaust. TK-151 detected the bitter fumes of burning coolant, even through the filter built into his helmet. Ignited by catastrophic failure in the repulsor turbines, the drive shaft transformed TK-290's speeder bike into an unguided, high-velocity missile.

An experienced outlaw racer would have been looking for a spot to dismount, hoping to survive the landing with their limbs mostly intact. But TK-290 was neither an outlaw nor even an accomplished amateur racer. At five hundred kilometers per hour, he had no chance.

GONE TO THE WINNER'S CIRCLE

He wrecked head-on into a stoic Endorian tree. Thousands of years old, the tree's root systems ran deep beneath the forest. Despite the force of the crash, the ancient tree barely moved, presiding over the collision like a tombstone above a freshly interred grave.

The explosion registered across TK-151's built-in helmet sensors in a hypnotic spectrum of infrared infernos. Fires from the explosion radiated outward from the center of the impact site and swelled into an erratic spiral that spread to the forest floor. In a few hours, the temperate dampness would snuff out those flames, leaving nothing more than a slight depression in the ancient tree and a charred halo across its hardened bark.

TK-151 winced. He harbored no hope for his squad leader's survival. The impact alone would have shattered every bone in TK-290's body, regardless of the protection of the polymer scout trooper armor. As the fiery images faded from his HUD screen, he suffered a pang of guilt. Had his aim been more deliberate and true, that rebel would have been grounded or dead, and not his squadmate.

"All right, wild card," the scout trooper whispered. "Let's see what you're made of."

He gritted his teeth until his jawbone cracked, swallowed any feelings of regret, and feathered the sensitive throttle to maximize his speed. Under his helmet, sweat poured across his black skin. He shook his head to keep the stinging beads from falling into his eyes. Carving a daredevil's path between the trees, he lured the rebel away. With any luck, the other scout trooper would outrun his pursuer and send out an alert that the Alliance had landed.

Experienced with racing through a multitude of complex obstacles designed to hinder and intimidate racers on course, TK-151 reveled in the overgrown forests of Endor. While on official patrol or out for sport, he took every opportunity to convert the planet's woodland labyrinth into his own private training arena.

Pressing his toe against the foot peg to finesse his control of the bike, he ducked down over the vehicle's engine mount and sped beneath the petrified trunk of a fallen tree as if it were the starting gate of a race. Damp mulch and underbrush spewed into the air from the exhaust blast and temporarily covered his evasive maneuvering.

Undaunted, the rebel dropped in behind him, weaving between the narrow gaps of the surrounding trees to make up for lost ground. He forced TK-151 into a disadvantage on the outside line and sped up until they were riding side by side.

In a synchronized turn, they swung around in unison onto a straightaway, and like a dirty lane stealer vying for lead position on the rail, the rebel deliberately crashed into him twice. The screech of metal hammering against metal reverberated above the high-pitched shriek of the laboring engines.

Swapping a little paint did little to affect TK-151's courage or his balance. He was riding speeder bikes and swoops before he could walk and racing for prize money before puberty. Such tactics were commonplace among amateur outlaws. But it was always done with a purpose among the pros, and not just for intimidation. The rebel, while skilled, was just another rookie hoping for glory.

TK-151 held his position. He could have outridden his rival, outmaneuvered him, or braked hard and let the rebel fly out of control into a tree. But he needed to see him, up close, and look into the man's eyes. The eyes of a traitor.

Like all rebels he looked haggard, piecemeal, dressed in a makeshift helmet and a dusty camouflage smock that would have been deemed unfit for a mudtrooper. There was an intensity in his face that marked him as a veteran soldier, but still a backstabbing Alliance

GONE TO THE WINNER'S CIRCLE

turncoat with nothing to lose. He was dangerous, as were all Alliance fanatics, a fact the rebel proved when he broke off, rolled the speeder bike sharply into a forty-five-degree angle, and slipped through a particularly narrow copse of trees.

After readjusting his position, the rebel glanced over his shoulder. He didn't have to look far. TK-151 was on top of him. Having seen the man for himself and found him undeserving, the trooper knew it was time to render judgment. He banked his weight to the off side of the speeder and crashed into the rebel. Being the more experienced rider, he knew the weak points of the 74-Z and how the slightest shift in the alignment of the directional vanes would destabilize the vehicle.

Remembering the countless hours his brother had spent in reinforcing these frangible areas, TK-151 installed aftermarket Starblight outriggers to strengthen the vehicle chassis of his speeder. Designed to withstand the rigors of uneven terrain and racing, the sturdier metal frames maintained their integrity while severely damaging the rebel's stock accessories. Each collision shifted the rods and resulted in the misalignment of the sensitive directional steering vanes.

With a cocky snort that registered only in his ears, TK-151 heard a rattling from the front end of the rebel's speeder bike. The battered outriggers banged unsteadily against the frame, shaken loose in the persistent hammering between vehicles. Whining in protest of the wind cutting across them, the steering vanes fluttered and failed, unable to sustain the punishment. As the vehicle stuttered forward, losing altitude and output, the rebel's blue eyes went wide.

Bearing down on a tree at four hundred kilometers per hour, the speeder's control unit seized from the onslaught of external damage. The impending malfunction and system failure were inevitable. The rebel's face went pale with that realization as the maneuver controls in his hands froze up. Teeth clenched in frustration, he leapt from the seat and landed in the underbrush with a defeated grunt. His speeder bike flew on, riderless, and collided with a tree.

TK-151 squinted against the fiery corona of the resulting explosion as he rode by with a callous smirk. "What a scrub!"

He couldn't wait to celebrate the rebel's death by cutting the first victory notch into his utility belt to pay homage to his murdered brother. Racing through a shower of sparks and debris that rained down on him like victory confetti, TK-151 pumped his fist exuberantly in the air. He leaned into a fifty-degree roll, manipulated the throttle to bring his speeder bike around through a triumphant bootlegger's turn, and accelerated back to where the rebel had dismounted. It was time to send the traitor to the winner's circle, a lowbrow racing euphemism for riders who died without finishing the course.

Propping his thumb over the Aratech 74-Z's weapon controls, TK-151 aimed his speeder bike at the fallen rebel and fired, intent on reducing him to a charred scorch mark on the forest floor. The smug smile etched across his face went crooked when his HUD detected an unusual energy surge, a streak of green plasma.

He dismissed it at first as a random flare from the fires of the wrecked vehicle, but the steady emission did not diminish. To his horror, it moved in precise, measured strokes, deflecting the blasts from the Ax-20 cannon.

A lightsaber? His only knowledge of the ancient weapons came from holocomics and the grifted whispers of story peddlers who regaled children and tourists with tales of the Jedi. From the lost and bygone era of the Republic, the Jedi were a disgraced order of charlatans and con artists that had turned their backs on Emperor Palpatine in the hour of his greatest need.

A cold fury shuddered through him. Like a fathier jockey in Canto Bight, TK-151 stood up, perched on the speeder bike's foot pegs, and

GONE TO THE WINNER'S CIRCLE

leaned into the maneuver controls while gunning the throttle. If he couldn't shoot the rebel, he would run him down. At high speeds, the speeder bike's directional steering vanes were capable of severing limbs. The instruments would have no trouble cutting down the rebel and bringing their race to a gruesome but dramatic finale.

TK-151 grinned, eager for the kill, and braced himself for the impact. But at the last minute, the rebel stepped to the side and swept the lightsaber down across the front of the speeder bike. The simple sweep of the blade lopped off the reinforced outriggers. Without the directional steering vanes to guide its passage, the vehicle spiraled in a series of gut-wrenching, out-of-control death rolls.

Bile spilled up from TK-151's stomach. The caustic acid burned his tongue and the sensitive lining inside his mouth. Obstinate resolve, honed reflexes, and centrifugal forces kept him pinned to the mangled speeder bike's seat. This race was over, and he had lost.

"*Can't win them all,*" he heard the voice of his dead brother whisper. Succumbing to vertigo, the scout trooper felt the weight of his older sibling's hand on his shoulder.

"No, you can't," TK-151 replied, tightening his grip on the maneuver controls. "See you in the winner's circle, partner."

He was still conscious, seconds after the initial impact. Long enough to experience the abrupt stop and then the intense heat of the speeder bike as the engine detonated, erupting in flames beneath him. The heat bled through the polymer of his helmet and melted through the less reinforced joints of the armor. A short-lived discomfort, the fire enveloped him with a nagging, tingling sensation of an itch he could never again scratch.

Before his HUD went black, he caught the crackle of the open comm coming back online. "TK-151, come in. This is base. What is your position?"

ONE NORMAL DAY

Mary Kenney

On Endor's forest moon, daybreak came hours after the sun had broken free from the horizon, and then only in scattered golden drops that filtered down through the dense canopy. Sheltered by needled firs, hand-shaped leaves, and silvery moss, the tree homes of Bright Tree Village were cocooned in cool shadow. This was why Wicket Wystri Warrick, a brown-furred, youngish Ewok, found it impossible to roll out of his soft, warm bed.

Not that this was the only reason. For an Ewok of his age, Wicket had experienced more than his share of adventures. He'd found a crashed ship from another world, saved children, and fought monsters. Even as a wokling, he'd ventured into a blizzard and tracked down a troll. But not today. Today, he snuggled down deeper in his fur blankets. Today would be his one normal day.

That normalcy, unfortunately, included an awful cramp that seized his left foot. Groaning, he rolled from the bed and hopped onto the other foot, over the threshold of his hut and onto the outdoor wooden platform. He stretched through the cramp, growling and baring his teeth as he wiggled each clawed toe. Wicket clicked his claws against the platform, and the stretching felt so good, he saw no reason to stop. He crossed his legs and plopped down. He scooted until he found a solid band of sunlight, a single spot of warmth on the cool boards, and arced his back, lacing his fingers together and stretching his arms overhead. He couldn't help but let out a soft coo as his muscles unknotted themselves.

The coo attracted attention. An Ewok with moonlight-colored fur was just stepping out of her hut when she heard Wicket across the platform. Kneesaa, Wicket's closest friend and the only child of Chief Chirpa, grinned. She pulled on her pale-pink bandanna and jogged to him, pointing to the sky as she approached.

"Did you see?" she was saying, punctuated by little squeaks and chitters.

Wicket, his legs still crossed, squeezed his eyes tight. "No."

"You can't see if you don't look."

He opened one eye and peered up. "I see leaves and a little sun. What else is there?" He shut the eye again and unbent his legs. He tried, unsuccessfully, to touch his toes.

"Ships!" The word burst out of her like a log broken free from a river dam. "There were so many sky ships!"

Wicket's eyes popped open without his permission. "Ships?" No, no no no. He did not want to feel this pang of curiosity. He did not want to chase after ships. He wanted one normal day.

But Wicket could tell it was already too late. Kneesaa hauled him

ONE NORMAL DAY

upright. He squeaked a protest, but she was already propelling him toward her own hut. The forest cover parted there, letting in a warm flush of sunshine, but as he watched, dark shapes blotted out the sun. It could be birds, he thought, but these flew in lines too straight, so uniform they made him uneasy. The ships came in colors one never saw in the forest: grays too shiny, blacks too dark, whites without a fleck of dirt on them. "Ships," Wicket said again.

"But why are they here?" Kneesaa said. She was nearly hopping with excitement, still tugging on his arm. "We have to know where they're going!"

He pulled his arm out of her grip. She stared at him. "What's gotten into you?" she asked. "You're normally the first one out in the forest when something exciting happens."

"I know, and I'm tired!" he cried, though he couldn't help but glance at the sky in case another ship passed. "I want a day to rest, Kneesaa. No adventures, no ships, no forest treks. I'm staying home." He spun on his heel and marched back toward his hut, hoping he'd made his point.

He hadn't. She trotted after him, gesturing at him, his hut, and the sky. "Home? What's at home? Chores and sleep? The ships could mean anything!"

"Exactly—the ships could be good or bad! At home I can cook, play, sleep, stretch, tell stories, sing songs," he said at random. He reached his hut and pushed aside the fur that covered the opening, glancing at her before he ducked inside. "No more adventures for a while."

She peered at him for a moment. Then her face broke into a smile, and she gave a delighted squeak. "I don't believe you," she said. "You'll break that promise by the end of the day, Wick-Wick. I know you. You're too curious to stay home."

It was true: Kneesaa knew Wicket better than anyone. They'd

trudged through the snow-blanketed forest, trapped monsters, and caught kublag together. If Wicket was the curious one, then Kneesaa was the fearless one; together, they were formidable.

But Wicket didn't want to be formidable today. Instead, he harrumphed at her. He hadn't been called Wick-Wick since he was a cub, and he didn't particularly want to reintroduce the nickname. "If the ships start falling out of the sky, come get me," he threw over his shoulder before disappearing inside. "Until then, I'm staying right here!" He tugged the fur covering closed on her peal of laughter.

With the door and windows shut tight, twilight darkness blanketed Wicket's room. He stumbled forward, tripped on his spear, and, irritated, kicked it into the corner. He would fill the hut with sunshine if he pulled back the door flap, but he didn't want to risk bumping into Kneesaa again. He didn't know if he could say no to her twice, and he had made a promise—first to himself, then to her—to enjoy his normal day at home. Promises were important.

His stomach gurgled at him, no doubt angry that he'd stretched and stared at sky ships without bothering to eat something first. In the corner he kept a little table stocked with dried meat, fresh berries, glossy leaves, and the soft, chewy inner bark of the sunberry tree. At least, he normally kept all these things. Today there was just one tiny leaf, a dried and crumpled thing. He pressed it to the middle of his tongue, and it gave a short-lived burst of nutty flavor. That only served to make him hungrier. He checked under the table, around it, in his bed, and even in the corner where he'd kicked his spear. There was no food in the house.

Well, he could still stick to his promise. He wasn't going on an adventure, really, just a quick trip to the forest to gather some fruit, maybe a leaf or two. If he found a nice rugger to make new strips of jerky, even better. But he wasn't staying out all day. Just the morning, then straight back. Completely normal.

He grabbed his favorite orange hat, the one with the straps that ran down past his chin, and crammed it over his ears. He fetched a leather satchel and secured it around his chest. Finally, he scooped up his spear and tried a few practice thrusts. Satisfied, he grunted and lifted it to his shoulder. He went to the door and peered outside. Kneesaa had gone, probably to look at the ships from one of the forest clearings that gave a better view of the sky. That was good; it meant he wouldn't have to explain himself when he crept into the woods, though he would miss having a hunting partner. Even so, he stepped out cautiously. When she didn't appear from around a corner, he sprinted across the platform, determined not to be seen.

It wasn't that Wicket hated adventure, he reflected as he brushed aside a low-hanging branch with his spear. It was that he'd earned a few days of rest. When was the last time he'd spent a day by the fire with his pipe, or sipped spiced sunberry wine while listening to stories? Too long. Still, his thoughts kept drifting to the sky ships. These weren't the first ships to visit Endor. The ones he'd seen before had been alone, boxy gray transports on their way to the planet beyond. He'd never seen so many ships together, so orderly, gathered up in unnaturally perfect lines that made him feel a little sick. Unlike the clunky transports, these ships had bulbous centers with flat plates on either side. Mean-looking ships, he decided, that seemed to glare down at everything they passed.

However, despite the distraction of the sky ships, the woods were proving kind. He'd been out only a few minutes when he found a lovely creeping bush, spread flat and curling along the forest floor. It sprouted cheery red and purple berries, warmed by a patch of sunlight. He crammed three in his mouth before gathering up more to tuck into his satchel.

Wicket was debating whether to head home or seek out the bright-red petals of the raven thorn plant, his favorite snack, when he saw them: a perfectly plump pair of forest frogs. Their backs were silvery, good for blending into the shadowy forest. Wicket licked his lips. They would go wonderfully with the berries. He wished Kneesaa were here. They could've each aimed for a frog and had a much better chance of bagging the pair. Still, if he could throw his spear just so, from just the right spot and at just the right angle, he could hit both. He crept to one side, then the other, trying to line it up. His grip tightened on his spear, then loosened. He took a breath, released it. Forest frogs were notoriously skittish. He had to be very, very careful.

He could do it, he decided. He could hit two with one spear throw. He scuffled to the left, lining up the shot while trying to make as little noise in the underbrush as possible. He lifted the spear to his shoulder and threw.

Wicket's furred face wore an eye-crinkling smile as he made his way back to Bright Tree Village. He chirped and whistled, his satchel heavy with a couple dozen berries and two forest frogs. He was dreaming of sauces, stews, and crisp smells over a crackling fire. The dream was interrupted by a hum and click, followed by a string of sounds he couldn't understand. He froze, then dived under a cluster of ferns, tightening the grip on his spear and holding his satchel close to keep his treasures safe.

The noises grew louder. Whirs like breathing. The heavy fall of feet on the leaf-carpeted ground. But these footfalls were wrong: It wasn't the soft sound of fur, scale, or skin smacking against the dirt.

ONE NORMAL DAY

These were hard, sharp. Curious, Wicket crept as far out as he dared to peer past the feathery fern leaves.

He'd never seen creatures like these and, in a sudden flash of dislike, hoped he never would again. They were shiny all over, an unsettling white like fresh-boiled bone, with bulbous black, shining eyes. Their heads were the shape of upside-down buckets, and out of these came the sounds of wheezy breathing and what he guessed were words. They held long black metal things cradled in their hands and arms. Spears? But they were too short, with nothing pointy on the end.

These creatures must have come from the sky ships, he thought. The perfect ships in perfect boxes and lines. Their bodies were similar to the ships, all sharp corners and flat planes. They didn't look right at all: no rolls of fur or muscle, no lips or teeth pulled into a smile or grimace. Nothing but clean white and black surfaces. As he watched, one of them lifted an arm and pointed all around them. It spun its hand in a circle and pointed overhead. More ships coming?

Wicket jerked back. What would Kneesaa say? No doubt she'd point out that adventure seemed to find him, even when he wasn't looking for it. He growled at that. He'd made himself a promise, and the sky people weren't his problem and they hadn't seen him. Wicket had handfuls of berries and two plump forest frogs; he was going home.

Delighted squeals and chirps greeted him when he returned to the village, but they weren't for him; they were for his bag of goodies. Kneesaa was sitting in a loose ring with Weechee, Wicket's older brother, and their friend Teebo. They'd been playing a game with twigs and flat stones on the platform boards, but they abandoned it to investigate the contents of Wicket's satchel.

"Berries?" Weechee scoffed. "I expected something a little more—"

"*Frogs!*" Teebo interrupted. "Look, Weechee! The fattest frogs I've ever seen!"

Wicket chuckled at Weechee's ill-hidden jealousy before turning to Kneesaa. "I thought you went to see the sky ships."

She heaved a sigh. "I searched *all morning*. Nothing. No landed sky ship, no ship people, no one, nothing." She grinned as Teebo plucked the frogs from Wicket's bag and Weechee grabbed a fistful of berries. They ran off to start a fire and fashion a spit, leaving Kneesaa and Wicket alone. She added, "Did you see anything while you were out hunting?"

Wicket turned toward his house, and Kneesaa fell into step beside him. He thought about the shiny people in the woods. Their great black bug eyes hadn't been much good at finding; he'd slipped right past them, through shadow and undergrowth. "I didn't look for them." That was the truth, even if it was incomplete.

Once they reached his house, he put away his spear and the remaining berries. They returned to the fire, where Weechee and Teebo had set up a spit and a fire guarded by a ring of stones. Wicket was designated to turn the spit already loaded with frogs, and he did this slowly, with intense concentration. The skins were cooked to perfection, shiny and crisp, when he took them off the spit. What followed was blissful silence as they divvied up the food and settled in to eat. The quiet was broken only by birdsong.

The next sound was as unlike a bird as a forest frog was unlike a coiled, venomous snake. It was a low groan, as if the sky itself was sick. All of them looked up, their meal forgotten. It was the sky ships again, but flying so low they ruffled the forest canopy. Their passage sent the birds scattering, fleeing for the lower, safer branches.

Kneesaa rose. "The trees!" she cried, her voice wobbling with anxiety. She pointed as branches snapped off and showers of broken

ONE NORMAL DAY

leaves fell from the sky like tears. Wicket rose and put an arm around her. She cuddled close, wincing as more ships tore through branches overhead.

In the aftermath, there was a long stretch of silence. Kneesaa squeezed closer to Wicket, then stepped away. Before, she'd sounded excited about the newcomers; now her voice was hard and angry. "We have to know where they're going. Who they are and what they want."

Wicket chewed the inside of his cheek, deciding how much to tell her. "I saw them. The sky people." He described their shiny white bodies, their bucket heads, and their empty black bug eyes. Kneesaa stared at him. Weechee and Teebo looked equally impressed and terrified.

Wicket expected a reprimand for his earlier lie by omission. Instead, Kneesaa cried, "Wicket, you found them! Show me where. We have to follow!"

"*No*," he snapped. Weechee and Teebo exchanged a look, then wisely busied themselves cleaning up after the meal, leaving Kneesaa and Wicket to argue.

Wicket rocked on his heels, back and forth, until he'd calmed down a little. "I wasn't looking for them; I just found them near the tree frogs, in the big clearing by the old fern patch. They were dangerous. They had weapons, like spears but without the pointy bits."

She snorted. "Doesn't sound so dangerous to me. What were they doing?"

He thought about it. "Pointing at things," he said. "Talking. Wheezing."

"Do you think they want to build a village? Live here?"

Wicket hoped not. "They won't be able to build in the trees if their sky ships knock them down."

Kneesaa scowled at that, but before she could say anything, Chief

Chirpa emerged from his hut. "Wicket!" he boomed. "I've been looking for you all morning. I have a job that needs doing."

"We'll talk after," Kneesaa growled as Wicket scuffled over to the chief.

Before long Wicket found himself lifting a heavy beam to reinforce the massive spit above the village's main firepit. This was used for feasts and holidays, when everyone assembled to eat, dance, sing, and tell stories. The spit needed regular maintenance: reinforcing the supports that held it above the bonfire, reordering the stones around the firepit, and cleaning out the old ashes. The spit's wood had been taken from every tree in the forest: silvery inner bark, red and brown and black outer bark. All singed, now, from the meat and flames, but still distinct from one another.

Wicket tried to block out his argument with Kneesaa and the threat of the sky ships and their bug people as he worked. This proved impossible when another groan overhead signaled their low-flying, destructive return. Ewoks pointed and chittered to one another, little sounds of distress as more tree branches were ripped loose.

A crash echoed across the platform. Wicket was sure one of the larger branches in the canopy had fallen onto the village. It took him a moment to realize that the crash was his doing: distracted by the ship, he'd dropped the beam straight into the firepit, sending ashes and Ewoks scattering.

Chief Chirpa waddled over, his walking stick tapping against the platform. Wicket twisted his fingers together, trying to think of an apology, but Chirpa spoke before he could say anything. "You're distracted today."

Wicket took a moment to reply. Chirpa had the same penetrating, wise gaze as his daughter, though his was more patient. "I saw the sky ships this morning. I found their sky people in the forest. They had white, shiny bodies, and they carried strange short spears."

ONE NORMAL DAY

"Their spears shoot red lightning, like a thunderstorm," Chirpa said. "Take care. They hurt even if they're not close. No one in the village should go near them."

Wicket didn't ask how Chirpa knew; the chief knew many things. "I don't want to go anywhere close to the sky people."

Chirpa peered at the tree canopy where branches now sagged limp and broken. "If they try to build their own village here, you might not have a choice." Chirpa frowned before turning back to Wicket. "Clear your head, or you'll be of no use to anyone today, least of all yourself."

Wicket glanced up at the sky, too, expecting to hear that sickly groan again. "Chief, why did they come here?"

Chirpa gave a smile that could've been a grimace. "There's only one way to find out."

"I thought you didn't want us chasing after them."

The chief chuckled and put a hand on Wicket's shoulder. "Someone's curiosity will get the better of them eventually, and most of us couldn't stand up to them. But you, Wicket Wystri Warrick? I can't think of anyone better to track them down and warn them off."

Wicket shook his head, feeling tired rather than annoyed. "I wanted today to be normal. I've had enough adventures."

Chirpa laughed in little puffs at that. "Adventure finds us, Wicket, not the other way around."

Back in the forest, Wicket moseyed this time, his spear held loosely in one hand. He'd tried to clear his head at home, but no luck; his mind was filled with images of the bug people, the sky ships, and the broken canopy. He wasn't searching for berries or forest frogs. He took in the stillness of the thicket, the rises and falls in the carpet of leaves, and the gentle breeze that set strips of moss swaying. He tried to still his mind. What awaited him at home was a dark, cool little room, stocked with fresh berries and warm furs he could burrow into. What did *not* await him was adventure, blasters, spears, and danger. As the chief had said, if he didn't go after the sky people, someone else would. Kneesaa. Kneesaa would.

At that, Wicket froze. He hadn't seen her since he'd admitted he'd found the sky people. That would've been enough for her to mount a search of her own. He gave a distressed little squeak and started to half run, half skip, headed toward where he'd found the forest frogs that morning.

The forest that had seemed so friendly and gentle just moments ago was now full of shadows and strange sounds. Wicket knew that was partly in his own head, but it wasn't just his worry. There *were* strange new sounds: whirring, clicking, groaning, no longer coming from the sky but from the forest ahead of him.

He found the sky people before he found Kneesaa. He ducked behind a tree and watched, trying to keep his jaw from dropping. They weren't building tree houses; they were building in the *ground,* in the *dirt,* like bugs. A building like a metal cave jutted out of the ground now. As Wicket watched, the smooth metal surface at the front of the cave split in two and slid open, so smooth and seamless it made him wince.

Everything about the sky people made him think of bugs: their smooth, carapace-like bodies; the fluid way they, their doors, and their ships moved; and their big eyes. Some of his friends liked bugs, either to befriend or eat, but not Wicket. Wicket hated bugs.

So, this was what one of their villages looked like. They had come here to live, maybe, but what for? Where did they live before this? As his mind filled with questions, he forgot his promise not to get swept up in an adventure.

And then the sky fell down.

ONE NORMAL DAY

There was a creak like an old board bearing too much weight, then a series of crashes and a sharp-toothed rain of splinters. The sky people (Wicket was considering renaming them "bug people" in the privacy of his own mind) shouted and pointed. Wicket lifted his own spear as the bug people (yes, that fit) raised their blasters. Red light burst out of them, showing Wicket the electricity the chief had warned him about. The red light wasn't enough; the entire canopy seemed to fall on them, their new building, and the whole clearing.

In the aftermath, an eerie silence as the forest held its breath.

The silence was broken by whooping. Wicket lowered his spear; he'd know Kneesaa's victory cry anywhere. She was with Paploo, her cousin, and the two were bumping chests and generally making a spectacle of themselves. As Wicket approached, Kneesaa turned and beamed at him. "Wicket, did you see? The trees fell right on them, and they couldn't do anything about it!"

Wicket planted his spear in the ground and leaned on it, the way he'd seen Chirpa do with his walking staff when he was angry. "I thought you were mad they were hurting the trees."

Kneesaa's smile grew. "I am! I used bits and pieces their sky ships had already broken off." Her lips curled in a growl. "Serves them right."

But the victory was short-lived. The bug people, as Wicket had renamed them, were shoving away branches and leaves, melting and burning with red zaps from their blasters. Their words had turned to shouts, and though Wicket couldn't understand them, he could feel their anger.

"Go back home. They'll be angry," Wicket warned.

Kneesaa and Paploo looked ready to argue, but at that moment, one of the bug people pointed his weapon at a thick branch and unleashed a stream of sunset-red lightning. The branch, which would've taken several tries for Wicket to light with his little flint, burst into a pale-orange fireball, coughing a mushroom of smoke. Kneesaa and Paploo nodded mutely, and the three set off into the woods.

Paploo strode ahead, but Kneesaa fell back to walk with Wicket. "I thought you were staying home today, after you were done helping my father."

Wicket sighed. "I tried. I couldn't stop thinking about the bug people. Sorry, I call them that because of—"

"The eyes," she interrupted. "And the shiny bodies."

He couldn't help but smile. They were so alike.

Someone else might have gloated at Wicket's admission that Kneesaa had been right all along about his "normal day," but she just nodded. "Well, I'm glad. It wouldn't have been right, hunting without you."

Wicket nodded at the Ewok trundling ahead of them. "What about Paploo?"

"He does his best, but he's no Wicket," she chirped.

Paploo let out a hissing *shhhh*, followed by a series of gestures. The Ewoks used two combinations of hand and arm movements to signal silence when they were out in the forest. One meant you were approaching prey. The other meant you *were* something's prey. Paploo signed the second one.

Wicket pointed at a hollowed-out log as big around as a borra beast was tall. The three rushed to it, piling inside. Wicket grunted as Paploo tugged his fur and Kneesaa stepped on his foot, but they were cozy enough inside—and, hopefully, hidden. There was a great crack in the bark, and through this, Wicket saw two of the bug people move faster than any living being he'd seen. They sat upright on long contraptions that looked like the chief's throne stuck on top of a bundle of sticks.

"They're so fast," Kneesaa whispered, horrified.

The bug people came to a stop, then swung their legs to hop onto the ground. The speeder bikes remained floating, still, as they waited for their masters. Wicket wondered if they were alive.

The bug people were walking in big loops, searching the clearing. Wicket recognized the pattern: They were hunting, probably for whatever sent the sky crashing down on them. Wicket glanced at Kneesaa and Paploo, and his grip tightened on his spear. He studied the clearing, and after a few breaths, he touched Kneesaa's shoulder and whispered in her ear. He pointed at the trees, the forest floor, the looping bug people. Kneesaa and Paploo's canopy trap had given Wicket an idea, though this version was far riskier. Even so, the three formed their plan.

Kneesaa and Paploo silently slipped out of the log, edging into the underbrush. Wicket held his spear and gave a little growl. His part was arguably the most dangerous, but he was armed, and they weren't.

Wicket rolled out of the other end of the log, making as much noise as he possibly could. He hoped the bug people wouldn't shoot lightning first and investigate later. He heard them shout in their strange language, heard the clicks of them grabbing their weapons, but no fire. He released a breath, rolled to his feet, and let out a series of short, barking growls, leveling his spear at the bug people.

To his relief and slight confusion, they lowered their weapons. They exchanged a look and a few words, nothing Wicket could understand. One pointed to the canopy. That was no good. Wicket needed them looking *away* from the trees. He barked again, lowered his spear, and charged.

The bug people let out startled yelps. This time, their weapons spat the stinging red beams, but Wicket rolled to one side. The zaps hit the ground and burned through the dead, damp leaves. Wicket leapt up and shook his spear at them, barking and baring his teeth.

Behind the bug people, two furred figures scurried up opposite tree trunks: Kneesaa and Paploo. They each held a thick, furred vine.

Wicket looked down and saw little V-shaped twigs planted in the dirt at the base of each tree. Wicket waited a few minutes more, checking Kneesaa and Paploo's progress in the trees. Kneesaa's white-furred paw waved; at that signal, Wicket launched his spear. It flew right between the startled bug men. They shouted and shot at him, but he was already rushing them, rolling forward to avoid the blasterfire. He retrieved his spear where it had stuck into the ground just behind them, never stopping his sprint, and heard heavy footfalls as the bug people chased him.

When he was between the two trees, he lightly hopped onto a fallen tree branch. The sky people didn't bother—and soon regretted it. As their feet hit the ground beneath Kneesaa and Paploo's perches, the trap sprang. The vines left in big loops at the base of each tree tightened, one around each bug person's ankle. The vines hauled them upside down and into the air. They dropped their weapons, howling in surprise.

Kneesaa let out a whoop as she slid down the tree, and Paploo did a little dance the second he hit the ground. Wicket was growling and laughing, pointing his spear at each of the bug people before chuffing at them. *You lose, good riddance,* that chuff said.

"Maybe this is what a normal day looks like for you, Wicket," Kneesaa observed as the three of them headed back to the village. "Adventure seems to find you."

"Your father said the same thing," Wicket groused, but he couldn't hide his glee very well. It had felt good to stop the bug people from hurting his friends and the forest. He paused, thinking. Paploo kept walking, oblivious, but Kneesaa turned, her furred brows up in a question.

ONE NORMAL DAY

"I think," Wicket said slowly, "we might not have any more normal days for a while." As if to prove his point, another line of silvery sky ships roared overhead.

Kneesaa growled up at them before turning back to Wicket. "I think you're right. So, what do we do about it?"

Wicket planted his spear and studied the sky. "You go tell your father everything we saw out here: the bug people, their building, and the traps. I'll search the forest and see if I can find out why they're here."

Paploo grunted his agreement, and Kneesaa smiled. "There's my Wicket, the adventurer and hunter of bug people."

Despite whatever desires he'd voiced for normalcy, those words warmed Wicket through. Kneesaa's approval, the title of hunter-adventurer, it felt good. *He* felt good. Like he was doing something important.

The words continued to warm him over many long days of searching the forest's cold, sunless heart. He discovered more silvery buildings, landed sky ships, and scores of bug people. They seemed disinterested in the forest and the Ewoks, something Wicket was grateful for, but they also showed no signs of leaving. The Ewoks tried to resume their normal lives: gathering and hunting in the forest and playing in the valleys, streams, and meadows. But a chill had been cast over their everyday lives. It was the knowledge that the bug people were here, they weren't leaving, and they could always be watching.

One day, long after their arrival, Wicket found himself alone in the forest. These days, he usually traveled with Kneesaa or Paploo, but he'd wanted a few quiet hours to think. He was mulling over how much his life had changed since those silver ships darted in perfect lines across the sky. The forest was colder and quieter. Even the air felt heavier, full of watchful eyes.

This disturbing thought was in his mind when he rolled over a log and saw something sprawled in the dirt. Another of the bug people, he thought at first. It was lying on the ground, sleeping maybe, under a cover of thick ferns. Maybe it was dead.

Wicket poked the figure with his spear and hopped back. Nothing. Probably dead, then. He poked it again, just to see.

The figure jerked up, very much alive and, he realized, not a bug person at all. He'd seen creatures like her before, many years ago, though they had been woklings—children, they called themselves. This one was much larger, probably fully grown. She didn't have bug eyes or shining white skin that clicked and clacked against whatever it touched. Instead she wore a cloak like the ones elder Ewoks wore in deep winter, when even fur couldn't drive the cold out. It was the color of the dappled forest, greens and browns.

Wicket hopped back and growled as she spoke. He couldn't understand her words, but she sounded angry.

"You stay away," he told her. She didn't reply, so he assumed she didn't understand him, either. He growled and snapped, "I'll trap you just like the bug people if I have to. Haul you right up into the air, whoosh!"

She sighed. She seemed very tired, and Wicket cocked his head, surprised. That, at least, was something he could relate to. She stood and walked to a log before sitting back down. Wicket growled all the while, but she didn't flinch or even look back. She didn't have a weapon that he could see, but she didn't seem to fear him. He hopped up on the same log, still pointing his spear as he studied her.

Something about her reminded him of Kneesaa. She gestured at him, then at the bark next to her, and that, at least, he understood. He

ONE NORMAL DAY

wasn't ready to let his guard down, but there was something warm and gentle in her speech, in the way she moved her arms and hands. Not bug-like at all.

When he didn't sit down, she reached into a pocket and produced what looked like a drier, crumblier version of rorkid bread. She held it out to him. He growled again and waved his spear, but she kept her arm outstretched. The smell reached his nose: warm, nutty, with a tinge of sweetness. She took a bite of it and held it out again, showing him it was safe. His stomach grumbled. Well, how bad could it be?

He snatched it from her and took a cautious bite. Flavor exploded on his tongue: It was the richest thing he'd ever eaten. Pleased and intrigued, Wicket plopped down next to her, forgetting his fear. Her food was good, and she seemed good. Maybe, he thought, just maybe, she was more like an Ewok than a bug person. After all, none of the bug people had ever offered him a snack. And anyone who shared snacks was worth getting to know.

DIVINE (?) INTERVENTION
Paul Crilley

The Golden One had abandoned them.

The Shaman Logray *knew* this—had seen the proof with his own eyes.

The deal their God struck with the Darkness—to share Endor equally—had been broken. The Adversary reached out with damp, spindled fingers to corrupt their world. Wind-riders dropped from the sky bringing invaders who ravaged their homes, wiping out entire tribes to build their shining structures. White ghosts sped through the forests on steeds that spat red death upon any who got in their way.

They were on their own, but Logray had to make sure no one else knew this, had to make sure the other Ewoks still believed the Golden

One spoke to him. It was the only way to save the tribe, something Teebo—Lograys's apprentice—was making increasingly difficult for him to do.

"We've prayed," said Teebo passionately. He stood in the center of the temple that had formed inside the Great Tree. He turned slowly to address the crowd. "We've *begged* the Golden One to help us fight off the agents of darkness."

Lograys studied the crowded room, trying to gauge the mood. The Council of Elders had been called two days ago, messengers sent to neighboring tribes when Lograys noticed an increase in the number of wind-riders dropping from the sky—wind-riders that ferried more of the tall ones, both the unmasked *and* the white ghosts. There was a feverish rush to the invaders' movements, as if they were preparing for something big.

All eyes followed Teebo as he moved toward the Holy Stone, the glowing amber orb gifted to them by the Golden One Himself.

"But our pleas are ignored. The Golden One stands back and allows the Adversary to destroy our homes. He watches while Ewoks are slaughtered by the white ghosts. He does nothing while the two-legged beasts flatten trails through our forests."

Teebo turned to face the council. "We tried to ignore them. We hoped they would leave us alone. Even when they slaughtered an entire *tribe*—"

The council glanced toward Romba, a refugee from a village that had been destroyed to make way for the tall ones' structures.

"—we stayed silent. Hiding. *Cowering*. But we've all seen how their numbers have increased over the past days. It can mean only one thing." He paused and looked around dramatically. Lograys could barely restrain an eye roll. Teebo always had a flair for the dramatic. It was why he would make a good shaman. "They're coming for *us*."

DIVINE (?) INTERVENTION

Logray slammed his staff against the floor to draw everyone's attention. "Which is exactly *why* we must leave the village! We need to find a new home. Somewhere far from the softskins. Somewhere safe."

"You want us to *flee*?" snapped Teebo. "He shook his head in disappointment. "I never took you for a coward, Master."

There was a slight inrush of breath from those gathered. Logray stared coldly at Teebo. There was a moment of heavy silence before Teebo blinked and looked away in shame.

"I'll put that down to the heat of the moment—my *apprentice*."

But Teebo wasn't finished. He looked pleadingly at Logray. "Master, *please* listen. It's *because* we do nothing that the Golden One does not come. But if we *fight*. If we defend our homes from the invaders—*that* is when He will appear and help us push back the Darkness."

Teebo's war party, his private inner circle, waved their axes and spears, shouting their support. Members of the council nodded in agreement.

Logray saw this with dismay and felt the future slipping away from him. Over the past few weeks he'd been having visions of the forest burning, Ewoks lying dead, slaughtered by the invaders' fire-sticks. He knew in the very depths of his soul that their fate depended upon the outcome of this council.

Logray leaned on his staff and moved slowly to the center of the room. All eyes were on him. This was his last chance to plead his case.

"We stand at a crossroads," he said. "Our entire future rests on the path we decide upon today. We've seen the armor the invaders wear, the fire-sticks they carry. We've seen their power. Their *ruthlessness*. And you want us to *fight* them? With our spears? With our axes and catapults?"

"Better than hiding away underground," said Asha Fahn.

Logray scowled. He should have done more to steer Teebo away from Asha. Ever since they'd become close, Teebo's confidence had grown. She was a bad influence on him.

"I'm not saying we hide forever. I'm saying we wait. We watch. Only a fool rushes into a battle against an unknown enemy."

"There's no *time* to wait!" said Teebo. "You've seen their moon. With every village that's destroyed, the moon grows larger."

The Council of Elders whispered to one another. Logray couldn't even argue the fact. The moon had appeared as the slimmest of crescents one day, barely visible. But it had grown steadily since then.

"It is a countdown," said Teebo. "Once the moon is fully formed, the Adversary will descend and reclaim his throne, banishing the light forever."

More muttering and nodding. Logray felt a hopelessness open up in the pit of his soul. The balance had shifted. Teebo's impassioned plea was winning the Elders over.

He needed time to think. Time to come up with a plan.

He glanced at Chief Chirpa. They had known each other for over fifty years now, ever since they were woklings. Chirpa's face revealed nothing. Logray couldn't tell which way he was leaning.

"I humbly request the council break until sundown," Logray said. "I need time to commune with the Golden One."

Asha Fahn snorted. "What for? He never answers."

Logray looked at Asha with contempt. "He answers. You just don't want to hear what He has to say."

Logray looked questioningly at Chirpa. The chief nodded.

"Until sundown," he said.

Logray felt his calmness return as he made his way through the lush, green oasis of towering evergreen trees. Sunbeams flickered and flashed through the dense canopy. Rustling pine needles created a

DIVINE (?) INTERVENTION

gentle chorus, a constant whisper that brought the forest to life. He arrived at his destination—a small clearing where an ancient tree had fallen over in some long-forgotten storm. The tree was still alive, its twisted roots embedded firmly in the ground. They formed cool cavities and fissures that Logray used when he wanted to be alone, where he could feel supported and embraced by the forest.

Logray stopped moving, standing still on a bed of pine needles and moss. Shafts of hazy sunlight dappled the clearing. He took a deep breath, inhaling the smell of earth, pine resin, musty leaves.

These were the moments when he doubted himself. Maybe the Golden One *hadn't* abandoned them. Despite the presence of the invaders, there was still so much beauty around them.

A bearded jax sat grooming itself, unaware of his presence. Logray watched the yellow-eyed creature, trying to take in the moment of peace. To hold it in his heart.

He wasn't sure how many more such moments there would be. As if to reinforce this thought, he felt a low vibration in his chest. Then the sound came—a deep, throaty roar. The jax bounded away. Logray looked up to see a wind-rider moving slowly by. Low, almost touching the treetops.

It was coming in to land. Logray felt a rush of panic. Why here? None of the invader's structures were nearby. The closest was about ten thousand meters away. There was no reason for the wind-rider to be here.

Logray set off in the wind-rider's direction, using his staff to shove the thick ferns and vines aside.

Logray arrived at the crest of a hill that descended into a wide meadow. The wind-rider had already landed, its mouth gaping open and resting on the grass.

Logray watched as the tall ones exited the bowels of the creature. They weren't like the invaders. Not the black-and-gray-garbed softskins *nor* the heavily armored white ghosts.

These tall ones wore clothing that helped them blend in with the forest. There were around twelve of them, all armed with death sticks. They moved as a unit, like Teebo's war band.

The two that came next were even stranger. A softskin with an air of arrogance that Logray took an instant dislike to, and a giant creature covered in brown fur. The two were deep in conversation.

"Whaddya mean it doesn't make sense?" snapped the softskin. "Of *course* it makes sense."

The fur-covered one raised its head and roared. Logray had no idea what it was saying but he got the impression it wasn't very happy.

"*Fly casual.* It means don't draw attention. What it *doesn't* mean is pushing the throttle open like we're in a podrace. You're lucky the Empire didn't revoke our clearance."

The large creature let out a series of growls that caused the tall one to look at it in amusement.

"The throttle stuck, huh? Admit it, Chewie. You were in a rush 'cause you were hungry. We all heard your stomach. It sounded like an acklay. A *big* one, too."

"Han, stop giving him a hard time. We made it. That's all that matters."

Logray shifted his attention to two more figures emerging from the wind-rider. They were wearing the same camouflaged clothing and helmets, but they carried themselves differently. Even from this distance, Logray could feel an air of serene calm about them.

What was going on? Who *were* these softskins? They *definitely* weren't like the invaders. They talked the same language, but that was where the similarity ended. If only they—

—Logray froze.

DIVINE (?) INTERVENTION

His eyes widened in shock as he tried to understand what it was he was seeing.

It . . . it couldn't be.

Could it?

Lograv watched in utter amazement as a stiff-legged figure exited the wind-rider. It glowed golden in the sunlight, highlights and haloes flashing from every part of its body.

Lograv stared in amazement.

The Golden One.

Could it really be Him?

He was exactly as He had been described in the stories Chief Buzza used to tell the woklings around the fire. The Golden One's form was cast in shining gold drawn from the sun's very own glow. Every time He moved, flashes of light blinded Lograv, glints and winks of reflected holiness.

But it was the eyes that captured Lograv's attention. Chief Buzza had said the Golden One's eyes gave off a soft and steady glow, like two tiny stars that had been plucked from the sky. From within, the Golden One could only *see* light. Darkness was defeated merely by Him *looking* at it.

The figure below perfectly captured this description.

"*Yupyup*," he said softly.

Rejoice indeed. The Golden One hadn't abandoned them after all. He had responded to Lograv's prayers and come to lead them to safety.

Relief flooded through Lograv's body, months of stress and worry melting away in an instant. He knew he'd lost the battle that morning. Most of the Treeta Dobra backed Teebo, letting their hearts rule over their heads in wanting to defend their homes against the invaders. But if they truly wanted to survive the return of the Adversary, they had to use logic. And the logical thing to do was hide.

No one would be able to argue with him now. Not when their deity had actually chosen to appear before Logray. Not when Logray led the Golden One—their actual *God*—into the village.

Logray had let his cynicism and bitterness color his outlook. He had seen the destruction all around him and couldn't understand *why* the Golden One would allow such things to happen.

But it had been a test of faith all along. A test he had failed.

Shame overwhelmed him. He could only hope the Golden One would understand his fears, would show him mercy.

Logray had to restrain himself from rushing into the meadow and prostrating himself at the Golden One's feet. He was everything Logray had ever imagined. A figure *glowing* with inner glory. A God who radiated light from his eyes, a God who—

—tripped on a tree root, falling face-first into the undergrowth.

"Oh my!" he exclaimed. "Someone help! I've fallen over! *Help!*"

Logray frowned. He couldn't understand the words, but there was no mistaking the tone. Why did the Golden One sound so pathetic and wheedling?

A small white-and-blue creature rolled down the ramp and stopped next to the prone figure of the Golden One. It let out a series of beeps and whistles.

"What do you mean, 'What are you doing?' What does it look like, you brainless hunk of scrap metal! I'm *stuck*! Oh, this is so undignified!"

The brown-furred creature made a mewling, questioning growl. His softskin companion glanced at the Golden One with barely disguised contempt.

"I dunno. We'd probably be better off leaving him here."

"Oh, General Solo! Have mercy!"

The large creature mewled again.

DIVINE (?) INTERVENTION

"*Fine.* But only if he promises to keep his trap shut. We're on a scouting mission here. He's gonna give our position away."

"Oh, thank you, General Solo. You won't regret it. I'll be as silent as a tooka-cat. As invisible as a—"

Before he could finish, the large creature grabbed him by the back of the neck and hauled him to his feet.

"Be careful, you mindless brute! That is *no* way to handle a droid of my standing."

The . . . Golden One? . . . turned his attention to the softskin. "As I was saying, you won't even know I'm here. I'll be as invisible as a wampa in a blizzard. In fact—"

He didn't get a chance to finish his sentence. He took a single step—*one!*—and got his foot tangled in another root, falling flat on his face for a second time.

"Oh, the *shame!*"

Logray slumped to the ground in disappointment. This wasn't the Golden One. This was just another of the strange creatures the tall ones used for menial labor. He hadn't seen any others with the same coloring, but there could be no doubt about it.

Logray leaned his head back against the tree. So much for a sign. The only sign here was that they were doomed. They were no match for the tall ones' weapons. If Teebo got his way, every single Ewok in Bright Tree Village would be slaughtered.

Logray sighed. Why couldn't they just *listen* to him? He hadn't steered them wrong in the past. Why did they have to choose *now* to doubt his wisdom?

But he already knew the answer. Teebo and his friends. This younger generation of Ewoks were different. They rebelled against the teachings of the Golden One, that peace and prosperity were the paths to enlightenment, not war and conflict.

There was a lot of movement and talk among the tall ones in the clearing. Logray wished more than anything that he could understand their language, but it was just an indecipherable babble to all the Ewoks.

Logray paused.

He thought about this for a second, then got up and scurried into the forest, heading back to the village.

Logray was at the head of the hunting party with Teebo and Asha. The others trailed behind, spears and axes held at the ready as they moved silently through the trees.

"I just don't understand why we had to come with you," said Asha. "You've never asked for protection before."

"We've never been in this position before," he said, trying his best to keep his voice neutral. "You were at the council meeting. We all heard about the rising number of invaders."

"Exactly. So what are we doing out here?"

"*You* are out here to protect your shaman and his apprentice. Teebo and *I* are out here to seek a sign from the Golden One."

Logray caught the brief look Asha and Teebo exchanged. Teebo shook his head slightly. Logray knew what they were thinking. *Just humor the old Ewok.*

One of the advance scouts appeared on the path and hurried toward them. "There are tall ones up ahead," he said urgently.

"*Here?*" said Teebo in surprise. "But we're not even close to their base."

"Did you see them?" asked Asha.

"No. But they're using one of our trapping paths."

Logray could barely contain himself. The Ewoks had traps baited with verkle meat all over the forest. The paths leading to the traps

DIVINE (?) INTERVENTION

were generations old, invisible to non-Ewoks. They had been curated and manipulated over time, vines, flowering bushes, ferns, and fallen tree branches all subtly guided into position over the years to lead the unknowing prey toward the trap.

"Show us," said Teebo.

The scout set off, Teebo and the others following.

Logray let the hunters pass until he was at the rear of the group, then he followed a few paces behind. This had to be handled *very* carefully.

It wasn't long before they heard a loud crashing sound from up ahead. The hunters held their spears before them as they edged toward the sound.

"Nice work. Great, Chewie. Great! Always thinking with your stomach."

"Will you take it easy? Let's just figure out a way to get out of this thing. Han, can you reach my lightsaber?"

"Yeah, sure."

There was a moment of silence, then Logray heard the fake God speak.

"Artoo, I'm not sure that's such a good idea. It's a very long dro-o-p!"

There was another crash. Teebo and the others rushed forward, spears extended as they formed a circle around the softskins who had somehow fallen from the suspended trap.

"Wha—? Hey! Point that thing someplace else." Logray recognized the voice. The cocky one he didn't like.

Logray moved behind a large fern so he could see what was happening. Unseen. Waiting for his chance.

The scouting party erupted into angry mutterings. Asha stepped forward and held a low conversation with Teebo. Teebo shook his head and pointed the spear back at the softskin's face.

"*Hey!*" The tall one grabbed the spear and reached for his firestick.

"Han, don't. It'll be all right." A different voice—the soft-spoken one Logray had seen earlier.

The hunting party confiscated the tall ones' weapons. When they reached the brown-furred creature it let out a growl of anger.

"Chewie, give 'em your crossbow."

Logray curled his fingers impatiently around his staff. Where was—

"Oh my head. Oh my goodness!"

Logray saw the glint of gold in the sunlight as the false God sat up. There was a gasp of shock from the Ewoks.

Logray moved up behind Teebo and Lonta Kay. "The Golden One," he whispered. "Our God has come to save us."

"The . . . Golden One," Lonta repeated softly. The Ewok to his left heard, and soon the words were spreading around the entire hunting party.

Lonta dropped to his knees and prostrated himself. The others followed his example, chanting their devotion. Even Teebo and Asha.

Logray grinned as he turned and hurried back into the forest. It would be hours before the hunting party returned with the "Golden One." Plenty of time for Logray to lay the groundwork for his plan.

He would tell the council he'd become separated from the others and that the Golden One had appeared to him in a vision, forbidding them from taking up arms. His instructions were for the Ewoks to leave the village and hide in the underground cave systems to the north. Exactly as Logray had advised.

All this would be discussed before Teebo and the others got back.

DIVINE (?) INTERVENTION

And then—surprise!—the Golden One Himself! He'd come in physical form to make sure his instructions were obeyed! And the best thing was, no one could doubt Lograyʼs word. Not even Asha Fahn. The Chief Shaman was the only one who could communicate with the Golden One. It had always been so.

Which meant by this time tomorrow, the Ewoks would be heading for safety and it would all be thanks to Logray.

He couldn't have planned it any better if he wanted to.

Lograyʼs pace slowed slightly as he thought about these words, a frown forming on his face. That was actually true. Everything *had* gone remarkably smoothly so far. Almost as if . . .

. . . Almost as if he'd had help.

Logray stopped walking. The fur on the back of his neck rose. It felt like he was being watched. He shivered and looked around, but he couldn't see anything out of the ordinary.

But still, he couldn't shake the feeling.

Logray took a calming breath and sent his senses outward, listening, watching.

Feeling . . .

Louder than everything—the overlapping symphony of the thousands of birds that called Endor their home. Musical trillings as they competed for attention. Shorter chirps and tweets echoing back and forth as birds flew from tree to tree. The querying calls of flocks keeping in contact. The peep and rasp of younger birds still in the nest, plaintive and begging. The sharp, piercing call warning of danger. The distant hoot of an antary, the nocturnal bird waking up ready for a night of hunting.

And then all around him—as constant as the sun rising—the susurration of spruce needles stirred by the wind, a sound so familiar to Ewoks its absence would be like losing a limb.

Deeper...

Lograv could feel the life presence of a pack of squalls, the rodents busy carving out a fresh burrow in the earth.

A lantern bird—invisible above the canopy of leaves, its passage causing currents in the air that undulated for miles around.

A munyip, gliding between trees, singing its own song and silencing the chatter of birds as it... passed.

A herd of bordoks, calmly grazing. A blue lizard scurried past, causing the entire herd to bolt in fear.

Deeper...

The waves of joy and awe radiating from the hunting party behind him. (Guilt, quickly pushed down.) The radiance of their spirits cast a glow Lograv could feel like flames from a fire.

But above all that, above *everything*... something else. Something expansive. Something greater than the combined life force of the entire forest. Lograv strained his senses outward but couldn't pinpoint the source. It was too big. It encompassed *everything*. It made Lograv feel like a raindrop in a summer thunderstorm—inconsequential, insignificant.

The presence... it felt...

It felt...

Divine.

Holy.

... Was it possible the Golden One *hadn't* abandoned them after all? That the shining creature had been sent by their God just when they needed help the most and that all this... all this was *meant* to be?

Lograv gave this some more thought. If that was the case, it meant Lograv's plan was really their *God's* plan. That Lograv was merely the instrument the Golden One had chosen to save the Ewoks and that he was right all along about leaving the village.

DIVINE (?) INTERVENTION

But . . . if the creature *hadn't* been sent, if the Golden One *had* actually abandoned them, it didn't matter. Logray's plan would play out exactly the same anyway, and he would *still* be a hero.

Either way, Logray realized as he stood among the trees, his . . . he didn't want to call them *manipulations*, but . . . his *actions* today meant *he* was responsible for *everything* that happened tomorrow.

He started walking again, a bounce to his step. A celebration is in order, he thought. Logray had already decided that the false god's companions would be sacrificed in the Golden One's honor . . .

Logray was looking forward to feasting on the cocky one. Arrogance lent a certain . . . spice to the meat.

He was sure it would be delicious.

THE BUY-IN

Suzanne Walker

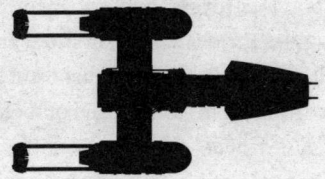

The Y-wing handles like a dream under Norra Wexley's touch, light and agile with the vast expanse of space pressing in around the cockpit. There's no comparison with the stalwart yet bulky freighter she's piloted for the Alliance these last three years, the *Violet*, though out of habit she still compensates for all its little quirks. She jerks a bit too hard on the Y-wing's controls in case they stick like the *Violet*'s; pounds the console needlessly when she fires up the targeting computer. The lights blink on of their own accord, and for a moment Norra revels in the joy of flight, the ease with which she weaves into formation alongside a smattering of other fighters. Nothing but her, the rush, and the stars.

Then she pulls the trigger, and the moment's gone.

The hunk of mangled durasteel they've grabbed for target practice explodes into satisfying pieces. Gold Eight's gravelly cheer crackles in her ear.

"Nice one. We'll make a gunner out of you yet."

"Eh." Norra shrugs, her doubt invisible behind the comms. There's a world of difference between space junk and a TIE fighter. Her close calls with the *Violet* each had someone else firing the guns while she outmaneuvered Star Destroyers and interceptors. Her stomach clenches as she imagines the death she'll dole out and witness tomorrow, the dank smell of her sweat-soaked flight suit all she breathes in the cockpit. Maybe she'll die herself, picked off before she even has a chance to act. *I'm just a pilot*, she thinks for the thousandth time, *that's all. A pilot, not a soldier.*

But the time for such distinctions has passed. The Rebel Alliance stands on the cusp of a reckoning, a last stand worthy of the old valachord ballads. And there can be no doubt at a reckoning.

"One more run." Lando Calrissian's voice glides out smooth even over the tinny, crackling comm system. "Then we're calling it. Last one to dock is on drink duty."

Norra huffs out a wry snort and soars into formation with the rest of Gold Squadron, all of them astonishingly in sync for the new roster's inaugural flight. At least if she dies, she can say she flew with the best of them.

"You did good." Wedge Antilles is there to clap her on the shoulder when she climbs down the ladder, an easy smile beneath damp helmet hair still plastered to his forehead. She gives him her own rueful smile before he turns his attention to Gold Six, a Kel Dor as new to the squad as she is. One by one he tends to all the rookies, jokes and

THE BUY-IN

reassurances mingling with the chatter. Across the hangar, a mix of Reds and Golds have gathered around Calrissian, perhaps waiting for some sort of dismissal or inspiring speech. Instead, the newly minted general catches the eye of Antilles, who detaches himself from the rookies and climbs back up on a ladder, one arm looped around a rung as he whistles sharply.

All fall silent, every eye or optic sensor on the veteran of Yavin. Norra catches the briefest flicker of weariness in Antilles before he squares his shoulders and surveys the assembled group.

"We'll get it done," he says simply. His soft voice projects across the hangar, soon drowned out by heckling and raucous cheers. "Just like before. Rest up and report back here at oh five hundred."

The pilots all intermingle in the changing room, distinctions of squadron and rank smudged out in the close quarters. Wes Janson throws a towel at Jake Farrell, while Wedge holds the attention of the other Gold Squadron rookies, bantha cubs in the shape of pilots. Like her, a solid third of the squad are new to combat, but she has at least fifteen years on the rest of them (or so she suspects—hard to tell with the Kel Dor). They all look upon Antilles with reverent awe: He *survived* the first Death Star, he'd stared down that behemoth and lived to tell the tale. And so they believe him when he tells them their skill and instincts and the generals' infallible plan will end in victory. That despite the casualties, despite the carnage, the outcome is assured.

Norra believes none of it.

Part of her wants to gently detach Antilles from the rookies, if only to give him some air, but before she has a chance Calrissian and his Sullustan copilot approach her. He slings an arm around her with casual ease. "I meant it, Wexley. Last to dock supplies the drinks."

Norra rolls her eyes and shoves his arm off her. "Weren't you some sort of baron? That's got to come with money, doesn't it?"

Calrissian gives a flourishing bow in response to her exasperated gaze. "While it's true I once was a prosperous mining administrator, I confess to have fallen on hard times. So I must beg the generosity of my squadron."

Nien Nunb says something in Sullustese that makes Lando punch him lightly on the arm. "Don't tell her that—you'll give her the wrong impression."

"There's not much he can do to worsen it." Norra fights to keep her mouth from twitching and presses it into a thin line, arms crossed in a look of arch disdain. Better that than admit the embarrassing truth: She enjoys Calrissian. He's the most entertaining rebel she's met in months.

"Don't make a parent cover the drinks, Lando." Antilles comes up behind them and shoves Calrissian lightly. The word "parent" hits Norra like a shock of cold water, an awful chill despite the humidity of the room.

Calrissian looks at her with some surprise. "You have a kid?"

"Yeah. He's back home with my sister." She struggles to keep her voice light amid the sharp pang in her chest. *Temmin*. Fifteen now, a wiry adolescent in place of the boy she'd left behind. She's been so swept up in the work, in preparations for the fight, that she can't remember the last time she sent a message home. Shame washes over her, and she lowers her head so they can't see how her cheeks have flushed.

Calrissian doesn't break his stride, merely thumps her on the shoulder again with a smile that's far more sincere. "Ah, don't worry about it then. I'll scam another rookie."

"Please don't," Wedge says with a soft groan. Lando winks at him before he strides over to a blue-haired pilot near the door, his arm soon draped around them in the same flirtatious manner. Temporarily forgotten, Norra watches as a put-upon Wedge follows him and enters another losing battle.

THE BUY-IN

She lingers in the changing room long after everyone else abandons it, elbows resting on her knees, a crummy, fourth-rate holoprojector cupped in one hand. Her thumb moves back and forth over the buttons, unable to find any words worth ferrying through five different encryptions halfway across the galaxy. Instead she studies the scuffed ridges of the floor, marveling at their relative cleanliness. *Home One* is in better condition than most rebel frigates she's found herself on, any grimy streaks beneath her signs of recent battle rather than decay. If they all survive this she should see about making a permanent—

No. What was she thinking? If they survive this, she's going home. Home to Akiva and her family. Temmin. She'll take him off that muggy mess of a world; bring him with her wherever she goes next. Three years and she hasn't found his father, hasn't come close to reuniting their broken family. She's found purpose, yes, found a cause she believes in more than Brentin, more even than Temmin. The galaxy's freedom goes before any of them. But she has sacrificed enough on her son's behalf. If she survives, he deserves his mother back.

And if you don't survive?

Nausea fills her with such force she fears she'll actually be ill. The room spins as she ducks her head between her knees, for whatever good that'll do. She can't do this. She can't leave Temmin alone for the rest of his life. Pain, dying, that's all one thing, but her son has already lost enough. It was beyond heartless to throw herself into the vanguard. Antilles played on her convictions to make her agree, on her sense of duty, but what duty could be more important than her son?

You abandoned that duty a long time ago, a cruel voice chides her. *And if you don't survive, he probably won't, either. The Alliance ends tomorrow, one way or another. It's got a better chance of rebirth if you get back in that cockpit.*

She barks out a short, humorless laugh. Usually her self-deprecation isn't quite so incisive. *Pull it together*.

Shoulders squared, she eyes the projector and thumbs on the recording.

"Temmin," she murmurs, then pauses. "If you're seeing this, chances are good I'm dead..."

She snarls and hits STOP. A violent urge to throw the holoprojector across the room overtakes her, but after a deep, grounding breath she steadies herself, rewinds the recording, and tries again.

"Temmin. I'm sorry I haven't called like I should. Things are changing. The Alliance is flying out to battle tomorrow. If I die, I want you to—dammit, no. *Stang*, what absolute garbage—"

"Having trouble?"

She jumps at the voice and turns to see Lando Calrissian in the doorway, his smile halfway between amused and sympathetic. With a groan she clenches her hand tight around the holoprojector. A dozen different excuses float up in her mind, humorous deflections she's used countless times to stave off more personal conversations with crewmembers on the *Violet*. Better to keep them at a distance than pick at the scab formed over her loved ones' absence.

"What do you even *say* to a fifteen-year-old?" she bursts out, scab picked wide open. "Goodbye, love you, sorry I parked you with your aunts for three years? Sorry if I die tomorrow?"

"Can't really say. Never had kids myself." Lando takes a seat beside her. "Never loved anything as much as living my life. Definitely not a lost cause like this."

She glances at him sidelong. "But here you are."

"Here I am," he agrees. They sit together in relative quiet, the clangs and mechanical whirs of the nearby hangar a familiar background in Norra's rebel life. At last Lando slaps a friendly hand on her knee and rises to his feet.

THE BUY-IN

"Listen, I promised Janson I'd teach him sabacc later. You should come."

"I hate sabacc," she exaggerates, just to mess with him. Sure enough, Calrissian emits such an indignant squawk that she bursts into laughter in spite of herself. The full-body reaction settles some of her jangling nerves.

"*Clearly* you've never played it right." He now takes both her hands and pulls her up. The faintest whiff of Chandrilan cologne makes her nose twitch, which in turn elicits a maddening wink from Calrissian. "As your general, I insist. I'll show you all a finer evening than the Alliance could ever supply."

Her face contorts wildly as she tries to hide her smile, earlier dread now morphed into a punchy sort of drive. She could spend all night on this blasted message, she knows from experience, but what good would it do her or Temmin in the end? A diversion would serve her far better, even one as frustrating as sabacc. And a night of camaraderie with her new wingmates could only help them once the battle came.

Her heart tightens as she remembers her husband's lonely work transmitting messages for the Alliance, locked for hours in a room sifting through code. It's a blessing, having these people around her, one she'd be a fool to ignore.

"Copy that, General."

Home One's central atrium always reminds Norra of home, or at least a vague approximation, lush vegetation that surrounds a large central pool, thick humidity pressed against her skin. Her crewmates all whine about the Mon Cal climate controls but she finds them a comfort, a sliver of Akiva in the cold vacuum of space. The reek of a dozen different species dissipates in the atrium's enormity, replaced by the scent of chemical water that, while vaguely unsettling, beats the changing room stench.

Calrissian holds court at a table half hidden by trees, moss creeping down its metal sides. Janson and Nien Nunb are already there, Janson's beady eyes narrowed as he peers over Calrissian's shoulder.

"This right here is straight staves. But wait—" Calrissian rolls a pair of dice and tosses them on the table. Janson's eyes widen. "That's double spikes. Now you've got to discard your whole hand."

"You've gotta be *kidding* me." Janson smacks his hand on the table. "After all that?"

"It's a garbage game," Norra comments as she takes her seat. Janson nods fervently and takes a long pull from his mug. "No skill at all. You only win if you stay in long enough."

Lando turns to her with mournful eyes, hand to his heart as if wounded. "Why, Norra, I'm offended. You think I won a tibanna gas colony only on luck?"

"Or you cheated." Norra winks at him, still punchy enough to indulge in a bit of harmless flirting. He shoots her that smooth grin and pushes a mug of spacer's ale toward her. With a nod of thanks she takes it in both hands, the metal cool beneath her palms, and tries not to scowl at the ale's engine room aftertaste. A bowl of spiced nuts sits beside the sabacc pot, all too likely the warra ones she's allergic to. She sighs and reaches into her flight suit for her bag of Devaronian cherries—a rare, expensive indulgence she's stretched out and savored over three long months. The bag of a hundred is now down to twelve, eleven after one slips past her teeth. The chocolatey tang melts atop her tongue, an odd mix with the ale but worth it nonetheless.

"Now, here's trouble." A wry voice echoes above them. Norra turns to see that Antilles stands behind her with two other rookies, the Kel Dor and a wiry, blue-haired human called Zyrka Tuhn. Antilles folds his arms, lips pressed together to keep from smiling, nothing but

THE BUY-IN

mockery for his old friend. "I can't believe Lieutenant Wesford Janson never learned to play sabacc."

Norra stifles a snicker. "Is your name really Wesford?"

"Just Wedginald's little joke." Wes makes a face at Antilles. "The Taanab monks forbid gambling, I'll have you know. Haven't had time to learn between flying X-wings, saving the galaxy—"

"Stinking up cockpits," Antilles finishes, but he smiles again and takes the vacant chair beside Norra. He beckons the Kel Dor and Tuhn to join them at the two remaining seats that flank Janson, the rookies indistinguishable from the vets. Tuhn leans forward, quiet intensity evident in the set of their shoulders.

"What's the buy-in?"

"We're too broke for a buy-in," Wes drawls. He tips his chair back so it teeters on two legs, so precarious it makes Norra wince. "I'm in this fight with twelve credits and some stale warra nuts."

"Sabacc is not a *fight*," Calrissian corrects him in mild indignation. He picks the card deck back up and begins to shuffle. His practiced fingers render the simple action an art form, the cards blurred from how fast he moves. Norra watches, mesmerized. "Sabacc is *life*. You can bring all the skill and cleverness you want, but there's always going to be that unknown factor, the parts you can't control. It's civilized in its chaos. The most civilized game in the galaxy."

Norra opens her mouth with a snappy retort but stops once his point truly settles in. She detests sabacc because of the chaos, that and her utter inability to keep a straight face. Far better are games of skill like dejarik, control of the outcome solely in her hands. But what was flying, if not trusting to chaos? It was half luck the day she outran a Star Destroyer, her instinctual maneuvers and a battleship that fell for her feint. If someone more clever had been at the helm, or if the *Violet*'s aft thrusters hadn't flared back to life after she rammed her fist against the defective console . . .

She shivers.

Wedge spots the movement, head tilted in mild concern, but everyone else laughs heartily at Calrissian's earnestness, Nien Nunb's wheezy chortles echoing above the rest. Wes gives a particularly impish smirk and tilts his chair forward with a loud *clank,* three credit chits slapped down on the table before him.

"All right, *civilized.* Let's see how you like certified Janson chaos."

The cards are worn and pliable beneath Norra's thumb, the designs faded from dozens of hands before her. As expected, she starts with miserable luck. A wince crosses her face before she can stop it and heat rises to her cheeks, embarrassed to have already slipped.

"Come on now, Wexley." Lando fixes that perfect, obnoxious smile on her. "Everyone's already watching someone as beautiful as you. Keep your tells away from your face."

"I am married, you know." Norra rolls her eyes in feigned indifference, leans back in her chair and attempts a more casual pose.

"I'm not." Wes tilts forward till his face is a hairbreadth from Calrissian's, eyelashes fluttering above a roguish grin. Zyrka Tuhn chokes into their mug of ale. Lando's eyes widen in brief surprise before he settles back into his usual, charmingly cavalier manner.

"Anything on the table then, Janson?"

"By the Force," Wedge mutters, face buried in one hand. Norra quickly stifles a laugh, all the more difficult when Wes catches her eye and sends a furtive wink. She owes him now—everyone else is so distracted that by the time the bets go down they've completely forgotten her terrible hand.

It's an absolutely pitiful pot, pieces of lint fluttering down when Nien Nunb adds four chits, a small red gem, and some scented soap marbles. Through Lando he explains that the gem is rather worthless, a hardened piece of lava from Sullust, but Tuhn's eyes gleam at the sight of it and they slap down an obsidian amulet to call. Norra

THE BUY-IN

pitches in half her remaining credits rather than give up her precious Devaronian cherries, though Wes eyes them with envy when she pops another one into her mouth. Ten left.

One by one the rest of them call, but then Lando rolls the spike dice and blows it all to hell. The Kel Dor folds, Wedge stays in with clear unhappiness, but Norra's now got a halfway-decent hand. She throws in another credit, just for good measure, only for her hope to deflate when Wes spreads his cards out on the table. His voice wobbles in uncertainty when he turns to Lando, who looks down at the cards with a dumbfounded glower.

"Is that right, Calrissian? Straight staves?"

Now it's Lando's turn to bury his head in his hand, cards tossed down on the table in defeat. "Damn beginner's luck. Not supposed to be real."

"Oh, I'm real, baby." Wes grins and collects the pot amid several groans. Norra laughs again, caught up in the furor of the game, and as the night wears on she dares to relax a bit. She even wins a hand or two, a first in all her years playing the blasted game. Another round of ale finds its way to the table and she indulges in a rare third drink to buoy the pleasant lightness in her limbs. Just enough to keep the tension at bay.

"Call." She drops the credits down on the table with a satisfying *clink*. "And raise five."

Lando raises an eyebrow and leans back with an impressed whistle. "That's the spirit, Wexley. Too bad it won't save you this time."

He spreads his cards out to display another pure sabacc. Norra lets out a frustrated groan, a sharp sting to her palm when she smacks it on the table. "Oh, you've *got* to be cheating."

"Never insult your general's honor, pilot." Lando scoops up his winnings with an infuriating grin. "And you're not out yet. Live to fight another day, eh?"

SUZANNE WALKER

One last day, Norra thinks sourly. She rolls her ninth remaining chocolate-coated cherry between her fingers, some of the residue coming off on the pad of her thumb. Probably wasn't a point to hoarding them, not anymore.

She banishes the morose dread with another drink of ale and places the cherry back in her bag.

At some point, Lando pulls out a bottle of Calamari Xinphar for the table, basking in the impressed whistles from Norra and Zyrka Tuhn. "From the admiral," he says, with a small nod across the atrium to where Ackbar sits with Mon Mothma and General Madine, a tactical diagram visible on the table, their heads together in deep conversation. Lando pops open the bottle with ease, eyes alight in satisfaction as he portions out the bubbling liquid.

"And this, my fine young friend, is why you should always cozy up to the brass," Lando says to Tuhn. He stands to twirl his cape with a little flourish, ignoring the long-suffering sigh from Wedge when Tuhn blushes and laughs. "Stick around and you'll find even more perks."

"Oh, we're great at perks." Wes grins. "After your ship explodes they buff your name up *real* nice on the side of the hangar. Might even name a drink after ya."

Norra chokes out an instinctive laugh, but she's the only one. The Kel Dor stares at Wes with his raspy breathing, expression impenetrable beneath the face mask, while Tuhn looks nervous, close to frightened. Once again, Wedge looks to be fighting off a headache. "Wes," he says quietly.

Wes looks around in bafflement before he shrugs. "What? I think it's great. Every time I drink a Klivian I think of old Hobbie."

THE BUY-IN

"Stars, I've had that." Norra wrinkles her nose at the memory of tuber liquor brewed in a hollowed-out R2 unit, torn between amusement and sorrow for the dead. "Figured a droid must have made it for how awful it tastes."

Wedge's mouth now turns up in a wistful smile. "Nah, the whole operation was Hobbie's. The rest of us just kept it going."

"The perfect palate cleanser." Wes is halfway between a smile and a grimace when he elbows Wedge up to his feet. "Go on then, Captain. A round of Klivians for everyone!"

A mixed chorus of protests follows Wedge as he heads out of the atrium, and the heaviness lifts from the table while they all argue about the drink. By the time he returns, Lando and Nien Nunb eye the dented tin jug in his hand as if it might come alive and bite their ears off. The unholy scent of citrus mixed with engine fuel engulfs the table, and Norra steels herself before she takes the jug from Wedge. Slowly it gets passed around, finally arriving at Wes, who pours out the last drop before he raises his mug. He meets each of their eyes in turn, good humor faded into grim acknowledgment when he locks on Norra's.

"To the squad," he says, uncharacteristically sincere. "No one gets a drink named after them tomorrow, got it?"

Norra knocks her glass against Lando's and downs the Klivian in a quick gulp. Everything explodes from within, her senses awash with a taste akin to carbon scoring. She swallows it with a choking grimace, gasping for air once finished, and reaches frantically for that ninth Devaronian cherry. The tart sweetness takes away some of the sting, though it still feels like a waste of a treat, gone to preserve her dignity in the face of the galaxy's worst drink.

Worth it for that, she reflects as she surveys the damage around her. Orange liquid drips down Wes's cheeks, courtesy of Nien Nunb's instant expulsion of the beverage. Lando's mouth moves in some spectacular contortions before he rounds on Wes in a not-entirely-feigned fury.

"What're you trying to do? Kill us all before we get there?"

Wes shrugs in a vain effort to keep a straight face, while poor Wedge has that same pinched expression he's had all night. The Kel Dor, meanwhile, sips almost daintily through a thin tube that's extended down from his face mask. Norra's respect for him skyrockets as he slowly finishes the drink, unbothered by the commotion around him.

"Quite excellent." His words croak through the face mask, deep and sonorous. "I think I'll have another."

The rest of the evening passes in a blur of pent-up energy, Norra barely caring that her pile of credits slowly dwindles along with the hours. She feeds off the audience they've attracted, onlookers exchanging side bets as Lando manipulates the players. At some point Sila Kott swaps in for Nien Nunb, but she's quickly cleaned out. In a last-ditch effort to stay in the game, she drops in an unopened box of Corellian ryshcate and loses that, too. With a resigned shrug she drops her cards on the table, muttering something about swindling card players and stacked odds.

"We'll give the ryshcate back," Wedge calls after her as she pushes her chair back. She waves a hand in cavalier dismissal.

"Give it back if we come back, Captain," replies Kott. "It's meant to celebrate life, right?"

Norra catches Wedge's eye just before he exchanges a meaningful look with Lando, but no one comments on the fact that the odds of coming back are about the same as Norra walking away victor for the night. Though those odds aren't *entirely* useless. She's closer to pure

THE BUY-IN

sabacc than she's been all night, close enough that she could get it if those blasted dice didn't make her discard her hand again.

"Ah, the spoils of Corellia." Lando adjusts the box so that its glossy edge catches in the light. "Gem of a world. Cuisine bar none."

"Speak for yourself." Wedge's mouth twitches. "I'd take some of Wexley's Devaronian desserts first."

"You would not!" Norra's tipsy enough that the words come out in a vexed little chirp, hand curled protectively around her bag. "These took me five months to get. You know how much other food in this galaxy I'm allergic to?"

"I didn't mean yours, specifically," Wedge chuckles, but Wes takes the moment to pounce, eyes gleaming.

"*I* did. Why don't you add 'em to the pot? Sweeten things up a bit."

"No! Here." In a fit of pique she tosses her remaining credits onto the table. "You can buy some yourself."

"In another five months? No thanks," Wes scoffs and calls her bet.

The rest of them go around, Wedge and Tuhn also down to their last credits. They each draw their new cards; Norra's hand improves a bit. She tries her best to keep her face expressionless, though she can feel the imperceptible arch of her brows. Lando looks at her, a dangerous gleam to his eye. Norra's spirits sink.

"I'll bet twenty." He drops the credits on the table with a smirk. "Those of you without credits may call with anything remaining on your person. Except clothing. If you want that, I hear Santage is running a different show in the ready room."

"What?" Wedge jerks his head up in such earnest alarm that Norra bursts into laughter with Lando and Wes. Wedge glowers at them all as he digs into his vest pouch.

"No respect for the captain," he grumbles and tosses in a datacard containing an old holonovel. Tuhn folds amid protests and heckling, a final silent toast to everyone before they disappear into the assembled crowd. Wes tosses in his final credits and a scuffed ring for good measure before he turns to Norra with his chin in his hands, all innocent smiles.

"Well, Norra?"

Norra glances at her cards, then back at the rest of the players in a last-ditch attempt to suss out her odds. It's a good hand, the best she's had all night, but she's thought that before. At this point, the cherries come down to the principle of the thing: She knows Wes Janson well enough to know he'll lord it over her the rest of their lives if he wins them. Even if the rest of their lives only lasts another eighteen hours or so.

An image of Temmin blooms in her mind's eye, or at least how she imagines he looks these days, all too-long limbs and a mop of unruly dark hair. Boundless energy compressed into a tiny child, that's how she remembers him, endless flights with toy starfighters and days he tried to run headlong into the jungle. The same way she ran for the Alliance, the way she runs to battle now. Instinct, pure and raw, a fuel that's sustained her all her life. A fuel that pushes her to tomorrow, no matter what it holds.

The dice fall on the table one last time. She doesn't bother to look at her new cards before she drops her bag on the table.

"Sure, I'll bet them," she says. "I'll bet them all."

THE MAN WHO CAPTURED LUKE SKYWALKER

Max Gladstone

Commander Altadan Igar walked the haunted moon, guided by the Death Star's light.

The cool gray glow made twisted paths through strangling trees, and it gleamed off the white-armored Gamma Squad troopers fanned out ahead. The light cast shadows, too, but they were hard-edged and clear. Igar knew those shadows and their dangers, as he knew his body, his weapons, and his squad.

The search for Theta Squad was in its fourth hour, and Gamma Squad was tired. The troopers would not say as much. It was a commander's job to know.

He pinged for reports.

"Segment clear."

"Segment clear."

"Segment—" A curse, a crash, a blaster twang.

He turned to Sector Three. "Trooper Dooze. Status."

"Fell into one of those crikking pits, sir. Some rodent-thing jumped at me. Ran off. Should burn this place to the ground if you ask me. Sir."

Poor discipline. A newly minted officer would have broken Dooze for it. But Igar knew that would only cost him his troops' respect, or worse, out here in these damn thick woods where whole squads disappeared without a trace. The men were jumpy, suspicious, all the words they'd say instead of *scared*. There were plenty of reasons an officer might not come back. Igar had seen it before.

"Dooze," he said, "language," and that was enough.

"Sorry, sir."

The echoes faded.

Dooze was a good man. He had been close with Scout Trooper Rell of Theta Squad. He might still be close with Scout Trooper Rell of Theta Squad, though the odds of that declined with every hour Theta remained out of contact. Third squad lost this week. They'd searched four hours without any sign. There were so many shadows. This moon ate you, the men whispered back at base, it ate you and it did not leave the bones.

"Convene, all units." He reviewed the topography scan. "Meet at the overlook north-northeast of my position."

Positive pings. Movement in the deep forest.

Igar climbed.

No sign of Theta. No sign of enemy action. Just like the others. Telemetry and comms glitched out in among those massive trees. Heavy metals in the bark? The boffins should have found a fix by now, if only point-comms through satellite like prehistoric colonists.

THE MAN WHO CAPTURED LUKE SKYWALKER

But the boffins were busy on the other side of the sky, building the future.

He crested the ridge and stared out alone upon the starlit night.

The sky above was clear, and the Death Star bright. Treetops silvered, like the crests of waves on a black sea. Down there in the deeps he had lost soldiers. He had seen so many forests, on so many worlds.

Should just burn this place to the ground if you ask me, sir. He understood Trooper Dooze. He had been Trooper Dooze, a long time ago.

Back in the Clone Wars, when the Separatists invaded his home and he joined his local militia to fight back, Altadan Igar had believed a war was won through blasters and turbolasers and courage and blood. He wanted to serve, and service eventually brought him to the stars, but he had worn out so many boots on so many worlds that he came to hate the ground beneath his feet. That young man was lucky. He survived to learn: Wars were won through clarity.

Your enemy was not the ground. It was the dark.

He gazed up at the Death Star, and breathed in the forest scent of Endor.

He was tired. That was all. He knew his squad. He knew this hungry moon. He knew the enemy.

"It is a beautiful night," someone said.

He did not know the voice.

A man in black stood beside him on the ridge, where no man was before.

The man in black was young, but his eyes were not. There was a curve to his mouth, a smile at a private joke. He did not seem to mind Igar's blaster barrel in his face.

Gammas crashed up the hillside. Igar heard them. He had not heard the man in black.

"On the ground, scum!" Trooper Dooze crested the hill, rifle leveled, perfect form. Igar raised his free hand, signing caution, care. The other Gammas caught up with Dooze and fanned out into covering positions, rifles leveled and primed.

The man in black did not flinch—either as a coward might, away from danger, or as a hero, toward it. He seemed resigned. Igar saw the Death Star glint in the cold blue pools of his eyes. "Who are you?"

"I am here," the man in black said, "to surrender to Lord Vader."

To Vader? Igar's grip on the blaster tightened. "You are a rebel."

"If you say so."

There was a knot in Igar's brain. He knew rebels. He had fought so many. There was something wrong about the man in black. He stepped away, and kept his blaster level.

"Search him."

Dooze worked the man over. It didn't take long. The man carried a few ration pouches, a broken comlink, and— "Some kind of hand torch?" Dooze asked. He raised the metal tube, turned it over, peered down one end. His thumb drifted toward a switch.

"Dooze," Igar said, sharply. "Hand that to me."

"Sir."

Igar took the lightsaber.

He had never held one before. It was lighter than he had thought, and heavier, too, in different ways. So many thousand years of history should have more weight, when pressed and rolled into a weapon. Nothing that killed so easily should feel so delicate in the palm. He remembered Celes IV, a long, long time ago. Rain hissed off a blade of green fire.

He realized that he had taken his eyes off the man in black.

"A Jedi's weapon," he said, coolly. "Or, it was. Their fire is gone from the universe. Their altars are cold. Their temples warp no more children. Since the Clone Wars, I have seen lightsabers in the hands of collectors, cultists, and fools. Which one, I wonder, are you?"

THE MAN WHO CAPTURED LUKE SKYWALKER

The man in black smiled. "Perhaps I am a fool."

"How did you reach this moon?"

"In a small vessel. Alone."

"You would have been scanned on approach."

His hands were by his sides. He spread them, palms up, slowly. "Here I am."

"The rebels would not have sent one soldier. We lost a squad in these woods today. That's the work of more than one man."

"The woods are thick," said the man in black. "Accidents happen. I met your squad today when I landed. They're dead now. Not far from here."

"Scum," Dooze muttered in a side channel. "Lying scum."

"There has been enough death in this war," said the man in black. "I must see Lord Vader. I must help him."

"Show us the squad," Igar said.

It would not be a long march, the man said. Three kilometers, maybe less.

Igar expected a trap, and ordered Gamma to guard against one. His soldiers flared like wings through the wood. In the center of their formation he walked, blaster ready, beside the man in black.

If the man tried something, Igar would shoot him. If Igar wasn't fast enough, Trooper Dooze was near. Gamma, spread to filaments, would find any trap before it sprang. And if the man in black was himself the trap, Gamma would close around him like a fist.

When Igar was a boy, he used to walk like this with his friends, through the woods back to their campsite, finding paths by memory in the dark.

He had hooked the lightsaber through his belt. It struck his leg as he walked.

The man in black was the first to speak.

"You served beside the Jedi," he said.

Igar surprised himself by answering. "I did."

"When you spoke of them, I heard your hatred."

He might have walked on in the darkness, with his blaster out. Perhaps he should have. But he answered.

"I was young when I went to war," Igar said, "and like you, I was a fool. I fought for my Republic and my home. It seemed romantic at the time, to be caught up in the battles of great houses, of wizards, counts, and queens. The Jedi—you idolize them. You rebels carry their tokens and tools as if you knew anything of their true nature. You say to one another, *May the Force be with you,* as if it would be a good thing for that to be the case."

"Would it not?"

The man sounded truly curious, where Igar might have expected resistance, even anger. He looked again at the stranger, into his dark eyes. He wondered if the man was as confident as he seemed, or if he was just as unsure as everyone else. That wonder itched, and he found himself speaking again. "I fought beside the Jedi once, on Celes IV, defending my home. A hard rock, a miserable rain, endless bloodshed, a great dark Separatist fortress too shielded to reduce from orbit. We were pinned down under fire without relief or support. The Jedi, she said the Force was with us. She charged into the rain, and we followed her."

"You won," said the man in black.

"We won the battle. We took the fortress. We freed the system. Many of us died. But we won."

"I'm sorry about your friends."

"There was no reason for it. Our position was impossible. No general, no soldier I have ever served beside since would have led that charge. Only a mad wizard, following the will of the Force." Wind whispered through the trees, and the Gamma's footfalls cradled him. "The Jedi way is madness. If the Force wants you to kill a chancellor, you kill a chancellor. If it wants you to hurt a child, you hurt the child. If it wants you to die, you die. It is destiny as a devouring mouth. We needed a new world. Clear and orderly and free, shaped by words and deeds and will and choice, not destiny and ancient magic. That is the galaxy we have built."

"You serve the Emperor. Is that freedom?"

"If you believe in the Force, what does it matter when your Rebellion fails? It is the will of a blind process. Your friends die, your dreams wither, and for what?"

"It matters."

Igar might have been walking alone in the woods, for a time. When the man in black spoke again at last, he chose his words with care. "You talk as if the galaxy is made of separate things. As if nothing binds you and me, this tree, that rock. Or your Empire and the Republic from which it grew. Your Emperor, and Vader, and the Jedi. The will of the Force is the power of choice—all our choices, the choices of the living and the dead. Back on Celes Four, you say no soldier you have ever served beside would have led that charge. You should have died there. But you did not. What is that, if not destiny?"

Igar looked up into the night. He could not see the Death Star.

He opened his mouth. He did not know what he would say, but a pressure rose within him, and he would answer it, with his words or with the cold blaster in his grip.

They emerged into a clearing. Igar stumbled, caught himself on a branch.

There, in ruin, lay the body.

Its armor was black with soot, and broken. Its limbs should not have bent that way. Half the mask had broken off. If you did not look at the part where the eyes had been, the face still looked like Trooper Rell.

It had not been a bad death, Igar thought. Fast.

The Gammas closed around them, rifles out.

The man in black stood over the burned body as if he remembered other bodies, also burned. For the first time, Igar realized that the man was not much older than Trooper Dooze. "I chased them on a speeder," the man in black said. "You'll find them scattered in this area. I can show you the others, if—"

He did not finish, because Trooper Dooze hit him with the butt of his rifle, in the shoulder.

The man in black staggered. Dooze hit him again, and the man let the blow carry him to his knees. Dooze screamed out a curse, and kicked him in the ribs. The man in black did not fight. He rolled over, and looked at Igar—but not for help. He looked as if none of this surprised him.

Another blow fell. Dooze would kill him, Igar thought. Igar would have killed the man in black himself, as a younger man. Now he would stand by and let it happen. The forest ate people. No one would question that.

Let his Force come to save him. Let the power he claimed to follow bear him up. Would it, here? Alone and unarmed, in the dark?

What is that, but destiny?

He watched the stranger's eyes. He remembered the cave, the hiss of rain off a lightsaber blade, and the Jedi, unsure, before she moved.

"Dooze," he said. "Stop."

They returned to base in the calm before dawn.

His soldiers marched in crisp array. The man in black did not speak, and Commander Igar did not address him.

THE MAN WHO CAPTURED LUKE SKYWALKER

After the forest, the halls were clear and bright. Igar's eyes ached with the change, as if the dark was in them still, waiting to grow again.

He did not know himself. He was tired. It had been a long war.

And then he stood before Lord Vader.

The black lenses of the mask turned upon him, and he heard the echoing breath that would go on forever, the breath of the Empire's sword, its perfect instrument. He felt seen. He felt the lines of the world bright and true, a galaxy made of separate things.

"This," Igar said, "is the rebel that surrendered to us. Although he denies it, I believe there may be more of them, and I request permission to conduct a further search of the area."

He held out his hand, and in it, the lightsaber.

"He was armed only with this."

"Good work, Commander," Vader said. "Leave us. Conduct your search and bring his companions to me."

Igar heard these words in his soul. He had his orders. He turned to carry them out.

The Death Star shone above beyond the sky, and all was clear.

He had made the right choice. His world was will and rule, and therefore free. The man in black was a rebel. Igar was a soldier of the Empire. There was no bond between them, and the forest within was bright.

Still he lingered, to hear Vader speak. To hear the wisdom with which he would confront the man in black, and cut through the confusion sown by that calm and level voice.

Just before the doors of the lift hissed shut, he heard Vader say, "The Emperor has been expecting you."

And heard the man in black reply: "I know, Father."

Ackbar
Jarrett J. Krosoczka

"May the Force be with us!"

In this moment, I won't have time to second guess myself—or my commands.

There is much at stake. We are going all in on this mission. Any misstep, regardless of how slight, will prove devastating to the Rebellion.

Every word, every syllable I choose, needs to ensure that my team moves with conviction and speed.

THE IMPOSSIBLE FLIGHT OF ASH ANGELS

Marieke Nijkamp

Arvel Crynyd didn't believe in anything.

Life was easier, he thought, without the crushing weight of hope, responsibility, and anger. For years, the closest thing he had to faith or spirituality was the constant hum of the engines from the starfighters he'd made his own, from the grumpy rumbling of his Z-95's retrofits to the smoother murmur of the A-wing's sublight engines. It was the sharp, tangy smell of titanium and durasteel.

It was the rush of hyperspace. The first time he saw the stars change around him, he felt like he was one with the ship and the space around him, and he vowed he would never let anyone take that freedom away from him.

It was the slow path, too. He loved the jump, but equally, he loved to find the darkness between stars. Those empty pockets of stillness, where it felt like only he and his fighter could see the currents of space around them.

He thought it had been enough. He thought he wouldn't get involved.

And yet he found himself in the Sullust system, surrounded by a fleet. Star cruisers. Gunships. B-wings. A-wings. Ready to jump to hyperspace. Ready to engage the Emperor's new battle station, orbiting the forest moon of Endor.

He felt the countdown in his bones. He'd felt the sense of possibility ahead ever since taking off from *Home One*.

Arvel Crynyd didn't believe in anything. And yet, here he was.

He wondered what had changed.

"Admiral, we're in position. All fighters accounted for."

It had to have been the spacedock, nearly four years ago.

An old, abandoned spacedock on the edge of the Western Reaches.

And Arvel should've known better. He should've kept his eyes on his own craft. He'd decided long ago his best chance of survival lay in ignoring the terrible pilots on either side of the war. Keep his head down, don't get caught up in anyone's attempt to change the galaxy.

He should have ignored the blundering amateurs who seemed intent on running their rebel starfighters into the structure and simply continued on his way. After all, he had a contract to fulfill. The Bacta Cartel paid him well to be a glorified messenger, and his Z-95 Headhunter deserved an upgrade. It'd seen him through tight spots. It'd helped him avoid many a confrontation, too. A good vessel could mean a pilot's life, and a good pilot took care of his vessel.

THE IMPOSSIBLE FLIGHT OF ASH ANGELS

Arvel judged people by loose bolts, oil smears, badly repaired laser damage.

Perhaps that was what gave him pause here. Not the pilots—judging by their practice runs, they wouldn't be able to identify a hyperdrive motivator if it flew in circles around them—but their starfighters. Three A-wings. Scarred, bruised, more salvaged parts than original elements—and immaculate. Elegantly mended. Lovingly maintained. They looked too sharp for this forgotten corner of space.

Curiosity was a dangerous trait for a pilot. And yet—Arvel paused to watch them fly.

He scrambled his comm frequencies until he could listen in to the chatter from the spacedock: "—won't impress the commander with those antics. Barely surviving a barrel roll won't convince him you're a pilot."

The comm crackled. One of the rebels laughed. "I'll settle for convincing my A-wing, Pieter."

"Your A-wing doesn't care about your antics, either," Arvel said, before he could stop himself.

His words were met with deadly silence. A beat. Hesitation.

The A-wings drifted closer, approaching some semblance of battle formation, and Arvel marveled at the pilots' vessels even as he winced at the pilots' skills.

Then, the same voice from spacedock. Clipped. Confident. "Identify yourself."

Arvel glanced at his nav computer, mentally plotting an escape if things got touchy. "Just a traveler, passing through."

"Sightseeing in a snubfighter?" one of the pilots scoffed.

"Hush, Raf." Spacedock. Pieter, was it? "Best to be on your way, traveler."

Arvel wondered why he didn't heed that advice. He kept his eyes on the fighters. "Your problem is that you're easing back on your throttle halfway through your roll. It makes it harder to control the pitch rate."

"And I suppose you'd know." Raf might not have been much of a pilot, but she was confident enough to challenge him.

Arvel sniffed. "It's a *rookie* mistake."

He marked Raf's fighter and reached for the throttle, accelerating directly toward the A-wing, before he barreled around her.

He felt the intricacies of the maneuver. He adjusted his path on instinct, leaning into the spin and easing back once he fell into the downward swing.

He followed the first roll with a second, tighter one, until he came to a sharp stop and lazily looped back to his original position. He'd passed by the pilots before they'd had time to react, and he savored their silence of a different flavor. Shock. Awe. Annoyance.

Of course Raf spoke up first. "Damn. Cool tricks. Why haven't you taught us those yet, Pieter?"

The reply was frosty. "I'll settle for making sure you can take off and land safely."

A fourth A-wing had left the spacedock and was making its way toward Arvel. If possible, this fighter looked even more like it was held together with glue and string and care, but the pilot flew with intense determination. "Like I said, traveler. Continue on your path."

"I will," Arvel said, knowing the words were a lie as soon as he uttered them. "You have lessons to teach and I have places to be."

He should go. He should . . . leave. The pilots would learn, or they wouldn't. He'd never known the galaxy to be merciful, and the war wasn't his purpose.

Arvel switched from open comms and hailed Pieter directly. "I have to ask, though. Are you responsible for the wings' maintenance?"

"Why?" Pieter's voice was softer, but no less wary. He'd circled Arvel's Headhunter, forcing him off course and away from the others.

THE IMPOSSIBLE FLIGHT OF ASH ANGELS

"It's rather hard to imagine you could take out a Star Destroyer with this."

"With courage and determination? With pilots willing to risk it all for a better future? It's not all sim pods and Skystrike Academy defectors. Not every farm boy from some Outer Rim black hole turns into an ace fighter, and not every rookie has the chance to grow into one. Some of these pilots will never join up with the rebel fleet, but if we don't make sure they get some training, they're dead before they can try," Pieter snapped, and the words sounded well worn, like it was an argument he'd had a hundred times before. Then he stilled. "I try to prepare them, as best as I can, because I always have. Out here, no one else will. I never know if it's enough."

Arvel opened his mouth to say something, anything, he didn't know what, but before he could the other pilot continued. "No, that's a lie. I know it isn't. *They* know it isn't. And still they fight. So as long as I have them here, I will protect them. From their own inexperience as well as suspicious outsiders, if need be."

Arvel glanced out toward the spacedock. The three pilots hadn't returned to their practice. The three A-wings were lined up close to one another, like silent spectators. They were built for reconnaissance, not for outright assault. "Do I look like an Imperial spy? Would I stumble into a practice run of three aspiring rebel fighters in a forgotten corner of the galaxy?"

"Are you seriously asking me if an Imperial spy would try to look as innocuous as possible?"

Arvel barked a laugh. "Fine. I prefer to keep a healthy distance between myself and the war, anyway."

"So keep a healthy distance between us, too. We'll consider your flyby educational and something that won't happen again." Pieter closed the remaining distance toward the Headhunter, a pilot's equivalent of showing someone the door.

And really, Arvel should have left it at that. A singular, educational event. But the words that tumbled out of his mouth were, "I could teach them to barrel-roll, your rebels. Before I leave. They'll be slightly better prepared."

"*Why?*" He never knew one word could hold impatience, frustration, and curiosity.

That was the question, wasn't it? Why had he deviated from his path? Why hadn't he left yet? He looked at the A-wing's cockpit, and Pieter stared back at him, eyes dark behind the visor of his helmet.

Arvel judged people by oil smears, starfighter upgrades, and welding burns. "Those blasted A-wings, they look like you raided a scrapyard, and by rights they shouldn't be flying. The fact that they do is a small miracle. They're stunning and they deserve pilots who can keep them intact, who can keep them safe." He was never one to speak his deepest thoughts. He was a natural when it came to flying. He could feel the shape of space around him. He breathed easiest when he folded himself into a cockpit. He was . . . less comfortable with trust or vulnerability.

But Pieter responded immediately. "So they will keep the pilots safe."

The third silence was one of understanding, of recognition.

Pieter breathed out hard. "One trick?"

"One trick."

"I have my eyes on you."

"I'm more worried about your laser cannons."

This time, Pieter was the one to laugh.

"One trick," Arvel assured him, and he wondered if they both knew they were lying. He wondered if they knew that one trick would turn into a dozen would turn into dozens. One spacedock would grow into a larger base, turn into another. Aspiring resistance fighters would become rebels.

THE IMPOSSIBLE FLIGHT OF ASH ANGELS

One gritty pilot would turn into many, and many would not return.

Those blasted A-wings.

Those damn brave fools.

Arvel Crynyd didn't believe in anything, but he knew how to teach a good barrel roll.

"Proceed with the countdown. All groups assume attack coordinates."

It had been the tavern, too. A year later.

Or rather, the walkway outside of the tavern. He met Demms Ryx on Koda Station, outside The End of the World.

Arvel had entered the tavern to meet with a representative of the Virgillian Free Alignment—a Virgillian woman who'd introduced herself as Dagger. She was the one who'd asked him there, promising a message from one of his pilots. Arvel didn't do glorified messenger runs anymore, but he'd made an exception for the invitation to come *sightseeing in a snubfighter*. After all, only one pilot had said those words to him, and he'd wanted to know how Raf was doing. He'd wanted to know, right up until the moment Dagger offered him a thin, burned sliver of durasteel and her sympathies.

Arvel hadn't been a stranger to loss, but he hadn't lost a pilot yet.

He'd stormed out.

Demms, ever the concerned, considerate bartender, followed.

The light streaming out from the door opening to the seedy tavern made the Volpai's blue skin seem brighter, almost cerulean, and the stripes along his face and arms shone like stars.

Those were the first words out of Arvel's mouth.

"You look like hyperspace come to life."

He knew his pilots would've laughed and laughed at that. *Raf* would have laughed. They'd been the ones who taught him to speak his mind more.

Mercifully, the Volpai had laughed, too. He could have walked away. He could have scoffed at him. But he'd laughed and reached out a hand, drawn him in. He'd warned him Arvel would catch his death out there. He'd offered Arvel a drink. And then another. And then, when their paths not so accidentally crossed again, another.

It was habit before Arvel realized it was more than that. He still needed hyperspace routes and coordinates to navigate interpersonal relationships, and without them he felt lost.

But Demms found him. Every time.

A drink. A smile. A tender word. A comforting arm—or four.

That first night, Demms had gently sent Dagger on her way, had called in another bartender to take over his shift, and he'd sat down next to Arvel.

"Tell me about hyperspace."

Arvel clung to the edge of the table in front of him, as though it was the only thing that kept him upright. He felt like the world was spinning with a vengeance. "It's beautiful. It's freedom. It's . . ." He shook his head.

"Tell me." Demms nudged him.

"Nothing makes me feel both so powerful and so insignificant." He'd never admitted to that before. Not even to himself. "It's *impossible* and somehow we make it work. If we can do such impossible things, why are we so intent on harming each other?"

"Careful," Demms said with a soft smile. "That's rebellious talk."

"I'm not a rebel, I'm a flight instructor," Arvel snapped, though he was quite sure the Empire didn't differentiate between rebel and flight instructor. And the truth was, he wasn't sure he could, either. Not today. Not anymore.

He tried to get up, but Demms put a hand on his shoulder. "Don't go."

"I have to." He didn't, but he couldn't stay, either. It scared him.

"Tell me about her."

Arvel hesitated before he downed his drink in one gulp. "I'd just taught her a Cru spin, right before she left."

He placed the sliver on the tabletop in front of him. "Just one trick."

"I'm sorry."

"Yeah." He was, too.

Demms considered him. "It mattered, even if it didn't change the outcome. It mattered that you taught her. It's an act of trust, to teach, to believe that we can be better than we were."

"I don't believe in anything."

"I doubt that very much."

Arvel managed a pained half smile. "That's rebellious talk, too."

Demms grinned and shrugged, four arms at once. His eyes sparkled. "I'm a bartender on Koda Station. I'm a rebel by definition."

"It must be easy," Arvel said, without thinking it through. "To know exactly who you are."

A shadow crossed Demms's face, and for a brief moment it was as if the deepest blue darkened further, as if his features sharpened. Then he smiled. "I thought we already determined, I'm hyperspace come to life."

"I *can* see the stars in your eyes," Arvel said, meaning every word of it.

Demms seemed to stare straight through him. "Then use those stars to plot your course, flight instructor. As long as you occasionally find your way back to me when you want to talk."

Arvel promised, but still it was Demms who found him first.

When Pieter dragged Arvel to Koda Station to negotiate a shipment of salvaged A-wing parts, Demms was there with a drink and a smile, like he'd been waiting.

He had been.

When Arvel returned to the old spacedock—and briefly considered that they should name the damn thing now that more aspiring rebel pilots found their way to it—Demms found his way there, too. Not immediately, nor confidently. He hitched a ride and showed up with a bag slung over his shoulder and a thousand questions in his eyes.

Arvel felt a pull at his core, the same rush he felt when hurtling through space. Fear and exhilaration, all at once.

"It occurred to me," Demms said, "that plotted courses work both ways."

Arvel glanced around the docking bay, at the pilots who adamantly didn't look in their direction. "You're not here to become a pilot?"

"I'm not. And I won't stay if it makes you uncomfortable. It's just—" Demms clenched and unclenched his hands. "You make a difference. I serve drinks. I want to do more."

"You don't," Arvel said quietly.

Demms frowned.

"You don't make me uncomfortable," Arvel added, stumbling over the words. In fact, it was *comfort* before he realized it was more than that. "What would you like to do?"

Demms's frown faded and a soft smile broke through, like the first starlight arcing over a planet. "I can cook. Quite well, actually. I like to make a difference, too. I want to feel like I matter."

"To a cause?"

"Or a person."

This time, Arvel reached out a hand and drew him in. "We could use a chef. If I have to look at another polystarch ration pack, I'll fling myself out an air lock."

"We couldn't have that," Demms muttered. "I just found you again."

"You did."

When the path was hard to navigate, it was so much easier to be found than to plow on. To reach for an outstretched hand. A strong arm—or two or four. Perhaps in that sense, they found each other. And they kept finding each other.

On a walkway outside of a tavern.

On a spacedock.

In a newly rebuilt RZ-1T A-wing, with Demms in the pilot's seat and Arvel as backup, with Pieter on their comms, occasionally reminding them he'd never refurbished a trainer starship before, so it might just fall apart around them. It didn't. They switched places halfway through and Arvel showed Demms the beauty of hyperspace.

On Hoth, where Arvel met with the Alliance High Command and other Alliance flight instructors for the first time. And after Echo Base fell, when Arvel left the still-unnamed spacedock, because it held too many names of pilots that would never return.

On a nameless asteroid, where Demms cooked for a small contingent of rebels and Arvel ran supply missions, until he got annoyed by new pilots messing up their barrel rolls and he taught them, too.

They found each other, and they kept finding each other, and it was love before Arvel realized the stars had never shone brighter. What was love became home, what was home became family.

One trick, one smile, one word at a time, Arvel Crynyd lost his heart to everything that was worth fighting for.

Those blasted A-wings.

Those damn brave fools.

That headstrong, rebellious bartender, who made the best rations in the fleet.

He understood what motivated them now.

Arvel Crynyd still didn't believe in anything, but he saw the stars in the eyes of his daughter, too.

"All craft, prepare to jump to hyperspace on my mark."
"All right. Stand by."

Or perhaps it had, quite simply, been the birds, three days ago.

He'd passed by Sullust on the trade routes a hundred times. He'd never stopped to go sightseeing; he'd preferred stars over planets. But the fleet had assembled there, all courage and determination. All pilots willing to risk everything for a better future.

You could take out a Star Destroyer with this fleet.

With his eyes on the barren, volcanic planet below, Arvel let the hum of his A-wing overwhelm him. He should've known better. He should've kept his eyes on his own craft.

But Starr had wanted to know about the birds, because Demms had told her they were the only featherless birds in existence. "They're impossible," he'd told their toddler softly, when Arvel visited them on Cerea, where they'd made their home safely away from the rebel fleet. "And it's exactly because they're impossible that they're worth holding on to." Demms had looked at Arvel. "Because it's creatures like these, my love, that make this galaxy miraculous."

So Arvel plotted a course to far below the obsidian surface, found himself a Sullustan naturalist—a short woman who introduced herself as Fenna Lev—and went to see the birds.

Because it was easier to think of his daughter than of what lay ahead.

THE IMPOSSIBLE FLIGHT OF ASH ANGELS

He'd dragged Pieter along. "For old times' sake."

"Watching featherless creatures stumble through flight? Nothing would delight me more."

Fenna Lev rolled her eyes at them but didn't say anything. She guided them to a small, raggedy shuttle that would bring them to the surface and listened to the two of them bicker, until they emerged from the subterranean city and toxic smoke surrounded the vessel.

A virulent lava river cut through the harsh landscape, hot bubbles of fire exploding from the surface.

"You should know," she said in weary Basic, cutting through Pieter's recounting the adventures of the most recent pilot trainees aboard the spacedock, "that ash angels don't stumble or blunder. You flyboys may think your starfighters are so elegant, but you have nothing on these birds."

She brought the shuttle to a halt above the lava river's estuary, and the red glow from the molten rock lit up the landscape around them. On the rocky, obsidian outcroppings to their right, tall gray birds sat with their wings outstretched—like they were drying them in the heat of the volcanic fumes.

One of the biggest birds toppled forward, and Arvel barely had the presence of mind to reach his holorecorder and follow along as the bird skimmed across the lava, gracefully avoiding touching the surface. The wings looked odd, like they were partially incinerated and shouldn't be able to sustain flight.

"They *are* impossible," Arvel commented softly.

"No," Fenna Lev said. "They are unlikely."

Another ash angel followed the first, rolling around it, diving between the first bird and the lava and corkscrewing around it, like a young pilot who finds their wings.

The bigger bird squawked, a harsh, guttural sound, and as it made a sharp turn away from the other one, the thin strips of tissue that covered its body and wings shivered in the heat. It left a thin trail of ashes in its wake.

They watched a fledgling tumble down, too, narrowly avoiding angry bubbles of lava as it crossed the stream and stumbled onto an ash-covered ledge. It rolled around in the ash, big flakes clinging to its skin.

Arvel made sure to catch every moment of it. "All the rules of physics should stop these birds from flying. The fact that they're up there . . ."

Pieter nudged him. "If I remember correctly, you once told me my A-wings shouldn't fly, either, and look where that got us."

Arvel shook his head. "Your A-wings obeyed the laws of physics."

"And these birds obey the laws of nature."

"What laws?"

Fenna Lev answered first. "Survival. Life continues, even when everything around it is deadly and dark, even when it has to adapt to ash or hunger. Life continues to find its path."

Pieter looked at her and smiled. "Exactly. Though I wouldn't call it survival. Survival is so crude and emotionless."

He turned to face the ash angels again, and for the briefest of moments, Arvel saw two Pieters at once. The one he'd met in a patched-up starfighter outside a reclaimed stardock, and the one who sat in front of him now, in his Green Squadron flight suit. They were quite a lot more similar than the Arvel he'd been then and the person he was now.

"What would you call it then?"

Pieter shrugged. "Hope."

"Ah."

"Yeah."

Arvel switched off the holorecorder and placed it to the side, looking out over the ash angels in the light of the lava stream.

THE IMPOSSIBLE FLIGHT OF ASH ANGELS

He ran a hand through his hair. "Damn brave birds."

"Blasted A-wings." Pieter held out his hand to him. "One more trick?"

He nodded. "One more trick."

Arvel Crynyd didn't believe in anything, but it didn't stop the birds from flying.

"All wings report in."

Arvel Crynyd didn't believe in anything.

Except in the pilots fighting for a better future—even if they couldn't barrel-roll. He'd stopped counting how many he'd taught over the years, but he knew all their names. He saw them now, appearing out of hyperspace, with Endor ahead. With a Death Star, too. He felt them. The ones who were present. The ones who came before.

He believed in the beauty of the galaxy, and in the people who kept his galaxy in the palm of their hands.

He believed in hope, even in the face of cruel impossibility.

Arvel Crynyd believed in anything . . . much.

But this was enough.

He opened his comms and prepared himself for battle. "Green Leader. Standing by."

ENDING PROTOCOL
Hannah Whitten

"Walking through this forest," GR-792 said, "feels like walking through the inside of a Hutt's mouth."

Riz cocked an eyebrow, though the other stormtrooper couldn't see it beneath her helmet. "How many Hutt mouths have you walked through, exactly?"

"Let me amend: Walking through this forest feels like how I *assume* walking through a Hutt mouth would. Humid and smelly."

The humidity she couldn't argue with, but Riz didn't think it was *that* smelly. Granted, not much got through her helmet. She refrained from telling Gir that he was probably just smelling his own breath.

Gir stumbled, foot tangling in thick green underbrush. His blaster, held carelessly in his armor-plated hand, swung out wide as he tried to regain his balance and struck Riz in the chest. It didn't go off—his brain wasn't so packed with nerf fur that he'd forgotten the safety—but Riz froze anyway, the sweat pooling on her neck going clammy and cold, her heart knotting up in her chest.

Being at the business end of a blaster—especially one from another trooper—made her twitchy, for more reasons than one.

"Kriff," Gir grumbled as he righted himself. "At this point, I would rather walk through a whole horde of Hutt mouths. Doubt I'd trip as much."

This was the part where usually she'd say something witty, fulfill the role she'd taken in the stretch of days they'd spent tromping around this tiny, overgrown moon, watching for rebels who seemed much better at blending into their surroundings than Imperial troopers ever were. But the *smack* of Gir's blaster hitting her armor had stricken the possibility of anything witty from her brain.

Gir's head tracked from the smudge on her white armor where the blaster had hit her to the weapon in his hand. With a sigh, he holstered the weapon carefully, then reached up and disengaged his helmet. His pale skin was sheened in sweat as he glanced at her, his eyes narrowed. "Blasters still bother you?"

Following his lead, Riz pulled her own helmet off. Her short blond hair was practically plastered to her skull, and the cool breeze through the trees felt impossibly good. She closed her eyes a moment, as much to enjoy the respite from her helmet as to avoid looking at Gir's face. "Yeah," she said quietly. "Still."

That, at least, was an understandable explanation for her jumpiness. Seeing your commander shot during what was supposed to be a simple interrogation wasn't something you just *got over*.

NE-034—Neo, they'd called her, cobbling together nicknames because none of them were particularly attached to the ones they were

ENDING PROTOCOL

born with—wasn't even supposed to be leading the mission. But the captain had been called away at the last minute, something about a special assignment to Cloud City, and Neo was the next highest in rank. Under her leadership, they'd been deployed to Nar Shaddaa for recon. A simple enough task, though they'd all been instructed to listen for any news of Luke Skywalker while they were there. Lord Vader was particularly interested in learning of his whereabouts.

Riz shouldn't know that, though. And she didn't, for certain. It was just a feeling she'd had, when the order came down from the higher-ups. A twinge in her middle that told her Vader's interest was more personal than political.

She'd always had what she interpreted as a strong intuition. Not necessarily a trait the Empire valued in its troopers, so she'd done her best to squash it down, to silence it. At least, she had back then.

The order came that morning to find a human woman rumored to know something about Skywalker, for reasons that command didn't deem necessary to share. Neo programmed the reported coordinates, and off they went.

Riz was uncomfortable through the entire march, a scattering of goosebumps across the back of her neck, a pitted feeling in her middle. She liked Neo well enough, but the other trooper had a reputation for going too far, sometimes. For relishing the brutal parts of the job.

Not that Riz had a leg to stand on in that regard. Not really. No one in her contingent spent much time sharing the stories of how they'd come to be in the Imperial military, but Riz suspected that many were like her—orphaned, nowhere safe to sleep, not knowing where their next meal was coming from. Hunger was sharp enough that you'd do anything to blunt its edge. It was only once you were sated that you looked guiltily back on what it had cut.

Maybe it'd started like that for Neo, too. Backed into a corner, seemingly no other way out. Maybe she'd just decided to keep the blade sharp, even after the hunger was blunted, the stability secured.

Either way, all of them were here, doing the same things, enacting the same violence. It came easier to some than to others, but there was no way to hold this job and innocence in the same hand.

The woman they were looking for lived in a warren beneath a skybridge, broken durasteel creating a makeshift door into hollow darkness, kept away from the glow of urban sprawl. Stepping through the jagged doorway felt like stepping into a waiting mouth.

She'd looked harmless. Thin and pale, as if she never got quite enough to eat, dressed in ragged layers of cloth that may or may not have ever been intended as clothing. Despite her thinness and her age, though, there'd been a glint in her eye that spoke of well-honed survival instinct, prey that had managed to evade the predator far longer than expected.

That look said the stormtroopers would have a hell of a time getting anything incriminating out of her.

Still, Neo began with what they'd been taught best. Intimidation.

Neo crossed her white-plated arms, making sure her blaster was clearly visible, rolling her neck as if loosening up for a fight. "Now," she said, her helmet flattening her voice to something cold and droidlike, "you're going to tell us everything you know about Luke Skywalker, Han Solo, and Leia Organa. And we know you know *something*, bantha-bait, so don't try to pretend."

Riz didn't usually like to watch this stuff. She'd close her eyes beneath her helmet, sinking into her own mind as if it could be an escape. She'd made a place for herself at the bottom of the barrel, thought of as too weak to carry out any important aspects of a mission, so she was never asked for much other than her presence. Still,

ENDING PROTOCOL

she always stood aside, a quiet witness who never stepped in, even when everything in her screamed that it was wrong.

The old woman's flinty eyes darted to a ratty curtain hanging over the back half of her makeshift home. They'd taken a cursory look behind it when they first forced their way in and seen nothing but dusty boxes. It didn't look like the boxes had been disturbed in years, and the other troopers hadn't bothered checking inside before declaring the all-clear.

But that intuition, that tug at her ribs, told Riz to look. Slowly, she backed away from formation, flicked aside her hand to open the curtain. A cloud of dust bloomed in the air; it made her glad of her helmet.

In the storage room, Riz carefully opened one of the boxes. It'd taken her a moment to realize what she was seeing. A mess of metal and plastoid, jumbled weapons in various states of repair. And in pride of place, set delicately atop the rest of the contraband, two silver-and-black hilts.

Lightsabers.

The woman was an arms dealer, then, and a collector as well. If Lord Vader knew she had lightsabers, he would've come here himself; the information must've been garbled along the way, twisted out of relic collecting and into her knowing about Skywalker. Such a thing would still bring her before Vader, though, and Riz couldn't imagine that would end well.

Maybe the woman did know something about Skywalker's whereabouts, but the tug of feeling in her middle told Riz she didn't. The knowledge was a rush of strange relief.

Riz eased her way out of the curtained-off storage room and into the back of the formation again, chewing her lip bloody beneath her white-plated visor.

Neo knelt, leaning closer to the old woman, her armored hand hovering over her blaster. "Start talking, lady, or things are going to get real nasty real quick."

With a lurch, Riz stepped forward. "Ne— Commander. A word?"

Even through the helmet, Riz felt her superior's confused stare. Neo's hand wavered, but then she stood. "You may have your word right here, trooper."

Riz got as close to Neo as she could in the cramped space, wishing she could take off her helmet and whisper, knowing that would be a catastrophic breach of protocol. She didn't have much in the way of a plan, and she was certain they weren't going to get anything out of this mission, anyway. But maybe she could at least spare the old woman some pain.

"You aren't going to get anywhere like this." The voice filtering unit turned Riz's whisper to a hiss. "Offer her immunity."

"Immunity for *what*?" Neo gave a slight shake of her head. "Listen, you can't just—"

"Trust me," Riz interrupted. "If you offer her immunity for past crimes, she'll tell you everything she knows. I'd bet the fleet on it."

Her incredulous look was hidden behind white plastoid, but Neo sighed, the sound a soft seethe through the filtering unit. "Okay. We—"

Interrupted, again. But this time, it was by a blaster bolt.

Riz remembered turning so fast that her neck creaked, but the images of that moment in her mind were all slow-motion. The spindly old woman holding a blaster, screeching as she fired off a few more rounds that went blessedly wild, the ember-bright bolts streaking through the air like comets. The chaos of the other troopers ducking, running, trying to wrest the blaster back from the old woman. Neo, crumpling, her chest a smoking hole.

ENDING PROTOCOL

Riz, patting at her side, where her blaster should be holstered, and realizing the weapon the old woman held was her own.

"RZ-440. GR-792. You are in breach of recon protocol; please replace your helmets immediately."

The cool, automated voice floated out of Riz's helmet beneath her arm, startling her back into the present. The present, where her blaster was snug on her hip. The present, where she couldn't bring herself to fire the damn thing, not for the entire week since Neo died and they were all reassigned.

"Damn." Gir shook his head, sliding his helmet back on. "That's the clearest the comms have sounded in weeks."

Riz didn't respond, though Gir was right. The comm sounded too clear.

Which meant that they must have sent someone else to fix it, for once.

The decision to start leaving the communications towers in disrepair had come almost subconsciously. Riz was one of the better mechanics in her contingent; wherever they were stationed, her two jobs were almost always perimeter duty and patch-ups. But ever since they'd been on the forest moon of Endor, she'd just . . . stopped. Left the comms the way they were. Let the signal crackle and fade.

Most of it could be blamed on the thick forest, and the Empire was so sure of their impending victory that a few jammed communications lines weren't of great interest. Riz still wasn't sure why she did it. It wasn't like it was making much of a difference.

When she lay awake in whatever hours had been assigned to her for sleeping, the only answer she could come up with was that she wanted this to *end*. The Empire, maybe. Her part in it, certainly.

She couldn't hold innocence, never again, but that didn't stop her from trying to reach for it.

Riz's helmet hissed as it sealed to the rest of her armor, blocking out the ambient noise of the forest. At least they hadn't seen any Ewoks today. Those things gave her the creeps.

"Look." Gir ignored the comm, his baritone voice tuned back to helmet monotone. "You were trying to help Neo. You can't blame yourself forever for the way things went."

He didn't say it wasn't her fault, Riz noticed. They all knew it was. She saw the sidelong looks, heard the mechanic hiss of whispers in the halls.

After Neo's death, everyone in her contingent had been sent to guard the shield generator protecting the new, improved Death Star. No time for mourning. No thought for the people who'd seen a friend die. Troopers were pawns, moved about the board at the will of their betters, and no thought was given to those inside the armor.

Something in Riz was withered, now. In abstract, she'd always known that she was barely a person to the Empire, valuable only for what she could offer them—a trigger finger and a body to use as a barricade. She'd always comforted herself with the thought that at least they were mutually using each other, she and the Empire. She got three squares and a roof, and they got war fodder. But that deal was lopsided.

So, the comm signals. So, this feeling brewing in her middle, a slow-growing determination that yes, the Empire was the villain here, and yes, she had been complicit in things she could never truly make up for.

"Think about this instead of blasters," Gir said, taking an exaggerated huge step over a tangle of weeds. "We just caught a handful of rebels. Maybe that means it'll be over soon, and we can get off this damn moon."

Over soon. That sounded nice.

Something in the distance. Sounds of scuffling, shouting. Faint

ENDING PROTOCOL

enough that Riz wondered if she was imagining it. Her stomach twisted, that *feeling* sparking to life, telling her to be watchful, be wary.

If Gir could hear the same sounds she could, he didn't seem fazed. "And you're going to have to use that blaster again eventually," he continued. They'd moved from the relatively open ground on the outer perimeter of their route to the thicker bramble that grew close to the bunker, reaching up nearly to his waist. "You can't just—"

A sound, too clear to be imagined this time. A blaster.

They broke into a run, eating up the distance remaining between them and the bunker.

Not just one blaster—*lots* of blasters. And Ewoks, too, chittering in their high, unintelligible language, jumping down from the trees to beat at stormtroopers with sticks. Blasters, and Ewoks, and scout walkers, shooting bolts of light that whizzed through the trees.

Gir dropped down into the tall grass; Riz followed, training taking over her muscles even though the sounds of battle had turned them all liquid. Her comm was shouting in her ear, staticky and garbled but in better shape than she'd left it, ordering all hands to the bunker, the prisoners had escaped, the bunker was under attack.

They crawled through the underbrush until Riz could see the bunker door through the swaying yellow-green grass.

Four figures. Two droids, one humanoid and golden while the other was a white-and-blue R2 unit, and two humans. One of the humans messed with exposed wires in the bunker wall. The other wore a green cape and had her hair braided in a dark crown, crouching in the corner with her blaster outstretched. Riz was too far away to see their faces.

Her intuition flared again, looking at the woman. As if she should recognize something.

Blasterfire zinged around the forest, harmonizing with the shouts of Imperials and the screeches of Ewoks, the whine of scout walkers. A bolt skidded along the side of the bunker, and the woman by the door returned fire. Rebels, then.

Riz hoped the woman's shot landed.

"I think I've got it!" the man at the door called triumphantly, wires sparking in his hands. Another blaster bolt hit the side of the bunker, just missing the woman crouched at his feet. She fired back—another white-armored body sprawled in the brush. "I've got it!"

He didn't. The bunker doors were doubled; he'd only managed to close the set he'd already hot-wired open.

Gir didn't hesitate. He lurched up from the ground, still at a crouch so he didn't emerge fully from the undergrowth, and fired.

His shot went wide, sparking off the bunker's side. But it got close to the woman, and she reeled away. Riz could clearly see her face for the first time.

Leia Organa. The woman at the bunker was Leia Organa. Which meant the man had to be Han Solo. The escaped prisoners, right here.

Next to her, Gir seemed to be coming to the same realization. He chuckled low, the sound made more menacing by his voice filtering unit. "The princess herself," he murmured, raising his blaster. "This will make me captain, for sure."

He raised his blaster. He centered his shot.

And right as he pulled the trigger, in a burst of movement that her brain barely considered before her body took over, Riz kicked out her foot.

Her boot knocked into Gir's leg, sending his blaster-arm swinging to the side. A cry from the bunker—Organa was hit, but just in the shoulder, her green poncho sparking as she fell backward.

Relief gripped Riz's chest in a cool fist.

Gir, surprisingly, didn't seem upset with her, apparently thinking it had been an accident. "Come on." He stood, tugging Riz along with

ENDING PROTOCOL

him, running at a bent-over crouch to the deeper cover of trees. "We can still get them, no one else is going to."

He was right. All around them, Imperial soldiers were falling, beaten back by blasterfire and Ewoks and a scout walker that appeared to be commandeered. The Empire was losing. *They* were losing. It was a shock, a possibility none of them had prepared for, and Riz felt strangely detached from it, as if she floated somewhere above her body, watching.

In the trees, Gir stood and looped around, heading back for the bunker. Riz glanced over her shoulder before following—the man still didn't have the door open, and Leia was still crouched in the corner. Riz couldn't see how badly she was wounded.

Her body felt as mechanical as her armor made her look as she followed Gir, threading through bodies sprawled across the forest floor. He didn't give them a second glance, intent on his prize. And this was how the Empire worked, wasn't it? United in violence, but when things went badly, it was every soldier for themselves.

Still, she followed, her head a haze of smoking blaster discharge and the smell of burning plastoid as Gir marched up to the bunker doors. "Freeze!" he snarled, blaster raised. "Don't move."

Her blaster was in her hands, the safety still flicked on. Her stomach was churning, churning.

"I love you," Solo said, crouched over Leia so they couldn't see her fully. He sounded awed.

"I know," the princess replied.

"Hands up!" Gir ordered, clearly annoyed that his captives were having a moment when this moment should be his. "Stand down!"

Like that day in the old woman's home beneath the bridge, the world seemed to stretch out into slow motion. Solo whirled away from Leia at the same moment that she raised a blaster from her lap. She pointed, fired, but only once.

The bolt caught Gir in the chest. He reeled back, fell.

And Riz went with him, driven by instinct that told her to lie down, to play dead, though only the barest spark from the bolt had hit her. She fell to the dirt beside Gir, and she tried to drum up something like sorrow for him, but all she got was blackness as her head hit a tree root and her consciousness narrowed to a pinprick, blinked out.

She didn't know how long she lay there. The comm must've broken when she fell; there were no broken orders in the humid dark of her helmet, nothing but the harsh grate of her breathing. At one point, she thought she heard heavy doors opening, booted feet, a high-pitched chorus of victory. But now, it was quiet, and she was trying to summon the energy to move.

With a heave, Riz pushed up from the ground. All her muscles were tense, the tendons in her neck felt like they'd been used to rein in a dewback, but nothing seemed broken or horrifically out of place.

Riz disengaged her helmet, taking a deep, heaving breath of clean forest air. It still smelled like smoke and death, but anything was preferable to smelling her own sweat.

The bodies hadn't been touched. White plastoid was left where Imperials had fallen in mangled heaps—troopers beaten by sticks, thrown back by blasterfire, brought down by laser bolts from the scout walker.

Complex grief clenched her heart in its fist and squeezed. This was what the Empire thought of them: letters and numbers and armor, bullet points on a report, easily replaced. Not people.

In a rush of compulsive movement, Riz tore out of her uniform, leaving her in only the skintight dark bodysuit all troopers wore beneath it. She didn't want to touch that armor. Didn't ever want to

ENDING PROTOCOL

wear it again. Once, it had been shelter and security, but now it felt like shackles.

They thought she was dead. Someone had been by to catalog the casualties, surely, and if not, if they'd never gotten that far—if they'd been beaten that badly—the Empire would simply count anyone on Endor as a loss.

She was free.

A noise above her head. A quiet boom.

Riz looked up.

An aurora of red and orange and yellow bloomed in the sky, bright against the blue.

When she'd first joined up, Riz had been told the tale of Alderaan. It was a quick story, one meant to boost morale—look how strong the Empire is, blasting entire planets out of existence, surely nothing can stand between it and victory. At the time, she'd taken it as reassurance. She'd chosen the winning side, no matter how its atrocities slowly revealed themselves to her, no matter how they began to crawl beneath her skin and settle like slow disease. She remembered the feeling in her middle sparking to life when she was told of Alderaan. Something mourning, so many lives snuffed out, all for want of power.

So many years spent trying to squash that feeling down. Rationalizing, knowing that she'd been a participant in countless terrible things, that there was no real redemption. But through it all, the intuition remained, a spark that wouldn't go out. A pull toward something different, if only she was brave enough to reach for it.

Maybe she was now. Late, later than she should be, but it was something.

The destruction of Alderaan had apparently somehow led to Luke Skywalker becoming one of the rebels, according to rumor. Every death meant a rebirth, somewhere.

Riz turned and walked into the woods. She followed the tug, letting it wind her through the trees, around the rocks and vines.

Eventually, she heard singing. Saw the flickering of a bonfire, figures dancing around it, Ewok and human and every manner of species in between.

Rebels.

And she knew what she should do, then. That there was no justice in hiding, in pretending, in hoping that everything she'd done would fade away. There was nothing to do but face it head-on, and accept whatever atonement she could find.

Riz stepped forward, out of the tree line, into the fading light.

"Hey!"

A man she didn't recognize, though his green-patterned clothes marked him as a rebel. His eyes narrowed, a blaster held tight in his hand. His eyes quickly took in her bodysuit and short hair; it didn't appear that he knew immediately what she was, but his suspicions weren't soothed. "Who the hell are you?"

The question of the hour. Riz had no idea how to answer. She spread her hands wide, showing clearly she carried no weapon. "I . . . I don't . . ."

I don't know.

But that part didn't matter, did it? She took a deep breath. "I'm here to turn myself in."

His hand tightened on his blaster, and his eyes went wide, but the guard didn't shoot. "Wait here." He seemed confident she would do as ordered; there was that, at least. "I'll get someone."

As he tromped off into the party, Riz followed his orders. She was good at that, following orders.

A few minutes, then the guard returned with Princess Leia.

She'd changed. Her hair was long, down instead of braided, and

ENDING PROTOCOL

she wore a dress instead of a military poncho. Her eyes gleamed as she took Riz in, lips pursed thoughtfully.

"Anyone you recognize?" The guard narrowed his eyes at Riz. "Wouldn't tell me who she was, but said she was here to turn herself in, so I'm guessing trooper."

Riz almost wanted to flinch, but she didn't let herself.

The guard's eyes narrowed. "I'm sure Han could take care of—"

"No." Leia gave Riz a long, searching look. Then, she nodded, almost to herself. "Go enjoy yourself. I'll take it from here."

The man didn't seem to like that idea, but neither was he willing to gainsay his superior. With one last appraising glance at Riz, he headed toward the bonfire.

Then it was just them, Riz and Leia, Riz and the woman who had every right to want her dead for all she'd done and all she represented, the woman she'd saved in a quick flash of intuition and impulse. One good deed that could never balance such a stacked scale.

Leia stared at her. She was beautiful, but not in a way that could ever be construed as soft—her face was strong angles, her eyes wise. "So." Leia gave her the hint of a smile. "What's your name?"

Riz took a deep breath. "Riz," she said. "At least, it has been for years. I left my old one behind when I joined."

And that was as good as a confession.

There was no surprise in the princess's face. "Where are you from, Riz?"

"All over, really. But I've been here for the past few weeks."

There it was, laid out without words. Her identity, such as it was, and her surrender.

Leia nodded, again, and for a moment, they were silent. Every ligament in Riz's body was held thrumming-tight.

Leia looked behind her, at the bonfire, the dancing. A deep breath, then she turned back to Riz, her face grave. "I think it's best if you stay out here while I confer with my other officers."

She understood that. "I surrender myself to whatever punishment you deem fit."

A nod, short and businesslike, but there was an unexpected softness in Leia's eyes. Not forgiveness. Not yet, maybe not ever. Riz could live with that, she thought. Forgiveness wasn't necessary.

But if there was any way she could fix it—anything she could do to repair the damage she'd done—she would take the chance.

"Just a moment." Leia nodded to a rock jutting up from the ground. "Sit tight, and I'll let you know what we decide."

Riz sat down on the soft grass. She looked up at the stars wheeling over her head. She thought of things ending, and things beginning.

THE LAST FLIGHT
Ali Hazelwood

Sila Kott is no master of the art of war, nor does she care to be. She is proud to fly with Red Squadron, proud to serve under Wedge Antilles and beside her wingmates, proud to join the fight against the tyranny of the Empire. And yet, military strategies, tactical affairs, large-scale assessment of conflict—for the most part, they all elude her. She trusts the High Command to act for the good of the Alliance, and whenever she is sent on a mission, a raid, an attack, she rarely knows beforehand whether it will be a crucial turning point in the war or just another inconsequential dogfight.

Endor, however, is different.

When she left Sullust and jumped into hyperspace with the rest of the fleet, she hadn't quite known what to expect. But once they drop into Endor system, she nearly recoils. There are swarms of TIE fighters everywhere. A Dreadnought, battle cruisers, Star Destroyers. Proton torpedoes ready to fire.

Above all, there is the Death Star. Impossibly large, a dull, sterile gray orbiting the forest moon of Endor. Not yet complete, but . . . soon. Very soon.

"Everyone ready?" Antilles's voice asks through the comm.

Sila exhales slowly—and then collects herself.

"Red Three here," she says. "I'm ready."

This battle, she knows, will decide the future of the galaxy.

The shadow in which Sila Kott grew up had long brown hair, a knockout smile, and more luck at sabacc than anyone in the Outer Rim had the right to be afforded.

Lante was younger, but only by a few months. Intelligent, but in an unpredictable way. Charming and easy to talk to, but not for Sila, *never* for Sila. Lante lived just a few steps down the road. She was different and dangerous and impossible to ignore, and Sila absolutely despised how everyone in their corner of Toprawa City would go out of their way to compare the two of them. And yet.

"Heard Lante sing with the band at the tavern last night," Sila's father told her one morning, adding blue milk to his caf. "Just leapt on the stage, grabbed the mic, and improvised five minutes' worth of gliz. Not half bad, unlike *someone else* under the sonics."

"She's a menace," the trapper who lived across the street said when Lante reprogrammed a discarded indoc droid to walk around playing aubade. His indulgent laugh spoke of awe.

"Isn't she just thirteen? Sila, you can barely fix the automatic doors of your father's ship when they get jammed."

THE LAST FLIGHT

"Don't you ever wish your hair looked shiny like that?" her brother—who would deny his crush on Lante for half a decade longer—asked her one night. "Instead of the entrails of banthas, like yours?"

"My hair is only as red and curly as *yours*," Sila hissed, hoping that the "nerf herder" she muttered while storming out reached him loud and clear.

Because Sila didn't see the point of putting goop on her hair, or cozying up to the technos, or having perfect pitch, when everyone knew perfectly well what the future held for her: She was going to become a transport pilot and take over her dad's business with her brothers. All Sila wanted to do was fly, which she was already damn good at, thank you very much. She'd always been quiet, respectful, mild-mannered. She forgave her cousins when they pranked her with that stormtrooper uniform and almost gave her a heart attack, just like she shrugged it off when her brothers went to visit the moss-blanketed ruins of the Ansharii Caverns the very day she had a cold and was stuck in bed. Sila was levelheaded. Not a bundle of joy, and certainly not the type to *like everyone*, but also not one to *dislike anyone*.

Except for Lante. Because for some reason, every centimeter of her skin simmered with loathing at the thought of Lante.

The worst of it was, Lante never reciprocated. She never understood why her existence was a pain in Sila's ass. Instead she would follow Sila around, a manka cat never letting her prey out of sight, the constant smears of grease and oil on her cheeks only making her look more . . . *more*. She'd grin and wave at Sila and say things like, *Wanna check out my new hydrospanner?* Or, *I fixed your dad's holopad, could you return it for me if you're on your way home?* Or, *Watch out for those new transponder buoys, I heard they did a charhound-piss poor job of setting them up.* Or, *Sila, will you—*

"Just leave me alone!" Sila finally erupted when they were sixteen. The explosion was a decade in the making.

"Why are you always so mean," Lante asked, head cocked, more curious than offended. And then, when Sila opened and closed her mouth several times like a fish, no answer forthcoming, Lante just grinned a stupid, brilliant grin. "Never mind," she said. "I know why."

The Imperial Research Station loomed.

No better way to put it—it was a sterile, malignant growth, mutilating the surface of a lush forest planet. Sila had no idea when it had been built. Before she was born, she imagined, because she had no memory of the landscape without it, and by that logic it should have felt as immutable a part of her life as the moons orbiting Toprawa, or her father, or the copilot's chair on the family freighter—but no.

Still, in Sila's world the hatred for the Empire was a lazy, distant thing. Their part of the Rim was sparsely populated, and not rich enough in resources to be anything more than an occasionally convenient afterthought, first of the Republic, then of the Imperial forces. The syndicates and the cartels . . . those were other matters. But when their civil war began, Toprawa's remoteness became more of a blessing than a curse, and being left alone started feeling like a gift.

Lante was seventeen when she impressed the right Imperial scientist and was recruited by the research station. In their corner of Toprawa, not an eye was batted.

"What would you have her do, Sila?" Gave, her eldest brother asked. "Run spice?"

"There has to be a middle ground between running spice and working for the Empire," Sila grumbled. Several others in their community worked at the research station, and Sila had never bothered to look sideways at them. Lante, clearly, inspired every indignant bone in her body.

"Such as?"

She shrugged to avoid admitting that she hadn't thought *that* far. "I don't know. Isn't she always fixing something? She could open a junkyard."

"You do need *some* capital to set up a shop, even one that's mostly refurbished garbage. And now that her aunt has moved to Otor's Hub, Lante's alone in the world. It's not like she has someone providing for her."

Sila hadn't considered that, either, which was more than a little embarrassing. She had grown up with a big family—dad, and three older brothers who were the bane and joy of her existence. Maybe Sila's memories of her mother were few and fuzzy, but the stories everyone exchanged at the dinner table every night made up for it.

As far as Sila knew, Lante never had parents, or any relatives aside from her elderly, ornery aunt who looked more like a great-great-grandmother. But Lante never acted like she'd known loss, and it was hard to imagine that she missed something. Sila suspected that she had sprung to life fully formed, walked out of one of the tall conifers in the Big Woolly, and instantly started puttering with plasma coolant.

"Still," Sila said, more sullen than she felt justified to be.

"Seems a bit hypocritical to judge her for helping the Empire when it's not like any of us are out there joining forces with the Rebel Alliance," her brother Set pointed out.

Sila rolled her eyes.

"Are you envious?" Corl asked. "Because she has an apartment at the research facility and creds? While you still sleep in your childhood bedroom and haven't been able to scrape that chaffir stain off your mattress for the past five years?"

Envy was wanting what someone else had, and Sila would not have traded lives with Lante, not for all the credits in the world, which was why Corl's words did not even deserve a reply.

"I think she is," Set agreed, before starting to singsong like a boy ten years his junior: "*Sila is jealous, Sila is jealous.*"

Jealousy was being afraid to lose something, and that felt . . . disarmingly accurate. So Sila spat, "Shut up, will you?" and went to check if the ship needed any maintenance work done, hating the way automatic doors could never be satisfactorily slammed.

"Long time no see," Lante said, hair even prettier than usual, blush just this side of crimson. The dark sleeves of her tech uniform were rolled up to show her strong, wiry forearms, and clearly the Empire was doing great these days: The rations must have been particularly generous, because Lante looked like she was filling out a bit, healthier than ever before.

Sadly it had been—a long time, that is. Since they'd last seen each other. It had been three months and two weeks and some change of days, and Sila had never been more baffled by her ability to quantify something. "Yeah," she said, feeling like her tongue was too big for her mouth.

"How have you been?"

Sila couldn't think of an answer that wasn't, "What do you want?"

"I'm looking for test pilots." There was something in the way she tossed back her dark waves, in the tilt of her long neck. It reminded Sila of Gave at the market, haggling with the old lady who sold tarsh maxers just to get a discount. *Look what I got for half price, Sila. Thanks to some harmless flirting.* "I seem to remember you were good at that?"

"Doesn't the Empire have their own tester?" Sila asked, a little acidly.

"Yes. But I need the best pilot I know."

Sila refused to feel complimented. She *was* the best pilot on Toprawa, and well aware of it. No need to get worked up over facts. "Why would I help the Empire?"

"For a nice number of credits. Don't you like credits?"

"Not as much as you do, clearly."

Lante's face didn't quite fall, but there was some slippage. "Come on."

"I don't like the Empire."

"Who cares about the Empire, or the Alliance, or whatnot?" Lante huffed. "That stuff is so much bigger than you and I. And if you don't do the testing, someone else will."

"Then let them."

"Fine. They'll pocket the Imperial creds you apparently hate. You okay with that?"

Sila was. Or at least, she said so.

Her brother Set ended up doing the test, and then used the credits to buy a new oxygenator for their freighter. The family business was apparently struggling more than Sila had realized, what with all the smugglers littering the Hydian Way. She'd always been more into flying than finances, but Dad was getting older and definitely more tired. Sila had noticed the way he seemed to doze off on top of the holopad lately, chin gradually dropping to his chest, sometimes when it was still bright outside. One day soon she and her brothers would have to take over, take care of him the way he'd taken care of them for over two decades.

A few weeks later she spotted Lante singing at the tavern, her voice throaty and beautifully curled around a ballad.

"It's getting late," Sila told her friend. She downed her drink, paid, and went home to bed—then couldn't fall asleep for over three hours.

Two months later, when Lante showed up looking to hire Set for more tests, Sila stared at her own feet and mumbled, "He's out on a job. I guess I could do it, though."

It was pilot stock that she came from, and yet, as far as she could tell, her father and brothers never dreamed of flying anything beyond a cargo freighter. Sila, however, had often wondered what it'd be like to do . . . more.

Lante was working on upgrading the performance of several types of Imperial fighters. Better speed, maneuverability, and visibility. Her instructions to Sila before the test were vague: "Push it as much as you can. Performance data will feed directly to me, but I'll want you to tell me the feel of piloting the ship once you're done." She seemed . . . anxious, perhaps. Nervous. Sila had never seen her be anything other than self-assured, and for a moment her brain hitched on this new version of Lante. "You know, *your* personal experience."

When Sila started pressing buttons for the prelaunch checks, electricity hummed between her fingers and the console.

The spaceport grounds shook underneath Sila's boots, a million dizzying jolts that almost had her losing her balance as she tumbled out of the fighter. She had to reach out and furtively lean against the hull, let the durasteel ground her.

The flight had been . . .

Lante ran in her direction, circling around a docking freighter. "Okay, first of all, excellent flying. Nice maneuvers. And the data I collected—really useful stuff, thank you." A frown appeared between her eyebrows. "What did you think about the general . . . feel? I've basically rebuilt the engine units myself, and I'm not really a pilot, so I'm a bit concerned that in practice the flying—"

"Amazing," Sila breathed out. She didn't even bother playing it cool. Simply couldn't.

"Yeah?" Lante grinned.

"Yeah. It's the best ship I've ever flown."

"Okay. Great. I . . . Thank you. It's really . . . thank you." Lante put a hand on Sila's shoulder, and—eighteen years living on the same planet, on the same *street,* and they'd never touched before. Somehow, they'd managed to avoid any sort of physical contact. And Sila knew this for certain, she knew that this was the first time, because . . .

The galaxy seemed to expand all of a sudden. Then compressed once again to a manageable size, but there was something left over from that little groundquake, something scalding that clutched tight around her heart.

Sila's world abruptly reoriented.

Ah, she thought. *Ah.*

Okay. So Lante had known about *this* before her.

Whatever.

This was not a competition.

A few nights before the Battle of Endor, Sila stares at Sullust from the viewport of the *Home One.* The veins of lava glow bright red, poisonous snakes contorting into darkness of space.

Beside her, Tomer and Antilles talk in relaxed tones, caf cups in hand, contemplating a galaxy in which the war is over.

"I think I'd like to be a flight instructor," Antilles says. "Maybe back in Corellia, where my aunt is. Or somewhere along the Trade Spine."

Tomer nods. "Sounds nice."

"What about you? Actually, don't tell me. I don't want to know about your future smuggling enterprises."

Tomer laughs and turns to Sila. "What about you?" he asks. "Where will you go once we're finally free?"

Sila traces a stream of lava against the transparisteel, but remains quiet. She has nothing to say. Above all, she has nowhere to go.

Once was an accident, twice a coincidence, *maybe,* but three times.

Three. Kriffing. Times.

"They know I've been wanting to go to the Ansharii Caverns since I was a child, they *know,* but they always make the trip when I can't go along." Sila's hand closed around a rock wedged on the soil between her and Lante. She picked it up and threw it into the lake, watching the surface ripple in expanding circles.

"Your brothers are nice," Lante said, noncommittally. "I like them."

"Right." Sila did her best to avoid a pout. It wasn't enough. "Well, they like you, too, so it's reciprocal. Glad you guys are best friends—"

"Not."

"—honestly, I'm surprised they didn't invite *you* to go with them—"

"My point is, *Sila.*" It felt weird, Lante saying her name. Like a shiver, but hot. "They're nice, but they're not the only people on the planet." Her knuckle brushed against the side of Sila's dirty palm, and it didn't feel like an accident.

Sila blinked. "What do you mean?"

"There are other options. You could go on that same excursion with others."

"Like . . . who?"

Lante's only answer was another of those wide grins. Her eyes were green, as brilliant and perfect a green as the leaves of the nearby bush.

Sila told her family that she wouldn't be around the following day, expecting questions or protests or some kind of reaction and receiving no more than a shrug. Lante asked her superior for leave and was answered with a resounding "Whatever," because most of her team was going to be testing something that wasn't flight-related anyway.

And then they were off.

Sila would remember it in bursts, that day. There had been a flow of events that she could reconstruct—arguing over who would drive the speeders, reaching the caverns, hiking, snacking, watching the sun set, and reluctantly agreeing to head back home. And yet their time together would live in Sila's brain not like a holovid, but in isolated moments. Unmoving, but as real as the ruins of a Jedi temple.

The wind in their hair as Lante's arms held tight around her waist.

Laughter after slipping over a sleek boulder.

The sweetness of the starfruits they packed.

Taking Lante's hand to cross a river, and forgetting to let go.

Cool fingers on Sila's forehead, blood rushing her cheeks, and an amused, "As scarlet as your hair. You always burned so easily," before a small jar of sunscreen oil was produced.

And then, finally, coming home.

To a shattered galaxy, and the words: "There was an accident, Sila. I'm so sorry."

"At the facility, they've been working on building some kind of laser to help with mining," Stefan explained to her that night, taking a seat at the table in the kitchen, a seat that had been Set's since he'd turned five. Stefan had been a friend of her father for many years. Worked at the Imperial Research Station for a few of them. "There was something wrong with the gas, and the laser malfunctioned during testing. And your family's freighter was... I wish it *hadn't* been where it was."

Gave and Set and Corl had been on that ship. Dad, too, and Sila couldn't grasp it, couldn't conceive a world where her noisy, importune, annoying, adored family was not surrounding her, suffocating her.

But Lante was there. She took Sila's numb hand under the table on that first night, and held it during the days that followed, squeezing it throughout the funerals at all the right times.

After everything was over, they lay down together in Sila's bed, heads close on her pillow, without even bothering to close the door. No one else lived in this house now. It was Sila's. Corl's beloved gyroball, the one no one was allowed to touch ever, not even the cleaning bot—that, too, was hers. Together with the racy holovids Set hid in his closet, and Dad's Corellian whiskey, and Gave's little cruiser. Everything was Sila's, because she was alone.

"I'm going to make sure it doesn't happen again," Lante promised against her ear. "I'm going to make sure that the research station doesn't screw up ever again."

Sila frowned. "How?" It was a genuine question.

"What do you mean?"

"Just... how? You're not going back there, are you?"

It didn't occur to Sila that she was making assumptions, not until Lante slowly sat up, slowly turned to look at her, slowly made a sorrowful, apologetic face.

"Lante. You're joking, right?"

Lante swallowed. "I'm sure they didn't mean it. It was an accident."

Sila sat up, too. "It was. But they didn't even acknowledge that they

THE LAST FLIGHT

accidentally killed *four people*. And tomorrow they're going back to building weapons that will kill more people, *on purpose*. Who gave them the right."

"But—"

"The Empire is taking over the entire galaxy, and you know what it means? It means that they'll have even more power, and they'll be able to do what they want, where they want, with no consequences."

"Maybe. But this is what the Empire does—what *everyone* does. The entire system is corrupt, and the war is bigger than you and me. We can only accept it. What is the alternative—going off with the rebels?"

Sila hadn't even considered it, and she said nothing, but apparently it was enough for Lante.

"Oh, come on, Sila. You can't really . . ." Her face was slowly crumpling with something that looked remarkably like fear, and pain, and the same loss Sila held in her heart in that very moment. "If you leave . . . If you leave me . . . You and I . . ."

Sila spent the night alone but did not sleep. Gradually, the numbness of the last few days dissipated, and among all of her hazy, possible futures, one in particular began to solidify.

The following day, she left.

The Rebellion was too busy saving the galaxy to be a family, and it certainly didn't feel like home, or even an approximation of it. But it was something to do, and the more Sila stuck with them, the more she grew to believe in their cause.

For the first few months, she felt like something that belonged in the bathroom. Then, little by little, the sharp pain of losing her family, her planet, dulled to a constant ache—hard to ignore, always present, but finally manageable. Cargo pilots always came in handy, and Sila had plenty of experience to provide. But when Commander Narra put her through the flight simulator, hoping to find someone who'd join the starfighter squadron, Sila threw the test on a hunch. The thought of taking a life—even an Imperial life—was too heavy to bear.

She tried not to think of Lante too much, but she still did.

More than she should have.

In the Endor system, Sila moves her starfighter into attack position, ready to strike the Imperial fleet, waiting only for Antilles's commands.

But her eyes fall on the *Executor,* and her mind goes down the usual, dangerous path.

How many crew does a vessel like that carry? How many troops and support staff? Hundreds of thousands, probably. And how many of them joined the Empire because they felt they had no other choice? How many of them have families, lovers, friends back on their home planets? If the rebels win and the *Executor* is destroyed, how many people will be left behind, haunted by grief and loss for years to come?

The Empire may have taken her family, but the idea of taking someone else's doesn't give Sila any satisfaction. Revenge is just a pale, inadequate imitation of what she really wants: justice.

There is no right or wrong, Sila is starting to suspect. Like Antilles once told her, there's only the hope of leaving the galaxy a better place than it is now.

It was Sila's second year with the Alliance. Someone tapped her shoulder when she was in the middle of cleaning the bathroom on one of the freighters. Not her favorite task, but decontamination was

THE LAST FLIGHT

a necessary evil, and it wasn't as though Sila hadn't grown up with three brothers who thought the height of hygiene was spraying themselves with cheap perfume.

"I have something for you, Sila."

She turned around. It was one of the rebel intelligence agents, someone Sila barely knew. But if she wasn't mistaken, he'd recently been sent on a mission to . . .

"From Toprawa," the agent continued.

"Oh." Sila had no one left on Toprawa. With one single exception, that probably didn't count. "Who is it from?" she asked, heart already beating faster.

"One of our informants. I met with her while I was gathering intel on the Imperial facility, just a few days ago. She asked me to give this to you."

He deposited a holoprojector in Sila's hand. Sila's steady, pilot hand, that immediately began shaking. She could have asked for the identity of the sender, but she had a good idea of who it might be. Except, the person she was thinking of would never serve as an informant for the Rebellion. Right?

She took a deep breath, and activated the holoprojector.

Lante's beautiful face instantly materialized in front of Sila, stealing the air from her lungs. She looked . . . very much like she always had: beautiful face, green eyes, ridiculously shiny hair. She also looked tired, and a little older, and as though she'd been crying.

Her voice sounded thin and faraway. "Sila, I . . . I was wrong. And you were right. And"—a warm, amused laugh—"right now I would give anything to hear you say *I told you so,* but I'm still here on Toprawa, still at the facility, and you are . . . who knows where you are? But it doesn't matter. I don't have a lot of time to record this. But I wanted you to know . . ." Her voice broke. Attempted to restart, but didn't quite manage. "I was *so* wrong. And I did . . . something. A thing that will count as an apology, I hope." There was a commotion outside of Lante's door. Her voice dropped to a whisper. "Sila, I have to go. And this is goodbye, but . . . I'll see you again, I know I will. I don't know when, but . . ." Tears filled her eyes, even as she smiled. "Why don't you surprise me?"

The message ended there.

Two days later, an Alliance agent brought back the news that the Imperial Research Station in Toprawa was no longer functional.

"Could be sabotage. But our forces had nothing to do with it, so we suspect an accident."

A list of the known casualties appeared on the holoscreen, not in alphabetical order. Sila read the third name, waited for her heart to start beating again, and excused herself. She didn't want to cry in front of her comrades, so she feigned the Dantari flu for the rest of the day. She spent it in bed, remembering Lante's arms looped around her waist and the mossy scent of the Ansharii Caverns.

A perfect day, it had been. The last of its kind.

Sila is no master of the art of war, nor does she care to be, but it's starting to become apparent that Endor was an ambush. At the very least, the Alliance was lured here by misleading intel. The Death Star is at least partially operational and shielded, the Imperial fleet has clearly been waiting for them, and Sila has never seen so many Star Destroyers in one place. She didn't even know this many *existed*.

The rebels are outnumbered. Swarmed by TIE fighters, interceptors, bombers. The space around them is a chaos of red and green laser bolts and debris. At the periphery of her vision, she sees the

THE LAST FLIGHT

Millennium Falcon destroy three TIE fighters, and exults in the cramped cockpit of her ship.

But then two more TIEs appear; that's when the order comes.

"Red Three, Red Two. Pull in," Antilles says.

He wants them to stick close and be as safe as possible. But Sila knows that what her wingmates really need is a diversion—and that *she* can provide it. She can lead the interceptors away from them, so she doesn't hesitate.

Or maybe she does. Just a fraction of a second before answering her commander—just long enough to think of her brothers. Her father. Her homeworld. Of everything that the Empire has taken from her, and everything that will be given back if the Death Star is destroyed. The kind of galaxy that will be rebuilt if the Alliance triumphs in this battle.

"Got it," Sila says, just before defying her commander's order.

Interceptors on her heels, she allows her flying instincts to take over. She dives abruptly, maneuvering toward the immense surface of the rebel cruiser. When the TIEs chase her, she feels triumphant, knowing that her plan worked. Until she realizes her mistake: The TIEs are much closer than Sila expected, and she's in their firing range.

The rest of the squadron manages to get away. That's why, out of all her mistakes, Sila would make this one over and over and over again.

Right before the Imperial lasers strike her, before her fighter explodes into a million atoms, before becoming little more than space dust, Sila is not scared. Her last moment is full of vibrant joy.

Lante. I hope you're ready to be surprised.

TWENTY AND OUT

Lamar Giles

Corr Lerrann inspected himself in the mirror, the squared-away image that would soon be a part of his past looking and feeling more surreal as the end of his watch grew closer. Would he miss it? he wondered.

Miss what? his insistent internal voice countered. The endless deployments? The cramped berthing areas that smelled like Klatooinian feet no matter how much you cleaned? The drilling, monotony, and bureaucracy that made up the vast majority of what it took to protect the Empire from evil?

"No," he told the voice he'd come to think of as the Veteran, a better version of himself that not only relished the thought of life after the Imperial Navy but had a rock-solid plan to thrive. "I won't miss any of that."

Corr smoothed the wrinkles in his black uniform, tucked his gleaming beetle shell of a helmet under his arm, and began his trek to the food district for a meal before reporting for duty at initiator laser cannon five.

He was a Death Star gunner, and after twenty years in the Imperial Navy, this was his last week on the platform.

"Lerrann!" Tay Kando, his platform partner, called from their usual table. A loose group of Imperial weapons techs occupied seats with an empty chair reserved for Corr. They were in unusually high spirits, the mood that infected anyone who'd been on the battle station for more than a few days and got a sense they were about to experience something new, or just different.

Was this about the Emperor?

Their entire hemisphere had been abuzz with the arrival of His Eminence. For most he was just a floating face in a holo. Given the vastness of the Death Star that was still all he'd ever be if you didn't know someone who knew someone that could get you assigned to the greeting party when he arrived at the hangar a full one hundred kilometers from where Corr stood.

He cringed thinking of that garrison stuck at attention to watch Palpatine walk past and ignore them. Row upon row of ego stroking for a man who barely bothered to look soldiers who'd die for his whims in the eye.

Careful, the Veteran voice warned.

Corr's patience for worthless pomp and circumstance had gotten as short as his time on this station.

But he was always careful. He'd not come this far to let his frustra-

TWENTY AND OUT

tions with Imperial leadership derail his plans. If all worked out, there would come a time when he might be in close proximity to the galaxy's elite, including the Emperor. Rumor had it you had to guard your thoughts when near the ruler, especially if Palpatine's Goon in Chief Darth Vader was present. They said the masked wizard could read minds.

Anyhow... no way the weapons techs hooting and hollering at his approach were this eager over Palpatine. They were all true believers in the *cause,* not the figureheads. So, what then?

"Is this my retirement party?" Corr joked.

"Not even close," Pog Degor, a tech who worked the firing station board on the other side of initiator laser canon five, said, "We're doing that in the southern hemisphere at Death Bar Two night after next."

Kando smacked Pog in the back of the head. "Surprise. Party. Ever heard of it?"

"Sorry."

Pog had already let the secret slip a week ago, but it touched Corr how into it Kando was. They'd grown close during their years as gunners across various vessels.

Kando turned his attention to Corr and said, "So is today the day you tell us or what?"

Corr's goodwill toward his friend decreased by half. He took his reserved seat at the center of the gathering and considered all the expectant gazes.

Kando primed the group. "Corr's got a secret plan to make a billion credits once he's a civilian. I've been waiting years to hear it."

There were chuckles of disbelief. Not surprising. Everyone who got out of the navy had a big plan, and most amounted to a new way of taking orders from someone they despised. Not Corr, though.

He'd kept his secret close for years because it was *that good,* and to let it slip when he still had years of service left risked someone older and quicker beating him to it. But with retirement looming, and preliminary connections to the proper power brokers already made, no one could filch his ingenious plan now. Why not let his best mates in on it? They'd all retire eventually, and maybe he could be the one they'd be taking orders from on the outside.

"Come on, Corr," Pog prodded, though he didn't have to.

Corr said, "All right. Fine. Question . . . what's the number four highest cause of trooper deaths in the Imperial military?"

Pog furrowed his brow, considering. "Well, number one is rebel scum. Everyone knows that."

"And number two is Vader chokes," Kando joked at nearly a whisper, getting absolutely no laughs.

Everyone else shrugged and grunted.

Corr let the silence linger for the sake of drama before he said, "It's falling off platforms. Catwalks. *Bridges.*"

More shrugs and grunts.

Kando said, "So what? How do you get a billion credits out of that?"

Corr leaned in, ready to fire the biggest weapon in his arsenal. "Two words. Safety. Rails. I'm going to start a business that supplies all the hundreds of thousands of Imperial facilities and ships with safety rails that will reduce the number of trooper deaths by a significant—"

There was more to say. Much more.

But Corr's teammates were laughing too hard to let him finish.

"I don't think it's a *bad* idea," Kando said. He didn't sound like he thought it was a good idea, either.

Corr clenched his jaw—not that Kando would notice since they'd

TWENTY AND OUT

both donned their helmets—and focused on the numbers ticking up in the turbolift display.

Kando continued, "All I'm saying is if the Empire cared enough about quote-unquote 'safety' to buy into your idea, they would've done it by now."

"No, no, no!" Corr snapped. "You're thinking about it all wrong."

"Enlighten me, then."

"This is wartime. Of course they're sticking to old models—the rebel threat won't allow anyone a breather for innovation." Corr held up his hand, his thumb and index finger millimeters apart. "We're *this close* to crushing the rebellion. Once the threat's eliminated, we're in peacetime. Historically that's when civilizations make leaps and bounds in all aspects of technology, customs, thinking. My idea will be so beneficial that anyone with half a brain will see the wisdom in providing a safer work environment for those who serve."

"In the next war, you mean?"

"Sure. I suppose."

Kando said, "Seems to me if everyone's making such big leaps in thinking, there shouldn't be a next war. But what do I know?"

Within ten levels of their destination the air began to change. The slightly scorched scent of ozone over increased artificial oxygen could overwhelm if you weren't used to it the way Corr and Kando were. Anytime you got close to an open port with only a force-field generator protecting you from naked space, you felt it with every sense.

The lift dinged and opened onto a small, narrow platform overlooking a yawning maw. Hello, initiator laser canon five! Corr and Kando stepped out onto their post, carefully, and gave a go-ahead wave to the guys across the tributary beam shaft in the superlaser firing station.

Pog snapped off a salute from his console. His voice crackled through the receivers in Corr's and Kando's helmets. "Safety rails," he said, laughing.

Laser cannon five was actually conduit five of eight. Eight conduits were spaced around the central amplification nexus at the center of the Death Star's superlaser array, the one responsible for propelling a concentrated beam of apocalyptic energy toward whoever dared challenge the Empire.

Every tributary beam shaft was identical. A tunnel running from multiple small beam generators powered by kyber crystals to the force-field-shielded exterior of the base. Corr knew everything about beam shaft five because all they'd done since deploying was study and test the superlaser. Dry fire. Single-beam fire. Four-beam fire. All working up to an eventual full-power, eight-beam blast whenever the Emperor made the call. Until then . . .

"What's on the menu today?" Corr asked the firing station.

"We are standing by," Pog replied.

Kando's helmet tipped toward Corr, signaling the same confusion Corr felt. If they were standing by, why were the energy readings on their platform monitor ramped up so high? They were in eight-beam range when they hadn't even tested a six-beam blast yet.

Kando said, "Should we power down?"

"I asked the same thing," Pog said. "I was told to hold steady."

Yeah! Sure! Don't explain decisions to the guys doing the work, the Veteran in Corr's head said. No. He wouldn't miss this.

Kando leaned on the board—the only thing you could lean on given the precarious nature of the platform—as annoyed as Corr. "Since we've got time to kill, walk me through it."

"What for? You're only going to have jokes."

"Seriously. I'm trying to understand."

"Leaning on our board like that, you should already understand. Wouldn't it be nice if there was a rail you could shift your weight to?

TWENTY AND OUT

Or a combination rail-and-glass partition so you could sit down safely and comfortably with full view of the conduit. Or, you'll really think I'm crazy now, but hear me out: What if our platform was a completely enclosed booth? No way to fall out of it."

Kando contemplated. "So, like another firing station?"

"Exactly."

"I don't know, Corr. Next thing you'll be saying our board should just be in the main control room to begin with. Clearly there are reasons for things being like they are."

"Are there, though?"

It wasn't like just anyone could get their hands on Death Star plans, but Corr often wished he understood the decision making that went into the more puzzling designs. Why so many seemingly bottomless pits?

"What else?" Kando asked.

"Well, I thought about some sort of netting, but I don't think that would fit the Imperial aesthetic."

"No! I'm only three years behind you and I want to hear about some fun stuff. What else do you have planned for retirement that's not more work?"

It was a difficult question. Corr knew because he'd asked himself the same thing many times. "I'm thinking of getting a dwelling on Coruscant. Maybe something in the Urscru District. I don't know."

"You must be real good with credits. I don't think I could afford a one-bedroom in CoCo Town."

"I mean, twenty years. One ship after another. I didn't spend hardly anything."

So many sailors burned through credits as soon as they got them. Usually at onboard bars, putting the funds right back into Palpatine's pockets. Corr always knew better, even in the early days. He never planned to give his all to the Empire.

"I know a waitress, a Zeltron. We had some fun over the years. Stayed in touch. Maybe . . . you know . . . she'll want to pick back up . . . maybe settle down."

Kando's smirk was only slightly envious. "Settle down with a Zeltron? That's your worst idea yet! If she happens to have a sibling, though, you can put in a word for—"

"BATTLE STATIONS! BATTLE STATIONS!"

Corr and Kando's training kicked in. They sprang to attention, no questions. Another unplanned emergency drill. An extremely realistic one. They would pass the test.

Kando shouted readings from the board. Numbers and jargon that would seem nonsensical to anyone who hadn't spent over a year in weapons training and multiple years working heavy weaponry on ships across the fleet, but Corr's fingers were nimble on the levers and dials, adjusting accordingly.

To fire.

These calculations were for an eight-beam shot. Not full power, but any hypothetical target on the receiving end of the blast wouldn't appreciate the courtesy of getting hit with only a quarter of planet-destroying power.

Even as the vibration of the beam generators grew enough to rattle teeth, and a glance into the control room saw Pog and the others in a frenzy, Corr still didn't believe they'd actually fire *all eight beams.* They'd had dry-fire drills before where they'd gone right up to ignition before the scenario was called off. Surely this would be the same!

Someone in the control room gave a sharp thumbs-up. Before Corr and Kando could brace, the beam fired! A green spear of hard light with bursting amber pulses at its core. It blasted through the force field at the end of the conduit where it would merge with the other seven beams and do what it was designed to do.

But Corr was less concerned with the particulars of the shot than

TWENTY AND OUT

he was with his platform partner, who'd overbalanced in the wake of the beam.

Kando's arms pinwheeled, one boot completely off the platform as he tipped backward toward the maw. Corr leapt forward, understanding too late that he wasn't anchored to anything and in grabbing his panicking partner, he risked toppling over, too. Kando grasped Corr's forearm, screaming, not intending to drag Corr with him, but the physics were not on their side. They'd die here. During what was maybe, maybe not, a training exercise, if Corr didn't . . .

He grabbed the power oscillation lever, a flimsy thing, but all there was to clutch. It wouldn't have been enough except Kando managed to wedge a toe on the vertical plane of the platform and thrust some of his weight back up, enough for Corr to lurch into a backbend and tow them both to safety.

They collapsed beside each other, gasping. Corr glanced at the control room where everyone pressed against the glass watching the near-death pantomime that couldn't have lasted more than a second or two.

Kando forced himself to his hands and knees, while Corr hinged at the hip.

"Safety rails," Kando said with a shaky voice. "I think you're onto something."

Corr said, "When I make my first billion, me and you are going to Zeltros. My treat."

"What happened to settling down?"

"Just saw my life flash before my eyes and I'm reconsidering. What did we shoot at?"

Pog's voice crackled through their receivers. "Rebels. The fools are attacking. We're lighting them up right now. Get ready. This might be our shot to wipe them out once and for all. And stay on the platform this time."

Corr and Kando burned with rage over how little regard their near demise elicited. That was life in the Imperial Navy, though. Do your job, try not to die. But if you do die, make sure your job is done first.

"No, not missing any of this!" Corr said.

"What?" Kando and Pog said at the same time.

"Nothing."

Kando returned to his post. Corr did the same. While he played his part at his station in this last battle against the rebels, the Veteran spoke in the back of his mind.

Seven more days, short-timer. One last battle! Then you're twenty and out.

And the galaxy is yours!

THE BALLAD OF NANTA
Sarah Kuhn

It all started with a tree.

Not the Great Tree, the majestic forest giant from which all Ewoks are descended. No, this one was but a scrawny runt, its lone uncertain branch forever reaching for the lush forest canopy covering the Endor sky.

Nanta first discovered this tree as a wokling toddling out of the Hut of Healing. He was sporting a fresh new wound dressing thanks to an unfortunate run-in with a jagged bit of stone on the forest floor. The way Nanta told it, said bit of stone leapt from the shadows while Logray, Bright Tree Village's head shaman, delivered an important lesson to the tribe's woklings about the healing properties of various native plants. It wasn't Nanta's fault the Nefarious Stone of Evil had chosen to target him (specifically his left foot, which had the misfortune of landing on the stone's most jagged point just as it emerged from the shadows), but it was certainly lucky that it had done so during the most excruciatingly dull portion of the lesson. Logray had shot him a long-suffering look and sent him to the Hut of Healing, where Nanta was already a regular patron.

He hadn't noticed the tree until that day, though. The sun filtering through the forest green was especially enchanting that hour, slivers of magic scattering golden light over that tree's single branch. While it was as tall as the mighty trees that made up so much of the village, it was not nearly strong enough to support even a single hut. It simply existed next to them, as if waiting for its chance at greatness.

Nanta found himself drawn to the tree because it looked like it was trying very hard to be a *proper* tree, and he could not help but feel something like kinship. He *tried* to pay attention to Logray's lectures about plants, to the chief hunter's teachings on gathering food, to all the stern drills on defending oneself from predators. But his mind always seemed to drift, to wander to things that were more *interesting*.

Like: What did the Great Tree *do* when she wasn't being worshipped or housing various important ceremonies or receiving the spirits who returned to her after death? And what existed beyond the canopy of trees, what lived amid the world of endless sky and stars? Why did his people never venture out there?

Nanta's mother and father could only give him pained looks—much like the one Logray had given him—when he asked these questions, *what* and *why* and *how*. They would tell him to hush. Things just *were*—no need for further explanation or exploration. Then they would tell him he needed to devote more of this endless thinking energy to topics that were useful. The memorizing of plants and the hunting and gathering and all that.

THE BALLAD OF NANTA

This was something else he tried very hard to do. Just like this tree was trying to be a tree.

Nanta realized his feet had carried him over to the tree, as if of their own volition. He stared at it for a moment, shifting back and forth, and winced as the dressing on his left foot rubbed against his wound. Perhaps it was his imagination (which, as his parents liked to remind him, was quite vivid), but the tree seemed to incline its lone branch toward him, as if asking . . . *What happened?*

Nanta hesitated, his paw curling around the jagged stone—Logray's apprentice had allowed him to keep it as a souvenir of his small adventure.

Tell me, the tree seemed to say.

Nanta was dying to tell *someone* about his run-in with the Nefarious Stone of Evil . . . and how, now that it was clutched in his paw, said stone did not seem *quite* as evil as it had upon first glance. He also knew that his mother and father and Logray and just about everyone else he could think of would be very uninterested in this story, and that he would likely see their eyes drifting closed as soon as he started telling it.

So he stepped into the tree's sacred space and raised the No Longer Quite as Nefarious Stone, its jagged edge glinting in the golden light. And he carved his story in the tree's rough surface, each word building to this moment.

Perhaps it was his imagination again, but he sensed the sun's glow brighten around the tree. And he could have sworn that single branch stood just a little prouder when he was done.

The day after he carved his first story, Nanta's parents made him return to Logray for a makeup lesson. Once again, he tried to pay attention. And once again, his mind wandered.

"Child," the shaman said at last, after explaining the difference between knettleroot and knettleberry for the third time, "this business of plants and herbs is clearly not of interest to you. May I ask what is?"

Nanta hesitated. No one had ever asked him that before.

"It is the . . . the why of things," he finally answered. "And also the how. And the what. But not as in, 'Which plant cures what malady?' or 'What is the best way to craft a spear?' More like . . ." He frowned, struggling to find the words. "Why are we here? Where did we come from and where will we go? And what exists beyond the stars?"

"Ah." A knowing glint sparked in Logray's eyes. "You are concerned with the greater questions of our people: our past, our future, our story as it unspools in Bright Tree Village and wherever our wanderings may take us. And I have certainly noticed your very, ah, vibrant imagination."

Logray tilted his head at Nanta, one fuzzy ear twitching as he assessed the wokling.

"Have you ever heard of a Storykeeper?"

"No," said Nanta, even though he could feel his own ears perk up. Something about that word sent a certain undeniable feeling through him—as if he had once again stepped into his scrawny tree's golden light.

"It is not as official a mantle as shaman or chief," Logray said. "The tribe does not require us to have one at all times—we do not have one now. But we have at different points in the past, and sometimes we have had more than one. Where do you think all of our tales and songs came from? The ballads that are sung around the fire, about the Great Tree and our most fearsome battles against the mighty Gorax?"

"Storykeeper," Nanta said, wondering how a single word could sound at once mysterious and like the answer to a question he'd never known to ask.

THE BALLAD OF NANTA

"Storykeepers hold all of our greatest legends—both true and made up and sometimes a little bit of each," the shaman explained. "And they often craft their own—again, both true and made up."

"And sometimes a little bit of each," Nanta murmured.

"These stories are passed down among our people, so that we never forget how we came to be and who we are," Lograg continued.

"Or *why* we are," Nanta said thoughtfully.

Lograg's eyes got that knowing glint. "Indeed. You know, it has been many seasons since our village had any Storykeepers. But I sense we will soon need one."

Nanta didn't say anything. He was too busy thinking. But later, after he left Lograg (having finally memorized the difference between knettleroot and knettleberry, sort of), he found himself drawn to the scrawny tree behind the Hut of Healing.

And once there, he carved everything the shaman had told him into its surface.

From there, one might conclude Nanta's path was set. But stories—be they true or made up or a little bit of each—are funny things.

As the seasons turned, Nanta devoted himself to the business of Storykeeping. Whenever something interesting happened—to him or a fellow tribe member or Bright Tree Village as a whole—he carved it into the tree. And once in a while, he would cast his gaze toward that endless sky and carve a new tale that was entirely made up, about a curious wokling who ventured into the stars. He felt sure such a fantastical journey would provide many new stories.

As the tree's trunk began to fill with Nanta's painstakingly carved words, sometimes he would set them to music, crafting ballads to sing around the fire. His very first—"The Ballad of the Astounding Quest of the Not So Nefarious Stone"—did not make much of a mark, but he kept at it. Slowly but surely, many of the villagers started clamoring for his works, and after his rousingly successful introduction of "The Ballad of Logray's Fearsome Fight Against a Particularly Poisonous Knettleberry," he could barely write fast enough to meet demand. And yet, Nanta hesitated when it came to asking the village elders to grant him the mantle of Storykeeper.

I will know when I am worthy, he thought. *I will feel it in my blood as surely as I felt the call of my tree bathed in golden light.*

When the Skull Ones swooped in from the sky, setting up camp and destroying a neighboring village, Nanta wrote furiously, even as tears for the slain inhabitants streamed from his eyes and matted his fur. It seemed especially important that no one forget what had happened.

And when the Golden One was brought to Bright Tree Village, Nanta channeled his feelings of awe into a ballad that was to be performed at the celebratory feast. The feast was unfortunately cut short when the Golden One protested the menu, though Nanta could not help but feel that the main course of Fleshy Ones looked quite delectable. Still, he was able to refine "The Ballad of the Glorious Golden One" for a later performance.

That night, when the Golden One told the full story of his people and their journey, Nanta was enthralled. He admired the Golden One's way with words—perhaps he was a Storykeeper as well. But more importantly, Nanta was swept away by the potent swirl of emotions the Golden One's tale evoked. He was overcome with wonder learning about so many new worlds. He thrilled in the descriptions of all the incredible things that could be found in that vast sky of stars. Just as he'd always believed, there was so much out there. So much to explore and experience and be inspired by, beyond the canopy of the forest.

So many stories.

THE BALLAD OF NANTA

And as the Golden One continued, rage sparked in Nanta's heart at all the horrors the Skull Ones and their leaders had visited upon innocent beings. When Chief Chirpa announced that Bright Tree Village would aid the Golden One's fight, Nanta's voice joined with all the others in a cheer that shook the treetops.

As the village elders began constructing tactical plans, Nanta bolted out into the night and found his tree, eager to carve the story of what had just transpired. He was surprised to see someone else there, another Ewok he did not recognize on sight. Usually, Nanta was the only one who paid this tree any mind.

"This is yours," the other Ewok said by way of greeting, gesturing to all the words carved into the tree. They now covered nearly every inch of bark Nanta could reach. "I've been hearing of the Ewok who writes tales in this tree—a future Storykeeper, they say."

"That is me—I am called Nanta," Nanta said. "But I am not Storykeeper just yet."

"I can see that you will be," the other Ewok said, turning back to the tree. "I am called Romba. I am one of the few survivors of the Skull Ones' invasion."

"From the village that was destroyed," Nanta realized, tears rising in his eyes. "I offer many sorrows for your losses."

"I can see you felt it quite deeply," Romba said, gesturing to the section of tree where Nanta had recorded the tale of the destroyed village. "Thank you for preserving our story, so it will not be forgotten. I am moved that you have captured not only the tragedy, but also the many joys our tribe celebrated before the Skull Ones came."

"It would not be a complete story otherwise," Nanta said, his tears threatening to spill over. "Will you join the fight tomorrow?"

"I will," Romba said, drawing himself up tall. "And you?"

Nanta hesitated, turning back to the tree. He had never been the most battle-ready Ewok—that was apparent early on, when his little wokling self had such a hard time paying attention to combat drills and spear-making lessons. And as he'd dedicated more of his life to Storykeeping, he'd had less time for such things.

But he couldn't deny the fury the Golden One's story provoked in him, or the sadness that threatened to overwhelm his entire being when he thought of Romba's destroyed village. All of those feelings knotted together in his chest and pushed a single word from his throat.

"Yes," he said, meeting Romba's eyes. "I will be there, to help right many wrongs and hope that further tragedy is prevented. And Romba..."

He paused, allowing his gaze to wander to the stories he'd fully made up—the fanciful tales of a wokling exploring the worlds beyond the forest, catapulting into those beautiful stars. Finding new stories without end.

"Once we have defeated the Skull Ones and their leaders, do you think Ewoks might venture into the sky, just as the Golden One described?"

"I think it is a very good possibility," Romba said, a twinkle appearing in his somber eyes.

"I must train tonight," Nanta said. "I am not the most skilled in spear making. Or any aspects of battle."

"I will make you a pact," Romba said, giving Nanta a solemn nod. "I am a veteran of battle. Tomorrow, we will stay together and keep eyes on each other. We will go through this fight as partners, whatever it may bring. And once it is finished, you will write the story of our triumph in this tree—after that, I don't believe you will be able to deny your mantle as Storykeeper any longer."

"Yes," Nanta breathed, a slight smile tugging at his mouth. He could not exactly explain it, but as soon as Romba said these words,

THE BALLAD OF NANTA

he knew them to be true. His entire life had been building to this moment, and he felt it as surely as he'd felt his first connection to the tree.

After tomorrow, he would be Storykeeper. And then he would explore the stars. He would discover the stories he'd always dreamed of.

Everything was so loud.

Nanta was no stranger to noise, bustle, chaos—Bright Tree Village had all of these things in abundance. But it was different in the heat of battle. The smoke that curled into his nostrils had the acrid singe of a destructive explosion, rather than the homey scent of campfire. Raised voices shattered with raw desperation, rather than joy or anger. The constant need to run and leap and dodge and hit skittered through Nanta's bloodstream, forcing him to simply react instead of thinking anything through.

And yet exhilaration blossomed in his chest, that precious sense of being alive in the world—perhaps more alive than ever.

Romba kept to his word, sticking by Nanta's side as they darted around trees and ducked under errant branches, trying to escape the blasts from the Skull Ones. He could see how skilled Romba was in battle, finding hiding places that seemed to appear out of nowhere and launching well-timed attacks that were so cunning, Nanta wondered if he practiced sorcery.

"Come . . . this way!" Romba hissed, placing a paw on a low stump and vaulting over it. Nanta attempted to replicate the move and only stumbled a little.

Romba then raised a finger to his lips and crept toward a clump of Ewok scouts that had clustered up behind a pile of fallen rocks. Nanta followed, perking his ears so he could hear the whispers among his compatriots.

"We're going to ambush the Skull Ones," Romba murmured, immediately picking up on the plan. He gestured to a group of Skull Ones positioned behind a large fallen tree, using their rough weapons to send blasts of sparks and light toward the Golden One's people. "They are unguarded from behind and have chosen their formation poorly!"

Nanta nodded, huddling with Romba and the others and raising his spear. That exhilaration was blazing through him like wildfire now, making his heart beat so loudly, he wondered if the Skull Ones could hear it.

He stayed in the middle of the pack as the Ewoks shuffled forward, their feet soundless against the forest floor. He wondered why everything about the Skull Ones seemed designed to stick out as much as possible in the quiet greenery of his home—the stark brightness of their armor, the harsh metals of their weapons. It did not appear to be the best battle strategy—he'd definitely have to describe that in the story he would write about today.

Nanta breathed deeply and focused on the Skull Ones, who were still firing their weapons with careless abandon. He attempted to memorize every detail of this moment—the way the Skull Ones were so out of place in his world, the steely determination he could feel emanating from Romba, the wild beating of his own heart.

Two more deep breaths and they were upon the Skull Ones and Romba was yelling, "*Now!*"

Nanta felt strangely disconnected from his body as his spear swung through the air, a cry of rage erupting from his throat. It was as if he was driven by instinct so pure, it powered him forward before his brain could form a thought. And when he and Romba brought their spears down on the heads of the Skull Ones and watched them fall, triumph ripped through him, a sense that they were avenging Romba's lost village and everyone else who had been hurt by these invaders.

THE BALLAD OF NANTA

"We did it!" Romba exclaimed, breathless. "Now let's head for the Skull Ones on the other side of the clearing and do the same!"

Nanta tightened his grip on his spear, purpose flowing through his veins. He could already see the words of his story carving themselves into the tree, stirring descriptions of Romba's assured leadership and the sensation of becoming an essential part of the forest as he and his fellow warriors moved as one.

What would he call this tale? "The Ballad of the Epic Battle Against the Skull Ones"? "The Ballad of Romba's Revenge"? "The Ballad of—"

Suddenly, the ground began to shake.

Nanta whirled around, his head whipping back and forth as he scanned an expanse of trees so tall, they were like giants.

But then a different kind of giant emerged.

It was nearly as tall as the trees, a dingy gray color, and made up of surfaces that looked similar to the hard, unyielding armor of the Skull Ones. Its eyes were empty black squares, uncanny and strangely unseeing. And its mouth boasted an odd protrusion that looked like a collection of harshly angled things that did not go together, a bizarre mockery of a tongue.

It stomped forward on wobbly legs, its massive feet creating little groundquakes on the forest floor.

"Walkers," Romba breathed, his voice threaded with fear. "Abort the plan—we need to run."

The walker stomped the ground once again, sending reverberations through the trees that made even the most stately of branches shake.

The Ewoks scattered, running off in different directions, and Nanta turned, aiming himself toward what looked like a very leafy bush that might make for a good hiding place.

"No, Nanta, that will only delay you getting stomped underneath the walker's mighty tread," Romba said. "And remember the pact:

The two of us stick together! Come with me—we'll lead them away from the Golden One so he can complete his quest and drive the Skull Ones from our world!"

Nanta followed Romba as he crashed in the other direction. His legs moved so fast he thought they might run away from the rest of him. He no longer knew exactly where he was in the forest. He only knew he needed to keep Romba in sight, even though Romba could run much faster. He raced between trees, wincing when the merciless sun sliced through the forest canopy to rain heat on his back. The ground trembled as the walkers lurched closer, their unwieldy legs tearing through the forest.

"Watch out!" Romba yelled over his shoulder.

Nanta glanced up just in time to see one of the giants release a blaze of red-orange fire from its strange mouth.

And then another. And another.

The fire lanced toward the ground—a deadly sword that scorched everything in its path—exploded into a spray of sparks, and left a smoking cloud of debris in its wake. Nanta coughed, turned back to the path in front of him, and refocused on running.

He and Romba were moving so fast, the forest around them became a blur. The fiery blasts from the giants—there was definitely more than one now—cut through the muddy surroundings, bright and relentless.

Nanta dragged air into his lungs, his vision clouding around the edges. He'd lost his spear at some point—when had that happened? And it looked like Romba had lost his, too. What would occur if they came upon more Skull Ones, if they had no way to defend themselves?

Nanta shook his head, hopping to the left to avoid more of the giants' fiery breath. They would figure it out, he decided. They'd kept their pact to stick together in battle, and they were doing just that.

Depite their dire circumstances, Nanta could not help but smile.

THE BALLAD OF NANTA

Wasn't it something that he had found such a stalwart and fast friend as Romba? And look at them now, flush with the euphoria of fighting for a noble cause, aiding the Golden One in liberating their world, creating a new tale with every step they took.

What a thing it was to *live* a story as it was happening.

Nanta spared a glance up at the sky, imagining all the stories he might live after this day. After he carved all of this into the tree and shared it with Romba—and then the whole village. After he finally ventured to the stars.

He could practically see the title of his future story as he and Romba scrambled down a dirt-strewn dip in the forest floor.

"The Ballad of the Very Curious Storykeeper and His Exciting Exploits in Worlds Beyond His Own—"

He heard the blast from the walker before he felt it.

In an instant his world exploded and everything was that fire, that smoke, that spray of sparks. Pain crashed through him, pain that was somehow red-hot and freezing all at once, pain that stretched to the tips of his ears and the ends of his toes. An anguished cry ripped itself from his chest, echoing through the green.

He felt himself fall, cradled by that dip in the forest floor, and Romba's face swam above his. He was vaguely aware of his new friend shaking him, trying to get him to stir.

"*Nanta!*" Romba screamed.

But Nanta could not hear him.

Even though fire surrounded him, even though pain was everywhere, Nanta knew what was happening.

I am a Storykeeper, he thought. *And now my story is ending.*

He lay on the forest floor and gazed up at the sky, smiling as he dreamed one last time of all the adventures he was about to have.

That night, after Bright Tree Village and the Golden One emerged victorious and banished the Skull Ones, Romba returned to Nanta's tree. He studied it for a long while, even as the sounds of celebration wafted through the village. Then he searched until he discovered the perfect stone, sharp at one end.

Romba found the spot where Nanta had carved his most fanciful stories and began to write—but not a new story. No, Romba simply added bits around all the things Nanta had already written, weaving in a few words here and there to bring the tale to its ending.

He wrote about a brave Ewok who, though not born battle-ready, fought like a warrior. An Ewok who selflessly gave himself to a noble cause, who became a staunch friend, and who dreamed up wondrous tales in that way only a true Storykeeper can.

He wrote about how this Ewok perished courageously and how his spirit returned to the Great Tree. And then he wrote about how the Great Tree released this Ewok's spirit to the stars, where he could explore forever, dream forever, and discover all the stories he was meant to find.

The people of Bright Tree Village sang this story later in the night—and for many seasons to come. It became the stuff of legends, one of the most enduring and celebrated tales of Ewok bravery ever to be heard.

And it was called "The Ballad of Nanta."

THEN FALL, SIDIOUS

Olivie Blake

The galaxy never chose me. Why should it? Power bends to mastery, not destiny. Instead I called for triumph and the stars themselves obliged.

(10—)

Perhaps they now call him the Chosen One as they once did you. Is that what crossed your mind when you saw him standing over you, your death a promise in his hands? I must admit it is a pretty story, the fates so graciously aligning, but hope is a pendulous blade, a slow-acting poison. For what can come of it but pain?

A Jedi, he says, like his father before him; bodies set in orbit by some benevolent design. Perhaps his elders have failed to teach him how I orchestrated the Republic's fall and watched its martyrs falter. That the nostalgia that drives young Skywalker's rebellion is a myth, a foolish longing for a world that has never been. Before the Empire was not some tranquil state of nature—some golden halcyon peace. Before me was the tyranny of corruption, the despotism of politics fought among the margins, in the shadows. What I brought to light I did not to subjugate, but to rule.

Because I have been inside the monster; seen its heart for what it is. The nature of all beings is as entropy itself, a slow but certain decay. Peace is the rebels' claim, born from trance-inducing dogma meant to stifle more enlightened threats. What is love but weakness, an illusion, the trick of an unfocused mind? In this the Jedi are correct to remove themselves from its temptation, to isolate their young. What is it they say—there is no passion, only serenity? No chaos, only harmony? How restful the indoctrination to mediocrity. How eloquent the reluctance to do what it takes and lead.

Good. Greatness calls for something sharper, born from something more than anesthetized subservience. Humanity is not nothing. It gives us passion that drives achievement, strength that arms us with clarity, to see the bonds of servitude forged by such perilous smallness of thought.

What is a prophecy but doom to the same cycle, unable to break the chains of the world it was born to save? What is a legacy but the invocation of ghosts? This boy on the brink of death, he cannot understand what I would have ultimately shown him—that love is a powerful soporific. And peace an unequivocal lie.

THEN FALL, SIDIOUS

(9—)

A Jedi, he says, like his father before him. Only perhaps it would pain you both to hear that you do not resemble him at all.

I remember you as you once were—or rather, I can still taste it. The anger that gave you focus. The hatred you have always felt; the violence you craved but were denied. The chance at victory over death, which you chose not from wisdom, but from desperation. The rage you were told never to wield; that gift that I alone would give you. Freedom, without which you might never have been great.

You, the Chosen One, you needed me; need me still. It is symbiotic, this thing between us, the push and pull of master and apprentice, together a dual-sided weapon of the Force. There can be no dominance without power. No greatness without control. Our bond does not live on a foundation of fidelity, on the paltriness of oath. I raised you from the ashes of your pain; I built you on the backbone of my vision.

I remember you as a boy. The fresh grief, newly cleaved from your mother. A simple flaw, the sliver of a weakness your mentors recognized for the danger that it was. They tore you from the only safety you had known and then they told you to be grateful. They told you to be peaceful and yet mistrusted you, letting fear make a mockery of their own code.

I remember you, so hungry to learn, so desperate to matter, to fulfill some shallow mythology of yourself. *The one who will bring balance to the Force*—how quaint, how precious, as if the Force is something to be audited by blood alone. What a mantle they placed on you and yet withheld from your own grasp. How eager you were, how trusting, how corrupted by insincerity and lies. How tormented by the loss they did not allow you to feel.

Born a slave with untold power and still so unwilling to overthrow your masters. It did not surprise me when I called you to my side, and you knelt.

(8—)

A Jedi, he says, like his father before him, resembling you most now that nothing is left in him but pain. I honor it, sanctify it in its way, by personally seeing to its destruction. When he is gone we will continue on unchanged. Another so-called Chosen One will be born and die. The suns will rise and set on ruination, moving on as time has always done.

You will be more mine than ever after the death of your son. Without him your legacy will have to lie with me, beside my deeds and with my Empire. Such pain, I feel it even now. You have been my right hand for so long that I can feel your fingers clenching, burdened with the misery that has always been yours. You are no stranger to pain, Darth Vader. It is as much a part of you as your connection to the Force, or the taste for darkness in your veins. What world could the Jedi have offered you that you would have accepted? Harmony, balance, order—what inconsequential nothingness is that to a boy without a mother? To a man who has loved with such precious sparsity only to watch all that he loves die?

Your truth is that you are weak no matter what you do, regardless of what you choose, because even before you came to me you were already broken. I have tried to make you great and I have done so, as much as I could have done for an apprentice still in subservience to ghosts. Do you think I, who have done what no Sith or Jedi before me has done, cannot feel the basic substance of your soul—your remorse? Your regret? Your guilt? I allow it because it empowers you, feeds the hatred I need you to feel. But I tire of the flavor.

THEN FALL, SIDIOUS

There is something in you that remains eternally undecided. The mark of a man who was chosen but never truly chose.

(7—)

He is dying now, Skywalker. A Jedi, he says, like his father before him. So, he chooses not to break, but to shatter. There is valor in that. It will lie interred with his bones.

I must admit that I cannot enjoy it, the feel of him giving way beneath the power I possess. To call upon the dark side now is still not without its demands. I still must channel my own malice, my fury, my wrath, and my contempt. The shame of such a crushing disappointment. The rot that is my enmity, my growing resentment of the stagnant bond I've tied to you.

Because you do realize, of course, your inconsequence had Skywalker given in to his hatred and chosen me? There can only be one master, one apprentice. I do not forget the significance of this, the constancy of violence. Present at all times between us is a stalemate only compromised by death, yours or mine. Heavy is the crown, and yet worn only by the apprentice who outlives the master. For all those with whom I've shared the secrets of this power, I alone have lasted. I alone know what it truly means to win.

The power of the dark side is like holding lightning in a bottle. Like trapping the galaxy between my hands as I have always done. I am a vessel of stellar fusion; of unlocked secrets of the Force that I have shared with you, and kept from you. You cannot yet imagine the mastery I hold, the power that will only be yours when I allow it. When I condone it.

Which perhaps you are beginning to realize will be a day that does not come.

(6—)

A Jedi, he says, like his father before him. A man I resurrected from nothing; who, without me, would be nothing once again.

I am gifted with clarity, more so than power. That I earned, shaped by my two hands, and the mastery of the dark side that I so carefully harnessed. But before I became Darth Sidious, I was not without my blessings—not prophecy, but perception. Vision. If I have a destiny, it is hand-wrought like a weapon. It is a map measured by insight, by certainty and observation. I can see a being for what they really are.

Take Padmé Amidala, for example, whom I trusted to craft her own tragedy, and so she did. Even the virtuous will compromise their ethics in moments of fear. The question is never if they will betray themselves, but when, and how soon. Thus, a life spent fighting tyranny still launched an empire; how ironic that the legacy of the Republic's greatest champion would be my reign.

And you.

(5—)

There is a taste in my mouth: Metal. Iron. A coppery wash of salted blood. Without passion there can be no power. Without chaos, no control. Without pain, there is nothing. I am human, I am the vessel, I am the answer, I am the blade. Like his father before him, Skywalker says—this the final legacy he claims—and yet I, who hold his life in my hands, was never so prettily chosen. My fate was never written in the stars. Stars die and so do saints, so do cowards. But I am hunger. I am wrath. And by my own hand, I am divine.

What can come next but drudgery? Rebellions are no small thing. The idea of mutiny, should it succeed in any way, cannot be unplanted. It will have to not only fail, but be decimated. Many will die. The brutality of this does not delight me. Despite the meritless qualms of the Jedi, the dark side is not a simple matter of carnality or lust for blood. If I wanted nothing but destruction I could call it forth at any moment. Already I extinguish planets with the motion of one finger; I can drain a young man of a long life for little more than the inconvenience of standing in my way. But power is not violence, even if it requires violence. An empire demands stability. This is what the Jedi, with their foolhardy promises of justice and morality, could never have successfully delivered. There is no justice. Good men suffer. Bad men triumph The way of the universe is not some unachievable balance from which only peace will remain. Inevitably the masses will be disappointed, and from that unrest will only rise more unmasterable chaos, like the turn of a tireless wheel.

What others do not understand is that strength is not a fist, but a burden. I will do what must be done to make this galaxy great because it is what I am called to do. Because I came of age in a world of stone and left it one of gleaming marble. Because I chose this crown, forged it myself, when no one else could bear it. Because I have chosen impossibility; because serenity is not where the human lives; because I was born not with prophecy, but with vision.

I told you once that all who gain power are afraid to lose it, but I lied, because this thing in my chest isn't fear. It's faith.

(4—)

When he is gone you will carry the body.

(3—)

Perhaps this thought is just occurring to you. I feel it like a glimmer from my periphery, a blur in my vision, a stirring in my chest. It is disorienting, the sudden movement, because I am—have always been—undeterrable, unshaken. It is this that calls me to lead; this that spurs me onward. The steadiness of my pulse; my certainty of greatness. Where others would falter and err I am immovable; unmoved. Others have failed this world with assailability and impermanence. I am clear-eyed and enduring. I will not do the same.

But the taste on my tongue is richer now; different. A Jedi, he says, like his father before him, but no saccharinity of goodness could ever be your flavor. Yours is pierced through with causticity, bitterness with no release. The constancy of your suffering, the tribal drum of your rage remains, but the timbre of it is different, raucous, changing; realigning from the fragments, futures joining up with pasts. It does not grow louder but deeper, illuminating from the marrow, coalescing like a chord. Your brokenness—should I have feared it? From the viscera of your power I can sense a key is turning; crackling at your margins is a rapid-burning flame. It is an old wound, vestigial; dormant in the fragments of your secrets, the irreparability of your truths. It is fear—no, it's agony—no, it's terror, wonder, awe. It is loathing and revulsion; heartbreak and despair. It is raw, and it is rapture. It is ecstasy. And I, like all your masters, have missed it.

It is not good or evil, light or darkness that made you and unmade you.

It is love, and it is grief.

(2—)

A Jedi, he says, like his father before him. Is this what you are made of, my apprentice, after all? You are flayed and hollowed out with tenderness that softens your purpose, vines of tired grace like dormant weeds to strangle your resolve. It does not make you strong, the invocation of your clemency, but it has made you volatile. I can feel it

THEN FALL, SIDIOUS

in you now—the change, the rift—but there can be no outlet for your agency, no salvation for your change of heart.

So there is goodness in you. My hearty congratulations. It will not save you now.

Perhaps I was wrong to think you broken, but not wrong enough to deny the cracks that yet remain. You crave the peace you were once promised, but it is a peace you will never be allowed, not in this lifetime or the next. Not with your choices, or your losses. Not with your unwavering regret. Yours is a prayer left eternally unanswered. Even now, as prophecy lies once again before you, can you say the fate they offered you could have ever been enough?

No. This—can't you see?—it's your tragedy and now mine: the stars that call for you, that crown you with the dulcet lies of destiny, bartering your freedom for your happiness from the start. Their promise of balance has always come at the price of your precious so-called peace. The stars, they will not redeem the life they stole from you, because unlike me, they are inconstant. What will but mine can possibly absolve you—what world but ours can satisfy you? Prophecies will remain indifferent to your losses, unfeeling to your pain.

The stars do not chart your course or mine, Lord Vader. They are ever-changing, ever lies. You may try in the midst of suffering to change your path, but you forget that I am constancy; I am victory. I am ruination; I am fate. I am hunger; I am fury. Death is not an answer. Death is not deliverance. With as much death as you yourself have witnessed, do you not already know it? That there is nothing after death but emptiness and loss.

No act of redemption can rewrite the blood on your hands. No martyr's end will cleanse your sins. What choice is this, love over life, when all it means is strength forfeited and legacy forgone? My power is not yours to take. As a vessel you will not survive it, and so the only answer left is doom.

Tell me, oh Chosen One, do you dare strike the divine? When I am gone there will only be darkness. Cut me down and all you leave behind is unfinished glory and an empty throne. The strong will always emerge, the weak will always be subjugated, some other father will die at the hands of some other son one day. The way of the galaxy is the turning of a wheel, with only power left unchanging. Heroes come and go, your story readily forgotten.

A Jedi, he says, like his father before him. So be it. There can be no turning back from here.

If this is your fate, what was your purpose?

If this is your choice, what was your meaning?

If this is your end, what was your story?

What will they say of you, Anakin Skywalker, when you are dust and gone?

(1—)

What is a legacy?

I am the one who will decide.

IMPACT

Sean Williams

Sound doesn't travel at all through a vacuum, but it travels very well indeed through durasteel. The shock wave of the impact of *Executor*'s fore weapons station against the quadranium plating of the second Death Star raced aft through the Super Star Destroyer's hull at a rate fifteen times faster than through air. It took only three seconds for the deafening echoes of the explosions to reach the command bridge.

Anyone there who might have heard it, however, was already dead.

Less than a dozen seconds earlier, the commander of *Executor*'s combat information center was trying and failing to wrest control of the giant vessel from the chaos following the destruction of the command bridge. Internal comms were down: She had tried everyone she could think of, from Admiral Piett all the way to Bridge Officer Jhoff, with whom she shared shifts and occasional meal breaks, and whom she found good company in a taciturn, inwardly focused way. She had only just learned of his death, and the deaths of Admiral Piett and everyone on the bridge through garbled eyewitness accounts from outside the ship.

There wasn't time to grieve. In theory, full control of *Executor* should have automatically devolved to her station at the CIC, buried safe from harm, deep within the mighty vessel's protective skeleton. There, ensuring the physical safety of everyone aboard was first of a long list of priorities, slightly ahead of determining the new chain of command . . .

Now, though, her final moments were slipping away, and those priorities became irrelevant. She could only watch in horror through instruments as the crosshatched surface of the incomplete battle station loomed large before her. There was no way to change course. All she could do was wonder how this had happened to her and Jhoff and everyone else aboard. And why.

Whoever was responsible, she cursed them to a long and painful death.

For the *Executor* and everyone aboard, the Death Star wouldn't need its superlaser. It just needed to be a profoundly immovable object.

Less than one minute before impact, Bridge Officer Kasva Jhoff flung his arms up to protect his face—a futile gesture, since the explosive energy of a rebel RZ-1 A-wing would burn through his flesh as easily as air.

IMPACT

His fate had been sealed a breath earlier, once the final commands had been input with a decisive series of taps on his bridge workstation. *Rat-a-tat,* like a military drumbeat. As a child, the rhythm he had first heard on Abridon had frightened him with its promise of violence and the loss of loved ones. Now it reassured him.

No room for doubt. No turning back.

"Follow your present course," said the voice in his memory.

Executor would now do just that.

Task complete, he glanced up and saw Captain Gherant leap with a cry of "Too late!" from the command walkway, Admiral Piett desperate in his wake. The hull of the spinning A-wing loomed large in the main viewports. There wasn't time to see the motif of the world on which it was manufactured, but the thought it might be Jhoff's own had irresistible poetry.

Jhoff flung his arms across his face—and a split instant later was vaporized along with the admiral and everyone else on the command bridge, the sound of their brief and violent deaths ricocheting through the interior of *Executor:* a portentous signal of its oncoming demise.

So much for the CIC commander's curse.

Jhoff was dead before she uttered it.

Two minutes before impact, Jhoff had been busy severing all command systems from navigation and drive controls, using overrides that existed to protect the ship from insurrection: Had the crew ever tried to take over, these were the steps Admiral Piett would have ordered to ensure no one outside the bridge could wrest control from him. Jhoff had memorized the emergency protocols during his training but never expected to use them.

"Intensify forward firepower!" cried Admiral Piett again.

Normally confident in his authority—and with good reason, given the firepower at his command—Admiral Piett had never sounded *alarmed* before.

Quickly, Jhoff told himself. *Quickly!*

The voice of his father, faint in his memory now but not forgotten, urged him on.

Rebellion against the Empire never made newscasts until it was defeated; this was something Jhoff's father had bitterly noted in the days of the Republic, but with Separatist movements on planets Jhoff had never heard of. Rumors spread, now as then, and officially none of them were true. Even the newscasts were doubted, sometimes, because everyone knew that misinformation was occasionally disseminated through official channels to throw off the enemy's plans. As a result of this, there were still believers that the first Death Star hadn't been destroyed at all, that it was out there, patrolling ghostlike on the galaxy's outer fringes, awaiting the order to strike the decisive blow against the Rebellion. This despite the emergency conscription of over a million officers like Kasva Jhoff to serve on the second one, which was already being built in orbit around Endor.

Reports, one year before the impact of *Executor,* of a violent nationalist insurgency on the mountainous world of Abridon followed the same pattern. Whispers circulated, to which Jhoff attended with superficial disinterest, careful not to display the alarm they caused him. As far as he knew, his grandmother was still alive. She was an old woman now, bordering on the infirm, still bitter and angry for reasons he hadn't known as a boy but had come to understand as an adult. He had thought for a long time that she was angry at his father; now Jhoff knew that anger had been directed at the rulers of Abridon, whether they wore the uniforms of Republic or Empire. Until recently, they had exchanged brief messages when his duties allowed. He sensed her disapproval about his work, although she never openly criticized him; she knew he had been enlisted against his will as soon as he was of age, along with so many others. It wasn't his fault he worked hard, and well, and had learned not to see what he shouldn't.

If she had been in the wrong place at the wrong time and been caught in a crossfire . . . or worse . . .

When news of the uprising finally reached public notice, much of what he had already heard went unreported. Nationalists, said the grapevine, had briefly taken full control of Abridon, but all the newscasts announced was that resistance had been crushed and all rebel leaders captured. The planet and its critical shipbuilding facilities were once again under full Imperial control.

Jhoff didn't care about the facilities. He pored over the list of those executed for insurrection. Amnen Jhoff's name wasn't there, which came as a quietly held but immense relief—but why did she still not answer his messages?

And why did subsequent rumors speak of ongoing bombardment of the planet, as though resistance continued unchecked?

He dreamed of his family's nerf runs burning, of mountains falling, and felt deep stirrings of homesickness, which he had thought long suppressed.

Two minutes and twenty seconds before impact, a vibration rocked the bridge, its source shockingly close.

"Sir, we've lost our bridge deflector shields!"

Jhoff felt a rush of adrenaline. He didn't know who had sounded the alarm. Someone behind him? He was too focused on exploring options while at the same time giving the impression that he was doing what he was supposed to be doing. Wasn't that the mission of every Imperial officer? To be seen in the correct light? And to see no distance at all beyond that light.

Well, Jhoff was seeing now. And what he saw, he disliked immensely. Uncertainty everywhere. Deception. Fear.

Once seen, he couldn't unsee them.

"Intensify the forward batteries," barked Admiral Piett with his usual imperiousness. "I don't want anything to get through."

What if something *did* get through? Jhoff couldn't help but ask that question. What would it mean to him and the hundreds of thousands of people aboard the ship—and maybe hundreds of quadrillions outside—if the admiral and everyone on the bridge were killed?

This was a possibility, now that the bridge deflectors were down. A remote one, but a real one. He could take advantage of it, this instant, or it would soon be taken from him. One lucky shot could be enough to behead the ship's command—and given the fire *Executor* was taking, that shot could come at any moment. The rebels were giving it everything they had. There was no reason why he shouldn't do the same, by stopping a new head from growing back.

He was sick of lies. Here, there was at least the possibility of truth.

Twelve hours before impact, he had been on traffic control duty, overseen by Admiral Piett, when the first suggestion that even here, at this critical juncture in the Empire's fight against the Rebel Alliance, when every thought and deed was supposedly united in common purpose, nothing was as it seemed.

Executor had been holding station in orbit with two smaller ships near the incomplete Death Star when a *Lambda*-class shuttle emerged from hyperspace, requesting a landing on Endor.

Jhoff identified the vessel and followed standard protocols, vigilant for any sign of deception.

IMPACT

"Shuttle *Tydirium*, transmit the clearance code for shield passage."

The reply to his request came immediately. "Transmission commencing."

As the data flowed into his station, a heavy presence joined the admiral's careful watch of his activities. Jhoff didn't need to look up to recognize Lord Vader himself. The dark shadow of the Emperor's right hand had been hanging over *Executor* for days, filling every thought with the threat of hot metal and reprisals for failure.

"Where is that shuttle going?" Vader demanded.

"Shall I hold them?" the admiral responded, eager to please his master.

Hesitation.

Jhoff felt something cold crawl down his spine. Vader *never* hesitated. It was as though the normal operation of the universe ceased, just for an instant. His breath stalled in his throat.

Finally came the instruction: "No, leave them to me. I will deal with them myself."

Jhoff's breath returned, and behind him he felt even the admiral relax minutely.

"As you wish, my lord. Carry on."

Obeying the order, Jhoff broadcast, "Shuttle *Tydirium*, deactivation of the shield will commence immediately."

Without consciously realizing until later where the words came from, he added, "Follow your present course."

Vader strode off, radiating a sense of hidden purpose, and the shuttle accelerated into the formerly protected sector of space around Endor, leaving Jhoff profoundly rattled.

Hesitation. Suspicion. Uncertainty.

These feelings were old acquaintances on the bridge of *Executor*. But never before had he suspected that Vader knew them, too.

Did everyone? Even the Emperor?

One day before impact, a message arrived through the usual channels from his grandmother.

"I am sending you a gift," the readout said, as though these few words didn't break a year's silence in the face of a dozen attempts to communicate from him, none of them answered. "In the name of your father."

What gift?

His *father*?

Was it even her?

Whispers on the grapevine only compounded the mystery. Of a new rebel leader and freedom regained on Abridon. Of the foundries turning out A-wing starfighters for the Rebel Alliance instead of the Empire. Of hopes and fears he dared not express aloud.

Maybe his grandmother felt the same way when talking to him. Some things just couldn't be said when a knee was on the throat of someone you loved.

He thought of his grandmother's tight-lipped silence whenever he, in his youth, had asked about his father's fate. She had been protecting him, he now realized, from the revolutionary streak that ran red in his family. What had his father done in Abridon's name? What rules had he broken?

Eventually he stopped asking so she didn't have to lie.

In every other respect, too, all his life Jhoff had done as he was told in the firm belief that it was the right thing to do. "Follow your present course" was his mantra, never looking beyond it, but who set that course for him? First, it had been his father, then his grandmother, then the Republic and the Senate, then the Empire.

He sensed a tide turning under him, tugging him in directions unknown.

If his grandmother really was alive, and speaking to him now, on the eve of this critical battle, perhaps *that* was her gift. A new question.

Did anyone have to tell him where to go at all?

Or maybe it was a cruel lie, and she had been dead all this time.

Five minutes before impact, as the rebels intensified their attack on *Executor,* ships and energy bolts flooding in from all sides, on the screen of his bridge station he glimpsed what might have been the motif of Abridon emblazoned on one of the rebel A-wings, near the sensor jamming array.

Then he *knew,* with a surprising stab of pride for the revolutionaries who had raised him, that his grandmother was still alive.

She had chosen her own course. Why couldn't he?

Jhoff had been all of seven years old during the annual migration of his family's herds from hilly southern paddocks to the flanks of Geah Mountain. At the time, he had known little of the Republic, let alone Separatists like his father and the troubles they were causing. The closest city to the family's nerf runs was Sayan, and he had never been there. His grandmother forbade politics from mealtimes. The little he had gleaned from overheard conversations when his father sat outside with friends and talked in hurried whispers suggested that people were unhappy, and his father was one of those people. Young Jhoff didn't know why. But the booted *thud-thud* of Republic soldiers patrolling nearby roadways put him on edge, as did the beat of a recruiting officer's drums, seeking conscripts for distant battles that herders like them had no stake in. Once a week, those drums sounded, while Jhoff's father Harclew fumed and his grandmother Amnen urged silence.

On that day, during the migration, Jhoff and Amnen rode one

scooter, his father another under a sky busy with air traffic. The herd had been divided as it always was around the upraised rocky blade of Jolson's Promontory, and Harclew issued patient commands as they coordinated their progress. Nerfs were good-natured but dim beasts, prone to startlement and occasional fusses. Getting them moving was the easy part; stopping them could be much harder. The stink of them took some getting used to, too.

Jhoff's attention was on the beasts around him, not the air, so he didn't immediately notice the cause of their growing restlessness. Republic airspeeders were rising and falling like birds on the far side of the promontory. Where his father was.

"Harclew, what's going on?" Amnen asked over the transponder.

"An ambush," he came back with. "Something's got the powers that be riled up."

"What have you done this time?"

"Nothing." A crackle came over the transponder. "Don't worry. Follow your present course."

The fliers descended. Jhoff's father fell silent.

Young Jhoff craned his neck as they came around the promontory. All he saw was the other half of the herd stampeding toward him, terror in their eyes. The fliers were gone, and so was Harclew.

Thirty-two years later, at the moment of impact, the echoes of his father's final words still sounded, slower than explosions through durasteel, taking much longer to reach their destination, but firmly striking their mark.

Kasva Jhoff had chosen his own course, at last. For Abridon.

TROOPER TROUBLE
Laura Pohl

TK-423 LOG—DS-II—ENTRY 1

First day on the new post aboard the Battle Station DS-II. That's short for "Death Star." Not a particularly good name for a station because it's not a star. Further, you'd think they'd have retired the name after the first one blew up. But every officer here assures us that this one is bigger and better, and the newly recruited troopers have nothing to worry about except following our duties.

It does have a minor gravitational pull, and currently orbits along one of the many moons of the planet Endor, which is inhabited by some sort of primitive life-form—no concern to the troopers stationed in space. The plan is for the Death Star to be "fully operational in thirty days' time. New arrivals are to station all posts to represent the might of the Empire." (This is word for word what was written on the orientation datapad, though I have taken the liberty to correct the unseemly grammar mistakes.)

TK-423 LOG—DS-II—ENTRY 3
Have been through my whole section of the floor now and assigned all the official duties while aboard the station. The officers sorted the new recruits first to check who had been through training protocol and were shocked to find that apparently we hadn't been through shooting practice. The shock solidified into outrage when they found the reason behind it (the training base was out of E-11 power cells), and said that whoever was in charge of the onplanet recruitment process should be shot, if only they had ammunition to spare.

TK-534, a member of my unit who is clearly stiff and eager to please, asked if we were going to go through shooting drills now aboard the base, but was quickly dismissed. *Shoot or be shot,* said the officer. *It's that simple.*

Since this seems to be the most helpful advice our superiors will offer, recording it into my personal logbook to register for posterity in the hope that one day its utility becomes clear.

TK-423 LOG—DS-II—ENTRY 4
The principal duties of my unit consist of standing around when an important officer arrives at the station so they have a welcoming committee and feel valued by the Empire. We cover landing bays 1 to 12. Other units have been assigned to the other landing bays on the opposite side of the station. There are plenty of landing bays and plenty of important officers, so this means we stand around at least three

hours a day until General, Moff, or Admiral makes an appearance, and we're not allowed to drink water or go to the restroom while we wait. One important officer we were meant to be welcoming forgot the access codes to unlock his cargo hold, and had to keep trying old codes until one worked. TK-534, after bothering our officer to stand in front of the line, passed out in the fourth hour. He went to bed very sullen.

TK-423 LOG—DS-II—ENTRY 6

TK-293, who is assigned to my unit and who is also my bunkmate, warned me to stay off the path of the most disagreeable people on board, but failed to mention that some of the aforementioned people are droids. Unfortunately I have met such a person today, the astromech assigned to our floor, R2-Q9.

Like all astromechs it is crafted chiefly out of durasteel and solidified spite. It has refused my polite apology after making the mistake of thinking that I could ask it to be the holoprojector for our captain, who wanted to show us the ending of his new favorite holovid *Officer & Commander*. R2-Q9 informed me in Binary that I was merely a stormtrooper and therefore the lowest and most pitiful item on the food chain, using such foul language that even my younger cousins would have had a hard time competing, and badgered me endlessly until the heat alarm on my helmet was going off from my burning cheeks.

That small blunder has cost me my dignity since I have now been locked out repeatedly from my room, and I have no doubt as to who should be held responsible.

TK-423 LOG—DS-II—ENTRY 7

We have been out of caf for five straight days in the cafeteria. It is also the seventh day of our assignment at the DS-II and everyone is still eager to reassure the newcomers that the station is flawless. However if we do happen to find flaws it is key to fill out a form reporting said flaws, or are welcome to fix them ourselves if doing so is within our capacity. Though *how* one single person could fix the faulty caf importation of the station is anyone's guess.

We were also told our wages would be late in coming even though the promise of recruitment for stormtroopers is for a weekly salary. This means it can be easily sent back home to support our families (along with a few other bonuses that have been generously increased since the first Death Star was destroyed). TK-848 was about to make a ruckus over this delay, but a fire alarm rang out on one of the upper floors and we were all rushed to help smother it before it spread through the steel cranes, which were imported from Mustafar and took weeks to get here and we couldn't afford to lose even one of them if we wanted the construction finished on time, and we do want the construction finished on time because that's the only thing every single officer from the upper echelon seems to concur on.

TK-423 LOG—DS-II—ENTRY 8

TK-534 has passed out once again while waiting on another committee on landing bay 4, and we have started a betting pool on the back of the assignment board. He says he suffers from low blood sugar and we should not make fun of him for this. TK-293 is against the betting pool but only because we all know TK-534 is the one who will pass out first and that takes the stakes away from the game. We have now decided to bet on the minutes it takes for TK-534 to, as TK-848 put it, "fall flat on his ass" (please excuse the language, some troopers were born in the Outer Rim and it shows). Since the only thing everyone knows about the DS-II is that the officers are constantly asking for more personnel and parts, they are keeping TK-534's service

TROOPER TROUBLE

despite his unpleasant demeanor and innate clumsiness until such a time when his services are deemed redundant. We can only hope this day will arrive soon.

TK-423 LOG—DS-II—ENTRY 9

TK-534's steadfast bootlicking got him promoted out of our floor, which means he has to actively work on the construction, which he seemed happy with. Our unit continues to stand around when someone arrives and put out fires when needed. Huzzah.

TK-423 LOG—DS-II—ENTRY 9—UPDATE

Unfortunately, once TK-534 was promoted above, he was asked to perform some shooting to get rid of an unexpected infestation of mynocks. He evidently failed, which meant that by night he was back in our rooms to bunk with us once more. This was for the best, since R2-Q9 had locked me out again from the room after I left to shower. I would have gotten back in sooner or later, however, since TK-848 had been out meeting some other stormtrooper units and arrived past our curfew, so I did not feel the need to thank TK-534 very effusively.

TK-423 LOG—DS-II—ENTRY 11

There is still no caf in the cafeteria. One would think this elementary since it is impossible to spell one without the other. When I mentioned that this may be due to lack of planning on the part of the Empire to the unkind worker behind the counter, TK-293 told me to shut up because we will get into trouble, and troopers who get into trouble get sent through the air lock, which explains the lack of personnel the officers are constantly complaining about. I don't want to point fingers but perhaps the solution for the "we need more men" problem would be not to throw all available men through the air lock once they complain there's no caf.

TK-423 LOG—DS-II—ENTRY 12

Locked inside the refresher on our floor, no doubt the diligent work of R2-Q9. Hammered on the door until someone opened it for me, all while hearing it malignantly beep on the other side.

TK-423 LOG—DS-II—ENTRY 15

Not only has the caf not arrived (although promises were made, excuses were given, the shipments aren't what they were in early Empire days, the ISB has prioritized their own offices' supply first, etc., etc.) but the wages are still late (more promises were made and further excuses were given, the ISB has been prioritized over other workforces, etc., etc.).

TK-848 was none too happy when discussing this later in the evening in our quarters, saying ships had been set on fire for much less on his home planet. According to his words, "We signed up to be here but there were conditions, and these conditions aren't being met," which quickly jumped to "we are being exploited" and then to "I've been talking to the other troopers about forming a un—" which was interrupted by TK-293 telling him that "the commanding officers don't like the U-word."

I was deeply confused, and expressed this by telling them I could not see how any Ugnaughts could relate to our situation. The conversation ended abruptly when TK-534 told all of us that TK-848 was an agitator and that we'd all be getting a Considerable Scolding if we didn't stop all this Ugnaught talk at once.

TROOPER TROUBLE

TK-423 LOG—DS-II—ENTRY 16

Never mind all that, today Lord Vader showed up, so instead of us getting a Considerable Scolding, it was Moff Jerjerrod's turn. Other troopers had warned us (TK-848, actually, who apparently knows everybody and everybody's business) of Vader's reputation, but said he never bothers with the stormtroopers, and only keeps his threats to important commanding officers.

"Now, *that's* class solidarity," said TK-848 after Moff Jerjerrod had made the usual "we need more men" speech (which I had on my card, "claims lack of workers," for the betting pool), and then Vader mentioned the Emperor (which TK-293 had on his card, "namedropping"). All in all, we got to be the audience for one of Vader's famous threats, which is a real treat if you're not on the receiving end of it. Fortunately, we did not witness a less appealing Vader management method, the choke hold, which makes all officers unhappy and scared and thus more prone to screaming at the lower chain of command (i.e., us).

Moff Jerjerrod affirmed we'd be *back on schedule*, which apparently means we'll have longer shifts of waiting around and pacing corridors. Most important, we now have Standing There for the Emperor's Arrival to look forward to. It'll require a lot of stormtrooper units, which means the betting pool is larger for how many will pass out from dehydration.

TK-423 LOG—DS-II—ENTRY 17

Still no caf.

TK-423 LOG—DS-II—ENTRY 19

I reported R2-Q9 for its latest behavior (crossing the corridor at high speed when my unit was coming through, causing more than one accident with this reckless conduct; everyone knows the unspoken rule of the Death Star is that we do not run in the corridors), but the pernicious droid has right up and vanished the form I filed from the system. I fear the droid and central computer of the Death Star are in collusion.

TK-423 LOG—DS-II—ENTRY 21
Promised wages still have not arrived, and neither has the long-heralded caf. I begin to think the beverage is a hallucination created by my mind to placate my worst instincts. There was nothing much that could be said in regard to this, except what was so vehemently put by TK-848: "Honestly [automatically redacted] the ISB, and [automatically redacted] the TIE they flew in on" (direct quote).

TK-423 LOG—DS-II—ENTRY 22
Was late to report to duty in another match against a door that would not budge open, but the unit covered for me, and I renewed my complaints about the cause of this. "It hates me particularly," I said. "None of you ever get locked anywhere."

"You should stop pushing its buttons," said TK-534, which said by anyone else in the galaxy would have been met with the groans of an audience listening to a tired joke, but was instead met with the groans of an audience hearing TK-534 open his mouth to speak.

"That's your useful advice?" asked TK-293, who sounded increasingly ironic but was still too opaque for TK-534's comprehension.

"We all look alike, it can't be picking you from the rest," TK-534 insisted. "You're being paranoid."

This was later proven wrong when we had been marching as a full unit and TK-293 had traded uniforms with me, and R2-Q9 still picked me out on this lineup and ran over my boot.

TK-423 LOG—DS-II—ENTRY 24

Someone mixed up all the landing codes for the moon nearby and sent them in the all-personnel daily dispatch, which meant that everyone on board had every single security code to breach the place, and thus we were all assembled in the hangar and made to delete it from our datapads in front of the supervisors. While at it, they decided to drone on about "indiscipline" and "irresponsibility" and "lack of work ethic" and that we had been "lucky to be recruited to be part of this massive initiative" and that the troopers had "compromised the victory of the most magnificent project of the Empire" and would be severely punished. After that nasty reprimand, we were all unhappily marched back to our bunks.

"It was not even our fault," said TK-293, still revolted. "Why do they always blame us somehow?"

"Because it's easy," replied TK-848 immediately, and not even TK-534 could counter that one, even if he would have liked to. TK-848 was still running about with the other stormtrooper units when he had free time. TK-534 would love to have called him incompetent, but he was the most diligent in our unit, and the only person the officers seemed to bother listening to. His voice never sounded annoying through the helmet speaker, which was the case for 98.8 percent of the rest of us.

"One would think they would value us more," I said after careful consideration, "since although they order us, we are the ones to follow through. If we aren't here, they have nothing. Without stormtroopers, there can never be any storms."

"TK-423, you are a poet," was the appreciative reply of TK-848, to which I answered "Why, I *never*." Not even if it was the last profession available, which coincidentally was the reasoning behind enlisting in the stormtrooper units since there hadn't been that many options at hand.

TK-423 LOG—DS-II—ENTRY 25

The Emperor arrived, and it was a fanfare like we'd never witnessed before aboard the station. Someone had planned a fireworks routine, which was canceled midway through after one almost blew the Emperor's retinue out of the sky. Someone would be hearing a lot about that later, and if it were me, I'd quickly dispatch the unused ones to the ground and get rid of the boxes so no one else knew I was to blame for it.

My unit was sent to the very back of the ranks, thanks to the dutiful efforts of TK-534 whose low blood sugar continues to be a plague upon the efficient machinery of the Empire. It was still easy to spot the Emperor's Royal Guard, wearing the blood-red uniforms, which made all of us writhe in envy considering ours are white. According to regulation, it should be spotless, a task nigh impossible considering how much heavy lifting near grease and metal we have to do.

TK-293 was mostly excited to get a look at the Emperor's personal ship, though to his disappointment it was only a *Lambda*-class T4— a shuttle, and not even a modified one at that. "Now if *I* were the Emperor," he said later ("But you aren't so why bother," interrupted TK-534, who'd turned all the energy he'd put previously into bootlicking into antagonizing us after that one transformative admonition yesterday), "I'd never leave home without taking at least a *Delta*-class."

We heard not a word from the Emperor himself, considering he was

TROOPER TROUBLE

too far away, and him being an old man, he took about an hour to go through the whole hangar. When he got to the door we were all bored stiff already and didn't even try to catch a glimpse beneath the hood.

TK-423 LOG—DS-II—ENTRY 26

If we thought things would change with the arrival of the Emperor, we were sorely wrong. Our shifts got even longer, fourteen hours a day with fewer breaks in between. With the Emperor here everyone wants to appear busy, which is different from actively being busy, so Vader shouts (or chokes) all the commanders, and all the commanders (unable to resort to choking) shout at the captains and all the captains shout at the officers and all the officers shout at us, and being stormtroopers there is no one to shout at (except the droid, which I daresay is out of the question).

After a long and unrewarding shift, I went to pick up refreshments in the cafeteria and was actively assaulted on the way back. R2-Q9 made me give everything I'd picked to him and failure to comply meant getting hit with the arc welder.

"This is workplace harassment, I'll have you know," I told R2-Q9 as it beeped gleefully through the corridor and threw all the refreshments down the trash compactor. TK-534 did not complain I hadn't brought the food to our rooms, and even went so far as going himself to the cafeteria to get replacements for all of us.

TK-423 LOG—DS-II—ENTRY 28

After three days of fourteen-hour shifts (and not even the distant promise of caf, as if they, too, thought it was now an illusion beyond our far and wildest reaching dreams), we returned to our bunks truly exhausted. We all took the helmets off, which we were only allowed to do when going to bed, otherwise it's against regulation protocols. TK-293 put his blaster down on the bed and said, "I've had enough."

"I think we should go back to our Ugnaught talk," said TK-848, raising his eyebrows meaningfully and meeting TK-293's eyes. "They've been getting all the glory, and we don't get anything at all for the work we put in."

"*What* work?" said TK-534, which I believe was meant to be critical specifically of TK-848's posture, but had the regrettable side effect of criticizing every single stormtrooper's work. Although working aboard the DS-II may sound light, stormtroopers are always the first on ground attacks, and always the first to be sent when there's a gas leak somewhere and they don't want to send upper personnel to get asphyxiated or plummet to their death.

"They would have sent you home ages ago if they didn't need you," TK-293 pointed to TK-534, who seemed unhappy at being used as an example to prove a valid point.

"We're *essential workers*," said TK-848, "or else they wouldn't need this many of us, and there wouldn't be all those nice incentives and benefits they promised. They need us, but we don't need them." (Inspirational, albeit untrue. Lack of job offers is running rampant throughout the galaxy, and the only steady offers come from the Empire itself.) "The Empire basically just buys us with the benefits, and now they don't even bother to try and win our cooperation since they aren't keeping any of their promises. I say it's time."

After a long, dramatic pause, TK-293 asked, "Time for what?"

TK-848 acquired a gleam in his eye. "Time for revolution."

TK-423 LOG—DS-II—ENTRY 30

TK-848 has not let go of his idea, and was up early for his machinations and meetings with the other troopers as always. He somehow

TROOPER TROUBLE

already had a list of all the stormtroopers on board and their commanding officers, and by late afternoon he was in an entirely different stage of megalomania much to TK-534's chagrin. "You can't go through with this. Not when the *Emperor* is on board."

"And that is why we have to go through with this, or nothing will change."

"Nothing *ever* changes," came the exasperated reply.

"That's not true. Changes only come when they're demanded, through inconvenience and, if it comes to it, violence."

"Do *not* suggest blowing up this battle station," said TK-534, who was articulating emphasis in all his sentences like he was narrating a particularly challenging game of dejarik. "A peaceful protest is *more* than enough."

"The Empire doesn't understand peace," said TK-848 darkly. "Alderaan wasn't built in a day, but it sure was destroyed in one."

TK-423 LOG—DS-II—ENTRY 31

TK-848 finally confessed today that he had been waiting for this moment a long time, and all of his running about the station previously was to articulate the conditions for this purpose. He reported that all the other units were just as unsatisfied as the rest of us (many had complained about the lack of caf, proving that this was a reasonable upset on my part, and not a childish hyperfixation, as had been suggested by TK-534). The units on the forest moon protecting the shield are also feeling dejected. There had been one major problem, and that consisted of the fact that no one wanted to believe a stormtrooper alone could change things as they were currently.

"Of course one stormtrooper doesn't change anything," TK-848 said impatiently when this was brought to him by the head of the unit on the floor below, in a meeting our unit was finally allowed to join now that we were all included in his plan. "But it isn't just one stormtrooper. It's all of us, together. And if all of us are together, then they're in trouble. Isn't that what they train us for?"

TK-423 LOG—DS-II—ENTRY 32

It's a busy day, but even with only ten hours of assigned rest, we have managed to send messages all through the station to the other stormtrooper units. Ideally we'd get to talk in person but this station was built only to be "fully operational," which means it contains a death ray but no turbolifts in logical places that might allow everyone to move within this planet-sized labyrinth.

One of my mother's many pieces of advice was to never trust an engineer, which proves how sound of mind she always was, although her counsel has led me to this job that doesn't offer a solid career path (something that TK-848 assures me can be negotiated with our employers, along with a retirement plan. TK-534 is convinced he's delusional). Either way, TK-848's first plan of action is simple: a strike. A full day of no stormtroopers, where we all sit down in the hangars and wait for the officers to come to the negotiation table. TK-534 could not object since it is peaceful in nature, and decided that he'll stick with us after all.

TK-423 LOG—DS-II—ENTRY 32—UPDATE

It's all set. The weather for tomorrow: a tempest.

TK-423 LOG—DS-II— ENTRY 33

The plan had to be delayed because today, of all days, the Rebellion decided to mount an attack on the Death Star and we've just received

TROOPER TROUBLE

the warning. The upper floors are in turmoil. Could not have been worse timing.

The last-week recruits are all trembling in their armor, though I understand that with the states things are in, it's not unreasonable to imagine that the Empire has not, in fact, fixed the flaw of whatever allowed the first Death Star to explode. I am left to assure them that it's unlikely the rebels will blow up the biggest battle station ever built (again). The other problem is that many units have been called for ground assault, including ours, and the officers have conveniently forgotten that we *still* have not been through shooting drills. For my part, I was so irritated by this sudden break of routine and TK-848's plan being postponed that I mostly forgot to be worried.

Lord Vader had left to go to the command ship, but suddenly showed up not an hour later, as one would do when they forgot to change into their favorite cape. We barely had time to disperse the units for those assigned to ground assault before he'd already returned to leave once again, and thankfully didn't notice the formation was entirely out of order, and that some of the troopers were wearing socks and not their boots.

TK-423 LOG—DS-II—ENTRY 33—UPDATE

This is the *second* time *today* Lord Vader has left and returned. We were forced to scramble the unit at the last second as he came back in. I wish the man would make up his mind. There were only half the usual troopers to receive him since the other half had already been sent down to the forest moon to capture some rebels, which are also making a ruckus down there as well as up here.

TK-293 has already been sent down with the rest of the unit while I stayed to bring the rest of the equipment, but from the latest update I received, they've landed on the opposite side of the place they were supposed to land in (evidently, TK-534 insisted on piloting, which explains everything). The commander has been shouting at them for the last twenty minutes, though apparently there's been trouble down in the forest so it's all for the best that they're not present for it. Besides, we were planning on going on strike. Our desire was to be more intentional about it, but I suppose this will do.

The loudspeakers won't stop blaring every five minutes with a new alarm. If I hear "fully operational" one more time I will follow my estranged uncle's example and go live as a hermit in a swamp (I was told it does wonders for one's peace of mind and skincare routine). I can't find the blaster and the equipment I'm supposed to bring down, and I have been walking in circles for an hour searching, sweating profusely and half worried both for myself and for every colleague down on the forest moon.

TK-423 LOG—DS-II—ENTRY 33—UPDATE

I've found the blaster. The confounded thing had been moved to the other side of the floor, but now it's almost impossible to return to the hangar with the fire alarms blaring and doors being shut due to the defensive protocol. I believe the rebel attack has already started and the shields are down. The TIEs are making such an infernal noise outside it's impossible to hear myself think. I dearly wish they'd kept the atmosphere bubble more confined to the base itself so we don't have to hear the blasts and explosions in space. Supposedly it helps keep our wits about what's happening, but all it does is make everyone jump every two minutes looking for the nearest fire, which is not helpful since there are dozens of fires and they are growing in geometric progression.

It doesn't help my nerves either that everyone I cross paths with is

TROOPER TROUBLE

always looking out the viewport to watch how the space battle fares, and half of them have taken their helmets off to throw up what we had for breakfast likely due to the turbulence (and also because of someone's dim-witted idea of serving sour blue milk with the cereal).

I collected the blaster and the equipment, but before I could progress any further, I saw R2-Q9 coming in my direction with murder in his one black eye. He barreled down the corridor and I jumped out of the way at the last minute and securely made it into one of the outer sections of the floor, but before I could advance he had almost shut the door on top of me. I ran down the corridor with the equipment in hand going through any open door as they were violently snapped shut a hairsbreadth after I was through, until I'd made it into the escape pod corridor, and there was no exit strategy to be found there.

I jumped inside one of the pods in the hope that I could slice the doors from this side, but by then it was too late. The droid had followed and, in a last antagonistic movement, used its scomp link to shut this last door.

Unfortunately, R2-Q9 was steps ahead, as it had always been. Even before I could react and try to crawl out, the signal started beeping and I saw the launch button being pushed from outside as it had shut me out completely from the controls. In a sudden, jerked movement, the pod ejected itself. The last thing I saw through the hatch window was the fiendish droid, getting smaller and smaller as the pod distanced itself and was launched straight into a battlefield.

TK-423 LOG—ESCAPE POD—ENTRY 33—UPDATE

This is starting to feel like one of those days where I should have simply never gotten out of bed.

LAURA POHL

TK-423 LOG—FOREST MOON OF ENDOR—ENTRY 33—UPDATE

The pod crash-landed safely into what seems like a naturally occurring net on the forest canopy. I woke up with a resounding headache and my helmet smelling like wet sand after being hit by a stray shot from a TIE and blown off course. Sky outside is inexplicably filled with fireworks (probably reused after the Emperor's disastrous welcome). Managed to get out of the pod only to be met with one of the furry life-forms that inhabit the place, and immediately had to lock myself up in the pod again due to its incessant banging against the metal, and menacing attitude.

I have sent the communications with my location to my fellow survivors, and hopefully will be reunited with them soon. TK-293's message was short but reassuring: "Coming." There is something to be said of what TK-848 calls "class solidarity," but might really be simply called friendship. I use the word with utmost care here (mostly for TK-534's sake, who one day might be optimistically promoted to cordial acquaintance after today's ordeal).

This is likely the last update, since the enemy outside is intent on my capture and I am not quite sure how long the battery of the datapad will last for me to log things. Perhaps, with some luck, there will be caf wherever we go next.

TO THE LAST

Dana Schwartz

In the moments after the rebel starfighter crashed into the bridge of the ship he commanded, and the world around him became a chasm of glass and flashing lights and screams sucked into the void of space, Admiral Piett wondered if maybe he had made a mistake.

No, he thought, before his lungs constricted and the whooshing sound consumed him, I did everything right.

He had been promoted to fleet admiral by Lord Vader himself—fleet admiral aboard the *Executor*, Lord Vader's personal flagship: a gleaming Dreadnought sharp as ice, with a titanium-reinforced hull and the most sophisticated turbolaser system in the galaxy. His promotion had been sudden, and unorthodox, sure, but still, Piett relished the way the lesser officers averted their glances when he walked down the long, gleaming hallway. The squeak under his shoes as he walked at a clipped, professional pace made him smile and stand up taller. *If only Ozzel were here to see me.* The words entered Piett's head before he realized what he was thinking and shook them away. He was in charge now. Ozzel was gone.

There had been a whisper that Piett's sudden promotion had made him the youngest admiral in Imperial history. If the Empire hadn't been at war, there probably would have been time for a promotion ceremony, for medals, speeches. Perhaps his mother might have flown in from Axxila. How proud she would be to see him, uniform pressed and hair combed, her little boy *important and powerful*.

But Piett was a practical man. A team player. He understood that with the Empire under threat, his promotion was honor enough. A verbal promotion from Lord Vader himself—surely, that was more impressive than any sterile, lifeless ceremony with an audience of jealous officers rolling their eyes beneath their caps. It was a battlefield promotion! There was a certain *rogueish* romance to that, Piett liked to think. It made for a good story. It was only a matter of time before he was made a moff.

You don't become an admiral unless you're special. That was what Piett had muttered to himself in the mirror that morning as he straightened his cap. They would reach Endor's moon within the hour, where they would finally wipe out the Rebellion for good. The rebels had fled and this was their final chance: a desperate move to deactivate the Death Star's energy shield. But the Emperor was smarter than they were: The full force of the Imperial Navy would be waiting for them, and then . . . the second Death Star.

Piett almost felt sorry for the rebels, misguided as they were: They

TO THE LAST

were a crew of fools and outcasts—untrained and disorganized, on an uncivilized forest moon—about to face the full steel and discipline of the Empire.

The *Executor*'s assignment was delivered by Moff Jerjerrod the previous day when his hologram had appeared on the bridge for the first time since Piett had become admiral. Jerjerrod had cold eyes that Piett found unsettling, and he spoke in a droll, casual sort of way, as though the Empire's naval strategy were a lunch that had already disappointed him. He spoke, Piett thought, like a man who had been wealthy his entire life. His previous moff, Tarkin, had been the sort of leader Piett respected, a man *hardened* by battle. Piett had served as a junior officer under Tarkin for two years, and in that time had only gotten the man to quirk a corner of his mouth up into something resembling a smile once. (Piett had filed the reports on possible dissenters on Ferrix a day early and—unprompted—in alphabetical order.)

But when Jerjerrod finished orders, "straight from the Emperor," Piett had saluted. "Sir."

The *Executor* would be making no offensive maneuvers. That was the Emperor's strategy. They were instructed not to fire unless fired upon. Piett understood: The Dreadnoughts were there as a show of force, as intimidation, as distraction. They just needed to occupy the rebels long enough for their shields to be breached so that the second Death Star could do what it was designed to do and eradicate them once and for all. It would be a clean and awe-inspiring victory; Piett found his mouth almost salivating at the thought of the black sky suddenly, dazzlingly, becoming bright with the power of the superlaser. There would be the satisfying swell of the moon, and then—nothing. Dust disappearing into the ether. Let them scramble like insects on the surface of a pond; the rebel cause would become a footnote, a memory, a joke.

How lucky he was, to be an admiral at the Empire's greatest moment of victory. Everyone involved would be promoted. He might even be a moff by the end of the week.

Confident, aren't you? came the whisper that only he could hear. It was a soothing voice, a familiar one. *I was confident, too, Firmus. I had years more experience than you have. I was better than you. And remember how easily he disposed of me?*

Piett closed his eyes and willed the imaginary ghost away. No, he assured himself. I am a good admiral. I am a *better* admiral than Ozzel. That is why he's dead, and I'm in charge of the ship he once commanded. Admiral Ozzel had made a fatal mistake, and so Vader had punished him. There was nothing wrong with that. Piett had *warned* Ozzel that their maneuver back at Hoth was risky, hadn't he? He had told him that there was a chance the rebels would be able to erect a defense shield if they came out of hyperspace too late. He had been a perfect first officer. That was why he was promoted.

And yet . . . he couldn't stop playing the scene in his mind over and over again. He dreamed of it almost every night. The nightmare begins the way it had in life, with the two men speaking to Lord Vader on a display screen. In his dreams, he sees the way Ozzel's eyes had widened in surprise, how his hands lifted to his neck and tugged at the invisible strings that were tightening around his throat. The veins had bulged in his forehead and across his scalp; when he was alive, Ozzel had pretended he was insecure about going bald at his temples, but he always ended his complaints with sly winks at Piett. Ozzel's scalp was visible when he had fallen to the floor—his cap had rolled away, under a control panel.

Had Piett watched him die? Or had his attention immediately gone back to the screen—to Lord Vader's face as he killed Ozzel from a dozen parsecs away? Piett couldn't remember. The medic aboard had come in quickly enough, had covered the admiral—the former

TO THE LAST

admiral—and pushed his gurney away before Piett had to think too much about what had just happened. But in his dreams, Piett would stare at Ozzel's face: He saw it purple and swollen as a jogan fruit, a tongue lolling out, grotesque and terrible. In his dream, he knows Ozzel is dead, but his eyes are open. His mouth moves slowly. Ozzel is always trying to tell him something—to *warn him*—but he can't manage the words out of his broken windpipe.

Most mornings since the promotion, Piett wakes up gasping. Once he found he was clutching at his own throat. But nightmares frightened children. Piett might be the youngest admiral in Imperial history, yes, but—he chuckled to himself at the thought—but he wasn't a child. And by the time he dressed and reached the bridge, the memory of the gasping, choking sound had left his mind entirely, and he was ready to work, his spine straight as an arrow and his resolve firm.

Firmus Piett hadn't always known he was destined for great things. When he was a child on Axxila, he was—loath as he was to admit it—a little, well, ordinary. He was the only child of older parents, a couple for whom having a child had been an afterthought and who then discovered that they had accidentally inconvenienced themselves with an uninvited, rather annoying guest. His father, Pollus, worked in the ore mines in the cliffs to the north, one of the last few men who continued to descend into the dark, cold rock even though the mines hadn't made a profit in decades and most everyone else had left for other opportunities. His mother ran the only inn on the planet, a few rooms ready for an occasional mine investor or for a rare visit from an Imperial officer on a perfunctory tour of Outer Rim planets.

When Piett was young, his father had told him that back when the mine was fully operational, Axxila had been populated, even bustling. But those days were long since gone, and Piett spent a lonely childhood watching his mother sweeping, waiting for her to turn her back so he could run outside to climb the rocks.

"The ore is strong, but it's not strong enough to stand up to the Empire." It was one of Pollus's frequent refrains, almost a mantra, repeated nightly when he came home from work with nothing more than an aching back and a few credits. Piett recalled his father returning home, sighing and running a hand through his thinning hair, still black with ore dust. Pollus spoke about that a lot, that the Empire's demands for ore had stripped the mine bare.

One night Piett snuck out of bed in the middle of the night to find his father still awake. The yellow light of Axxila's three moons gave the room a hazy glow, and Pollus was slumped low in his chair, a cup dangling from his fingers. Without turning around, or even looking at his son, Pollus spoke, his voice thick and robotic: "Axxila is a ghost planet now. Carved from the inside out by strangers a galaxy away. I hope you make it off this husk."

Piett ran back to bed before his father could say any more, terrified without quite knowing why. The next morning, Pollus went to work without saying another word to his son. He died the next year and Piett and his mother had buried him close to the mines where he had spent his life.

Imperial officers occasionally stayed at his mother's inn, but it wasn't until Piett was twelve that he actually met one of them. By that age, his mother had stopped caring whether he ran away from home to climb on the cliffs. There was a ledge about halfway up the bluff where he normally stopped. This time, the day was bright and clear, he could hear his mother's singing voice coming through the window in the distance, and Piett decided to climb higher. Looking back, there had been no real reason why, on that day, he would do something different. It didn't even really feel like he made a choice at all. Once the notion of climbing higher entered his brain, it simply became the thing he was going to do.

And so he climbed—up the craggy bluff, his fingers getting colder and turning white from how hard he had to grip the increasingly sheer cliff face. He was too high to look down without getting dizzy. It was daylight, but one of the moons was still visible above the crest of the bluff, and Piett stared at it, willing himself higher and higher, toward it.

And then he fell.

His stomach pulled itself into his throat and before he could scream his body hit the dirt with a force that made his ears ring and his vision pop black. A sharp pain radiated from somewhere in his lower back; he tried again to scream but his mouth didn't seem to be connected to his brain anymore. It was getting so cold but he didn't know how he was ever going to get home.

It was nearly dark before the man arrived. He was an officer in the Imperial Navy, but Piett didn't know that at the time. Later he would know what the badges and insignia would have meant on the man's chest, but at twelve years old, Piett looked up and only saw a man with friendly round eyes and a ginger mustache. "Hello, chap," he said. "Looks like you took a nasty fall."

Piett just groaned.

"You must be Firmus," the man said, clucking his tongue sympathetically. "Your mum has been making a fuss over you not coming back for dinner. Do you think you can get up if I give you a hand?"

He leaned down before Piett had a chance to respond and swept his arm beneath Piett's back. The pain crackled inside him but soon he was moving, walking with his full weight on the strange Imperial officer's shoulders. Something tasted like blood in his mouth. His vision was still filled with blooming orbs of color but after twenty minutes, the officer had managed to hobble with Piett to the door of his mother's inn.

Piett never learned that man's name, or, if he did, it disappeared from his mind, but the memory of him, dressed in crisp olive, walking him back to his mother when he was sure he had been forgotten by the world, stayed in his mind for the rest of his life. When he was sixteen, he told his mother he was enrolling in the Imperial Navy.

She hadn't responded. She continued sweeping the floor, making no progress. "If your father were here," she muttered. She didn't finish the thought. Piett had burned with shame for a reason he didn't quite understand. Didn't his father want him to *make* something of himself? Hadn't he wanted him to get off this planet? By this time, the mine had been shut down for years. There was nowhere for Firmus Piett to go except the Imperial Navy, to wear a perfect drab cap, to salute, to see the galaxy. To become part of a whole that was setting right things that were wrong.

The *Executor* had arrived at Endor ahead of schedule, though neither Moff Jerjerrod nor Darth Vader bothered to commend Piett for it. The orders were simple: Lie in wait. Protect the defense shields from rebel attacks, but no need for aggression. The second Death Star was more than capable of dealing with the few criminals still clinging to the delusional dream of the old Republic. There was nothing that he was going to do wrong, Piett thought, his hand floating to scratch his neck reflexively. He knew his orders, and he was going to obey them. Why was his heart beating so fast? He was going to do everything right.

Didn't I do everything right, Firmus? It was Ozzel's voice again. His former admiral. His mentor. Piett tried to blink the hallucination away, but there he was, on the bridge, his lips bulging and blue, his eyes bloodshot. The bruise coiled around his neck from a hand that constricted but was never actually there. Piett squeezed his eyes shut. "*No!*"

Piett opened his eyes to see the baffled look of officers around

TO THE LAST

him. The ghost of Ozzel was gone and in his place was one of Piett's officers, looking concerned. "Apologies, Romodi," Piett said quietly. "Forgive me. Just . . . thinking." Romodi raised his eyebrows, but bowed slightly and left Piett alone on the bridge, staring at the forest moon. Waiting.

What was he waiting for exactly? Victory, of course. The moon to be destroyed. The mission to be finished. And then on to the next mission. He had devoted himself to the cause of the Galactic Empire; he wanted it to succeed, it was as simple as that.

When the rebel ships began to fly toward them, Piett had been surprised. These were suicide maneuvers! The rebels were *throwing* themselves at ships ten times their size to try to . . . what? Stave off the inevitable for a moment longer? When the second Death Star finished powering up, when Vader's plan came to fruition, it would all be over. He, Piett, was on the winning side. He *knew that*.

He gave the orders quickly, trying to keep away the wavering of fear that was creeping in at the edges of his voice. They were firing their weapons, but the rebel ships were too small, weaving between larger ships; they were being *smart,* trying to entice the Empire into friendly fire. "Hold fire!" Piett called. Piett began breathing faster. Could Lord Vader see him now? Was he displeased? Should Piett have kept firing? Or had he called for a cease-fire too early? It was becoming hard to breathe now. He wanted to run, to escape back into his bunk, but surely then Vader would kill him for cowardice. When he saw the rebel A-wing gathering speed as it flew straight toward the bridge, he was almost relieved.

I did it, he thought. I did everything right.

THE EMPEROR'S RED GUARDS
Gloria Chao

"Guards, leave us."

I never questioned Emperor Palpatine's orders. Though a part of me felt uneasy about leaving him. It wasn't because I didn't think he could take care of himself—of course he could—it was more that I felt better when he, the one around whom my existence revolved, was in my sights. And maybe I felt the most useful then, too, but it wasn't about me.

Tauk and I left as commanded, waiting just outside the closed door. But we stayed nearby, ready. It was our job. To protect the Emperor and to anticipate his future needs.

I'd sacrificed so much to get here. During training, it had been endless sparring, the daily threat of serious injury, then the final test—a fight to the death in The Squall before Emperor Palpatine. I'd never wanted to impress him more than on that day, and it's only increased since then. Since I was chosen. Since I earned my place. Now, years later, I'd worked my way up from retinue to personal security. I was the last defense before reaching the Emperor. Always on guard, always ready for a fight to the death.

I turned to Tauk and said, "Wish we were still in there?"

"Of course," he said dutifully. "Only to better serve our master."

"Of course," I repeated back. Tauk had the best traits of a soldier—and had gained favor with the Emperor exponentially faster than I had, though I would never admit that out loud—but sometimes it felt like there wasn't much else to him. Couldn't he be loyal and unquestioning without also being so droid-like? I was certainly more loyal than Tauk, the newer recruit who has been tested less, but I'd like to think I had a little more beneath the surface.

Even though I doubted it would receive much of a reaction, I added, "And if we were in there, we could've had a front-row seat to the action." We were always sent away at the most inopportune, juiciest moments, it seemed. Something dramatic was certainly unfolding on the other side of the doors. A fight? Torture? Drat. Never in on the fun.

Tauk didn't respond.

Overhead, explosions rang out. Tauk and I glanced out the closest viewport to see rebel ships bursting into a stunning cascade of fire and flying metal.

"A magnificent sight," Tauk whispered to me in awe. The faith and pride dripping from his voice filled me as I watched more explosions light up the darkness outside.

Then I felt rumbling beneath my feet.

"It's happening," Tauk whispered.

THE EMPEROR'S RED GUARDS

The rumbling grew, reaching its climax before disappearing abruptly. We were showing off. Demonstrating to the young rebel what our mighty Death Star could do.

A new wave of pride surged within me. This was what it had all been for. A superlaser unmatched by any other, capable of destroying entire planets, annihilating them in the blink of an eye. How could anyone be on any other side but that of a power like this?

Tauk must have been thinking the same thing because his grip on his pike tightened in excited anticipation as he said, "The Emperor must be trying to turn the rebel to the dark side."

Maybe Tauk wasn't so droid-like after all.

"What do you think his strategy is?" I asked, wanting to imagine every detail. Witnessing him turn Skywalker would not only be fun but inspiring.

"Whatever it is, it will be brilliant." Tauk didn't need to imagine more, it seemed.

"Do you think he'll push the rebel to attack Darth Vader? To tap into his anger." I stiffened suddenly. "What if he's encouraging an attack on *himself*?"

"Then that would be brilliant. A definite way to turn the rebel."

The Emperor knew best. So if that was his strategy, then it meant it was the best. But it didn't sit comfortably with me, clashing head on with my duty to keep him out of harm's way.

Suddenly, from inside the throne room, a crash rang out as if the ceiling was collapsing, followed by wails of anguish.

My muscles tensed on instinct, worried about the Emperor. But Tauk laughed.

"The rebel is getting what he deserves," he said. "Especially if he is resisting."

Of course. I shouldn't have even worried about the Emperor. My faith should carry me.

I wanted to return inside but would never go against a direct order. "Leave us," he had said. And so outside I remained. Besides, the Emperor could protect himself. Though sometimes I couldn't help wondering: If that was the case, why did the Red Guards exist? But no matter. The Emperor always knew best, always succeeded.

The sound of lightning crackled through the air, punctuated by the rebel's screams. His fate was sealed.

I gripped my pike, waiting. The sound of both the lightning and the screams notched up a level, the intensity making me clench my teeth in anticipation. It didn't matter how many times you killed or heard a kill—your muscles reacted instinctively.

The crackling of the electricity intensified. I could hear it and feel it reverberating in my skull. It was uncomfortable and satisfying at the same time.

It wouldn't be long now. The end was near for the young rebel.

Despite the closed door, screams blasted my eardrums. Screams of fear, of begging for mercy. I felt a smile creeping onto my face.

Suddenly, shouts of "No," followed by more screams. But as the yells filled the air and my insides, dread overtook me, my body reacting before my mind caught up.

Those screams did not sound like Skywalker's.

But that couldn't be.

I turned to Tauk. He returned my gaze, but he didn't move. He was standing there steadfast. Still, as always. Never doubting.

I didn't doubt, but I also couldn't deny my ears. My sharp, trained ears that served me in battle and were also homed in on the Emperor like a hound to its master's voice.

"Do you think—" I began, but Tauk interrupted.

"We were only told to leave, and we were not instructed to return for any reason." Following orders to a T, as always.

All my instincts were shouting at me. I had to check. It wasn't what the Emperor ordered, but this had to be an extenuating circumstance, no?

I opened the door before Tauk could question my choice. Only to be greeted by the young rebel dragging a limp Darth Vader.

Was he kidnapping him?

"Leave us," Darth Vader rasped, seeming on the brink. Those two words sounded so different from when the Emperor had said them.

Perhaps it wasn't a kidnapping?

I froze, unsure of what to do for the first time in my life as a Red Guard. My reactions had been drilled into me, but this was completely new territory. My training told me to follow Vader's orders, him being Palpatine's right hand, but my gut was telling me that something about what I saw before me was wrong.

Tauk watched them go, still standing guard as commanded. Was he continuing to follow orders or was he as confused as I was?

I needed more information. Even if the Emperor punished me, so be it. Because I couldn't live with myself if my failure to clarify the situation led to worse outcomes for the Emperor. Besides, Tauk was surely going to stay here—didn't we have both options covered between the two of us?

I ran inside, with Tauk yelling at me not to leave my post. But he remained outside. Whatever punishment I might face was mine alone.

Inside, it was eerily quiet. Not on the surface—the ceilings were caving in, and outside everyone was running wild—but there wasn't the underlying energy I expected. There was no sign of the Emperor. Had he left the room? I would have seen, wouldn't I?

An uncharacteristic shiver overtook me. Something was wrong.

I didn't see much out of the ordinary, so I turned to my other senses. My grip on my weapons tightened as I picked up the scent of burning flesh—a smell one could never forget, especially after smelling one's own. I eventually ventured far enough that I started to also see a few things—scorch marks, which I followed. The stench grew stronger, my nose and eyes leading in the same direction.

My eyes landed on the reactor shaft where the burn marks slashed angrily—the largest and deepest I'd seen yet.

Smoke billowed up from the opening.

No.

I fell to my knees.

An anguished cry surrounded me. After a moment, I realized it was coming from me.

I didn't want to believe it, but I already knew the truth deep down in my bones.

I should have come running when I heard his screams. I was too late. I'd failed the one duty that had been entrusted to me.

What was I supposed to do now?

I heard footsteps behind me. I turned.

Tauk, approaching. He slowed. He couldn't see my face, but from my position on the ground, he must have a sense of what had happened.

Or did he? "What are you doing? Where is the Emperor?" he asked.

I didn't respond. Couldn't. I just shook my head at him.

He didn't believe me. But then his eyes took in the scorches, and just like mine had a second ago, they locked on to the reactor shaft. Instead of falling to his knees, though, he gripped his pike in hand, determined.

"Let's go," he said. No uncertainty.

"Where?"

"To avenge him, where else?"

Of course. Where had my head gone to? Maybe I could stand to be more like Tauk. Channeling his conviction, I used my pike to pick myself up off the ground.

The new purpose centered me. With a shared nod, we took off in the direction we'd seen the young rebel dragging Lord Vader. Together, we ignored the alarms blaring, lights flashing, and other ranks falling apart around us. They were of no concern to our objective. I forced myself to also ignore the voice in my head asking again whether Skywalker had truly been kidnapping Darth Vader, and if so, why Vader would command us to leave them, allowing the rebel to escape.

Now was the time for action, not thinking. The time to be like Tauk.

Ahead, we spotted them. Lord Vader, not moving, collapsed on the ramp of a shuttle. Skywalker, kneeling over him, his back to us.

Did Skywalker kill Darth Vader? Even though he was worth more to him alive than dead?

The sight didn't make sense until the only possible explanation came to me.

"He did it," I whispered. "The Emperor succeeded. The young rebel has turned." Of course the Emperor had achieved his goal, which led Skywalker to kill both the Emperor and then Darth Vader. Was this somehow all part of the Emperor's plan, one so genius someone like me could never understand?

Tauk paused, unsure what to do now. I didn't know, either. Did we still avenge the Emperor? Did we embrace the rebel?

As we neared the two of them, Skywalker stood and turned to us. At the same time, Tauk and I halted out of sheer confusion.

The rebel had tears on his face. And even more surprising, after he wiped his eyes, he yelled, "Run! Save yourselves! The battle station is crumbling!"

We were still frozen in shock as Skywalker grabbed Vader's body and dragged him up into the shuttle.

All I could do was stare after them. But as I took in Darth Vader's fallen form, everything came to me all at once.

The damage to Vader's suit. The absence of a lightsaber wound. Vader's "leave us."

Skywalker hadn't changed sides. He didn't kill the Emperor. Darth Vader did. And he was killed in the process.

How could he? Why?

That wasn't even the most important part.

The Emperor had failed. Completely.

Tauk began following the rebel but stopped when he realized I wasn't following him. "What are you doing?"

I couldn't answer. The truth was, I had no idea. My head felt like it was splitting in two.

"You didn't attack him!" Tauk accused me.

"Neither did you!" I hurled back at him.

"Well, let's pursue!"

Skywalker wasn't even the one who'd killed the Emperor—we wouldn't be avenging anything. And more important, that was the least of my concerns right now. Didn't Tauk feel the enormous weight of what had just happened?

The Emperor was *dead*. Gone. There were no more orders coming from him. None of this had been part of his master plan. Our world had just been turned upside down and was on the brink of what felt like destruction. In light of all that, the situation didn't feel as black and white as before.

Hesitantly, I said to Tauk, "What does it mean . . . that the Emperor was wrong? He said he would prevail." He'd been completely, utterly wrong.

I felt my faith starting to slip away, but what kind of soldier did

THE EMPEROR'S RED GUARDS

that make me? And that was the only identity I had. Soldier. And not only was I a soldier, but I was the most loyal. The one handpicked by the Emperor himself to protect him.

And I'd failed. I'd been *outside the room* when he'd been killed.

"We failed," I said, my voice almost a whisper. "We failed him."

Tauk didn't seem to be having the same existential crisis as me. "That's why we need to avenge him!" So black and white. How was he able to hold on to that?

"The young rebel didn't kill him," I said. The next words tasted like sand coming out of my dry mouth. "Darth Vader did."

"How can you say that? Darth Vader would never have turned."

Except he did. I was sure of it. Darth Vader, Emperor Palpatine's devoted pet, had turned to the other side. If even he could . . .

"Tauk . . ." I said slowly. "Do you understand the gravity of what has happened? The Emperor *failed*."

Could it be? I couldn't say it out loud.

Were we wrong to have followed him?

That couldn't be. I'd dedicated my whole life to him.

Tauk shook his head. "We just can't see his whole plan. That's not our job. Our duty is to avenge the Emperor, then return to Coruscant so we can learn what plan the Emperor has put in place moving forward."

"Use your head, Tauk! The Emperor wasn't supposed to die! There are no plans. There is no Empire without the Emperor."

I'd been born to uphold this legacy, pushed to want this duty, and damn proud to have achieved it. But now, in the wake of the Emperor's death—his *failure*—I couldn't stop thinking about the other side.

A profound desire to save myself came over me. I started to move. But I'd only shifted my weight before Tauk was in front of me, pike drawn into battle-ready position.

"Tauk."

He lunged at me, pike tip thrusting through the air. "Traitor! You're deserting the Empire!"

"There are no rules for this!" I yelled back as I dodged his attack. But because of the surprise of it, I didn't manage to move fast enough and the tip tore through a piece of my red cloak. I parried his next few attacks, but I was struggling. He was in full rage, coming at me hard, hitting me with everything he had.

I blocked, always on the defensive, moving backward down the ramp of the shuttle, and toward a corner.

"Tauk, wait," I said breathlessly, but he ignored me.

We continued to strike, pike against pike.

My feet digging into the ground, I finally managed to put enough force against his weapon to cause a standstill, each of us pushing against the other's outstretched weapon but without movement.

Tauk released one hand from the pike, which allowed me to press mine closer. But then he used his free hand to grab his blaster pistol, forcing me to do the same.

Now we were both weapons drawn, arms outstretched, circling each other slowly. One step. Two steps. No sudden movements.

The last time I'd had to fight another Red Guard was in The Squall when I earned this position. I'd had to kill one of my closest friends, but such was the sacrifice. I'd won then. But so had Tauk. Otherwise, neither of us would be standing here.

"Tauk," I began, intending to find a way to get him to pause so we could breathe, think, talk about how I just needed a second to unwind the million thoughts in my brain that were battling to the death. Red Guards were unquestionably loyal to Emperor Palpatine. Who were we without him? And why was Tauk so unfazed?

Tauk's hand beneath his robe moved the slightest millimeter.

Without hesitation, I shot him with my blaster pistol. It was him or me. He didn't give me a choice.

THE EMPEROR'S RED GUARDS

I took off. I didn't look back.

But as Tauk went down, he must have managed to get off a blaster shot of his own. It bypassed me but hit a nearby ship. I heard the contact overhead, but there wasn't enough time. A piece of the ship broke off. I managed to run a few steps, but the giant slab of steel fell swiftly, crushing my legs beneath it.

I was going to die a coward's death, without having protected my Emperor, without keeping the faith to my dying breath. I should be going out in battle against the rebel forces, not a single doubt in my head.

I closed my eyes.

Suddenly, the pressure on my legs decreased, but only slightly. Maybe the adrenaline pumping through me was helping.

Then the pressure disappeared completely.

I looked up. Skywalker was standing above me, having used the Force to lift the rubble.

"Hurry!" he yelled as he continued to shift the surrounding debris blocking the shuttle's escape. Once the path was clear, he disappeared back inside.

As his shuttle took off, I sprinted toward the nearest ship. No time to think.

I flew off the Death Star without a second to lose. The explosion rocked the ship, sending debris and fire flying all around me. I navigated between the obstacles and forced myself not to look back.

But now that I had escaped, all I could do was think, about everything.

What now? What was the galaxy going to look like with the Emperor dead? How would it function? I'd meant it earlier when I told Tauk that there was no Empire without the Emperor. I didn't see how we would continue.

As I hurtled farther and farther from the disintegrating Death

Star, the most unwelcome thought appeared: How would I fit into it all?

The Red Guard life, the dark side, the Empire were all I'd ever known.

Yet . . .

Could I return to it after all I'd seen today?

Or . . .

I couldn't even say it.

Could I be a part of something else?

Would they even take me?

At least one of them would, a small traitorous part of my brain said, the same part that hadn't let me fire at the young rebel when I'd had the chance. And the answer felt obvious. The person who'd told me to save myself, then actually saved me so I could be sitting here right now, hating myself for all these thoughts, would certainly welcome me in.

I'd have a lot of information to offer.

Yet another part of me wanted to fly my ship directly into another one just for having the thought.

I couldn't make any decisions right now. And as much as I wasn't supposed to, I took a second to mourn my Emperor.

And I mourned for myself. Where was I going to go from here?

WOLF TRAP

Alyssa Wong

The forest always made Hoyel uneasy. He had been stationed on Endor for half a year, but each day felt like the first. The towering trees bristled with strange life, from long-bodied, iridescent lizards with too many legs to entire insect colonies disguised as winding vines. The leafy canopy blocked out the massive, partially constructed second Death Star, making it impossible to see from the ground. Danger lurked around every bend. Two weeks into his deployment, Hoyel had watched his Imperial commanding officer lean against a rock, only to be swallowed headfirst by camouflaged carnivorous fungus.

At least he was safe on his speeder bike. The vehicle was his most trusted companion; he knew every scratch in its paint, ding in its shell, and quirk in its nav system. They had a deal, Hoyel and the bike: He took care of it, and it took care of him. It hadn't let him down yet. As long as he stuck to his patrol route and didn't touch any strange life-forms, Hoyel kept this thought cradled tight as he zipped through the forest, surrounded by the comforting rumble of his speeder bike's engine.

He didn't see the woven-fiber cable stretched between the trees until it was too late.

The rope slammed into Hoyel's chest, hurling him from his bike. The speeder flew end over end, smashing into the ground and exploding behind him. Fiery shrapnel rained around Hoyel as he landed on the forest floor, shedding pieces of white trooper armor. The impact punched the breath out of him; he gasped for air, clawing at the dirt. There was soil in his eyes, his mouth—

His mouth?

His hands flew to his face. His scout trooper helmet was *gone*.

Hoyel struggled to sit up, panicked. He couldn't afford to replace the helmet, much less the speeder bike. Command would dock his wages until they deemed the equipment paid for, but how long would that take? One year? Two? Hoyel barely made enough to make ends meet and he sent every spare credit back home to Kavith III.

Aren't there more important things for you to worry about? asked a little voice in the back of his head. It sounded like Caya, as it always did. Hoyel scanned the area, shading his eyes against the blinding flames billowing from the destroyed speeder bike. At first, he saw nothing. Just his bike burning, a noxious plume of black smoke wafting into the air. But then he spotted a small, stout figure picking through the wreckage. They were dragging a netted sack full of looted pieces of machinery. The stranger picked up Hoyel's scout trooper helmet, bashing it experimentally against a nearby rock.

WOLF TRAP

"Wait," Hoyel croaked, holding his hand out. "That's mine."

The stranger turned toward him and he instantly realized his mistake. It wasn't a short human at all. No, this creature had small, rounded ears poking out of its leather hood. Its whole body was covered in thick, dark-gray fur, and it regarded him with bright, beady black eyes.

Oh, Light. It was an Ewok.

Hoyel tried to scrabble backward as the Ewok approached, tilting its head to the side and hefting a club in its paw. Many members of his platoon had gone missing while patrolling Ewok territory, and Hoyel was about to be added to that statistic. "No, wait, please! You can keep the helmet! I won't tell anyone—"

"Yub," the Ewok said decisively, and brought the club down on his skull.

Everything hurt.

Hoyel's head was filled with agonizing, radiating pressure. It felt like it was about to split open like a rotting moonfruit. His mouth tasted like bile and vomit. His ankles were bound, and he was being dragged backward across the forest floor. His remaining armor scraped over roots and stones, each jerky movement sending another wave of nausea through him. His arms flopped uselessly past his head. Whoever had captured him hadn't bothered to tie them.

Hoyel didn't want to open his eyes. But when he did, he was greeted by a nightmare.

He was surrounded by Ewoks, their wobbly, blurry forms doubled over and over again. He couldn't tell how many there were; he couldn't focus his eyes. But there were enough to haul him through the forest and walk beside him, guarding their prey from potential predators. The sun had set while he was out, and the only light came from the

Ewoks' torches. The fire glimmered in their eyes as they chattered to one another in an excited, chirping language.

Hoyel blinked up at the sky. But there was no sky here, just the cluttered, laced branches of ancient trees. Nothing around him would hold its shape; the Ewoks swayed into one another, the forest shivered and melted. *Concussion,* he thought distantly. Even that word cost him, pain lancing through his head, so he stopped thinking.

He was placed in a large, woven net and hauled up into the forest canopy. The Ewoks' voices grew louder as they raced up ladders and stairs, following Hoyel's net. More torches then. More Ewoks. A village? No, some kind of scouting outpost. A brief series of platforms built in the treetops, connected by suspended bridges. As Hoyel's net reached a landing platform, his gaze drifted past a series of spears decorating the area, each with a large, white stone mounted on it.

No, not a stone. Stormtrooper helmets. Every single one impaled on a spear, a sickening reminder of the Ewoks' hunts.

When Hoyel lost consciousness again, it was a mercy.

"Trooper! Wake up!" someone hissed.

Hoyel groaned, cracking his eyes open. He was slumped against a post, his wrists bound behind him with thick rope. The world was still blurry. The only thing he could focus on in the dark was a bonfire on a distant platform. A cluster of Ewok scouts danced around it, feasting and singing.

If Hoyel turned his head, he could barely make out a glinting white shape on his right.

"What's your designation?" Two large black eyes and a wide, disapproving mouth in a white, white face. It took a moment for Hoyel to piece them together into a stormtrooper helmet. His neighbor was

WOLF TRAP

a trooper, too. And there were three more, arranged in a neat line, all tied to individual posts just like Hoyel. "Answer the question, trooper."

"I . . ." *Does it matter?* Hoyel wondered. "I'm TK-814. You?"

"TK-830. This is TK-121, TK-246, and TK-093." The stormtrooper on Hoyel's right—TK-830—nodded at the others. "Wasn't sure you'd wake up. You've been out for a day."

A day? Hoyel felt a glimmer of hope. If he didn't report in, maybe the garrison would send out a search party to look for him.

But that hope dimmed almost immediately. These troopers must have been here longer than him and he'd never heard about a search party for them. "What happened to you?" Hoyel asked them.

"We were investigating rebel activity not far from here. The commander noticed ships coming in and out, near the Death Star shield bunker, so she sent us to collect intel." TK-830 shook his head. "We came prepared to deal with rebel scum, but these Ewoks ambushed us. We didn't stand a chance."

That was why their designations sounded familiar. "Your squad went missing last week," Hoyel realized. But that meant there should be ten troopers here, not four. "Where are the rest of you?"

TK-830 shuddered, turning his head toward the bonfire in the distance. "They've been eating us."

There were countless reasons to hate Endor. Hoyel counted them over and over, trying to breathe steadily and evenly, fighting his suffocating panic and the dull, stabbing pain in his wrists. *The humidity that soaks into your skin. The unreliable comms signal at the best of times. The boredom. The loneliness. The way everything here is always trying to kill you.*

But the biggest one, for Hoyel, was how it felt like there were no stars on Endor. The thick canopy of trees choked them out of the night sky. Without them, he felt lost. Unmoored.

Back home, there was no place to hide from the stars. Kavith III was a flat, icy, Outer Rim world cut through with black lakes and treacherous rivers. The sky stretched on forever, unobstructed by mountains or buildings. Villages were dug painstakingly into the frozen ground so people could shelter from the howling blizzards. Hoyel remembered staying underground for weeks, his family rationing their meager food supplies to make them last. He slept to escape his hunger, taking comfort in the knowledge that no matter how loudly the wind screamed, the stars would be waiting for him when it was safe to come back out again.

Once, when Hoyel was young, he emerged after a long snowstorm to check his family's trap line. He and his best friend, Caya, had gawked at the auroras streaking across the sky. Swaths of greens, pinks, and purples, dotted with brilliant pinpricks of starlight. The night was most beautiful after a blizzard.

So was Caya.

They trekked over the snow with wide, wooden slippers strapped to their feet, digging for game that was buried beneath the new powder fall. Soon they each had a brace of frozen hares slung over their back. But then Caya stopped in front of Hoyel, holding out a cautionary hand. The wind picked up, ruffling his long, blond hair. "Wolf," he muttered.

Sure enough, an enormous, white-furred Kavith wolf crouched in the snow, baring its teeth in a low, rumbling snarl. It was lean and narrow like other Kavith wolves Hoyel had seen before, easily as tall as his shoulder. The wolf's two tails lashed behind it. One of its hind legs was caught in the trap's metal jaws, pierced down to the bone.

The snow around the trap was packed down and streaked with

hard, frozen blood. The creature had been stuck here for a while, maybe days.

Hoyel approached cautiously to get a better look. "We can't just leave it here," he said. "It's starving to death." Its ribs were already hollow beneath its thick coat. It looked as hungry as he felt.

"If you free it, it'll turn on you!" Caya argued, drawing his hooded pelt jacket tighter around his body.

The wolf growled louder. Hoyel crept closer anyway.

Not all the blood was old, he saw. Some of it was; the rusty, dry smears on the trap and the wolf's fur were days old. But there was fresh, bright blood, too. Wet between the Kavith wolf's teeth, wet on the animal's leg. Wet on the torn flesh above the trap, and the gleaming bone peeking through.

"It's gnawing its own leg off," Hoyel whispered, stomach lurching. He grabbed for Caya's hand to steady himself. The village told stories about creatures chewing pieces of themselves off to escape from traps, but he had never seen it himself.

The wolf growled again, curling in on itself. This time, it sounded weaker.

"We have to kill it," Caya said, gripping Hoyel's hand hard. Hoyel knew what he sounded like when he was trying not to cry. "For its own good. We *have* to, Hoyel."

Looking back on it now, maybe he should have chosen differently. But that day, Hoyel drew his hunting knife and tried to ignore that the wolf's brown eyes looked like Caya's.

There was no water to drink. Hoyel's mouth was thick and dry, and his head pounded nonstop. The Ewoks weren't feeding them, either. Why waste food on food?

The Ewoks had taken two of the remaining troopers over the past two days. One of those troopers—Hoyel couldn't remember whether it was TK-121, TK-246, or TK-093—had screamed and fought until the end. The other had barely moved. Hoyel hoped he was unconscious by the time the Ewoks got him.

Their helmets had been added to the outpost's fence of trophies.

Hoyel wondered what would happen to him when his time came. Since he had no helmet, maybe they would just take his head.

"Stop thinking," rasped TK-830. He and the other remaining trooper barely moved anymore. *Conserving energy,* according to TK-830. "I can hear you thinking. Just trust that the garrison is looking for us."

Hoyel thought of the Kavith wolf, all those years ago. How long had it been stuck in the trap, slowly starving to death, before Caya and he had found it?

"Don't give up, TK-814. That's an order," TK-830 said sternly.

Hoyel heard what he was really saying: *Don't leave me to face this alone.*

"Yes, sir," he said. TK-830 had no official authority over him, but that wasn't important. The trooper was clinging to the last scraps of order he could hold on to, hoping it would save him.

"Good," sighed TK-830. "Save your strength."

Hoyel dropped his chin to his chest and closed his eyes, just for a second.

It was an old, well-worn dream, one that Hoyel had had almost every night for the past two years. Its bones were built from memory. He was nineteen again, sitting at the table in his underground home on Kavith III, watching an Imperial recruitment holodisk. His packed bag rested by the door.

WOLF TRAP

Footsteps sounded down the stairs behind him. Hoyel snapped the holo off, but it was too late. Caya stood in the doorway, holding a lantern to ward off the dark. He looked betrayed.

"You promised you wouldn't enlist," Caya said, descending the stairs. The lantern swayed, the light catching on his pale hair. His eyes shone like amber. For a moment, he wasn't Caya, but the wolf.

"It's the only way off this planet," Hoyel argued. "The blizzards are getting worse, Imperial taxes increase every year, and we barely make enough to scrape by. You wanted to leave. We've always wanted to leave!"

It was one of many promises they'd whispered together under the auroras. And it was special, because it was the first.

Caya set the lantern down on the table "If you sign yourself away to the Empire, I can't come with you," he said, cupping Hoyel's face. "Times are tough now, but we can keep saving without taking their credits. When we have enough money, we can catch a ship and start over somewhere new. We'll leave together."

"Or you could come with me," Hoyel offered. Caya's expression closed off, but Hoyel pushed on. "Enlist with me, learn the Empire's secrets, then defect with that intel to the Rebellion! We'll have enough money to start a new life *and* help the rebels win the war! Caya, this could be our chance to do something that matters!"

"You think it's that easy to escape the Empire?" Caya snapped. "When they catch you, they'll kill you—if not now, then someday. We'll never be able to stop running." The lamp light shivered around him. "Let the Rebellion find someone else to play the turncoat soldier. It doesn't have to be you."

"I'll be careful," Hoyel said, turning his face and pressing a kiss to Caya's palm. "I promise."

The lamp flickered, then went out.

"Don't go," Caya whispered. His fingers traced Hoyel's cheek.

Hoyel was glad it was too dark to see his expression; he would have caved. "Please, Hoyel. Isn't this enough for you?"

Hoyel held him that night, imprinting Caya's warmth into himself.

By sunrise, Hoyel was gone.

A fat, wet droplet hit his ear. Another landed on his neck. Then more, plinking off his armor and soaking into his clothes. Hoyel blinked, lifting his head. Beyond the tree cover, the sky was clotted with dark, heavy clouds.

It was raining. Beautiful, Light-blessed rain.

"TK-830! Wake up! It's raining!" Hoyel rasped, nudging the trooper with his foot. He opened his mouth to catch the falling drops, drinking as much as he could. The rain tasted like leaves and old dirt. Hoyel was so happy he could weep.

The wind picked up and the rain kept coming, hammering down on the outpost. Water rushed around the unprotected troopers, forming little rivers around their bodies and streaming off the edge of their elevated platform. They were soaked and cold, battered by the elements.

Hoyel had never felt so alive.

Something swept past his numb fingers. He managed to pin it with his bound hands before it was pulled away by the water. When its sharp edge bit into his palm, he recognized what the object was: a fragment of broken armor.

"What did I tell you?" TK-830 yelled over the storm. "Don't give up!"

"Yes, sir!" Hoyel shouted back, grinning so widely his face hurt. He felt halfway mad, giddy with adrenaline again.

"All you have to do is have faith! The Empire will come for us!"

WOLF TRAP

TK-830 pointed his chin at the sky, where the boiling clouds were starting to part.

The second Death Star stared down at them, huge and pale. A jagged, judgmental eye, uncaring and bleak.

"That's our Emperor's promise," TK-830 said. His voice was worshipful. "The promise of order throughout the galaxy. Freedom and protection for all."

Hoyel laughed, shaking and hysterical, his brief euphoria draining away. Finally, a star, he thought bitterly. One that would obliterate planets when its construction was finished, wiping out countless lives like they meant nothing. It looked so much more complete than the last time he had seen it.

What a fool he'd been. He'd hoped to be stationed somewhere he could gather important Imperial military intel to funnel to the Rebellion. Instead, he had been stuck on Endor with a speeder bike and no means to pass that information on, all while the Empire developed its superweapon. Stranded far away from Caya, of no use to anyone. About to be eaten by Ewoks. And none of it would matter; he was stupid to think he could fight back against the Empire in the first place, especially from the inside.

But.

But the Death Star wasn't finished yet. Neither were the rebels. And neither was Hoyel.

"Right." He said hoarsely, gazing up at the Death Star. "Freedom for all."

As TK-830 rallied the other trooper, Hoyel flexed his fingers until he could feel them again. Then he flipped the piece of armor in his hand and began to saw.

That day, years ago, Hoyel approached a trapped Kavith wolf with only a hunting knife in hand. Caya was at his back, his own knife drawn so he could protect Hoyel. Two gangly, half-grown boys facing down an injured predator, their hearts full of terror and mercy.

Hoyel had hesitated.

That was all the Kavith wolf needed. It opened its massive jaws and bit down on its own injured hind leg with a savage *crunch*. The bone cracked. The beast tore itself free, leaping out of the trap. Hoyel and Caya fell back and the wolf bounded away toward freedom, running on three legs almost as easily as four.

It left behind a bloody trail and its severed limb, still warm on the ice.

When the rain relented, the Ewoks took one more trooper, leaving only Hoyel and TK-830.

Hoyel didn't watch. Instead, he stared at the sky and gripped his makeshift knife until his palm bled.

He was so hungry.

He tried to block out the Ewoks singing, the crackling fire, the charred scent wafting through the air. How TK-830's groans matched Hoyel's own stomach.

Light above, he was so hungry.

The rope around his wrists swelled with rainwater, tightening.

He sawed.

TK-830 was saying something.

Hoyel tried to listen, but it was hard to focus. His headache was

WOLF TRAP

worse than ever and his hands were cold, trembling, and slick with blood. TK-830's face was a smear with no distinct features, his body a collection of shapes that made no sense. "What?"

"I said, a rescue party is coming," TK-830 wheezed. "I've been broadcasting an SOS from my helmet comm since we were captured and the garrison finally received it. They're coming to get us, TK-814."

Hoyel's makeshift knife slipped, slicing his smallest finger down to the bone. He swallowed a scream, gritting his teeth.

"We'll be safe soon. After the rest of the troops burn down this outpost, we'll be transferred to a medical facility. The Empire takes care of its own." Did TK-830 think that saying it aloud made it true? "It'll be all right, TK-814. We'll leave together."

And go where? Hoyel wondered. The Empire was everywhere. Even if he survived Endor long enough to desert, nowhere would be safe. He and Caya would be hunted to the end of the galaxy. The money he had sent over the past year and a half was barely anything; no shaky future was worth what he had left behind to obtain it.

If Hoyel never made it back to Kavith III, was that all Caya would have to remember him by? A few credits, their broken promise, and the aching shape of his absence?

Loud, rhythmic Ewok chanting rose through the trees. TK-830 froze and Hoyel sawed harder at his bonds. The tough fiber rope was finally starting to give, but it was still too tight to wriggle free. His hands were too big. He wouldn't be able to cut through it fast enough before the Ewoks reached him.

These ones were warriors. And there were so many of them, a blurry sea of beady eyes and chattering mouths. In Hoyel's blurred vision, their torches were a floating wave of flames and their bodies undulated, running at the edges like wet ink. Nothing felt real.

And they weren't alone. Caya and the three-legged Kavith wolf emerged from the trees, trailing the Ewoks as they crossed the suspension bridge to the captives' platform. Hoyel's breath caught in his throat. He was definitely hallucinating now.

Still, there were worse last sights than Caya. He stood amid the Ewoks, resting his hand on the wolf's back, silent and accusing.

"I'm sorry," Hoyel told him, blinking to keep Caya's image clear in his eyes. "I promised I'd come home, but I couldn't."

"Who are you talking to?" demanded TK-830, but Hoyel ignored him.

The lead warrior raised its spear, rattling the bones attached to the handle. The other Ewoks eagerly stepped forward—

—And a deafening explosion sounded overhead. The Death Star shattered in the sky, detonating into a fireball so bright that the whole world went white. Hoyel flinched against his bonds. The rope creaked, stretching but not breaking.

"No," whispered TK-830, horrified. When Hoyel opened his eyes again, the blinding glow was fading from the sky and TK-830 was staring at what had once been the Death Star. "Did the rebels . . . did we lose?"

Hoyel watched the pieces of the battle station catch fire and become brilliant, long-tailed streaks far, far above Endor. They looked like the meteors that Caya and Hoyel had pinned their wishes to long ago.

We'll leave together.

While everyone else watched the sky, Hoyel met Caya's and the wolf's gazes. The wolf bared its teeth in a savage smile, opening its jaws. Caya nodded.

Hoyel knew what he had to do.

The wolf bit down. So did Hoyel's knife.

Heart-stopping pain seared through his smallest finger as he drove the makeshift blade as deep into the wound as he could. And then it

WOLF TRAP

was done—his finger fell away and his hand, now smaller, slipped free of the rope.

Hoyel was up and running before he knew what he was doing. He shoved past the surprised Ewoks, stumbling across the bridge and down one of the winding staircases. TK-830 screamed at his back, but Hoyel barely heard him. He left him behind, feeling lighter with every stride.

The forest loomed around Hoyel, but he was no longer afraid. He ran, shedding his armor and following Caya and the wolf into the trees.

THE EXTRA FIVE PERCENT

M. K. England

There are only so many times you can deeply contemplate your own mortality.

The first few times Karie Neth was sent into danger on a mission for the Rebel Alliance, she did the usual soul searching, sending messages to family, crying, and praying. She joined up with the decimated Alliance just after the Battle of Mako-Ta, and in the three years since she'd deployed to half a dozen worlds, leaving destroyed bases and dead comrades behind on each.

After a while, she eased off the intensely earnest pre-mission messages to her brother. She stopped seeking out her favorite foods as a morbid "last meal" ritual. And, to the relief of her various bunkmates, she eventually abandoned her habit of midnight conversations about the meaning of life and the nature of the afterlife in favor of sweet, sweet sleep. Eventually, facing down the possibility of death became a background hum, tuned out in the same way as the faint vibration of *Home One*'s engines.

As morning broke on the day they would assault the second Death Star, Karie Neth did nothing more than drool straight into her pillow, soaking up every last bit of rest she could possibly get. It was a pre-battle ritual that she swore by these days, to the point that she could be (and frequently *was*) accused of needling her fellow rebels about their shoddy sleep habits.

Unfortunately, not everyone respected her now time-honored ritual.

Bee-BEEP. Bee-BEEP. Bee-BEEP.

It was *not* the alarm she'd set to ensure the perfect balance of sleep and mission readiness.

It was, in fact, Karie's best friend Lanna, proving that she had a death wish.

Karie snatched her datapad from under her bunk and squinted at the screen. There were only three words.

> Come find me.

Not nearly enough to justify her transgression. Karie's fingers, clumsy with sleep, tapped over the screen.

> Do you not want me to be rested for this battle?
> Do you want me to crash into a Star Destroyer?

Lanna must have anticipated her reaction, though, because the reply came so fast it must have been already queued up.

THE EXTRA FIVE PERCENT

> Those fifteen minutes of extra sleep will not make or break your combat readiness, Yellow Nine. I want to see you before the battle.

The warm glow from being referred to as Yellow Nine finally pushed the last groggy clouds from Karie's brain. She swung her legs over the edge of the bunk and threw on yesterday's uniform, fully intending to change into her flight suit in the squadron locker room before anyone had a chance to look too closely. She'd probably find Lanna there anyway, troubleshooting gear or consulting with pilots on the state of their ships. A week ago, Karie would have been right there with her. But she'd gotten a new assignment.

A spot in a squadron, flying an X-wing with Yellow Group. The thought still sent a thrill straight to her heart.

It was a small blessing that she and Lanna were stationed together on *Home One* for this, the war's largest and most important offensive push to date. They'd joined up together, two nineteen-year-old kids from Baraan-Fa looking for revenge and glory as fighter pilots. Three years of real work for the Alliance had scuffed the shine right off those delusions of grandeur and hardened them into something else entirely: the real, ugly, grease-stained devotion born of sustaining a war effort and staying alive when very powerful people wanted your atoms scattered in their ion trails. No less sincere or loyal. Just a bit wiser. They'd been separated and reunited over and over in that time, but it felt right to be together for this one.

For the first one where either of them would fly with a squadron.

For three years, it had been the same refrain: "We have more talented pilots than we have spaceworthy birds." Karie and Lanna kept up their qualifications, logged their sim time, took on recon and shuttle duty whenever it was available. But for the majority of the past three years, they'd worked ground crew and maintenance: supporting squadrons throughout the Mid Rim Offensive campaign, sending transports away on Hoth, scraping together functioning starfighters while the Alliance tried desperately to pull itself back together again. But now, as they hung in the space over the Sullust staging area, Karie walked through the door to the locker room not to tinker with someone's flight helmet, but to grab her own.

Karie entered the locker room to find it half full of pilots from both her own Yellow Group and their sister squadron, Green Group. Some were quiet, working through their personal mortality rituals or projecting the same sort of intense, focused demeanor Commander Crynyd was so known for. Most, though, were jostling each other and shooting jokes like turbolasers, coping with dark humor and almost forceful cheer. Several nodded or clapped her on the shoulder as she walked by, searching the rows for Lanna's familiar black braids and mischievous smile.

"Krayt!" a voice called as Karie finally reached her locker. She glanced over to see her new wingmate, Rowe Jascott, nicknamed "Torp," standing next to his open locker farther down the row. The top half of his flight suit dangled unzipped from his waist as he tied back his shoulder-length copper-brown hair. Karie rolled her eyes. She would've much rather gained her nickname via flying prowess or other heroics. Instead, she was yet another entry in the long history of pilots who had been named according to whatever people made fun of them for.

"Don't talk to me yet, Torp," Karie grumbled, playing into the bit. "I have to hunt down Lanna. Is she here?"

Torp gasped with theatrical horror. "Don't tell me she woke the dragon!"

"She did," Karie said grimly. "It's such a shame she's not going to make it through today's battle."

"I'll be sure to raise a glass to her memory at the victory party."

THE EXTRA FIVE PERCENT

"Good. Someone has to." Karie pulled open her locker and stared at the contents.

The empty locker stared back.

"Is now a good time to mention that Lanna *was* here earlier and that she took your gear hostage?" Torp said with a far-too-bright smile. "I'd try the flight deck if I were you."

Karie slammed her locker and pointed at Torp as she stalked away, lips twitching as she tried not to laugh at the whole situation. "Don't forget who's watching your back out there today."

"I trust you with my life, Krayt!" Torp called after her.

His tone made it a lighthearted rejoinder, but the words cut straight through her defenses. As she left the locker room behind, heading for the flight deck, they settled in her heart and set her blood rushing in her ears. It was a very different sort of pre-battle nerves than what she was used to. It was one thing to be a cog in the machine supporting the front lines and enabling others to fight. It was another to fly straight into the maw of the Empire with her own hand on the throttle.

Focus. One thing at a time. Find Lanna. Get her gear back. Attend the mission briefing.

Fly.

Karie tossed a salute to the deck officer as she stepped onto the flight deck of fighter bay three, scanning the wide-open spaces between snubfighters for any sign of Lanna.

There. *There* she was. Lanna, perched on top of a lift, head shoved halfway inside a wing-mounted X-wing engine.

And there was Karie's X-wing. The bird that would carry her into battle. Of *course* Lanna was working on it. As she drew close, Karie saw her flight suit and other gear folded into a neat pile under the starboard strike foils.

"Happy now?" Karie called up to announce her presence. Lanna jumped, knocking her head on the inside of the engine casing with a swear, then slowly wiggling her way back out. She swung her legs over the side of the lift and dropped the rest of the way to the deck, her daring grin and Karie's fake annoyed scowl like dogfighting X-wings between them.

Karie broke first. Her lip twitched, then both burst into laughter so loud they startled a passing Verpine mechanic.

"Yeah, yeah, fine, it was funny," Karie said when she caught her breath. "But I *will* have my vengeance."

After the battle was the unspoken echo at the end of her sentence. The beat of silence that followed overflowed with the giant unspoken *if* between them: *if we both survive*. The silence stretched into discomfort as Karie took in Lanna's wide smile, dancing brown eyes, and painfully lovely, familiar face.

"I always thought I'd have you on my wing, when the time finally came," Karie finally blurted. "You're just as good as I am. I don't know why . . ."

"Stop," Lanna said, cutting her off with a wave. "It's nice of you to say and all, but you're the better pilot. Captain Ribeiro made the right choice. As much as I'd love to fly, this is where I can do the most good. I want the best pilots watching your back, and that's not me."

Then, because the sincerity was too much, she continued. "And I want the best tech working on your bird, and that *is* me."

"Damn right," Karie said, pointing up at the still-open engine casing. "What are you doing to it? Isn't it a bit late for repairs?"

"Just a bit of a tune-up," Lanna said, spinning a hydrospanner in one hand. "Managed to squeeze an extra five percent out of the thrusters. It's not much—"

"But out there, five percent can be the difference between a near miss and a cloud of wreckage. I appreciate it, Lan."

The rush of affection, of gratitude, was too much. Karie slipped past Lanna to grab the pile of gear and get her emotions back under control. It had been a long time since a mission had really gotten to her, making her think about life and death and all that.

She looked back up at Lanna and their eyes locked, that *other* unspoken *if* rising to fill the silence between them. For the thousandth time, Karie wondered: *Have I done the right thing, waiting for the war to be over? Should I have said something sooner?*

Lanna wrapped her in a tight hug before she could chase the thought too far, crushing their bodies together like she could physically shield Karie from danger. Karie wrapped her free arm around Lanna and squeezed back, burying her face in Lanna's neck and soaking up the scent of engine grease and home.

"Be safe," Lanna whispered.

"Always." Karie pulled back just far enough to let Lanna see the determination in her eyes.

Her throat ached with the need to say more, to leave no truth unspoken, but she swallowed it all down. People loved to go on about leaving nothing unsaid before battle, about going in with no regrets, but Karie knew better. Distractions got people killed. Hope kept people alive. Better to hope for a beautiful reunion than go into battle nursing a wounded heart, never able to repair the friendship if a declaration went wrong and one of them died before they could speak again.

No. Better to leave it. Better to fly with a fierce and full heart.

Karie pulled back, squeezed Lanna's hand, then left for the locker room. The mission briefing would be starting soon. Time to cut herself off.

Once dressed in her orange flight suit, Karie slid into a seat right in the front row of the ready room, clutching her flight helmet on her lap. The sight of now famous generals like Solo and Calrissian casually talking only a few meters away would normally have provoked some level of nerves. Instead, Karie found herself calm, focused, and completely capable of holding a conversation with the Sullustan B-wing pilot who came over to congratulate her on her first flight with Yellow Group. The hunt for Lanna and the exchange that followed had burned off the last of Karie's nervous energy . . . which had almost certainly been the point. Lanna always did know best.

Karie sent a silent thank-you toward fighter bay three. And as Mon Mothma stepped forward to begin the briefing, Karie promised herself: *If we both make it out of this alive, I'm going to tell her exactly what she means to me.*

"Red Group, Gold Group, all fighters, follow me!" General Calrissian called over the open channel.

Karie Neth banked hard to port in pursuit of another TIE fighter, the wreckage of her previous target still flaring out behind her. She was definitely an ace by now, but the achievement felt more and more hollow with each report over the comm.

"Yellow Six is EVA."

"Yellow Five is gone."

"Eight, too."

And Torp. Her wingmate had died only a few minutes into the battle, caught by a turbolaser from one of the capital ships. Her astromech, a faded orange-striped R5 unit, gave a mournful whistle.

"Who's even left?" Yellow Seven said, his voice high and sharp with the bright edge of panic.

"*You're* left, Seven," Karie shot back, dropping onto the tail of another TIE. "Keep your head in it. We've got this."

Make it worth it, she wanted to say but held her tongue. Best to keep the comms clear.

The flight coordinator's voice cut through the chatter. "Green

THE EXTRA FIVE PERCENT

Group, Yellow Group, this is *Home One*. We have Imperial launches from the Death Star. Watch for evacuations, they may be trying to reach the forest moon."

As if summoned by the comm officer's words, a cloud of new TIEs launched from the Death Star and split into two groups, half in pursuit of Green and Gold groups and half in the opposite direction.

"Malena, on me," Captain Ribeiro's cool voice ordered over the squadron channel. "Screen the entrance to the structure, keep those TIEs from following our forces inside. All remaining Yellow Group pilots, I want you on the opposite side of the station to clear the way for Red and Gold groups to exit."

"Copy," Karie said, abandoning her target and setting her new heading. Almost over, *almost over,* just another few minutes. General Calrissian and Commander Antilles were inside that thing, racing to put a torpedo straight into its heart, and once they did, they could all go home. Just a *few more minutes.*

She checked her sensors and saw green dots for Yellow Seven, Eleven, and Twelve circling the Death Star along with her. Half the squadron was gone.

But half the squadron was still alive. And with any luck, they'd stay that way.

"We're going in hot, Arfive. Hang on back there."

Karie picked the TIE closest to the marked exit point and dived in, throttling up to take them by surprise. They caught on—but too late. She tracked her shot ahead and pierced the TIE's cockpit with a linked blast from two of her cannons . . . then had to slam on the port-side rudder pedal and haul back on the stick to avoid flying straight into the TIE's wingmate. Green laser blasts spattered her forward shields as she pulled up, then continued on her aft.

"Got one on my tail," she said, juking around a hunk of ex-Star-Destroyer as Arfive squawked in protest. "Little help, anyone?"

"On it, Krayt." Yellow Twelve came screaming into the fight, and the TIE broke off to tangle with him instead. Another TIE exploded somewhere off her starboard wing, falling to Yellow Eleven's quad laser blast.

Then Karie spotted them: a pair of TIE fighters heading straight for the exit point just as an excited voice broke through the comm chatter.

"All forces, this is *Home One*. Move away from the Death Star, repeat, move *away* from the Death Star!"

Karie's heart leapt, her breath catching in her throat. Did that mean . . . they'd won?

Then the implication of the announcement sank in.

"Is it gonna blow?" Yellow Seven yelped, diving away from the battle.

"You're welcome to stick around and find out," Karie said, dodging a blast from yet another of the seemingly endless TIE fighters. She checked her sensors and banked to put distance between her and the space station—only to have a second TIE fighter cut sharp across her bow, lasers flashing. She slammed the stick hard to the right and floored the starboard rudder pedal, avoiding the collision by a tauntaun's hair. Her aft shields lit up with green laserfire from a second TIE, herding her in closer to the Death Star.

"Do these pilots have a death wish?" Karie said as her shields dipped below 50 percent. "Or does the Empire just not care enough to warn their own people?"

Arfive gave a mournful whistle that summed up Karie's thoughts perfectly.

The exit point in the Death Star's structure began to glow a menacing orange-red as the TIEs forced Karie ever-closer. Every twitch of the stick, every feather-light touch on the rudder pedals, they hung right with her, peppering her shields with sapping darts of green

THE EXTRA FIVE PERCENT

light. She risked a glance to see if anyone was in range to help . . . but no. Everyone had followed orders. She was alone.

A single X-wing broke free of the space station, zooming out the entrance at full throttle, gone far too quickly to be of any help. The glow intensified, whips of fire lashing out from the exit point—would General Calrissian make it out in time?

Would she?

A split-second decision. Only time for one. Choose wrong and go up with the station. Choose right . . .

Lanna's face flashed before her eyes.

Karie cut the throttle completely, sending the two TIEs screaming past her ship just as the *Millennium Falcon* burst free from the Death Star in a ball of flame several klicks above. Her hands flew over the controls, putting the station in her rearview and throttling back up as she diverted all power from her laser cannons to her thrusters and pushed all her remaining shields to the aft. Her ship gave a violent buck as the light flared behind her—and the station exploded. The TIEs she'd slipped evaporated in milliseconds, but the hungry shock wave wasn't satiated. It chased Karie, gaining, gaining, and her X-wing shook and whined with the stress of the chase. Karie shunted all remaining power from shields and life support to the thrusters. Neither would matter if she didn't live through the next three seconds. R5 screamed from the back of the ship, dome spinning wildly as the ship strained, shrieked—

And all at once the shock wave dropped away, losing momentum even as Karie's X-wing gained it, rocketing away from the rubble field on the heels of the *Falcon*. She sucked in a gasping breath, nearly blacking out from relief as her comm lit up.

"Close one there, Yellow Nine!" General Calrissian said, a smile evident in his voice. "Glad you could join us."

"Me too, sir," she said, too wrung out to be starstruck. Karie slumped back in her seat, rebalancing the power distribution as the raging adrenaline began to ebb, the haze of battle clearing from her mind. It was only just starting to sink in that something immense had just happened. The landscape of the entire galaxy had shifted.

They'd *won*.

"Yellow Group, this is Yellow Leader. Congratulations on a job well done. You did something incredible today," Captain Ribeiro said, her voice going rough at the end. She cleared her throat and continued. "If you need repairs, report back to *Home One*. Otherwise, set down at the rendezvous point on the forest moon. There's talk of a serious party down there tonight."

"With pleasure, Captain," Karie said, her mind immediately flashing to Lanna.

Lanna, whose extra 5 percent thruster tune-up had probably just saved her life.

Lanna, whom Karie desperately needed to see.

She flipped her comm over to her and Lanna's private channel and hailed her once . . . twice . . . three times. A bolt of fear for Lanna stabbed hard in her gut—*Home One* had taken some serious hits. Had Lanna been hurt? Killed? Who could she call to find out? The official channels were probably overrun with communications, but maybe if she—

"Karie, thank the stars," Lanna said over the comm, then immediately burst into audible sobs.

"Are you okay? Are you hurt? I saw *Home One* take some nasty hits—" Karie began, but Lanna cut her off.

"I'm a bit dinged up, but I'm alive," she said, sniffling. Then her voice took on an altogether different quality. Softer. More intimate. "And hey. So are you."

They were both *alive*. And that meant it was time for Karie to make good on her promise to herself.

THE EXTRA FIVE PERCENT

Life as an Alliance fighter pilot was way too short to let things go unsaid.

"Catch a ride down to the surface, the first one you can find," she said. "I've got something I want to tell you, and I want to be able to see your face when I do."

And the smile, the *joy*, rang out clear as a Baraan-Fa sunrise when Lanna replied.

"I can't wait to hear it. I'm on my way to you."

Karie's cheeks burned with the force of her smile.

"I'll be waiting."

WHEN FIRE MARKED THE SKY

Emma Mieko Candon

The *Tydirium* winked into the black while Wedge could see it. He hadn't planned it that way. He was in *Home One*'s main fighter hangar conferring with Red Squadron's head mechanic and there, over the woman's shoulder, was the stretch of space between *Home One* and the medical frigate where the stolen Imperial shuttle hovered, the size of his thumbnail. He must have stared, because the mechanic trailed off and turned. By the time she did, there was only absence.

"Something on your mind, Commander?" she asked.

"Something, yeah." Wedge rubbed his eyes. A hundred somethings vied for his attention behind them, as they had ever since the briefing where he found himself staring down the schematics of a dead and vengeful thing: a jagged, spherical mass of congealing metal lengths.

It made a sick sort of sense to see the Death Star rise from its grave. The sheer enormity of its first iteration had made it seem like a dark, immutable rule of the galaxy itself. It certainly hadn't seemed like it should just disappear because one pilot made a once-in-a-lifetime shot. Of course it wasn't really gone. Of course it had returned to collect on its debts. Of course the resurrection of that grim silhouette made Wedge feel like a ghost himself. Some nights he found himself staring at the ceiling of his bunk, thinking that he couldn't really be there. He couldn't have survived the fight over Yavin. Not when nearly everyone he ate, drank, and flew beside was dead. It was plain inconceivable.

Yet even now, four years and dozens of hair-raising, stomach-turning, teeth-clenching dogfights on, here Wedge was, perfectly and inexplicably alive. Though as he watched the majority of the survivors of that one unthinkable trench run disappear into a future he couldn't see, he found himself feeling acutely small and unlikely.

The mechanic cleared her throat. He'd left her staring at him, and her mouth twitched down.

Wedge knuckled his brow. "Right, the exhaust issue—were you looking for new hoses? Any Incom model should have parts you can work with, right? Darpen knows where to find a couple of scrapped T-47s. We could have them here in time for the mission."

The mechanic nodded, but she had a look that Wedge associated with irritated medics, the one that said: *You're going to fall over the second I turn around, and it's not going to be* my *fault.* He didn't miss when, later that day, she pulled Wes Janson aside for a private chat in the mess. He was thus unsurprised when Janson leaned over the table to put another sweet Mon Cal sea-lime on his tray. Wedge took an extra seaweed roll from his own tray and deposited it on Janson's.

WHEN FIRE MARKED THE SKY

"I hear someone needs a nap," said Janson around a mouthful of roll.

"Already on the schedule."

"Might need another."

Wedge segmented the lime, frowning. "How was Zyrka Tuhn's simulation this afternoon? They correct for that leftward bias?"

"Sure did. Said they owe it to your kind critique. Or maybe some of that precious Antilles luck rubbed off on them."

Wedge winced. "Don't you start."

"Just reporting what I hear, sir. Wait till I tell you about the squadron who made a batch of good luck charms out of your toenail clippings." Janson's grin faltered as Wedge flicked a seed onto his tray. "But if it's starting to bug you . . ."

Wedge waved him off. "If they want to call me lucky, then I'm lucky."

Better "lucky" than "just that good." Wedge knew the worth of his skills, his experience, his instincts. He was, at this point, a veteran by any reckoning. But none of that explained why he was alive. Plenty of smarter, braver, and more gifted pilots were long dead. If he was still breathing, then yes, he was lucky. But you couldn't trust luck. You could only ever hope it would carry you where you were needed.

"You don't look like you feel particularly fortunate," said Janson.

"Do you?" What Wedge felt was that he'd spent too long lingering over a meal. He set to scarfing down the rest while he ran through a mental checklist for the next rotation. "Have the rookies do another round in the simulator rigs. Tell them I'll meet them there at fifteen hundred hours to review—after the formation briefing with the frigate bridge crews."

"Funny how none of that sounds like a nap."

"Really? You've been to formation briefings."

Wedge refused to make a face when Janson tweaked his nose. It was harder when the look on Janson's face held a shadow of genuine concern. "Careful, buddy. You keep this up and they're gonna get someone to drug you."

No one drugged Wedge until he drugged himself. Twenty hours before the jump to Endor, he was reviewing yet more formations with Shara Bey by the simulator rigs when Janson strolled by, telling Sila Kott, "Come on, it'll be a show. I'm going to lose so badly, your grandkids will be telling their grandkids about the day your lieutenant thought he'd learn sabacc from *General Calrissian*."

Shara Bey raised a brow and Wedge pressed a palm to his forehead. He had a habitual twitch related to the aforementioned general. It derived from a deeply ingrained memory of General Syndulla regaling a frigate mess hall with various tales of Lando "Thinks He's So Slick" Calrissian's early attempts to con her old crew.

"Your lieutenant really wanted you to hear what he's doing tonight," Bey noted as her eyes returned to her datapad.

"He's under the impression that I need a break," said Wedge.

"Does he know Calrissian stresses you out?"

"Oh, it's a threat." Wedge straightened and tucked his datapad under his arm. "Which is why he knows it's going to work."

"So you are going." Bey's studiously neutral tone was betrayed by the hint of a smirk.

"I'm going to go pour salt in his drinks all night, if that's what you're asking."

But Janson wasn't wrong. Wedge knew he was stressed. The Rebellion was less than a day away from yet another dance with total annihilation. Sure, it wasn't the first time they'd stood on that bleak precipice, and sure, Wedge had beaten these particular odds once before. But his gut told him that luck of that magnitude didn't favor

WHEN FIRE MARKED THE SKY

you twice. So, he was stressed. No one in their right mind was anything but—unless they'd already dived into the sea of "stressed" and found themselves on the distant shores of "oh, to hell with it."

Wedge was on the wrong side of that sea. He needed to cross it, one way or another, or he might as well strap a ticking time bomb into his cockpit seat for all the good he'd do his squadron. A round of sabacc would loosen him up. And anyway, someone needed to keep an eye on Janson while he made eyes at Calrissian.

"Pure strategy," Janson assured Wedge as they walked into *Home One*'s atrium. "If you want a guy off his game, shower him with distractions. The general *craves* attention."

"I suppose you'd know what that's like."

"Exactly. Now watch the master at work."

Wedge watched said master play a much better sabacc game than his earlier claims suggested he would have. He was so impressed he entirely forgot to grab the salt.

By the time Wedge remembered he was supposed to have his revenge, he dismissed the thought out of hand. He and Janson were making a round of the central atrium, noting which pilots had turned up to watch the show, which were still hanging around, and whether any of them looked like they needed a kind ear or a visit to the medical bay for a sedative. His eye caught on Calrissian, who was lingering over a bottle at their table with Zyrka Tuhn. Wedge left Janson with Sila Kott and Keyser Salm—deep in their own debate about who'd played the better round of sabacc—and made his way back, trying not to look too much like he was hovering.

As Wedge closed in, he heard Calrissian say, "I swear it. Go wild. Any design at all. You draw it, I commission it, I wear it proudly when they give me my next medal. A victory cape for the ages. Ah,

Commander Antilles!" Calrissian waved Wedge closer. "You didn't tell me your new recruit had such an eye for style. Sorely needed, in this day and age. Zyrka, why don't you draw a matching cloak for your commander? At least one Death Star, I think. Marked with a red X—an X-wing silhouette! Too gauche? No, no such thing. Have you *seen* the Empire? We need all the color we can get."

Against his better judgment, Wedge snorted. Tuhn hid their blush behind a glass but didn't seem upset by the attention. Wedge would have left it at a brief check-in and a "see you at oh five hundred" if Calrissian hadn't nudged his elbow.

"Join me for one last drink, Commander—something nice and rejuvenating for the road."

"If you mean water, that's complimentary, sir."

"Perfect."

The Mon Calamari had installed a water station by the edge of the atrium pool upon realizing their preferred humidity had a tendency to dehydrate their guests. Wedge fell into step as Calrissian led him there, studying the general through a new lens. For all Calrissian was a gambler, a scoundrel, and an inveterate flirt, he had proven himself to the rank and file; they knew he gave a damn whether they lived. In that sense, whatever he had to say was worth hearing.

As they went, Wedge caught himself scanning the room again. Shara Bey and Kes Dameron were whispering to each other between the fronds in the back—their faces were grim, but their shoulders were relaxed, so he wasn't too worried. Grizz Frix was ruminating by himself as he gazed into the waters, and could probably do with a shoulder pat and a joke.

"I'm half convinced we should scrounge up another round of Klivians for you," said Calrissian as he poured from the water dispenser. "You don't really turn off, do you, Wedge?"

"I'm not running repair checks in my head, sir. That's what we've got astromechs for. Just looking out for whatever might need attention." To Calrissian's skeptical look, he said, "They're my people. My responsibility. You know what that's like."

Calrissian raised two cups with a sigh. "I suppose everyone finds their own way to cope, advisable or otherwise." One cup went into Wedge's hand, and Calrissian beckoned over Janson, on whom he off-loaded the other. "You surely do have your hands full with the care and feeding of this commander, Wes," Calrissian said with a long-suffering tone. Then he grinned and clapped Wes Janson's shoulder. "But I imagine a man of your cunning is up to the task," he added before walking away.

Janson took the compliment with all the grace of a spooked tauntaun. "What?" he said to Wedge's curious look, sent from over the rim of the cup. "The general's a pro. Just wait until he decides he's going to flirt with *you*."

The praise proved inspiring. For the next half hour, Wedge had to do his damnedest to be the one to put Janson to bed rather than the other way around. If he lost this round, too, he thought he would probably die.

Tipsy as they were, Wedge kept himself focused by running through the list of repair checks he'd sworn were the purview of Arfive. Occasionally, they slipped through his lips in a mumble. Janson's arm around his shoulders shifted every time.

"D'you think they honestly thought 'Death Star' was intimidating?" Janson asked abruptly. "Everybody's downer cousin was in a band called 'Death Star.' Nobody's afraid of 'Death Star.' Might as well call it 'Ooooh Scary Murder Moon.'"

"Imps have no imagination," Wedge said. "If they do, it's ground out of them."

"Suppose you can't keep a hold that tight if you let people start thinking interesting thoughts."

Wedge grunted. Exhaust pipes. Coolant. Ballast.

"What do you think the Emperor's doing right now? Bathing in the blood of innocents? Getting a foot massage from Darth Vader? Chowing down on some cute baby animals?"

Wedge nudged his ribs. "What's going on with you?"

Janson sent him an oddly quiet look. "Listen, Wedge. If this is going to be our last real conversation, I'd rather it not be about *ballast*."

The fork at the end of the corridor led to two halls where the pilots bunked. Janson was stationed in one, while Wedge had chosen the other because it was closer to the hangars. At the end of the corridor, they swerved toward the latter.

Wedge was thinking: *He's trying to look out for me. I don't know if I've been looking out for him.*

Wes Janson was his executive officer and right-hand man, but long before any of that, he'd been Wedge's friend. They had their ways of showing it. They'd learned the value of remembering that one was still alive, and that one had a friend to be alive with. Wedge also trusted Janson to be the man he needed him to be. That didn't mean he could just expect it.

They were at Wedge's door when Janson let out a beleaguered sigh. "You're still doing it. This is what I get for learning how to read you." He rubbed his face, then clapped his hands on Wedge's shoulders. "Fine, then." He looked Wedge in the eye with renewed resolve. "Guess I can't wait to see who you are on the other side of that Murder Moon."

Wedge didn't really know what to do with his hands. He placed one awkwardly on Janson's elbow. "Now you think we're getting out of this alive? You've kind of been that downer cousin all night."

WHEN FIRE MARKED THE SKY

"Sure." Janson nodded to himself. "I've decided." The last thing he did was squeeze Wedge's hand in his own. "You're going to take the damn thing down with a single shot—just you wait."

From the moment the forest moon of Endor came into view, everything that could go wrong went wrong. The battle was what battles always were—dark, desperate, and sweaty, then light and then dark, screeching electronics and yelling people—but it was worse. When they wheeled away from the Death Star's active shield only to face the Imperial fleet, Wedge had the thought he never, ever let himself have: *Ah. We're going to die.*

Sila Kott drew off two TIEs on Wedge's tail; they killed her quick. Keyser Salm had dispatched the threat before he even realized she was gone.

Wedge didn't see the first rebel cruiser go down. Light flared overhead, and when he dared to look, there was an explosion of absence where the ship had been.

They lost Grizz Frix and Will Scotian; Cinda Tarheel and Tomer Darpen. His squadron of twelve was down to seven, then six. The Death Star's shields wouldn't come down, the fleet was dying by the hundreds—the thousands—

Wedge hadn't felt so calm and clear in days. Weeks. Years.

They were going to die. *He* was going to die. And that was no surprise. Luck didn't last.

Even when the shield finally broke, and Calrissian gave the order to plunge into the forbidding bowels of the Death Star, Wedge was still thinking: *We're dead. I'm dead. Any second now. Any second.*

Yet the thought wasn't fearful. He flew as well as he ever had, quick and sure, even as he found himself outside himself, because he had lost the ability to believe he wasn't dead *yet*. He was unclouded, hurtling through a lucid dream, because it didn't matter what he believed—or what he didn't. All that remained was the way forward, and a prayer that luck would see him through. That he'd die only after he'd done his part.

Nothing was so crystalline as that moment drawing up on the reactor, when Calrissian directed him to the power regulator and Wedge said, "I'm already on my way out."

The words left him mechanically. He fired just one shot.

Wedge didn't look back to see if it hit. Didn't think to. There was no sound but for the ringing in his ears. The directive now was to get out of the beast and into the black. Until then, there was no knowing what came next. So until then, he was empty.

The first thing he saw when his fighter shot out of the Death Star was a line of engine lights, dwarfed by the glow of the Endor moon. The rebel fleet was running. It had to, in order to escape the blast radius. Because the nightmare was collapsing into fire and dust. Because he had done his job, and because everyone, alive and dead, had done theirs—

And so they would survive.

Wedge's first thought was therefore pretty ungrateful: *Now what?*

Now everything. An accounting of survivors; search and rescue through the debris; a debriefing, then another; crowing in the hangars, the decks, every corner of *Home One;* and everywhere Wedge turned, someone who wanted to shake his hand, slap his back, offer a tearful hug—

It became a lot. Wedge retreated to the last place in the galaxy he liked to be: the office he'd been assigned upon assuming official command of Red Squadron. Janson was surprisingly quick to find him there, hunched over his desk and reading a Pathfinder report.

WHEN FIRE MARKED THE SKY

"You've got shore leave in an hour," Janson announced as he sat on the desk. "Get dressed, hero. You want to look your best for the locals."

"Did you submit that request with my name on it or did you assert babysitter's privileges?" Wedge asked without looking up from the datapad. There were signs that the Imperial base on the far side of the moon wasn't going to surrender. Troubling.

"You can thank General Calrissian for that. Guess he thinks you deserve a treat."

Wedge snorted. "Don't hold back on my account."

He received silence. That made him look up, wary of however Janson was about to protest. But though Janson's expression was certainly annoyed, he put out a hand for the datapad. Wedge handed it over slowly, prepared for Janson to skip outside and chuck it down a garbage chute. But Janson only scanned the report with a deepening frown and said, "Right. Guess we're volunteering for a flyby."

This made Wedge feel a bit of a heel. He sat back in his chair and hadn't sorted out what he wanted to say, let alone how to say it, when someone new darkened his door.

It was Zyrka Tuhn. They wore a practiced blank look that cracked at the edges, crinkling with the energy zapping through the ship, and they had another datapad for him. "Commander, a proposal for your consideration."

Wedge feared they had drawn him a cape. They hadn't. The contents still left him silent.

"We've spoken with the techs and mechanics," Tuhn said, a nervous frisson seeping into their tone, "and received approval from the quartermaster, of course."

Wedge nodded slowly. Janson leaned over to read the proposal and raised his brows.

"We just need you, sir," they said. "To lead the flight."

Wedge frowned as he reread the list of acquired supplies.

Tuhn's posture straightened. "If you're willing, of course."

Wedge scrolled down the list a third time. Janson slid off the desk, readied to reply, when Wedge surprised them both by saying: "This is good, Tuhn." He pushed the datapad across the desk toward them. "But I'd like to see you flying lead on this one."

Tuhn struggled to keep their face still. They didn't seem to know whether this was a reward or a scold. "Me, sir?"

"You've got the eye," said Wedge. "And I need my feet on the ground. Can't have all this attention going to my head."

Tuhn retrieved their datapad, dubiousness giving way to a flicker of anticipation. They were one of those pilots who dreamed of being in the cockpit for reasons other than Death Stars. Wedge dreamed like that, too, some days. Not often. Not recently. That just made Tuhn even more the right choice.

As Tuhn saluted their way out the door, Janson peered at Wedge, brow creased with suspicion. Wedge sniffed the air and wrinkled his nose. "Is that you, Lieutenant? Do us all a favor and shower before you board the shore leave shuttle."

When they reconvened in the hangar, Wedge was confronted by an open stare. "You told me to dress nice," he said.

Janson looked meaningfully at the helmet hefted under Wedge's flight suit–clad arm. "I should've guessed you wouldn't know what that means."

On the way to the Endor moon, Janson proved downright twitchy. He talked up every being on the transport, but his gaze always tracked back to Wedge.

Wedge thought himself pretty uninteresting. He stuck to his seat and exchanged words with anyone who came by, but mostly he sat with his thoughts. He probably looked calm. He hoped so. He didn't feel it.

The buzz in his gut worsened when the transport jolted into atmo. It didn't dissipate even when they touched down and the hatch opened into the crisp Endor evening.

They'd landed on a rocky outcropping that overlooked a valley. Bonfires dotted the darkness below, until the valley met the trees where the Ewok village lay. There was music. Shadows stretched long, dancing in celebration. But when Wedge stopped on the path where it began to slope toward the fires, he found himself looking up.

Onworld dark was so different. Not the light-hazed gloom of a cockpit, but a distant and enveloping promise that breathed.

It was probably beautiful. Wedge couldn't stop thinking of battle debris. Big, hot, careening through the atmosphere . . . Pretty, for a bit. And then?

The buzz had crawled up into his chest. The lists in his head blurred into static then flared into clarity. There were still so many things to do.

"Hey, Janson," Wedge said. His lieutenant had assumed a steadfast lurk at his left elbow. "What's wrong with me?"

Janson made a face. "I get the feeling you're looking for a serious answer."

"That a problem?"

"Not really my purview." Janson crossed his arms, head bowed. "What do you think is wrong?"

Wedge smiled. He wasn't sure why. "Honestly? I think maybe being alive."

Wedge couldn't see Janson's expression in the growing dark, but there was a faint tension in his friend's voice as he asked, "Do I need to get a medic?"

"Nothing like that." Wedge considered the helmet under his arm. "Just starting to wonder if I really remember how to do that. Live."

Wedge didn't think he was the sort of person who had a lot of opinions about death. Every soldier learned how to wrestle with the specter of lost comrades. Most learned to look their own end in the eye, too. So of course Wedge had thought about dying. It presented a practical concern. He hoped he would leave usable gear, and that he wouldn't get too many more people dead in the process. It wasn't a sad thought. A little frustrating. Easily dismissed. Because if he wasn't dead, there was always something more to *do*. And so long as there was something to do, he couldn't just stand there, twiddling his thumbs and enjoying the stars.

But this sort of thought made more sense before a battle. After? For all the Rebellion had lost today, Wedge had, in the most objective and unimpeachable terms, just lent a hand to the destruction of a superweapon the likes of which the galaxy had never seen—to say nothing of the monstrous men who'd dreamed it into existence. Yet here he was, unsettled down to his bones, desperate for anyone to ask him his opinion on ballast.

Janson scrubbed his hair and groaned. "Cards on the table, Wedge, this is what's got me worried about you. Don't get me wrong—I've seen you happy, now and again. But you always seem to feel most like yourself when you're up there." He jerked his thumb at the star-pricked sky. "So I don't know why, given the option, you decided to be down here instead."

Wedge followed Janson's thumb upward and found himself smiling again. This time he knew why. "I'm testing a theory."

They only had to wait another minute or so. Then streaks of light and sound tore through atmo: Three fighters sliced the sky, and in their wake, fire cracked and boomed. Not lasers, and explosions only in the most technical sense. Fireworks. Light for light's sake. Sound made because there was something worth sounding for.

Whoops shot up from the valley. For a second, Wedge wanted to join them. His feet were firmly anchored on the ground, but his chest was thrillingly weightless. It was the sudden exultation of *possibility*.

Small, fragile. Real.

"All right, then." Wedge started back down the path. "Come on, Janson. Let's mingle."

Janson was at his side after only a breath, matching him step for step. "We're in for a good time tonight, I can tell. Have you seen those Ewoks? Tiny, fuzzy—hugest, most adorable eyes—and the most powerfully disproportionate bite force you've ever seen. Apex predators. Don't know how the Imps ever thought they stood a chance."

Wedge laughed, and that felt real, too. He didn't think he could hold that feeling of possibility for long. He suspected he might get better at it, over time, though his grip might not ever be good. But he was starting to understand that he could help others hold the feeling themselves.

They were alive, and so there was celebration. Even if that didn't bring Wedge much relief, there were ways to bring a measure of peace to others. All he had to do was stand in the light.

It would mean something for Wedge to be seen by the fire, just like it'd meant something in his chest when the *Tydirium* winked into the black, and like it had when General Calrissian cajoled the troops and drank to his own future. Like it had meant something when fire marked the sky in the name of elegy and victory.

So Wedge went to the light looking like a man who'd survived the Death Star, and he shook hands with all who found him there, greeting those who'd lived, and remembering those who'd died—because tonight, at least, he could afford to wait for tomorrow.

THE CHRONICLER
Danielle Paige

I have never held a lightsaber or shot a blaster or ridden on a dewback—and I probably never will. I rarely ever leave *Home One*. But I am a part of the Rebellion. And everyone from the littlest astromech droid to Mon Mothma herself has to share their story with me—so that their experiences might live on—even if they do not. Because starting today, I am a chronicler, one of the Rebellion's historians.

The briefing room was filled with rebel chroniclers from all around the galaxy. Tele introduced me to Garan from Coruscant and Lignu from Daiyu before Tele and I took our seats. But I was barely able to focus on shaking their hands, I was too nervous. Before today, I had spent years solely compiling and disseminating intel about the Rebel

Alliance as a data collector, helping to create and preserve a history of the Alliance from its inception. I was uniquely suited for data collection, but then again so was Tele. And Tele had made the transition from stat collector to chronicler long before me. We both have eidetic memories, meaning whatever we saw and heard we could remember forever. Why Mon Mothma had chosen to finally make me a chronicler in addition to my archival duties I did not know.

When Mon Mothma took her place in front of us all, the briefing room went still. I wondered what it would be like to command a room like she did. I was always more comfortable in the back of them. Outside the room, the rest of the ship was abuzz with activity heightened by the most recent arrivals.

Mon Mothma began, "I'll start by confirming the rumors that are already circulating. Han Solo has been rescued from Jabba the Hutt's clutches on Tatooine. This was a personal mission, and thankfully successful. And its participants, Leia Organa, Luke Skywalker, Lando Calrissian, and Chewbacca, were unharmed."

I recalled everything I had heard swirling since their arrival. I received daily official and unofficial reports from all over *Home One,* including a tip about the *Millennium Falcon*'s return. No one had mentioned Luke Skywalker being part of the rescue mission. And I'd not seen any report of his arrival with the others. Where was Luke Skywalker?

Mon Mothma cleared her throat and cast a serious glance over all of us. Despite the happy rescue, Mon Mothma was even more stoic than usual.

"With that issue addressed, as you may have noticed we have a few extra faces today. You all carry on the history—the memories—of the Alliance forever. Never forget that. After the full briefing, you will conduct your interviews. And I cannot stress enough the continued importance of your work, especially today."

THE CHRONICLER

Beside me, Tele dared to whisper, "Ten credits Mon Mothma will warn us about the end of the Rebellion . . ."

"I won't take that bet. You know I don't like losing."

"The way I see it, you win either way—"

"How's that—"

"If this is the end, you get to spend the end with me . . ."

An unconscious lick of the lips from him inspired a sharp intake of air from me as he shifted his chair closer to mine. I knew that this was how Tele handled the Rebel Alliance always being on the edge of extinction. His sense of humor covered any fear he felt.

His eyes twinkled. Was he flirting with me? Lately I was aware of Tele in a different way than I had been after so many years working together—his movements affected me, when he ran a finger through his hair, the way he smiled. The way he looked at me. Tele filled the space now where before he had once just been part of it. He had grown tall along the way. And muscular. And somehow he now filled up the whole room so that there was nothing but him. And a single gesture of his was now somehow seismic. He could run his fingers through his hair across the room and I would feel a quickening in my heart as I sat before the monitors meters away.

I looked down at my datapad—

It couldn't be.

Chronicler Dora Mar
Interview Subjects, Location: Home One
Home One
Han Solo
Lando Calrissian
Leia Organa

On my first day, I was going to interview Leia Organa. What would I ask her first? What would she say? What would she be wearing? Leia was a fable come to life. A hero to me and countless other beings across the galaxy. One who had risked her life for the Rebellion in a series of death-defying acts.

I'd heard from Tele about moments in his time as a chronicler when the subject had been less than their stellar reputation. I was sure that couldn't be the case with Leia.

Before I could show Tele, Mon Mothma pressed on.

"Everyone involved in this mission from the top generals to the support staff will be interviewed. No one is exempt. I want you to capture everyone's story. Not just in regard to today's briefing but every detail from the moment they joined the fight against the Empire."

Tele's eyes widened. And he showed me his own datapad.

Both Mon Mothma and Admiral Ackbar were on it along with a list of X-wing pilots. Tele's memory was like mine but he also had a real penchant for battle plans, so his assignment to talk with our pilots was no surprise. He had General Calrissian, too, for a tactical briefing. But Mon and Ackbar taking time to be interviewed when they were apparently planning a mission wasn't protocol.

I raised my hand.

"Yes, Dora Mar?"

"A full briefing? There's nothing on our datapads about a mission today."

"Representatives from our sector will be meeting back here in about an hour. I will expect you all to be in attendance."

"Which sectors?" I asked, an alarm bell going off inside me.

"All of our sectors. We are committing all of our forces for this mission. To attack and destroy the second Death Star."

Silence blanketed us for the briefest of moments. My eyes met Tele's for a second, finding him serious for once. He must have felt it, too—the opportunity, the excitement, and the danger sinking in all at once.

THE CHRONICLER

Mon Mothma dismissed us. Tele leaned over and looked at my tablet. "Sometimes dreams do come true," he whistled breaking the tension. Tele knew how much I admired Leia—

"Promise me something, Dora," he said earnestly.

"Anything," I said, sounding more breathless than I liked.

"That you'll still talk to me after hanging out with the princess."

Tele gave a little bow and I found myself smiling at him. Again, a little too wide. We had come from different planets. We had different histories, but now he was the closest person to me on any planet. And I think I wanted to be closer still. But I didn't know what he thought.

Mon Mothma stopped me at the door.

"A moment please, Dora Mar."

Tele nodded at me as if to indicate he'd see me back in our shared work chamber and moved on down the corridor alongside the other chroniclers.

"I know that the first day of being a chronicler is daunting. And it has likely been made doubly so given the timing."

"Mon Mothma, I would totally understand if you need to change my assignments . . . I can't believe you gave me the princess?" I said, filling with pride and also hoping that there hadn't been any mistake.

"You have the most complete archive about her of any chronicler. No one knows Leia like you do."

"But another chronicler already interviewed her—?"

"You know that I like to rotate chroniclers so that more of you carry the stories firsthand."

Mon Mothma always put weight on what we did, but her tone was decidedly more grave than usual.

"But . . ." I began, and I stopped myself looking at Mon's somber expression.

"Dora, most of the tasks I have accomplished for the Alliance, seemed impossible at first."

"So how did you accomplish them?"

"Sometimes it's in the doing that we find our way and our strength. I have no doubt you will do the same."

Again, I couldn't help but notice the dire look behind her smile.

"Mon Mothma . . . keeping records and interviewing subjects are so very different. Any advice?"

"Dora Mar, you do so much more than that."

She nodded and then added, "Lando will be charming. Han will be gruff. Princess Leia is capable of responding to every question without actually answering a single one. Be direct but respectful. Remember what I said in the meeting; it is the totality of their experience we need to preserve. The reasons for their service, however varied, are meaningful to the Rebellion and for posterity and inspiration."

To my surprise, Mon Mothma didn't rush off to prepare for the briefing. Instead, she paused again. "I don't envy you, Dora Mar—everything's on the surface for you, all the time."

I shrugged. "I haven't known any other way."

"But I added to your burden by giving you so many memories about the Rebellion."

I shook my head, an unexpected rush of emotion welling in me. The first memory I had of Mon Mothma's face coming to the surface. The shame I'd felt when I'd learned from her the Empire I grew up trusting wasn't what it seemed.

"You gave me a gift. You saved me from being part of a regime that builds planet killers. I will never have any memories of serving the wrong side. Besides, whatever happens, I get to interview Leia Organa."

THE CHRONICLER

I was sixteen when the course of my life changed forever. I was a student at the top of my class at the Imperial Academy, and once I matriculated, I would find my place somewhere in the upper echelons of the Empire, most likely as an intelligence officer, where my particular set of skills could prove essential.

In my village on my planet, my gift rivaled that of the droids. So much so that my teachers would test my memory's capacity against theirs. To their surprise and mine, it seemed that even their outdated droids could not keep up with my recall. I could remember every face, every date, and everything that I could see or feel or touch. When I first realized that no one else in my village could do what I could, I had mistakenly thought my gift was the Force. But I soon learned that my mind's gift was limited to memory. I was disappointed, but my memory still gave me an incredible edge that would lead me to success in the Empire.

I had thought I was going to serve the Empire. Not help dismantle it. But everything changed when I met Mon Mothma, and she helped me see the truth of what the Empire really was.

When we first met, I was on a junior Senate tour of the Galactic Senate Chamber, exploring a potential career in politics. Mon Mothma was the senator I got to follow for the day. She was everything I wanted to be—poised and gracious and commanding. I'd gushed over the Empire and how lucky she was to serve and be a senator.

"I came to the Senate the same as you did—full of gratitude and optimism," she said. The senator complimented my accomplishments but then added, "You are happy to be chosen by the Empire, but you forget—you get to *choose* the Empire as well."

At the time I thought she was trying to inspire me to be more inquisitive—to think deeper about the Empire and its mission. Much later, after the destruction of Alderaan, I was called home via an urgent message to visit my family. When I arrived I once again found myself face to face with Mon Mothma, then a fugitive. It was then that she showed me a holo-map of a debris field, where Alderaan *should* have been.

"They saw the seeds of dissent in Alderaan and they had to crush it. They want minds they can bend to their will, not minds who will never forget their sins. You have a power that is of little use to the Empire but of great use to us. The Empire does not want anyone to remember the truth of their deeds—we seek the opposite."

"Who are 'we'?" I had asked, Still reeling from the revelation that the Empire had destroyed Alderaan. I had been a loyal, ambitious student of the Empire and in an instant Mon Mothma had wiped away all my plans and hopes for the future and replaced them with the chilling reality.

"The Rebellion. And we need you, Dora Mar."

"What do you think I can do?" I asked, still reeling from what I had seen.

Mon Mothma said, "Someone once said that the victors get to write history. We do not know if we will be the victors, but our story will be written—by you, if you choose."

I had once been destined for the Empire's darkness but now we were destined for the Rebellion's light.

I raced back to the work chamber I shared with Tele and began to prepare.

I looked at the wall of screens in front of me and ordered my temperamental but reliable CZ series droid to help.

"Seezee, pull up all Leia Organa materials. Include notes, interviews, cams, everything." I remembered everything, but physically looking at the files somehow made me feel more ready.

THE CHRONICLER

Images and recordings of Leia filled every screen around me.

I had watched the princess wave on the cam from when she was small and I was smaller. Now I watched her brandish a blaster in footage from one of the cams; somehow she seemed equally at home with both gestures.

The blaster footage had been lifted from a visit to Alderaan's consular security forces. Leia had only held the blaster for a moment, but a journalist had captured it for the rest of us to see. Leia couldn't have known then she was going to be part of the Rebellion. Now it seemed almost prophetic.

Most of the elite class had chosen another way than Leia and Mon had—their privilege had allowed them to hide and wait to take the side of the Rebellion or the Empire, whoever emerged victorious. Leia didn't have to be here. She *chose* to be here.

Some of the information I'd gathered was from cams, some from interviews Leia had given when she was debriefed, some from others around her: friends, servants, fellow politicians, and other royals. My job was to capture the most accurate portrait of Leia's life, filtering out all the gossip and rumors that swirled around her.

I got up and straightened up the table before me. The objective of a chronicler was to make their subject comfortable so that they would share as much of their tale as possible. I had raced around the ship and scavenged and bartered for some supplies—foods from their home planets and things that might make them more comfortable. I set out a spread with something for every one of my expected guests. Alderaanian biscuits, colo claw fish, and blue milk from Tatooine. The table was ready. But was I?

My datapad beeped. The hour had flown by. I raced back to the briefing room. Tele and I took our place in the back as Mon Mothma made her speech to the assembled rebels. I watched as Leia sat next to Han who sat next to Chewbacca who sat next to Lando. Leia lit up when Luke unexpectedly joined them, and she rose and put her arms around him.

When the briefing ended, Mon Mothma held the chroniclers back for another word. Now that we knew the full scope of the mission, there were no jokes about this being the possible end of the Rebellion from Tele. I could see from the serious faces around me we all acutely felt the weight of what was about to happen and our small but supporting roles in memorializing it.

"As always. You are expected to honor your code of secrecy and to follow evacuation protocols. No heroics."

Evacuation protocols for chroniclers meant we were to stay until the last possible viable moment for *Home One* and then go directly to the escape pods in which we would be transported to safe locations. We were not to engage with the Empire in any fashion. Even if our fellow Alliance members were in danger. Until this moment, the idea of abandoning ship had seemed distant and theoretical. Now it seemed far too close.

"I want to be clear: What you carry for the Alliance is where your heroism lies. And the Alliance, myself included, are grateful for your efforts," Mon added.

I was right, and Tele was wrong. This was different. Mon Mothma wasn't sure if anyone was coming home after this.

First was Han Solo. He was somehow even handsomer than I expected. But handsomer still when he smiled his crooked smile. I must have stared too long because he began looking quizzically at me.

"Don't tell me, I missed some sand," he said, taking a drag of his

THE CHRONICLER

hand through his hair. When I looked at his face, I imagined it frozen in carbonite as a trophy of Jabba the Hutt.

His eyes fell on the table covered with food.

"There are two ways to get someone to talk. Feed them or starve them."

"What about torture?" I asked reflexively.

His eyes clouded over for a moment. I wondered if my words had brought to mind his carbon freezing on Bespin and his time at Jabba's palace. Both traumatic experiences must have affected him and, I assumed, were with him still. After all, his time in carbonite must have felt as if it had just happened over the course of mere days not a year. But when he finally answered, his words did not belie any trauma.

"That works, too. I definitely prefer the food." With that, he took a scoop of colo claw fish eggs with his hand and deposited it in his mouth. "That's the stuff."

"You are easier to bribe than I thought . . ."

"I'm a huge fan of bribery if I'm on the right side of it," he said, grabbing a biscuit from the tray then taking a seat and leaning back and making himself comfortable. "I've been told this isn't a normal debrief. This is the soul-baring one—right? What if I told you I didn't have one."

"Your actions tell another story," I countered.

"You haven't seen all my actions," he deadpanned.

"Droids record more than you think," I retorted.

He laughed then. And I was again grateful for my memory because it was definitely a sound that I would play back.

"Well, lucky for me, I've spent most of my time in the company of a Wookiee."

"Then let's talk about what brought you into the Rebellion's fold in the first place . . . everyone has different reasons for joining up. And only you can tell me your true motivation."

"I'd have to say that coin or lack of it has informed most of my decisions."

"Can you elaborate?" I prodded.

"No," he deadpanned and then laughed again.

But then he grew serious. "I've flown all over this galaxy. Walked through a lot of doors before I ended up here. Usually, I found a reason to walk back out of most of them."

"Sounds like you've found something of a home in the Rebellion."

"Is that what your datapad tells you about me?" he asked, eyes sparkling, as he leaned in and picked up one of the Alderaanian biscuits.

I paused. I knew I wasn't supposed to share my conclusions with my subjects *during* an interview. But Han had asked. And Mon had never explicitly forbidden it.

I thought about him and Leia. Their coming together from such different beginnings felt like something more than chance.

"It tells me that you went from a thief to a man who helped destroy the first Death Star. That you are a man in flux. Once a rogue, now a trusted member of the Alliance," I offered.

"Flux, huh? And what do you think caused my flux?" he asked as his lip curled around the words. Was he trying out my assessment of him or preparing to launch a defense?

"All of the data suggests to me that meeting Leia Organa is the inflection point of your life thus far. Before Leia—your decisions were morally questionable. And after her, still, but you stayed with the Rebellion. You deviated from your usual pattern, which was putting yourself and sometimes Chewbacca first, and continued to widen your circle of friendships. From the moment you met Leia on, the people you were willing to risk your life for has grown."

THE CHRONICLER

My next question fell out of my mouth before I could second-guess it. "Is that why you volunteered to lead the mission on Endor? For Leia?"

"For Leia yeah. But I'm doing it for all of us. Look, the Empire has to fall or none of this matters. We have to make a stand. It's the Death Star or us. And if we lose, there's nothing on the other side. No more questions, or flux, or growth . . . no more inflection points . . ."

Han stood up abruptly and began backing toward the door.

"Where are you going—the interview isn't over—" I said, getting to my feet.

"Like you said—I'm growing. I think I just outgrew this interview, kid."

While waiting for Lando Calrissian, I was surprised when Luke Skywalker entered the room. His face was somber. He seemed older than he had in the few images I'd seen of him. And more stoic.

"Dora? Mon Mothma said you have some questions for me."

The first stories I had heard of the Jedi had been of their betrayal of the Empire. But my time with the Rebellion's files had shown me the incredible true history of those who wore the Jedi robes or wielded lightsabers. Now, Luke Skywalker stood in front of me. The first Jedi I had ever met.

I gathered myself and looked down at my datapad for any notes I had on Luke, and asked the first question that came to mind.

"You didn't grow up expecting you would become a Jedi. What has that been like?"

"The war has accelerated time for us all. Without the luxury of time to study and prepare, we must take leaps and trust we are ready," he said simply.

He forced up a smile, which I presumed was for my benefit.

"Where shall we begin . . ." he asked.

We began on Tatooine. With Luke detailing his childhood with Beru and Owen Lars and ending with his daring rescue of Han with Leia and Luke and Chewbacca and the droids.

"I wanted adventure. But my aunt Beru and uncle Owen wanted to protect me. They also gave me a strong sense of right and wrong. Back when my old friend Biggs told me he planned to leave the flight academy to join the Alliance because he wanted to be on the side he believed in . . . it was such a surprise to me. It was the furthest thing that I could conceive of for myself. But after Ben was gone, and I saw Leia and the other rebels so willing to fight and sacrifice for what they believe in, I finally understood. And now here I am."

"So do you think you would have ever joined the Rebellion if it were not for Leia?"

"I'd like to think I would have found my way to the Rebellion no matter what. I guess the Rebellion found me first. Ben Kenobi was undoubtedly the catalyst. Leia is something else."

"What is she?"

"A beacon, a guiding light maybe . . ."

He smiled at the thought; then the smile faded again.

"Luke? Pardon me, but you look as if the weight of the galaxy is upon you . . ."

I knew we were all worried about what came next but I wondered if it was something else. Something related to Leia.

"Recently, I lost a friend, saved a friend, and found something I never knew I had."

"Can you tell me more?"

"Not until I tell someone else," he said with a gentle smile.

"I'm sorry. I didn't mean to be indelicate."

THE CHRONICLER

"You have a duty to do. And I understand that it is indelicate by its very nature. I'm sure you've found as I have that answering questions is almost always more uncomfortable than asking them."

"General Solo . . . um . . . left before I could get down all the details about Tatooine."

"That sounds like Han all right. He can be slippery with new people. What do you need to know?"

Luke filled me in on the rest of the rescue. It was even more harrowing than I'd imagined. Jabba had attempted to execute Han and Lando in the Sarlaac pit. They had narrowly escaped, and Leia had dispensed with Jabba using the chain that had once held her.

When he was done, I realized I had been holding my breath even though I knew that they had all escaped.

"Thank goodness you all made it."

Luke nodded appreciatively.

"Before we conclude, I am supposed to review the important moments of your journey with the Alliance without judgment, for posterity. But . . ."

"But there's something else that you want to ask? Something that isn't on your tablet?" He cocked his head, curious.

"Are you in love with her?" I blurted. Even though I knew I should have followed up with something more along the lines of how it had felt for him to be back on Tatooine.

"That's your question for me?" Luke laughed. "Your questions say more about you than about us."

"But what is the answer?" I asked. I had not imagined these interviews having such an impact on me—I had not imagined myself to suddenly be the subject. I had broken our rules again.

"I'll tell you this. From the second I saw Leia in that shaft of light—in the message she sent through Artoo-Detoo to Obi-Wan—

I think I knew that she would be a part of my destiny," Luke said with a faraway look in his eyes.

"That's so romantic . . ." I began, then added, "Are Jedi allowed to be romantic?"

He laughed again. "Jedi are allowed to be a lot of things. But that is your word, not mine."

It still wasn't the answer I wanted about Luke and Leia and Han, but I couldn't help it—he'd piqued my interest. I had to ask. What he meant about me.

"And what does my question say about me—" I asked, unable to resist.

He just gave a knowing smile.

I sighed and glanced down at my screen. My notes were sparse because Luke, at turns, had been inscrutable. When I looked up he was gone.

While Luke had exited without a sound, Lando Calrissian entered with a laugh.

If Han was the sun, and Luke a calm but confusing moon, then Lando was a magnetic field. He entered and kissed my hand.

"Just like Mon Mothma, to keep me away from meeting you until now. My last interviewer wasn't half as pretty as you."

"Thank you." I smiled, knowing that Tele had also interviewed him about the logistics of the upcoming mission. I offered Lando a seat.

"So you're charged with writing our obituaries. Which Lando Calrissian will you memorialize . . . smuggler, sportsman, or hero . . . ?"

The term "obituaries" caught me up short, but Lando's tone was light.

THE CHRONICLER

"No obituaries. Living memories, if you will . . . and if you permit me, I'd like hear about all of them."

"Mon Mothma and her contingencies . . ." he said, relenting.

"I'd like to know what sparked your conversion. What brought you fully into the Rebellion?" I began.

Lando considered his answer, his flirtatious smile never leaving his lips.

"I like to play, I like to win. And when all is said and done, I like to sleep without any bad dreams of my own making waking me."

So Lando, unlike Han, was willing to admit to having a conscience. Lando told me of his youth with zeal. He was good at being a smuggler, better at being a gambler, and he used the skills he had learned as both to be the hero he was becoming today in the Rebellion.

"Do you sleep well these days?" I asked, impressed by his honesty.

"Better than I have in a long time."

"Both you and Han have changed so much through your experience with the Rebellion. How do you think Han sleeps?"

"How or with whom?"

"I didn't mean . . . I mean . . ." I stammered.

"Ah, you're curious, too, who isn't?" he said with a flirty glint in his eyes.

Was I that obvious? How did he even know what I'd been asking Luke? Had Han told him?

"If you'd asked me a couple of years ago, I would have said the only one my old buddy would end up with is Chewie."

"And what do you say now . . ."

"Han and a princess shouldn't make any sense. Royalty's different from people like us. Hell, a whole other species. But then, Leia's different from any royal I've ever met."

"So you think they're a match?"

"Depends on how the cards fall. You can have the best hand in the galaxy, and still lose. You ever been in love, Dora Mar?"

"I . . . um . . . am not supposed to share personal . . ." I began, but my mind went directly to Tele.

"Ah, you have . . . I can see it. Then you know what war can do to it. It strips away all the excuses. But it might make you more vulnerable. It might just save you from a prison of carbonite . . . but what do I know. I haven't been dealt that hand . . . yet."

Blushing again, I looked back down at my tablet. "I just have a few more questions regarding Tatooine. What about the rumor that you served Han up to Jabba as payment of your gambling debts?"

"Look at the time. I just realized I have another briefing with Ackbar." Lando rose from his seat and began to move to the door.

"This is just as necessary as any briefing," I countered.

"That's the beauty of the Alliance. Everything we do here is voluntary. And I have to volunteer out there."

"If this were an obituary, would you really want your life summed up by a game of sabacc?" I offered, trying to get him to stay.

He paused and looked back at me.

"You want to know my truth . . ."

I nodded.

"I got old," he said in a quieter tone.

"You're not old," I said, surprised.

"War makes you old. Makes you choose. There's a point when you're too old to have the excuse that you are too young to know better. This war is so stark that children already know better. Look at you, at what you do, taking in all our stories . . . they're written all over you . . . you've seen and heard too much already. I hope on the other side of this thing, you get your chance to play some sabacc, too. Hell, if we make it through this, I'll teach you myself."

With that, Lando was gone.

THE CHRONICLER

I looked down at my interview notes. Remembering was sometimes easier than interviewing. The door beeped and slid open again.

It was Leia.

She wore a sand-covered jumpsuit, her sleeves rolled up. Her hair was wrapped twice around her head to create a double crown and tiny buns on either side of the nape of her neck. Yet even in the rebel jumpsuit she was every bit a princess. She smiled wider for my benefit and extended her hand. I stood up from my seat and took her hand. I bowed my head the slightest bit, and she stopped me with a laugh. How many times had I stood in front of any screen at home and pretended to wave to an invisible crowd of onlookers? How many times had I wrapped my own hair around my head—to match hers?

"Your Highness, what do I call you, Princess, . . . Senator . . . ?" I began.

"Try Leia," she said with an easy smile that I had seen a million times—but it was different seeing it up close.

We stood like that for the briefest of moments.

"Where are my manners—please, have a seat and anything you like."

Leia's face lit up as she picked up one of the Alderaanian biscuits.

"Where did you get these? I haven't had them since before—mmm . . ." she concluded, taking a bite. "A single bite and I'm six again . . . You really do have everything about me in that file of yours, don't you?"

She smiled and her eyes twinkled as if she was recalling a specific memory.

She leaned in and whispered, "If you have more where that came from—it could be useful in securing future allies."

I wasn't sure if she was serious or not. She was known for her sharp wit. But I did know that Leia's mind was always on saving the Rebellion.

"Is everything fodder for the cause?"

"Almost everything . . ." she said with a smile, taking another bite. I looked down at my tablet where I'd written my questions.

"The jumpsuit is very different from your old wardrobe on Alderaan—the absolute finest of fabrics. Was it an adjustment to wear the uniform of a rebel?"

"It wasn't an adjustment at all. It's an honor to wear this uniform . . . just as it was an honor to wear my Alderaanian gowns. Everything I wore back then was a representation of my home, my family, and now what I wear represents my new family . . . and the home we hope to create for all of us."

"In some ways your journey is the farthest of any of the rebels—from princess of Alderaan rubbing shoulders with the upper echelons of society to rubbing elbows with the rogues and the common folk."

"I think that the people I rub shoulders with now are the finest people in all the galaxy," she said without missing a beat. "And for what it's worth, I may have grown up in grand halls, but I have always preferred to be in the trenches with my fellow rebels."

Leia's gaze was unblinking, and I was sure that her disapproval was evident. I shifted in my seat uncomfortably and reoriented myself with a new topic, hopefully one that would not further offend.

"Let's talk about Jabba—the Tatooine ordeal," I said, keeping my voice steady.

"I can still hear the band that was playing endlessly," she began, her brow furrowing as she remembered.

"Some find that sharing their tale helps them put it behind them," I offered.

"Really? I find moving on to the next mission helps."

THE CHRONICLER

"You disapprove of the chronicler mission?"

A line formed in Leia's unblemished forehead.

"I believe in it in theory. But keeping our operations in the shadows has served us this far. Keeping a record . . ."

"I assure you that I can be trusted."

"Mon trusts you. So I will trust you. But even the trusted can be forced to share their secrets."

"You managed to mitigate that situation when you were questioned by Darth Vader. I hope if I ever find myself in such dire straits I will follow your example," I said, hoping that referencing perhaps the most tragic moment of her life illustrated how gravely I took my mission.

"I hope for your sake that you never have to," she said quietly.

"Where were we . . . ah, yes, Tatooine—Jabba's palace. You posed as Boushh—a male Ubese bounty hunter," I began again.

Leia's face relaxed, and she seemed more comfortable telling this part of the tale.

"We had intel about Boushh that I used to my advantage. Along with the fact that he and I were roughly the same size and height."

Leia described her ordeal and I peppered her with questions. She told of Jabba and his endless party; of her subsequent capture and the indignity that followed, literally chained to the beastly Jabba as if she were another of his pets.

"Do you speak Huttese? Could you understand him?"

"A little, but even if he hadn't spoken a word his body language was clear. And Threepio was there to translate. Jabba lived in excess in every respect. He collected things, people, droids, and fear itself. I am glad I never gave him the satisfaction of showing him mine."

"You were literally chained to your captor. For anyone that situation would be harrowing and demeaning, but for you—a princess who has proven herself to be fiercely independent, to have your freedom restricted like that—" I pressed.

Leia shook her head, "There is no 'but for me,' Dora. You were right at the start, it would be an indignity for anyone. Period."

"Of course, I meant no disrespect."

"I just don't want there to be any ambiguity in the record. Now, where was I? You asked how I felt being at Jabba's mercy? Emotionally, I was . . . determined . . . to find a way out of the palace," she deadpanned.

Leia stirred in her chair. I had overstepped. How soon until she bolted from her seat and back out into the corridor just like Han, Luke, and Lando before her?

"What did you say to Han when you unfroze him from the carbonite?" I blurted out.

Leia paused as if remembering.

"At first I was just making sure his airway was clear and that he could speak. I explained to him that he had carbonite sickness."

"And what did he say to you?"

"It was unintelligible."

"Oh," I said, trying to hide my disappointment. If there was ever a moment to profess one's feelings . . . wouldn't the moment of rescue be it?

"Leia, I don't mean to pry . . . As a chronicler I am charged with trying to preserve the Rebellion's history for all beings, especially those who will come after us. Not just the facts, but to create a record that is as vivid and tangible and accessible and real, so those who might read it can imagine themselves in your place. So that they might one day relate to what you and General Solo and the others went through. To know your struggle and ultimately your triumph . . . so that they might one day triumph, too," I pressed.

THE CHRONICLER

Leia paused, considering.

"Beautifully put, but like I said, his answers were unintelligible."

I sighed, realizing that we had reached an impasse.

"Mon Mothma said the mission was personal. I just want to get down why it was personal."

"I'm sure if you search your memory you'll see that there are a lot of other personal missions. Not a first for the Rebellion—or for me."

"But Han isn't just any rebel to you, right . . . ?"

The princess laughed. The kind of laugh that was practiced to sound effortless. But I was sure it was the opposite.

Leia got to her feet.

"Princess, er, Leia, I have a few more . . ."

"I'd like to revisit one of your earlier ones."

I felt my heart beat against the walls of my chest.

"You asked me about my time with Jabba—I'd like to amend my answer."

"Yes?" I asked, leaning in.

"I was mad. No, I was infuriated. Not just for myself but for the other women caught in Jabba's orbit. When I was first taken prisoner, another woman there, Jess, helped me get dressed. She thought I was in denial about getting free, but even still she used our time together to try to help me survive."

"How?" I said, genuinely surprised by this turn.

"She told me to keep my head down. And she told me about Oola."

"Who's Oola?" I asked, mentally sifting through what I had so far in my Tatooine file.

"Another of Jabba's dancers . . . That chain that was around my neck tethering me to Jabba had been Oola's only a few hours before.

"Oola had kept him entertained by dancing until he grew bored with her. Jess had done the same with her music—I did not have those skills and Jess knew that. She was grieving her dead friend . . . but she took the time to warn me. I only spent a few hours with her, and we argued briefly, but her instinct was to help me. I don't know if Jess survived. I know Oola was dead before I could meet her."

"Oh, your Highness . . ." I whispered.

"What's not in your story . . . what's not in your memory . . . what's not in your datapad are moments that the cams miss, and the interviews miss. I want them on the record."

Leia was right. I did not know the whole of their stories, and I had not sought them out.

"The Empire has its eyes on us. And we have our eyes on the Empire. But everything in between, everyone in between—they were smugglers—thieves—mercenaries. And then there were the performers, dancing for their lives. Just caught in the net . . ."

"The women you named . . ."

"Jess and Oola," she repeated firmly.

"Jess and Oola . . . are . . . were not part of the Alliance," I offered weakly.

"But they are part of the story . . . From what I gathered from Jess, Oola was a Twi'lek. She had been tricked into coming there. And her very last moment, her very last dance, was one of defiance. She pulled away from Jabba, and he punished her by feeding her to his rancor. I want to make sure that they have as much space in our record as someone like me does. Because Oola will never get to love—or grow old, or decide if she is going to be a wife next . . . If Jess survived somehow, I hope she gets that chance."

"I'm . . ." I began, an apology on my lips.

"Don't be sorry . . . be prolific. From what Mon tells me, your mind is so expansive you can hold an unlimited number of stories. Make room for theirs," she said, getting to her feet. She smiled a knowing smile.

THE CHRONICLER

"The Rebellion is bigger than the list of names we have that have joined us. Anyone out there can join us or betray us. Anyone can become a rebel anytime. It's never too late. It's the smallest action that gets us from being a group of rebels making tiny holes in the Empire to a free and glorious union capable of wiping the Empire out. Every tiny decision, every moment of resistance, is how we cross that threshold. And we take no one and nothing for granted."

Leia began walking toward the door, but suddenly she paused and turned back. Before I could protest, she scooped up the rest of the biscuits and left.

Leia's words rocked me to my core. From the first day I had joined the Rebellion, I had been proud of my work—but now I only felt shame. I felt as if the galaxy were pushing in on me. The Death Star itself had put a shadow over all of us . . . but I had an additional shadow of my own making now.

"Mon, do you have a minute?" I asked, as I caught up with her in the hall of *Home One*. She had a screen in her hand and was glancing down at it as she walked toward the assembly room. She was clearly going over her speech for the rebels, assembling momentarily. She looked up from her screen with a barely perceptible sigh.

"I have offended the princess." I showed Mon my interview notes while she waited for the rest of the contingent to assemble.

"I passed Leia in the hall."

"What did she say?"

"It wasn't what she said; it was how she smiled. I know that smile. It can be a weapon or a salve that covers myriad emotional wounds. Leia's been covering hers for longer than most . . . but we always knew that she would have reservations about this project. Let me see."

Mon's eyes traveled over the notes that I'd written. She reacted with a tiny smile of her own.

First she skimmed through the notes on Han, Luke, and Lando.

"You got a few actual sentences out of Han . . . that's not nothing. Lando will never abandon the card game metaphor . . . that was to be expected . . . the Luke interview will fill in some blanks . . . let's see . . . Leia . . .

"*Leia Organa—princess, junior senator, hero . . . she's given us so much. But what of her heart?*" Mon read aloud.

"It was as if every question I asked was more wrong than the next."

"There are no wrong questions . . . but in this context, questions are meant to elicit answers confirming facts and ideally reveal truths. The questions are not designed to in any way affirm the questioners preconceived beliefs and tangential interests."

"What do you mean?" I knew that Mon Mothma was disappointed in me, but this seemed even worse than I thought. Tangential interests? Was she saying that I had lost focus?

"As always your attention to detail is commendable—these notes are a departure from your other work . . ." she said. "Do you know why we don't just have droids record our history?"

"Because they can be sliced into or destroyed?"

"While they get closer every day to true sentience, right now they will inevitably misinterpret context or misconstrue emotion. Because they cannot yet grip the full understanding and depth of our experience."

"After Leia's reaction, I am not sure if I do, either," I admitted.

"You do realize that the most beautiful thing about Princess Leia is not the braids she winds around her head. It's what's underneath it."

"Her dress?" I asked facetiously, even though my heart wasn't in it.

THE CHRONICLER

"Her brain," she corrected.

"I know how brilliant she is . . . I covered her many accomplishments."

"And yet you devoted half your notes to musings on the status on Han and Leia's relationship . . . and another few screens to the performers in Jabba's palace on Tatooine. I know with your gift you remember ever detail. But not every detail belongs in the story."

"That's not what I was . . ." I began but Mon Mothma continued.

"I want you to focus on what's important. Leia's accomplishments, not a holodrama rooted in gossip and hearsay."

"But aren't our motivations part of the story? And Lando confirmed that there is some kind of connection there."

"Lando Calrissian is your source—! I don't mean to be indelicate, Dora. And I say this without judgment or interest. But there are those all over the Rebellion finding comfort in one another right now. Comfort is not necessarily love. Without some kind of formal declaration from any of the principals, those details do not belong in Leia's record. But you know what does . . . She has led and inspired our Rebellion. Do not reduce her to just her emotions. Do you understand?"

That wasn't what I was doing. Was it? I opened my mouth to protest, unable to articulate what it was that I was trying to say in Leia's story. What I was trying to say now.

"The people need hope. Love is hope," I said, digging in.

"And Leia has proven her love for the entire galaxy, not just one man in particular. None of us need to be distracted by specific entanglements, real or imaginary. There is only one engagement we should be focused on. The one with the Death Star," Mon said, her voice cracking almost imperceptibly.

But before I could form the words, the tone sounded again—it was time.

"I have to get back to the assembly room to meet with Ackbar—I'll see you there," she said curtly, as if I had forgotten that chroniclers were required to attend all meetings and functions.

"What you write now may be a guide for the future—for whoever survives. Do you want to leave them a love story, however romantic, or the whole of a hero's arc? There is a difference between the stories we tell through propaganda and those we tell here. This is a place for the truth unvarnished. Somehow you have made each of these stories less than heroic.

"We have to be worthy of their sacrifice. We have to make every moment—every action—count."

She handed me back my datapad. It felt heavier than it ever had before.

My CZ droid looked up at me. "Would you like me to load the next scan?"

After a pause, the droid persisted, "Dora Mar? Is something the matter?"

"Give us a moment, Seezee," a voice said as the door to my room slid open. Tele was in the doorway still typing on his datapad, not even looking up, a smile on his face. He'd interviewed Admiral Ackbar and a bunch of the pilots who were readying for the assault on the Death Star. "I'm pretty sure that Lando and I are going be friends. He even invited me to have a drink with some of the pilots," he boasted. His face was lit up with pride.

"The princess hates me and Mon Mothma thinks I'm writing propaganda," I blurted.

"Oh, Dora," he began, and then suddenly he picked up the tray of eggs that sat on the table. I assumed he was going to offer me one to try to make me feel better. But instead, he dumped them over his head.

"What are you doing?"

"Bringing you back to the present," is what he said. But what he meant was that he was giving me something else to remember. I felt myself smile and my tears dry up.

I thought of Oola again. How had I not done her story justice? How had I really failed Leia? And failed the Rebellion that had saved me from the Empire.

I closed my eyes momentarily and then tried to focus on Tele there with his sparkling eyes and those dimples. That image was chased with guilt that I felt even temporarily better.

"You know it's not really possible for me to forget . . . anything . . . but I do appreciate the effort."

As Tele wiped up the mess with a tea towel. I could see the musculature of his biceps pressing against the sleeve of his jacket.

"It's not possible for me to forget anything, either," he said looking up at me.

"So . . . how'd I do—is it working?" he pressed, stepping closer to me.

"Um . . ." I began, forcing myself to look up from his arms to his incredible hazel eyes—which proved to be equally distracting.

Despite his sweet stunt, our previous declarations remained in the air between us—I remembered every minute of him and me and he did the same. If this moment went south, whether we had hours or years left, the rejection would be forever on the surface.

It felt like he was going to say something. Or do something. Would he lean in and kiss me, or put a platonic hand on my shoulder?

"Dor . . ." he stammered and his face flushed. Did that mean he—

I took a step back. If Tele rejected me, I would remember it forever. And so would he. And that moment would be between us—never fading. I could not bear it.

An alarm sounded across the ship—it was time. There would be no more attempts by Tele to distract me from the indelible memory of my failure. We rushed to the bridge to watch.

I watched as the Rebel Alliance boarded their ships. I watched as we pulled back because the shields were still up. I watched as they came down just in time. And I watched as the Death Star was destroyed. I watched as we went from a ragtag Rebel Alliance to topplers of the Galactic Empire.

And as I watched I felt fear for my fellow rebels but also shame for myself.

As the cheers erupted around me, including Tele, I joined in the revelry. Finally, a victory—a definitive one. The Emperor and Darth Vader were dead and gone, and a new chapter for the Alliance had begun. We were no longer stuck in the shadows, constantly trying to claw our way into the light. We were the light.

I celebrated with the rest. But there was something gnawing at me that I couldn't let go of as I sipped some Polanis red. I felt like I was watching the celebration from the outside in. I hadn't done a thing to help create this victory—I was just an observer.

While everyone continued to celebrate, I slipped out and back into my chamber to begin Leia's story.

Tele stuck his head in a few minutes on. "Everyone's celebrating on the bridge. Don't you want to come join us—?"

I shook my head. "I'll be there soon. I just have a couple of more lines—"

Whatever happened next, I wanted to get this right.

The door slid further open, and Tele came and stood before me. "Do you mind if I sit with you?"

"Don't you want to be out there with everyone else?"

He shook his head and sat down next to me. If this was the end or the beginning, we did not know. But he somehow knew that this was where he wanted to be.

I smiled at him and he sat down next to me. I began to type again.

Later, as we descended in the transport toward the forest moon of Endor, Mon approached me and Tele. Understanding, Tele excused himself with a nod and moved away to some other rebels.

"Do you think I have pushed you too hard?" she said, looking out the window of our transport, her face glowing in the reflected light of the stars and the remnants of battle.

I shook my head. Realizing that she wasn't looking at me, I said, "None of us would be alive if not for you." My answer was automatic. This was new territory in more ways than one: Mon doubting herself. And us finally in a galaxy free of the Emperor.

"That wasn't an answer," she said without looking away from the view.

"The Rebellion itself is an act of faith. We have all had to change—to do things that we never imagined. Change is perhaps the only constant from the moment we stepped off the Empire's path. I thought you were looking backward, being nostalgic about the days when clothes and social graces were all that seemed to matter. But I see now you were embracing something else, a new future, and a new hope. Their love—a rogue and a princess—represents our future. Just as much as the farmboy-turned-Jedi or any of the countless other unlikely stories out there that could not have existed before this moment, before the Rebellion Mon Mothma, you were right about what I should be doing. But I can't do it here."

I shook my head and shook off her words, not allowing them to penetrate my guilt.

I handed Mon Mothma my datapad.

"I think I've written my first and last story as a chronicler. And as part of the Rebellion. Mon Mothma, you were right about what I should be doing. But I can't do it here."

Mon looked down at the tablet and began to read. When she was done, she looked up at me, her face full of surprise.

"That's too bad, because I think you've written your best yet."

In the end I had written three stories: one about Oola, one about Leia, and one about Jess.

"Those stories about the women at Jabba's palace—I didn't assign them. Neither of them are technically part of the Rebellion."

"I know that, but after talking to Leia, I thought—"

"But you make a powerful argument to include their story—to include Oola. And Jess. And to include the countless others who have aided our cause even when they haven't officially joined us."

"And?" I asked—filling one of Mon's famous pauses.

"Save them all to the record. Don't change a word," Mon said with a smile finally.

"I still think maybe my efforts could be better made elsewhere. Something more tangible."

"Whatever you decide there is always a place for you here, Dora Mar. It's been a pleasure."

I gave Mon a small bow. She stopped me and gave me the briefest of hugs before wafting off to the celebration.

Over her shoulder she called, "I'll make sure Leia reads your stories. I'll think she'll be pleased."

Taking a deep breath, I crossed the tree house's walkway to do something I hadn't done—but had been waiting to do for a long, long time.

I didn't have to be a princess to be brave. And perhaps the Force was not with me. But Tele always was. I found him standing among the crowd, having just accepted a drink from Lando Calrissian.

"What's with the weird look? You didn't really quit, did you? Everything is just beginning."

I took his hand, and his face lit up. This moment was mine and Tele's and no one else's.

CHRONICLER LOG

Subject: Dora Mar

I grew up in the outer reaches of the galaxy, and when I was young I thought I had a power that would take me to the very highest levels of the Empire. And I grew up reading tales that turned out to be propaganda.

But when I grew up I learned that the Empire wasn't what I thought. And that my definition of hero needed expanding.

I cannot lift even a single pebble with my mind. I cannot control another's will. I cannot defy death itself and walk between the dead and the living. I cannot wield lightning or lightsabers.

No, I did not have the Force. And I didn't belong in those stories I grew up loving. Because I had something else. A power that wasn't in the stories and a place in the real battle that I could never have imagined. I was meant to write different stories. Ones that included all of us . . . Not just the princesses, or the Jedi, or the rogues, but everyone and anyone who chooses to be a hero at any moment. Maybe even this one.

THE VETERAN

Adam Lance Garcia

Dexter Jettster thought of the boy he had met on Lenahra and all that the boy would never see. He thought of the warrior the boy had become and the war that had been lost.

The war Dexter Jettster had helped start.

A pirate holonet channel, the last bastion of a free press in the Imperial Center, was playing the destruction of the second Death Star on a loop, the shock wave blooming like a flower. Outside they were celebrating, a jubilant roar echoing through the chasms of Coruscant.

The Empire had fallen.

The Galactic Civil War was over.

Dex had heard this song before, played to a different tune but familiar all the same. He heard it when the Nihil had been defeated, when the Republic became the Empire, on countless worlds for countless reasons. The song of hope. Dex knew better; he had learned the hard way that hope was a hollow thing, promising everything and granting nothing. Hope was for the foolish, and tonight the fools were feasting.

Tomorrow, they would wake to empty stomachs.

Dex limped over to the holoprojector and switched off the feed. He had seen enough. Besalisks lived long lives, not as long as some beings, but long enough that Dex wondered if he had lived too long.

He still remembered the shape of the Kamino saberdart, the sharpness of its durasteel embedding prongs. The dried blood that covered its injector needle. He had been so proud, so eager to impress his young friend. He could never have known where it all would lead, that the Republic would fall, that the light of the Jedi would be extinguished, that billions would die. Dex bore the weight of every life lost, but none more so than the boy he had met on Lenahra.

Dex wasn't sure whether the warrior had died on the front or during the Purge, though he prayed it was the former. He couldn't bear the thought of his friend being gunned down by his own men. Dex could never forget how the Jedi Temple blazed in the night, how the smoke billowed days after the fires were quenched, how the air tasted of ash, and how soot covered his diner for weeks, no matter how frequently he and Wanda cleaned.

Nearly a thousand years of peace, reduced to dust.

"It'll be fine, honey, you'll see," Wanda had said, reminding him that droids rarely saw beyond their programming.

She broke down three years later.

He lost the diner soon after.

THE VETERAN

Now, two decades later, his sensory whiskers bristled, the faint scent of smoke wafting through the vents of his cramped Level 2401 apartment. The air was never clean this far down, but Dex knew the smell of fire brought on by laser blasts and what it portended. He tilted his head and listened. Beyond the cries of celebration, he heard the faint echo of blaster rifles. He cursed under his breath. He told himself he should stay put, that it was safer and smarter to remain where he was; that he was tired, so very tired.

But Dex never listened to anyone, especially himself.

He tugged on his old mining jacket, the edges ratty and torn. How long had he had it? Since Nar Shaddaa? Since Athus Klee? So many different worlds, so many stars, they all blurred together. Maybe it was right before Lenahra, before he met the young Jedi Padawan who had lost his way. Dex wondered what the boy would have thought of this day and everything that had preceded it. If the price had been worth the cost. He was practically a pup when Dex last saw him, but his eyes . . . they had seen too much. Dex winced at the thought. He'd punished himself enough these last twenty-five years.

He stopped at the door and turned back to strap a blaster pistol to his hip. He hated the kriffing thing but needs must. There was no civility in a blaster, which was probably why the Empire loved them so much. They could kill scores without ever needing to look anyone in the eye. The Emperor took that mentality to the extreme, crafting bigger and better blasters until he made a device so nice that he built it twice. The Death Stars. Dex scoffed. He remembered the Starlight Beacon when those in power worked to build things in the hope of creating unity and peace.

How foolish they had been.

Dex punched the control panel with his lower right fist, and his apartment door slid open with a frustrated hiss. He ducked his head so his crest cleared the top of the doorway and stepped out into the hall, which was already bustling with beings reveling in the Empire's defeat. A resounding cacophony of languages from Basic to Huttese. The faint scent of liquor, primarily refined coolant, wafted across his sensory whiskers as the revelers knocked glasses together in merriment. Dex couldn't help but smile at the sight. The great thing about Coruscant was that it was a melting pot. Beings from across the galaxy came here for a better life. Biths, Chadra-Fan, and Nazzar all lived in relative harmony with humans, Twi'leks, and Mikkians. That was the thing the Empire never understood with its human-centric policies and personnel. The galaxy was better because of its diversity, not despite it.

"Mister Jettster! Did you hear the news?"

Dex turned to see the young Nautolan who lived down the hall. He smiled broadly, his large black eyes excited and eager, filled with the naïveté of youth.

"Don't know how I couldn't, Kamose," Dex said. He gestured to revelers filling the corridor. "The noise everyone's making."

"They're saying the Emperor was on board the station when the rebels blew it up."

"The rebels can say whatever they want," Dex grumbled. "Unless I see a body, I ain't believin' anything. Ask yourself, when was the last time anyone saw the Emperor outside a holo?"

Kamose scrunched his face in thought. He didn't have an answer. "What do you think he was doing there on the station?" he asked instead. "Seems kinda silly to be there if he knew the rebels were coming."

"The way I remember it, the senator from Naboo played long games. If he *was* on the Death Star—and I ain't saying he was—it's because someone finally outmaneuvered the old monster."

Kamose nodded in understanding, but Dex could see in the boy's eyes that he didn't. "A bunch of us are heading to the Imperial Palace.

See what we can get for ourselves. Old man Palpatine's probably got a lot of stuff we can sell. Maybe we can knock around a stormtrooper or two on the way. Show 'em who's in charge now."

Dex noticed the rusted vibroblade sheathed at the boy's waist. He sighed and placed a hand on the boy's shoulder.

"You want my advice, kid? Stay away from the Imperial Palace. In fact, stay far away from crowds or anyone who talks about knocking around any Imps."

"But—"

"But nothing." Dex gripped the Nautolan's shoulder tighter while his lower right took Kamose's weapon. The kid meant well but was too young to know how violent a revolution could be. "Go take care of your mother. No matter how you're feeling tonight, she's gonna need you more tomorrow."

"But . . . *you're* goin' up to celebrate . . ."

Dex shook his head. "I'm goin' to see which direction the wind is blowing."

Kamose firmed his lips, looking as if he was thinking of how he could take his weapon back. But Dex, despite his advanced age, had a reputation and Kamose knew better than to defy his wishes.

The young Nautolan boy nodded, albeit reluctantly. "You think it's gonna get bad?" he asked as Dex tucked the vibroblade away.

"These things usually do. Head on back to your ma," Dex replied.

"But Jettster . . . that blade *belongs* to my mother . . ."

"And she'll get it back tomorrow once I know for certain that you didn't go and do anything . . ." Dex hooded his eyes with just enough menace to let Kamose know he was serious. ". . . foolish."

With that, Kamose spun around and raced down the hall toward his apartment, tendrils flapping anxiously behind him. Dex allowed himself a satisfied smirk before turning into the crush of revelers so he could make his way to the surface. Someone spilled liquor on him and fumbled their apologies, but Dex waved it off. Let this be the worst thing that happened tonight.

The lifts leading to the upper levels would undoubtedly be shut down. It wouldn't stop the celebrations from spreading, but it was one of the few ways the Imps could slow them down, and it meant Dex would have to take the long way up.

In another life, Dex had been a smuggler—and many more seedy things in between—and learned much that had kept his days at the diner significantly more interesting than the Great-Works-inspired décor implied.

Coruscant wasn't just canyons and stratum of durasteel, permacrete, and transparisteel. It was a honeycomb, with networks of tunnels—some intentional, most not—that connected everything from Level 0 to Level 5216 if you knew where to look. And Dex knew better than most.

Making his way to the end of the hall, Dex ducked into the narrow utility closet. Back when this building scraped the starless Coruscanti sky, this closet was used as a charging station for maintenance droids. As droids advanced and the city grew over the centuries, the closet became another useless appendix, a dead end for anyone other than Dexter Jettster. He pulled open a small hidden panel, keyed in an ancient code, and the far wall slid away with a rusty groan, revealing a slanted conduit leading up into the adjoining building. The Aurebesh letter *senth* was carved into the conduit's wall, indicating the smuggler's route. Dex ducked his head down and began his journey to the surface.

The winding path took him through meer-rat-infested halls from the time of the High Republic; through the classiest cantinas of the underworld; and along perilous, wind-whipped, rusted causeways that creaked beneath Dex's feet and threatened to drop him into the abyss of the forbidden levels. Throughout his sojourn, Dex could hear the cheers of the liberated and the blasterfire of despots.

THE VETERAN

By the time he was trudging through the CoCo Town sewers, his skin was wet with sweat, his knees ached, and he was breathing heavily. He wasn't the young smuggler he used to be. Reaching with his upper hands, he shoved aside a durasteel panel and climbed into what remained of his diner's kitchen.

His heart broke at the sight. Kitchen equipment had been torn free, several windows had been broken, and graffiti covered the walls. It had been years since he closed the doors for the final time. Back then, he thought it would only be temporary until he could get things sorted, but temporary things have a way of becoming permanent. He ran a hand along the dust-covered counter and allowed himself a moment to mourn a dream lost before stepping outside.

The thrum of celebration that had echoed throughout the city was now deafening. Airspeeders flew overhead, dropping confetti. Somewhere a gong was being rung. The sun was beginning to set, leaving the sky a bruised purple. In the distance, the Imperial Palace was alight. Beings filled the streets, shouting, jumping, screaming with joy. Some were banging on impromptu noisemakers, pots, pans, and in one case, a stormtrooper helmet. Dex's gaze lingered on the helmet, recalling the first time he had seen the clone troopers on the holofeeds from Geonosis and the pride he had felt. The warrior had found his missing planet.

That was before they spread over the galaxy like a virus.

Dex walked with the crowd for several minutes, returning smiles that were offered, embracing those who embraced him. He couldn't deny it was all very contagious, like being able to finally breathe. For a moment, Dex felt the urge to join fully in the celebrations, to cheer along with the hopeful as they made their way toward Monument Plaza. Maybe it was all finally over; maybe the Emperor was dead; the Republic would be restored.

Maybe Dex's mistake had finally been corrected.

He pushed that sanguine thought away and began walking against the current of the crowd, his eyes scanning the edges, shifting to rooftops and dark corners where riot troopers could be amassing. He could feel the tension building in the air. On the edge of the joy and relief was a sharpness of anger and malevolence. If the Emperor was *really* dead, the Imperials would do everything they could to hold on to power; if the Rebellion had indeed won, there was no guarantee that they would rule with benevolence. Dex had seen it before. Power was a death stick, just as addictive and just as lethal.

A high-pitched scream rang in the distance. Towering above most of the people marching through the streets, Dex turned to the sound and saw a pack of humans carrying a stormtrooper over their heads. It was the stormtrooper who was screaming. Dex looked to where they were heading and saw the platform's edge, the deadly drop beyond. They were going to throw him over.

Dex had no love for the Empire and little compassion for those willing to fight for it, but he knew what was right. Using all four arms, Dex shoved his way through the crowd.

"Hey!" he shouted. "Hey! Put him down!"

But those who caught sight of Dex chose to look away. Who would listen to an old Besalisk when there were tyrants to overthrow? Dex felt a hole open at the bottom of his stomach. He couldn't let this happen, not after what he had done and everything he had failed to do.

The stormtrooper was begging, voice distorted by his helmet speaker. The rioters ignored his pleas. Several of them were actually *smiling*. They planted their feet and readied themselves to throw the trooper over the side when a young human girl appeared in front of them, her arms spread wide like a bolo-ball player at the goal line.

"No!"

Her appearance caused the rioters to lose their balance, dropping the stormtrooper unceremoniously to the ground. With no way of egress, the trooper scrambled to the edge as the girl moved between him and the rioters.

"Get outta the way!" one of the rioters barked.

"No," she repeated, her almond-shaped eyes steeled with purpose. "This is not who we are!"

"I had family on Jedha!" another rioter shouted, unleashing a torrent of grievances from the others. Names of those lost, planets that had been decimated. Decades' worth of injustices were shouted out in angry, spittle-flecked, expletive-filled cries.

But the girl stood her ground.

"The Empire killed billions in the name of peace and security," she agreed. "That's how they *ended*. It's not how we're going to *start*."

The man who lost his family on Jedha drew a crate hook from the loop on his coverall leg and stepped forward. He raised the tool over his head, ready to drive its curved blades into the prone trooper's armor. Maybe he hoped it would be enough to scare the girl away, that the threat of such violence would cow her.

Instead, she met his gaze and dared him to strike.

Dex moved to intercept when the stormtrooper pulled off his helmet. He was a terrified boy, no older than twenty, if that, his face wet with tears.

"Please," the boy sobbed. "Please, don't."

The rioter's jaw dropped open, and he fell back a step. The Empire had worked so hard to dehumanize its soldiers that it was a shock to see a veritable child beneath the soulless white helmet. The rioter looked from the girl to the stormtrooper and the improvised weapon in his hand. He dropped it to the platform.

"This isn't who we are," Dex heard him whisper. He turned away, shaking his head, unable to meet the shocked gaze of his fellow rioters.

The girl knelt and tentatively reached for the boy's arm. "Are you all right?"

The stormtrooper batted the girl away. "Don't touch me!" he shouted as he stumbled to his feet. He ran off, helmet in hand, in search of asylum. He knocked past Dex, the harsh scent of sweat and fear lingering against Dex's sensory whiskers.

A sudden volley of blasterfire echoed up from Monument Plaza. Spinning around, Dex saw the recently toppled statue of Palpatine, the straw that broke the bantha's back. Just as Dex had feared, Coruscant Security Forces had come out blasters blazing, firing at anyone who crossed their path. Some who weren't immediately gunned down were running for cover, but many more were throwing pieces of the shattered statue in a misguided attempt to fight back.

It wouldn't be enough.

Dex felt his lower right hand drift to his blaster but stopped short. The crowd around him also heard the blasterfire, turning the mixture of rioting and celebration into a panicked stampede. The Imps wouldn't need to fire any more shots to cull the rioters' numbers; they would do it themselves by simply trampling one another to death. Dex wouldn't give the Imps the pleasure. Inflating his wattle as far as he could, he barked out a command that boomed over the discord.

"FOLLOW ME!"

Enough of the crowd heard him, stopping several of them in their tracks. Waving his left arms, Dex gestured toward CoCo Town, where the alleys and cross-level passageways would allow everyone to escape the Imps and, maybe, a chance to fight another day. Dex helped several people who stumbled near him, whispering to them places they could hide, forgotten causeways and levels where the security forces would dare not go. He felt a shot wing his shoulder. Besalisk hide was denser than that of many other beings, so Dex only winced in annoyance. Better the blasterfire hit him than any of the people he was helping escape. A few other rioters joined his effort, helping those who fell and carrying those too injured to walk toward safety.

THE VETERAN

One of them was the man with the crate hook. Their eyes met, and they shared an unspoken moment of solidarity; this was who they were.

Dex was the last off the platform, an unconscious decision but one he would have made all the same. He took one last look behind him as the security forces continued to march forward. He saw too many bodies sprawled behind him, the scorch marks of blasterfire evidence of their demise. Dex found it a cold comfort that none had died being trampled underfoot.

Dex thought of Kamose and prayed the boy had indeed stayed with his mother.

He limped his way back toward his diner, new wounds and old joints protesting a night meant for younger people. Night had fallen, and the streets were now mostly empty, with only a few protesters lingering either to nurse their wounds or to aid the fallen. Security force speeders tore high overhead. Dex could hear marching and more blasterfire in the distance and smell the familiar, hateful odor of smoke and ozone. The worst part was that none of this surprised him.

Dex was wheezing by the time he reached his diner. Practically falling inside, he leaned heavily against the entrance as he tried to regain his breath. That was when he heard someone crying, soft and muffled. They were doing their best to hide and failed in the effort. Dex pushed himself from the entrance and took a tentative step forward.

"Who's there?" he called, underscoring the concern in his voice.

The sobbing stopped with a sharp, panicked breath.

"It's all right. I ain't an Imp." He held up all four of his hands to show he was unarmed. "I came here to hide, too. This place, it used to be mine, so you ain't trespassing. At least, not the way I see it. I just want to make sure you're okay."

"Then why do you have those?"

Dex stopped short and realized they meant his blaster and Kamose's vibroblade. He had forgotten he had them. He sighed heavily. "Precaution," he admitted. "The thing about civil wars is that they don't end just 'cause one side says so. Right now, one side knows they won, and the other doesn't believe they lost."

There was a moment of weighted silence, and Dex worried if he had only made it worse. Then there was the shift of fabric, the sound of boots scraping along dirt and detritus as his guest stood up from behind his old counter. Dex's small eyes went wide, recognizing the girl from the platform.

"What's your name?" he asked.

"Vekin . . ." she said, almost under her breath. "Vekin Menez."

"Dexter Jettster," he said, touching his right hands against his chest and stomach. "I saw you defending that trooper."

The girl coughed a laugh. "You're gonna tell me why I shouldn't have?" she asked as she wiped away her tears with the back of her trembling hand. "I let him go just as the Imperials started shooting." She scoffed, angry with herself as much as the world. "Can you believe that? Trying to do the right thing . . . for what? Just so they could turn around and kill us all."

Dex shook his head. "I want to know why you did," he said, answering her initial question.

Vekin took a heavy breath. "That used to be the Jedi Temple," she said, looking beyond the diner's shattered windows to the Imperial Palace. "The Emperor tried to reshape everything into his image, but he couldn't reshape *that*. He made the Temple his palace, tried to shroud it in his darkness, but he couldn't stop it from being what it always was . . . a beacon of light."

"You don't look old enough to remember the Jedi."

"I grew up hearing the legends," she said.

THE VETERAN

Dex couldn't help but growl a laugh. "Legends . . . The Jedi were just as flawed as you or me."

"You knew Jedi?" Vekin asked in disbelief.

"Many, but only one I called a friend," he said with a mournful smile.

"Did your friend . . . ?"

Dex shook his head. He wanted to tell her how much he blamed himself; how he had wished he had lied that day; that no matter how much he tried to help after the Purge, it had never been enough to wash away the guilt he felt upon waking and carried with him until he cried himself to sleep.

Instead, he said, "You never really answered my question. Why did you protect that stormtrooper after everything the Empire did?"

"Because the Jedi were like stars," Vekin said with a shrug. "I've never seen a star, but I've been told they're out there. No matter how dark my night gets, they're still there, burning, making someone's way lighter." Her voice caught in her throat; eyes pinched shut. "That's why I did it . . . because it's what a Jedi would do."

Dex's gaze dropped to the ground. He knew Vekin was right. A tiny spark of something lit in Dex's chest, but he wouldn't let it become a flame. Not yet. Outside, the voice of the Emperor's grand vizier Mas Amedda boomed over loudspeakers, reminding citizens of the curfew and that the Empire still reigned.

"Do you think they'll ever come back?" Vekin whispered. "The Jedi?"

Dex's wattle deflated as he let out a heavy sigh. He'd heard rumors that a Jedi had blown up the first Death Star, but this far from the fighting details were scant, and Dex never trusted information he didn't learn firsthand.

"I don't know," he said aloud, shrugging all four of his shoulders. It wasn't the answer she wanted to hear, but it was the only one Dex could offer. "You should get home, kid, before the curfew." He began walking toward the kitchen, where the entrance to the smugglers' route awaited. "And you ought to stay there because tomorrow is gonna be worse."

Vekin looked away, knowing he was right. Dex sighed and shook his head. She was too full of hope, too foolish to understand how the galaxy worked.

Dex's knees popped as he lifted the panel leading to the CoCo Town sewers. He stopped to look back at the girl standing in his doorway, staring at the murky sky. She'd risked her life to protect an enemy because she believed light could shine through the darkness. The sort of thing that boy he had met on Lenahra would have done, an attitude for which the warrior had undoubtedly died.

If this was where Dex had helped extinguish the light of the Jedi, then it only seemed fitting that this could be where their fire could begin to burn again.

"There is truth in legends," he said.

Vekin turned to look at him, curious.

"This here's a route that crosses the entire city," he said, nodding to the smugglers' route, "leading to places the Imps would never know to look for. Could make a difference in the days ahead. I could show it to you if you'd like."

He told himself the glimmer in her eyes was just a reflection of the neon signs, but it burned all the same. "I think I would like that," she grinned.

"It's a lot of walking," he warned, "but while we do, I'll tell you about my friend, Obi-Wan."

BROTHERHOOD
Mike Chen

In the end, all things died.

Even *stars* burned out.

And the Sith? Even the Sith were consumed, evaporated into the barren nothingness of the void, where a generous and patient darkness completed the inevitable: a relentless, gradual claim over everything and everyone.

That darkness always won, and yet a closer look into that void revealed its one weakness.

Somewhere across the stars, amid the collapsing debris of a planet-destroying battle station, the mutilated half-machine body of Darth Vader fought for one, possibly two more final breaths. Vader's fiery rage and consuming fear subsided, a gradual withering until the most unexpected thing appeared.

A spark.

A single flame.

And from the flame, words. They struggled to form, dying organs failing as much as cybernetic implants. But the words found life, one last push to express the most important things Anakin Skywalker had ever said in his life.

"Tell your sister..." he said as he gazed upon the soft, compassionate eyes of the man who saved him.

His son.

"...you were right."

With that, Anakin sank into the void of the Force, guided by only that single flame. But in the middle of this nothingness, the unexpected occurred.

Anakin *felt* the flame within him, a growing intensity and radiance strong enough to break the darkness. Even as organs stopped and mechanisms fell silent, within the Force he burned like an old Tatooine bedtime myth:

The sun-dragon, a creature that could withstand anything, even dwelling within the smoldering core of a star. Over and over, Anakin's mother told him this story, the tale of the beast with the furnace heart powerful enough to protect anything and everyone it loved. "You are the sun-dragon," she had told him. "You have the strongest heart. Always believe in it."

Years of living half dead under layers of bulky armor and breathing machines made him forget that. Buried, ignored, that memory was as good as destroyed. Yet that was the thing about the sun-dragon—it could not be snuffed out. Not in the stories of myth, not in the Force.

Not even within himself.

BROTHERHOOD

His mother was right all along. And where he was now, this was more than an endless landscape of nothing. He was where he'd always been, fighting the ocean of the Force, its currents pushing and pulling, his dragon self whipping its tail and flailing its wings. He reached, the Force tugged; he soared, it grabbed; he roared, it silenced him. The more the currents raged around, the more he fought to be stronger than the Force itself.

And then everything snapped into place, a connection beyond time, beyond space, beyond worlds.

He didn't just see. He heard. He felt.

"I know there's good in him." His wife.

"He is the Chosen One. Train him." His first master.

"I know Anakin. Your vision is flawed." His Padawan.

Words and images wove around and through him, making him the center of his own orbit, his own gravity strong enough to tilt the very axis of the galaxy.

Shmi. Padmé. Qui-Gon. Ahsoka.

Obi-Wan.

"He was the best star pilot in the galaxy, and a cunning warrior." Anakin took in the voice, an aged gravel that felt like the Obi-Wan Kenobi he'd known for years and yet also different. Older, weary, and somehow content, a stark contrast to the person who'd left him to burn on Mustafar or the stoic wizard who'd confronted him on the Death Star.

This voice carried an unexpected steadiness beneath the pain. "And he was a good friend."

A *friend*. When was the last time Anakin had heard anyone call him that?

In the Force, the thought brought calm, flames from his furnace heart collapsing into a steady rhythm.

And in response, the strangest thing happened:

Anakin had spent decades fighting to control the Force itself, an aggressive tension that often lashed back in struggle. Here, this single drop of calm offered something different, a surprising tranquility that allowed him to drift. In that space, the currents calmed and Anakin Skywalker simply existed, a gradual acceptance of so many surprising things:

A warmth without temperature.

An embrace without touch.

A belonging despite isolation.

A *quiet* that revealed.

That quiet. How long had it been since Anakin found quiet? Even beyond the Force, mechanical thrums had surrounded him for years upon years, a droning repetition that often was his sole companion. And now?

Nothing.

Anakin always wondered if peace might lie beyond the noise of Darth Vader. Yet this absence of sound created anything but that, instead leaving only his thoughts and one clear, harsh truth.

So many terrible things had happened. And he was the cause.

He had brought destruction to the galaxy. He had brought pain to his apprentice. He had brought betrayal to his brother.

He had brought death to his wife.

In this intangible space, the subtlest of shifts happened, a single intention to break the quiet and ripple outward into the Force.

No.

He would not stand for this. He would not accept that his story was over, that it ended on a single act of choosing light over dark. Because he had so much left to undo.

Anakin Skywalker *refused*.

And he felt it—the fiery heart of the sun-dragon, the heart his mother told him could conquer anything if he just cared enough, the heart that would simply find a way. In the ether of the Force, the furnace roared with flames, and nothing—not even the Force—could smother it.

Because Anakin refused to accept that things should conclude this way, this history of destruction, this life of pain. A determination grew, an intensity ready to overcome whatever stood in his way. Anakin would not die. He couldn't. A galaxy of wrongs had been committed by him, and it was up to him, the Chosen One, the Hero with No Fear, the boy with the sun-dragon heart. He would make amends and bring justice to the pain he'd unleashed.

"Anakin."

A voice. Yet this was different, clearly not a specter of the past. This didn't come with any memories or visions of things gone by. Instead, it was as if the words whispered directly into his ear, as if he wasn't a phantom lost in the oceans of the Force, but whole in body and spirit as he once was: a powerful Jedi Knight, combat-ready with drawn lightsaber and wide stance, staring down dozens of battle droids without a single worry.

In fact, this *felt* just like that. But different.

Because this came right now.

"Anakin."

That voice.

"Obi-Wan." He said. Or perhaps he thought. Somehow, he communicated far beyond this plane of existence.

The last time he said that name, it came with fury, guilt, arrogance. Now? A plea.

"Still trying to be the hero," Obi-Wan said, followed by a warm chuckle, one carrying the grace and wisdom of age. "There's no holonet here to make you a poster boy."

"I'm not a hero," Anakin said. "I have done such terrible things. I have caused suffering across all corners of the galaxy." He felt Mustafar, the fire in his lungs and the burns on his skin, and Obi-Wan's broken face staring down as ash swirled around them. "I have failed you. Taken from you—taken from the galaxy, from the Jedi."

Back in that moment, Obi-Wan called him a brother, declared his love. And Anakin had only snarled in return, a fury taking over what remained of his body. "Obi-Wan," Anakin said quietly, like the two men could have been sharing a quick meal at the Jedi Temple refectory or sitting at an uncomfortably small table on a creaky transport. "There's something I never told you."

"There are many things we keep to ourselves over the course of our lives. Those choices are not the sum of who we are."

Always the wisdom—and sometimes, Anakin even listened to it. "When we buried my mother," he said after a moment. "On Tatooine." Suddenly he was there, collapsing to his knees. The intense dual-sun heat on the back of his neck. The grit of the sand between the fingers of his hand—his right hand, flesh and bone born of Shmi Skywalker, shortly before it was replaced by the first cybernetic limb of his life. "I swore I would be powerful enough to save people. And instead I did the opposite. I spread fire and pain to anyone in my path."

"Anakin, one person alone cannot burn down a galaxy. Or a Republic." They existed, and yet they did not. Formless and separate, and still one with the Force. Somehow, he felt Obi-Wan's hand on his shoulder, as real as it had been many times when Anakin was a lonely boy, when he was a brazen Padawan, when they stood as equals. "One person may pull a string. One person may light a spark. However, all the pieces don't move into place by themselves. Years upon years compound, one bad choice followed by a good choice followed by a well-intentioned mistake. The will of the galaxy, of people, is different from the will of the Force. Their intentions, their actions, and those that preyed on them, it is a collective. Not preordained. And not the mark of an individual. You do not bear the guilt of the galaxy. Only for your own choices."

"But I *made* those choices. To kneel to the dark side. To storm the Temple.

"To fight you."

"You did. Those belong to you," Obi-Wan said, though his tone came with surprisingly little judgment despite the words. "But so does something else. One moment that led to immense consequences."

"Obi-Wan, I—"

"Anakin. I have asked you many times to be patient. And listen." That laugh again, a sound so familiar and yet different, a change that only wisdom and age could bring. "I have one final challenge for you. Do you trust me?"

This was Obi-Wan Kenobi, negotiating his way even through the strange, endless void of the Force.

Of course he would do that. And of course Anakin would listen.

In the end, that was who they were. Who they always would be. Kenobi and Skywalker. Skywalker and Kenobi.

Because even though Anakin rarely admitted it, Obi-Wan was often right.

A sudden single light broke through the nothingness, a lone beam piercing the darkness. Then another, and another, so many that the veil of empty began to give way into something physical, something real. Except the transformation went further than the space around them; it reached into *himself* and brought him somewhere new.

Trees. Layers upon layers of trees, a dense forest where silhouettes blended into the dark of night. Above, the burning remnants of the Death Star still lingered, smoldering trails streaking downward. Another streak came, not the gradual descent of debris raining into the atmosphere, but a sudden blur whipping from side to side.

X-wing fighters.

They didn't come shooting red-orange blasts or glowing proton torpedoes. Instead brilliant colors burst forward, festive sparkles lighting the sky, and with that, a raucous cheer, voices of all kinds mixing into a frenzied joy that transcended languages.

Beneath the fireworks sat a landscape with so many flickers of light, the natural glow of flame. Around each, silhouettes moved in celebration, the galaxy's exhilaration captured in a single glance.

One glow, though, stood larger than the others, not just in size but also in shape. While joy surrounded most of the fires, this particular one had a stoic lone observer.

Anakin recognized the helmet on the pyre.

More important, Anakin recognized the *man* in front of it.

This was not an exorcism, nor a purge. It did not mark the extermination of Darth Vader, Dark Lord of the Sith and weapon of the Galactic Empire. No, this moment was the opposite. Here, Luke Skywalker did the unthinkable.

Luke had stared directly into the pain and rage of Anakin Skywalker, and somehow managed to see past it all. Now he stood alone, a son offering compassion to his fallen father.

"When he called out, you answered," Obi-Wan said. "You chose him over the Emperor. You chose empathy over power. You chose a future for the galaxy, to break the rule of the Sith.

"You chose to bring *balance*."

Anakin watched, the heat of the flames consuming the technology that had kept his broken body alive for so many years. Luke watched, too, sharp creases on his face. What must he be thinking? Not just about the galaxy on the verge of change, but the legacy burning away in front of him?

"He is a leader," Obi-Wan said. "He is both the present *and* the future."

The statement came so definitively, precisely chosen words by someone who knew how to wield them as weapons. The future, with so many risks both known and unknown—the types of risks that used to keep Anakin awake at night, his mind racing at ways to solve every problem.

And the present—the one thing that Anakin always seemed to overlook in his worries.

"Do you see?" Obi-Wan said, though the gravity of his words soon shifted into a more playful tone. "It took a lifetime for you to arrive. From your days on Tatooine to your life at the Temple to everything beyond that. But now you are here. It is your final lesson."

For so long, Anakin Skywalker had been the one who would simply *find a way*.

Such a lofty goal. Such a quaint idea.

Anakin watched as Luke turned from the burning mound that held Darth Vader's armor, Anakin Skywalker's body. He moved with purpose, but this was not a walk of regret or mourning.

Luke headed to the next step—to his friends.

The handsome caped man dancing to the beats of Endor's native species. Captain Solo, the person Anakin had tortured and put into carbon freeze, shaking hands and hugging one compatriot after another. R2-D2, the droid that served both Padmé and Anakin so loyally and now one of Luke's closest confidants. C-3PO, the very droid he built in a cold Tatooine hovel.

And Leia. A brave, bold woman, her face a perfect mix of her parents—not just in structure, but also in the fierceness of her eyes and the wisdom in her smile.

Anakin no longer needed to find a way. Others already had. And they trusted in one another, a bond so clear that it made complete sense that they defeated the Emperor and his planet-destroying weapon. Not because they were a ragtag group of pilots, smugglers, and dreamers, but because they were *this* particular group.

Anakin watched as Luke embraced his sister. And as he did, he understood the message that was stated so many times by so many people. Obi-Wan, Yoda, Ahsoka, his mother, *Padmé*. They all urged him in their own ways.

It was, in the end, the only thing that Anakin ever needed to do.

"They are the best of both of you," Obi-Wan said.

As if they stood side by side, Anakin instinctively turned to Obi-Wan, a motion that surprised him given that they existed only in the Force.

What surprised him more, though, was what he saw in front of him.

His friend, familiar wry grin beneath a beard, not quite a fully formed body, but a shimmering transparent glow of the old man in Jedi robes struck down in the Death Star.

Obi-Wan offered a smile, his eyebrow arched as he looked Anakin over. "That's new," he remarked.

Anakin looked down, and the fact that he existed in the same shimmering glow as Obi-Wan didn't surprise him. He stood there, his body re-formed, the weight of his feet on the solid ground of the Sanctuary Moon. But stranger still—and what must have caught Obi-Wan's eye—was what draped *over* his restored limbs.

Like Obi-Wan, Anakin existed in the Force wearing Jedi attire.

Not the dark tunic that he wore as he fought Count Dooku or dashed stealthily into Padmé's quarters. But lighter, traditional Jedi robes, the kind that so many masters of the Jedi Order wore—Yoda, Mace Windu, Ki-Adi-Mundi.

And of course, Obi-Wan.

BROTHERHOOD

"I'm as surprised as you are," Anakin said, looking down at them again. "I didn't choose these. I didn't choose any of this."

Obi-Wan's head tilted, his hand coming up to stroke his white beard. "Well, then, old friend. Perhaps those chose you."

Both men looked up to see Luke Skywalker, his mouth curled up in a weighty smile, like he could hear this conversation, a brotherly banter that Luke must have enjoyed with so many of his rebel comrades.

Anakin locked eyes with his son, an acknowledgment that things were different now. Things were *better*, and things would get better. Anakin glanced down one more time, and when he looked ahead, he watched as she arrived.

There was Leia Organa, putting her arms around her brother as bright cheeks framed a wide smile, yet with a familiar glint in her eyes. Anakin recognized it right away.

Leia, like her mother, was already planning for the hard work ahead.

"Theirs will be a long journey," Obi-Wan said.

"Bold their future is," a new voice came, one that Anakin hadn't heard in nearly two decades. "But uncertain."

Master Yoda. Anakin didn't ask how or why. He simply existed in this time and space, letting only a small thought wonder if Qui-Gon Jinn endured here as well.

Probably. Qui-Gon was never far from him. He just didn't recognize it until now.

Brother and sister walked away, leaving Anakin with his thoughts, a strange and unfamiliar comfort at the very nature of *acceptance* of all things.

"Did he see us?" Anakin asked his former master.

Obi-Wan's chin dipped quickly with a nod.

"What about her?"

"She has taken her first steps. But what she does on her journey, that remains her choice. Leia has many gifts beyond the Force."

Anakin felt his heart roar again, a fiery buck that called to him to do *more,* but he tempered it, grounded in his resolve. Luke and Leia, the children of Anakin Skywalker and Padmé Amidala, would outlive and grow beyond the legacy of their parents, with strengths and passions balanced by both the experience of the Galactic Civil War and the support of those closest to them.

"I have faith in them," Anakin finally said. As if that phrase unlocked the universe, the forest began to fade from his view, the feel of his corporeal body dissolving into the Force and leaving him with a single realization—an insight for the ages, so simple and yet so profound.

At that moment, he chose the only thing he ever needed. It just took one final nudge from Obi-Wan to get here.

Finally, Anakin Skywalker let go.

THE STEADFAST SOLDIER

Adam Christopher

The sky was full of lights, and his heart was full of pride, and it was all he could do to bite his tongue, to stop himself just laughing at the sheer, exhilarating joy of it all.

This was *it*. A single moment, a single point in time, *years* in the making. A moment of celebration and unity. Of triumph and of history.

A moment of victory.

A moment when Coruscant, the jewel in the Imperial crown, the bright center of the galaxy, *really* got to shine.

And shine it did. Brilliant and exquisite and wonderful, the lights of the ecumenopolis blending with the lights in the sky, melding into one glorious, planet-enveloping glow.

It was a wonderful night, a wonderful moment.

Right here, right now.

Finally, the laugh came. He couldn't hold it back any longer. He looked up at the night sky, watching the fireworks, watching the crisscross of ion trails left by speeding starships as they skipped in celebration across the planet's mesosphere high above, and higher still, the streaks of meteors as the celestial show grew.

He looked up and laughed. For a moment, the Coruscant night was as bright as day. Then his laugh died and he relaxed, allowing his jaw to slacken in sheer wonder, his vision and his mind lost in the lights, in the colors, in the glory of the moment.

Right here, right now.

They had won.

They had—

Enric Pryde coughed, his body jerking hard against the soft dirt, the back of his head thudding dully against the loamy, moss-covered bank. He screwed his eyes shut tight as his chest convulsed, his lungs on fire, his mouth filled with something hot and sour.

"You okay?"

Pryde waved vaguely in the direction of the gruff male voice, his focus now on merely trying to get his breath. Tears filled his eyes and he lay back, the coughing fit finally subsiding. The ground was soft and comfortable, and he felt light-headed. He opened his eyes, blinking into the too-bright glare of the sunrise visible through the dense forest. Looking away, he lifted his chin and stared up into the still-dark apex, where the last stars could be seen. Stars and other lights, ones that moved, quickly and slowly, a thousand flashes and flickers and streaks visible through the canopy. It was nothing like the spec-

THE STEADFAST SOLDIER

tacle of the night before, but even the morning sun didn't seem bright enough to completely hide the display.

This was not glory. And it most certainly was not victory.

They had . . . lost.

Pryde felt his heart kick into high gear as he remembered, the shock suddenly bringing him out of his daze, as effectively as a jab from a bantha prod.

They had lost, and the lights in the sky, visible despite the dawn, were not fireworks or meteor storm. They were the last burning remnants of the greatest fleet the Empire had ever assembled, the blasted debris raining down across the entire Endor system.

Pryde didn't know how long he had been asleep, and was both annoyed at himself for dropping off and pleased that he had at least been able to get *some* rest. He remembered hunkering down in the hollow with the other two, trying to hide himself from the intense firestorm in high orbit. Oh, he had seen space battles from the ground before, several times, but the intensity of this one had been something quite awesome in its ferocity. And then had come the catastrophic nova of the Death Star's destruction, lighting the entire forest. Even now, as he looked up again, the streaks and flashes and flares seemed almost brighter than ever. He guessed that the debris from the battle station, and other, larger ships in higher orbits, had now begun to finally enter the atmosphere, their ignition a rainbow blaze even the rising sun couldn't blot out. In the immediate aftermath of the Death Star's destruction, he remembered watching as the rebels put on a display of their own, deliberately misaligned engine plates on those wretched X-wings trailing sparks and colored smoke as hotshot pilots spun celebratory arcs. Then, later, the overflights took up another pattern, sequential patrols following a clear grid as they surveyed the area, trying to round up whatever surviving Imperial forces were still at large in the forest.

Survivors including, thought Pryde, swallowing the bile in his throat, himself and the two stormtroopers he had found himself with.

"Here," said the male voice again. "Have another. Will do you good."

Pryde blinked and, turning his gaze from the sky above, tried to focus on the object the stormtrooper was holding out to him, a small transparent cylinder half filled with a red liquid.

At the sight of the death stick, Pryde grimaced, feeling the bile rise again, his head pounding in time with his heartbeat. *Now* he remembered: the almost dreamlike feeling of shock and awe after witnessing the fleet's demise, the claustrophobic desperation as the trio hid from rebel patrols, the two troopers looking to their officer for orders, for answers, for a *solution* that he didn't have.

FS-451 had an answer, his own way out. The stormtrooper had produced the illicit cache and offered Pryde sweet oblivion, at least for a short while.

Despite himself, Pryde hadn't hesitated.

"No, no, no," he muttered now, shaking his head. "I had enough last night. More than enough." He closed his eyes and leaned back, trying to get comfortable in the ill-fitting gray metal breastplate he had been assigned at the last minute back aboard the *Steadfast* as he was unceremoniously ordered to join the ground assault.

Ah yes, Commodore Scaanos. Yet another name to add to Pryde's list of Imperial officers who deserved their commission aboard the *Steadfast* far less than he, and who would one day be made to pay for the way they treated him.

Ten years of service on that Star Destroyer, and Pryde's list was long. And now, with his armor's power pack dying—taking the heat-

THE STEADFAST SOLDIER

ing unit with it—he lay against the side of the hollow formed at the base of one of the gargantuan trees and felt the anger grow. Here he was, marooned with two stormtroopers—one a psychopath addicted to death sticks, the other a quiet woman who at least did what she was told—when Pryde suddenly realized that the rebels might just have taken care of most of that list for him.

That anger began to mellow.

"Now, there's irony for you."

"What?"

Pryde opened his eyes, not even aware he had spoken aloud. FS-451—his helmet off, his head bald and bullet-shaped—was still holding the death stick out. Pryde looked the trooper up and down. Oh yes, psychopath was right. Despite everything—the firefights, the escape, the hours crawling through the forest in the undergrowth—the trooper's armor was gleaming white. FS-451 had cleaned it during the night. Part of Pryde admired the commitment and sense of duty, even in the most trying of circumstances, and wished these were attributes he possessed himself.

Oh, it wasn't that Pryde wasn't committed—ten years aboard a single ship was proof enough that he was a lifer, dedicated to serving the Empire and serving it well.

But his lifetime of servitude wasn't mindless obedience. Pryde could see that in FS-451, the dark glaze the death stick cast over his eyes still unable to quite hide the fanaticism the stormtrooper clearly had in abundance. No, for Pryde, serving the Empire was all part of a plan. A plan that not only involved power, domination, and mastery, but something far simpler, too.

Survival.

He'd managed it well enough so far. From academy cadet to naval captain, Pryde had carefully carved out his career to avoid exactly the kind of situation he now found himself in. Of course he was combat-ready, and he even had some experience—all officers did. But it had taken Commodore Scaanos to mess everything up. Pryde had never liked him, and he knew the feeling was mutual. What he hadn't expected was that Scaanos would use those personal feelings to try to get rid of a fellow officer he clearly saw as an irritant.

It was infuriating, it really was. Pryde was the longest-serving crewmember of the *Steadfast,* and Commodore Scaanos had been parachuted in after his predecessor had carelessly managed to get himself killed at the Battle of Ponolapo. And from the very start, Scaanos thought he owned the place, stretching the boundaries of his command in ways that, to Pryde at least, seemed deeply, deliberately antagonistic. That Pryde had managed to endure four long years of the new commodore was something of a miracle, the two officers butting heads with depressing regularity.

But finally, Pryde had had enough—it wasn't just a personality clash, two equally rigid but opposing interpretations of Imperial doctrine causing the two officers to clash. No, for Pryde, this was personal, because Commodore Scaanos was *foe*. Pryde had a plan—a very long, very complicated, very *clever* plan that involved him being in charge one day—and the arrival of the new commodore had very much put that plan in jeopardy. So Pryde made his feelings known through official channels. Commodore might have outranked captain, but the *Steadfast* was Pryde's ship and he was going to make damn sure the upstart newcomer knew it. True, maybe he could have been a little . . . smarter about it. Worked around the rules rather than adhering to them, and, yes, Pryde could admit he sometimes acted upon the occasional rash thought (*hello, death sticks, my old friends*). But still, it was done. No regrets.

Until now. Until Endor.

Above the tree canopy, something flared, magnesium-white.

THE STEADFAST SOLDIER

Pryde glanced up, imagining the shard of disintegrating debris was Commodore Scaanos's eminently flammable backside.

It was all a matter of survival. That was Pryde's dedication and duty. Not self-sacrifice, not mindless devotion—like FS-451—to a cause. Because causes got you killed. *Belief* got you sent to the front lines, where you could bare your teeth and scream your allegiance to the heavens in the microsecond before you were atomized by an enemy whose belief was just as strong as yours. That FS-451 had survived this long was perhaps nothing short of a fluke, the same kind of unplanned development that had led Captain Enric Pryde of the *Steadfast* to be sent down to the forest to shoot at rebels on the ground while the Empire destroyed the Alliance's fleet above.

Pryde's plan hadn't so much gone awry as been shattered altogether. A plan that had started so many years ago, ever since he was a teenager working to get into the prestigious Alsakan Academy. It was a plan not only about power and control of others, but about control and power over his own life.

His own destiny.

A plan that rather depended on staying as far away from the battle lines as was physically possible during a Galactic Civil War. Coruscant would have been the safest option, of course, but that meant a desk job, and while it was a fine, even necessary career for thousands of officers, he knew he was above such menial tasks. As much as Pryde was dedicated to his own survival, he also knew he was a damn sight better than the average Imperial drone. To be stuck on Coruscant or some other Imperial base was, quite frankly, beneath him. And while it might have served his grand plan, it would most certainly have been the long way around.

Pryde was cleverer than that, and he knew it. The Empire owed him something far, far better.

Pryde sighed and pressed his face into his hands, surprised at how cold his face felt, and then he realized he couldn't feel his face at all. He worked his lips, but they, too, were strangely absent.

He dropped his hands. "My head's gone numb." He looked at FS-451—more specifically, at the death stick in his hand. A memory of the previous night's overindulgence on the luminescent little horrors swam into Pryde's mind. He closed his eyes, tight, and shuddered.

FS-451 was a *bad* influence.

Fighting against the rising swell of nausea from his stomach, Pryde opened his eyes and looked up at the trooper. "What in all the Typhonic Nebula have you spiked those with?"

At this, FS-451 grinned. "Have another and it won't just be your head that's numb," he said before flipping the death stick into his own mouth. "Helps with the cold."

Pryde noted that the trooper had stopped adding "sir" to the end of every exchange. He would bring that—and several other things, perhaps including smuggling of an illicit substance supply to a superior officer—up later.

If there was a later. Because they were stranded, and would remain so until they were either rescued or found their own way out. Given the continued rain of burning wreckage covering the sky, Pryde suspected they were very much on their own. Option B would have to be it.

"What would help with the cold, *trooper*," he said, unable to contain the snarl in his voice, "is heat." He nodded past FS-451. In the middle of the hollow at the base of the tree sat a small heap of twigs and brown pine needles. "I thought you wanted to be an incinerator trooper. Look at you. You can't even light a simple fire. We're going to freeze to death on this ridiculous planet."

"It's a moon, sir."

Pryde looked up as the third member of their party appeared over

THE STEADFAST SOLDIER

the embankment, her electronically augmented voice far too loud for Pryde's liking, the trooper's dirt-caked armor a sharp contrast with FS-451's pristine plastoid.

"Moon, planet, I couldn't really care any less, trooper." Pryde coughed again and sat up straight, determined not to let another fit take hold. He closed his eyes, like sheer willpower could bring it under control. To his surprise, it actually worked. He opened his eyes and spat a wad of mucus onto the ground by FS-451's boot before leaning back against the bank again. "Why," he said, with infinite tiredness, "is this *moon,* as you so accurately and pedantically describe it, so cold and wet."

The other stormtrooper slid down the incline and into the hollow, her blaster hanging from one hand. "Maybe another of Endor's satellites is a tropical paradise. *This* one is cold and wet," she said with a slight shrug that Pryde found utterly infuriating. This trooper wasn't from his regiment—he and FS-451 were the sole surviving members, as far as he knew, and they'd found TK-111 alone in the woods—but that didn't mean she wasn't supposed to show the respect due to a superior officer.

"How very observant of you, Tee-Kay-Triple-One," said Pryde, scowling. He went to stand but slipped and fell onto his back. He swore and craned his neck down, his numb fingers slipping over the wet, slimy clasps on the side of his stupid breastplate that was now nothing more than an impediment. "Next you will no doubt tell me how perfectly adapted the Ewoks are to their environment, how a primitive society such as theirs exists in perfect symbiosis with their forest and—"

His finger slipped, the tip sliced by the sharp edge of the breastplate clasp. Pryde swore again, squeezing his finger to stop the bleeding, before examining the tiny cut and putting it in his mouth.

Wonderful. Now he was going to get an infection as well. This mission couldn't be going any better.

"Where have you been, anyway?" Pryde asked, sucking his cut finger. "You've been gone for hours."

"You were asleep, sir."

"Don't be impertinent."

"Thought the furries turned you into stew," said FS-451.

"Yes, very good, trooper," said Pryde. "Very droll." He turned a sharp eye on TK-111. "Well? Give me a report, and it had better be good."

"I can do better than that, Captain."

Pryde paused, his eyes narrowed. Captain? That was better. But there was still something in her voice he didn't like.

"Spit it out, trooper."

"I'll show you. Follow me."

Despite his sleep, Pryde felt tired. And cold. And hungry. His head spun, and a trek through the forest was the last thing he felt like doing. He was about to stop and reprimand TK-111 for wasting a superior officer's time when she came to a halt herself and ducked down behind the hulk of a fallen trunk, gesturing for Pryde and FS-451 to follow suit.

And now he was looking at . . . what was he looking at?

"I'm waiting for an explanation, trooper," he said.

In front of the fallen tree, over at the other side of the clearing, was a pile of blackened, burned wood, surrounded by scorched ground, the remnants of a good-sized fire. It was still hot—Pryde could actually feel the heat, even from this distance, even though there was nothing left but embers and charcoal. Even as he watched, a fat spark spat out and floated, glowing, up into the haze of smoke and steam

THE STEADFAST SOLDIER

that rose from the ashes. He frowned and turned to the stormtrooper crouched beside him.

"Well?"

"Lord Vader."

Pryde blinked, his forehead creasing in confusion.

"What about him?"

TK-111 indicated the smoldering pile with a tip of her helmet. "Lord Vader is dead. The rebels must have captured him. They burned his body. I saw it."

Pryde stared at her blank, monochrome faceplate. What she said made no sense whatsoever. Not only was Lord Vader *not* on the forest moon, there was no way the pathetic rebels would have been able to capture him, let alone *kill* him. Pryde had seen Vader in action himself, the black armor reflecting the blaze of the red lightsaber as he cut through dozens of enemies, destroying all opposition that came within his reach . . . and some that lay *beyond*.

Darth Vader was unstoppable. Pryde was about to remind TK-111 of just these facts, but instead he just sighed and slumped on the ground.

"How many death sticks did he give you?" he asked.

The trooper tilted her helmet in the opposite direction. "I know what you're thinking, sir, but I'm telling the truth. I saw it. Lord Vader is dead. His body is just over there. What's left of it, anyway."

Pryde opened and closed his jaw, undecided whether TK-111 was a lost cause or . . .

Or was telling the truth.

Surely not? *Surely* not.

Pryde gritted his teeth and turned, looking over the top of the rotting log. Ahead, smoke curled gently into the morning air from the remnants of the fire.

And then . . . he saw it. A shape, something that wasn't burned wood, perhaps more an outline than a still-intact object, left in the center of the pile. The shape was long and thin, a hollow lined with ash and residue that looked artificial, shiny like burned plastoid.

TK-111 was right about one thing, it *was* a funeral pyre—

"Told you," she said, shifting on the ground beside him, her voice an electronic purr.

—but whether it really was *Darth Vader's* funeral pyre was another matter altogether.

"Perhaps," said Pryde. He turned back to the scene, the corners of his mouth downturned as he assessed the possibilities of TK-111's discovery.

"You have a plan, sir?"

Pryde's gaze flickered over the stormtrooper's helmet. It was back to "sir" now. That was better. Much better. Then he glanced across at FS-451. He was kneeling on the ground, his body upright but swaying a little. Pryde's sour expression tightened even more as he saw the trooper's face.

FS-451 was smiling. Pryde found the expression possibly the most frightening thing about their whole situation.

"Beautiful," said FS-451, his voice a whisper.

Pryde snorted. "At least the rebels know how to make a fire, trooper," he said.

FS-451 didn't respond. He just grinned, his gaze dead ahead but unfocused. Hanging from the fingers of one hand was an empty plastic cylinder.

"He's out of it, sir," said TK-111. "His mechanism's gone. Too many death sticks."

Pryde sighed. He turned back to the pyre. That it was still warm, even now, meant it was fresh. They were close to the Ewok village here—a little too close—but the forest was silent, the rebels and

THE STEADFAST SOLDIER

their disgusting furry allies sleeping off the depraved celebration Pryde had been able to hear on the other side of the forest the previous night. He lowered himself behind the tree trunk as he considered.

A funeral pyre, yes. For a single body, yes. But Vader?

Impossible. No, more than that. *Preposterous.* Pryde didn't know what TK-111 thought she saw, but it most certainly was not the final end of Darth Vader.

So, if not him, then . . . who?

The battle was only just over, there would be many bodies to bury, friends to mourn. To take the time to build the pyre, in the middle of a celebration, meant that the person for whom it was built was important—*very* important. Perhaps a high-ranking rebel offer, maybe even a general? Pryde wasn't sure . . . wouldn't someone like that demand a more elaborate, more ceremonial send-off? On the other hand, these rebels were a peculiar bunch; who knew what they thought was appropriate.

But . . . yes, someone important. It had to be. Someone the Empire knew. Someone the Empire wanted *dead.* That list was long, but there were some names near the top that even Palpatine himself took a keen interest in . . . and if Pryde was the one who could bring back evidence, something to confirm the identity . . . something he could claim to have taken in battle himself . . . then it would prove to be an important bargaining chip when it came to reestablishing himself in the Imperial hierarchy. He didn't know the *full* result of the battle that had taken place over Endor, but given the decimation of the Imperial ground forces Pryde had witnessed firsthand—and only just escaped from—and the very visible destruction of the Death Star itself, there would clearly now be many, *many* gaps in that hierarchy that would need filling.

This great rebel victory could, Pryde realized, be worked precisely in his favor. He allowed himself a microsecond to thank Commodore Scaanos for inadvertently steering his personal plan onto this rather advantageous, and totally unexpected, path.

What was that about destiny?

"I'm going to take a look," he said, lifting himself up, but keeping to a low crouch. TK-111 lifted her blaster, ready to follow, but Pryde waved her back down. "Cover me." He looked at FS-451, who was still in his trancelike state. He jabbed a finger at the stormtrooper. "If he does anything foolish," said Pryde, "you have my permission to shoot him."

"Sir."

With a nod, Pryde turned, checked the way was clear, and, keeping low, darted across the forest clearing to the funeral pyre. As he got closer, he slowed, raising an arm to shield his face. After he'd spent the night skulking in the chill of the forest, the warmth of the dying embers was surprisingly intense.

Pryde ducked down and scooted closer. Ideally, he'd be able to salvage some kind of souvenir—a rank insignia would be most likely to survive, he thought. Even better would be an ID tag, something that actually had the dead officer's name.

On his hands and knees, Pryde stretched forward and, selecting a tree branch that looked relatively untouched by the fire, pulled it out from the pyre's base. It came free, sending a cascade of fresh sparks into the sky as the sudden influx of oxygen made the embers flare. Pryde stumbled backward, dazzled by the burst of bright light as part of the charred structure collapsed, the gout of flame surprising but thankfully brief. Pryde shielded his face with both arms, wary of any further flashes of re-ignition. When none came, he lowered his arms, the short, partially burned branch held in one hand.

THE STEADFAST SOLDIER

His eyes went wide. He could feel them dry out almost instantly, but it didn't matter. Nothing mattered anymore, because...

It wasn't.

It *couldn't* be.

It...

Captain Enric Pryde finally blinked.

TK-111 had been right—although there was no body, there was... *evidence,* revealed by the collapsing pyre. There, in the center of the pile, the charcoal was coated in places with heavy patches of melted plastoid, thick and black and not because it had been burned by the fire. In a couple of places, the plastoid retained at least part of the original shape. As Pryde cast his eye over a nearly intact square fragment, he could see a clouded, pill-like shape embedded in the stuff. A light, from the chest unit of—

Pryde's throat closed up, his breath catching, his limbs—his entire body—suddenly feeling like deadweight. He dropped the branch then dropped to his knees and stared.

It was *him.* Or, as TK-111 had so accurately put it, what was *left* of him.

Darth Vader. *Lord* Vader. The Emperor's right hand. The enforcer, the leader, whose mysterious power—and oh, what power it was—Pryde had seen for himself, so many years ago.

Lord Vader was dead.

Lord Vader was *dead.*

It... it didn't even make any sense. Vader was here? How was Lord Vader here? And—

Vader was here (impossible) and if the rebels had somehow captured him (impossible) and if the rebels had somehow killed him (impossible) and Vader was dead (impossible) and it was impossible it was impossible it was impossible and and and

"Sir!"

He blinked, snapping out of his spiral of thoughts. He looked up at TK-111. She gave a faint nod, perhaps in recognition of what she must have known was running through Pryde's mind, what must have run through *her* mind when she bore witness to the lit pyre itself.

It was impossible . . . but . . . yes, it had happened. It was real.

Pryde rocked back on his haunches, wiping his face, running sooty fingers through his hair, pushing the storm of emotions somewhere deep, *deep* down.

It had happened, Vader was dead, which meant the balance of power in the Empire—the *remnant* of the Empire, he now realized with shocking clarity—had shifted to a degree he couldn't possibly have believed, even as he'd watched the great fleet burn in space.

And it felt . . .

It felt good. Maybe it was the aftereffects of the death sticks, maybe it was the stress and the fatigue, or maybe it was just the restoration of some kind of balance as Pryde's mind cleared, a strange, almost joyous sense of calm taking hold as he began to comprehend what the full impact of the Battle of Endor might be.

Opportunity. Oh glorious, oh wonderful, *opportunity*.

"Hand me that stick," he said.

"Sir?"

He reached out to her, snapping his fingers. "That branch, there, pass it over."

Her helmet angled again, but she obeyed the order, bending down to pick up the charred branch Pryde had dropped. "This?"

Pryde sighed and snatched it out of her hands. Then he turned back to the funeral pyre and poked the branch experimentally into the collapsed core of the pyre. Then, satisfied the structure was stable enough, he grabbed the end of the branch with both hands and began digging.

THE STEADFAST SOLDIER

"Help me," he said, still focused on his work. He pointed to his right with an outstretched hand. "Start over there."

He dug a moment longer, then turned. TK-111 hadn't moved.

"I gave you an order, trooper."

TK-111 moved closer to the pyre. There was a pause before she said, "What are we looking for?"

"His lightsaber," said Pryde, resuming his work. "It'll be here somewhere."

"You want his lightsaber? Do you even know how to work it?"

Another long, long pause. Pryde stopped again and this time he stood and marched over to her, looming over the much shorter stormtrooper.

"Do we have a command problem here, Tee-Kay-Triple-One?"

She snapped to attention. "No, sir!" came the reply, barked like the trooper was on parade.

"That's better."

"Permission to speak freely, sir."

"Permission denied," said Pryde. He paused and considered the stormtrooper standing in front of him. If he was to pull this off, he was going to need allies. *Insiders.* TK-111 may just have been a stormtrooper, but she had shown at least some initiative, and their current circumstances had also demonstrated the fact her personality hadn't been completely drummed out of her. And her operating number was low, indicating seniority, maybe even rank.

She could be useful, perhaps, for what might come next, as Pryde's grand plan suddenly accelerated.

"What's your name, trooper?" he asked.

"Tee-Kay-Triple-One, sir."

Pryde frowned. "No, your *name*. Or did they brainwash that out of you at the academy?"

She didn't answer at once. But despite the blankness of her helmet, Pryde could sense... was that just a hint of fear?

Good. *Good.*

Finally she spoke. "Karenza Masus, sir."

Pryde's lip curled, a nasty smirk forming on his face. "To answer your question, Karenza Masus, I wouldn't have the faintest idea about how to wield a lightsaber, but that is entirely missing the point. I don't want it as a weapon. I want it as a symbol. I want it as a *totem,* a ferrocrete demonstration of the transfer of power. From him—" He stabbed a finger toward the pyre. "—to me," he concluded, jabbing the same finger into his own chest. He took a step closer to the stormtrooper, pointing now to sky above. "Do you understand what has happened, up there?" he asked. "Do you have any comprehension of how the galaxy was changed in just one night?"

"I... I don't understand, sir. What's happening?"

Pryde's smirk widened, his gaze meeting the black eyepieces of TK-111's helmet. The pair stood for a moment in silence. Behind Pryde, there was a crack from the disturbed embers of the pyre. And then, in the distance, he could hear a heavy, primitive drumbeat, the Ewok village slowly waking in the new morning.

Still, he said nothing. He looked at TK-111, but he didn't *see* her. He was lost in his own mind, the shock of Lord Vader's apparent death, the new ambition that had been sparked within him, and the lingering high of the death sticks spinning his thoughts into a quiet hysteria.

The drumbeat got louder, and now there were voices. TK-111 turned to face the sound. It was distant, but the funeral pyre was very exposed. As were they.

And then... Pryde laughed. It was high, a childish giggle.

The hard plastoid back of TK-111's gauntlet struck Pryde on the cheek. He toppled backward and lay on the ground, blinking away

THE STEADFAST SOLDIER

tears, wondering why he could taste blood, wondering where he was, and what was happening and . . .

"Snap out of it." The same gauntlet that had hit him now appeared in his vision, this time offered as an open hand. Pryde stared at it, his jaw working, no words coming out.

The armored glove closed around his collar, and Pryde felt himself pulled up. He lost his balance and stumbled forward, his nose smacking into the muddy faceplate of TK-111. He gasped, and immediately felt blood, hot and wet, stream from one nostril.

"How many death sticks did he give *you*?" asked the stormtrooper.

Pryde pushed away, nearly tripping over his own feet but managing to remain upright.

"That's enough insolence," he muttered, wiping the blood from his upper lip.

In the forest, the drums continued. There was a rustle and a crack. Rebels or Ewoks or both were near. TK-111 turned in a circle, scanning the forest, then motioned to Pryde. "We need to leave," she said. "The Ewok village is too close and the rebels will be all over us if we don't move. Let's go."

She grabbed Pryde's wrist and went to move, but he jerked out of her grip and fell to his hands and knees. He looked up, into the smoldering pyre.

"No," he said. "The lightsaber. I want the lightsaber."

There was an electronically filtered sigh from behind TK-111's faceplate.

"Sir, there isn't time. Besides, nothing could have survived that fire."

Pryde, his eyes wide, stared at the pyre, felt the latent heat of it on his face . . . and heard, elsewhere, the approach of the enemy. She was probably right—about the lightsaber, about the rapidly increasing chance that they were going to get caught.

"Sir, we're moving, *now*." TK-111's voice was the sharp snap of a drill sergeant.

Pryde slammed a fist into the soft ground, then got to his feet. "Very well." He glanced back across the clearing, to the fallen log and, still kneeling behind it, the motionless form of FS-451. TK-111 followed his gaze.

"What about him?" she asked.

"Collateral damage," said Pryde. He glanced sideways at TK-111. "Deal with it. *Quietly*."

The stormtrooper did not acknowledge the order, but she ducked quickly across the clearing and disappeared behind the log.

Pryde turned away and looked up into the sky, craning his head back as far as it would go. The fall of burning debris had abated, but there was still a ragged, glowing patch where the Death Star had once been. He stared up at the point. He felt light-headed, his vision tinged with white sparks.

"The old order changes, giving way to the new," he said, his voice a murmur. "Oh yes." He nodded to himself. "Oh yes."

Opportunity. Oh glorious, oh wonderful, *opportunity*.

TK-111 returned to his side. "It's done."

Pryde's lips twitched into a grin. "Excellent, he said. "Now . . . let's get off this moon."

RETURN OF THE WHILLS

Tom Angleberger

Each time I am called on to serve, the burden is great, but the responsibility greater. This time, I must answer the questions left by an Empire's fall.

To write in clear Aurebesh what I have learned from the legends and tales of many voices, many languages, many planets.

I must settle into a unified vision, a single Truth.

Seeking balance and clarity, I have hidden myself away from all others as I write another entry in the immortal Journal of the Whills. The complexity of this galaxy-shaking moment requires my complete focus without even the fear of interruption.

May the Force Be with Me as I—

"KNOCK KNOCK!"

"What? I asked not to be disturbed!"

"You're supposed to say 'Who's There?'"

"I know who it is! Every time I try to write in the Journal YOU show up to hassle me!"

"I just want to be sure you get it right this time. And to do that you have to say 'Who's There!' KNOCK KNOCK!"

"You are making a mockery of a sacred duty! But I'll say it if you promise to leave."

"Sure! KNOCK KNOCK!"

"Who's there?"

"Al and Tim."

"Al and Tim who?"

"Al and Tim ago . . . in a galaxy far, far away."

"That doesn't even work. Now go away and let me get started . . . Now where was I. Oh, yes . . .

"REVENGE OF THE JEDI."

"Oh come on! You're not going to call it The Revenge of the Jedi, *are you?"*

"You promised to leave!"

"How can I leave when you obviously need my help? Have you even been paying attention? Don't you know anything? Revenge leads to the dark side! Revenge of the Sith, maybe, but never the Jedi."

"Hmmm . . . you actually have a point for once. Let me start again . . .

"THE RETURN OF THE JEDI!"

"Meh . . . it'll do."

"Luke Skywalker has returned to his home planet of Tatooine—"

"You're not starting on Tatooine again, are you? Half the chapters in this journal are set on Tatooine! There are other planets, you know! About a million of them!"

RETURN OF THE WHILLS

"Look, this is a hero's journey. It started here and so it has to come full circle sooner or later. Who knows, Tatooine may yet have more stories to tell."

"All right, but do me a favor and skip the sandstorm, will you? I hate sand."

"Who doesn't? Consider it skipped. Ahem—"

"Luke Skywalker has returned to his home planet of Tatooine in an attempt to rescue his friend Han Solo from the clutches of vile gangster Jabba the Hutt."

"Yes! Jabba's palace! The thugs, the monster, the dancers, the band, and most important . . . Joh Yowza!"

"Er . . . I wasn't really going to mention Joh Yowza."

"What? He's the poet of his generation! I simply cannot imagine Jabba's palace without him!"

"Oddly enough, I can. Anyway,

"Little does Luke know that the GALACTIC EMPIRE has secretly begun construction on a new armored space station even more powerful than the first dreaded Death Star—"

"Wait, hold up . . . ANOTHER Death Star? They're going to build ANOTHER Death Star?"

"Not 'going to,' they've already built it. And it's smart. If you spent all that time designing a Death Star and it turned out to have a single fatal flaw, then it makes sense to build another without the single flaw. Besides, it's a trap. Now let me wrap this up . . .

"When completed, this ultimate weapon will spell—"

"Whee! A weapon that spells! What a thrill!"

"—will spell certain doom for the small band of rebels . . ."

"Hey that's actually a nice touch: 'small.' And the true heroes of this story, the Ewoks, are small. It's great foreshadowing."

"Thanks, I wasn't sure anyone would notice."

"Well, I'm kind of obsessed with the Ewoks."

"Me too! I know some of the other Whills don't like them, but they're totally awesome! The apex predators on a hostile jungle world!"

"Yes! Clobbering stormtroopers, then chowing down for the strength to go clobber more!"

"Yeah! And their courage! It's like a whole . . . caravan of courage!"

"I . . . I never knew we both felt this way about the Ewoks. You're cooler than I thought."

"So are you! Maybe . . . you'd like to help me write their story?"

"It would be an honor! You know, this could be the start of a beautiful friendship."

"Yeah. Too bad this is the last chapter."

"No . . . there is another . . ."

"Really? You'll have to tell me all about it!"

"Well, I was thinking maybe we skip ahead thirty years. OR, hear me out, what if we go BACK thirty years? You know, I still haven't forgiven you for omitting Darth Maul from all of this."

"He had already been killed! Twice!"

"Sounds like a heck of a story to me! We start with the taxation of trade routes AND THEN . . ."

"It does sound pretty good, but I'm busy with this one. Maybe YOU should write it."

"Me? Do you really think I'm worthy?"

"Sure! And once I finish this up, I'll check in and give you some pointers . . . maybe a little constructive criticism . . . a few edits . . ."

"Oh . . . uh, that'll be great."

"No problem, now where was I? Oh yes . . . 'certain doom.'"

"Certain doom for the small band of rebels struggling to restore freedom to the galaxy . . ."

ABOUT THE AUTHORS

SALADIN AHMED is the Eisner Award-winning writer of *Marvel's Spider-Man: Miles Morales* and *The Magnificent Ms. Marvel*. His novel *Throne of the Crescent Moon* was nominated for the Hugo and Nebula awards and won the Locus Award for Best First Novel. He lives with his children near Detroit.

CHARLIE JANE ANDERS is the author of the Unstoppable trilogy, beginning with *Victories Greater Than Death*. She's also the author of the short story collection *Even Greater Mistakes* and *Never Say You Can't Survive* (August 2021), a book about how to use creative writing to get through hard times. Her other books include *The City in the Middle of the Night* and *All the Birds in the Sky*. She's won the Hugo, Nebula, Sturgeon, Lambda Literary, Crawford and Locus awards. She co-created Escapade, a transgender superhero, for Marvel Comics and wrote her into the long-running *New Mutants* comic. And she's currently the science fiction and fantasy book reviewer for the *Washington Post*. Her TED Talk, 'Go Ahead, Dream About the Future' got seven hundred thousand views in its first week. With Annalee Newitz, she co-hosts the podcast *Our Opinions Are Correct*.

TOM ANGLEBERGER is the author of the *New York Times* bestselling Origami Yoda series. His other *Star Wars* books are *The Mighty Chewbacca in the Forest of Fear!* and a novelisation of *Return of the Jedi* subtitled *Beware the Power of the Dark Side!* (Yes, the exclamation points are part of the titles.) He lives in Virginia with his wife, author and illustrator Cece Bell.

K ARSENAULT RIVERA is the author of the Ascendant trilogy and various *Magic: The Gathering* stories, including *Midnight Hunt* and *Crimson Vow*. She still has her childhood copy of *The Empire Strikes Back* for the SNES, a game she never actually beat. She lives in Brooklyn with her two partners. Her fantasy romance novel, *Oath of Flame*, released in 2024.

KRISTIN BAVER covers *Star Wars* news as the associate editor of Star Wars.com and the host of *This Week! in Star Wars*. The author of *Star Wars: Skywalker – A Family at War*, *The Art of Star Wars: The High Republic* and *Star Wars 100 Objects*, Kristin is also a contributor to *Star Wars Timelines* and *Star Wars Year by Year*. She previously worked as an award-winning journalist covering crime and social issues in central Pennsylvania, but now lives with her family in San Francisco, California.

OLIVIE BLAKE is the *New York Times* bestselling author of the Atlas series and *Alone with You in the Ether*. As Alexene Farol Follmuth, she is also the author of the young adult romcom *My Mechanical Romance*. She lives in Los Angeles with her husband, goblin prince/toddler and rescue pit bull.

AKEMI DAWN BOWMAN is a critically acclaimed author who writes across genres. Her novels include William C. Morris Award finalist *Starfish*, Locus Award finalist *The Infinity Courts*, *Summer Bird Blue*, *Harley in the Sky*, *Generation Misfits* and *Where the Lost Ones Go*. She has a BA in social sciences from the University of Nevada, Las Vegas, and currently lives in Scotland with her family.

EMMA MIEKO CANDON is the bestselling author of *Star Wars: Ronin*, an expansion of the *Star Wars Visions* short 'The Duel' that revisits the *Star Wars* mythos through the lens of Japanese history and folklore. The first book in their original debut series, *The Archive Undying*, pits queer rebellion against brutal police states who forge mecha from the bones of dead AI gods. *Star Wars* consumed Emma at a young age, and given their childhood fixation on Rogue and Wraith squadrons, they're thrilled to finally make their way into the canon proper via Wedge Antilles. You can find Emma airing unimpeachable anime opinions on X at @emmacandon, on Tumblr at @emcandon, at emcandon.com, or wailing about video games under the bushes of the nearest boba tea joint.

OLIVIA CHADHA writes novels and comic books for MG, YA and adult audiences. She has a PhD in literature and creative writing and her research centres on the history of exile, precarious borders and boundaries, global folklore and the relationships among humans, machines and the environment. *Balance of Fragile Things* is her debut adult literary novel. *Rise of the Red Hand*, her YA debut, was awarded the Colorado Book Award for Young Adult Literature. It's followed by book two of The Mechanists Series, *Fall of the Iron Gods*. She is a contributor to the YA folk horror anthology *The Gathering Dark* (Page Street) and the desi anthology *Magic Has No Borders* (HarperTeen). When not writing she's searching for butterflies on a hike in Colorado. She can be found at oliviachadha.com.

GLORIA CHAO is a screenwriter and the critically acclaimed author of *When You Wish Upon a Lantern*, *Rent a Boyfriend*, *Our Wayward Fate* and *American Panda*. Her award-winning books have received starred trade reviews and were Indie Next List, Junior Library Guild, YALSA Teens' Top 10, Amelia Bloomer List, Epic Reads Recommends for Target and Common Sense Media selections. After a brief detour as a dentist, she is now grateful to spend her days in fictional characters' heads instead of real people's mouths. When she's not writing, you can find her on the curling ice, where she and her husband are world-ranked in mixed doubles. Visit her tea-and-book-filled world at GloriaChao.wordpress.com and find her on Instagram and X: @GloriaCChao.

MIKE CHEN is the *New York Times* bestselling author of *Star Wars: Brotherhood*, *Here and Now and Then*, *Light Years from Home* and other novels. He has covered geek culture for sites such as Nerdist, Tor.com and StarTrek.com, and in a different life, covered the NHL. A member of SFWA, Mike lives in the Bay Area with his wife, daughter and many rescue animals. Follow him on Instagram: @mikechenwriter.

ADAM CHRISTOPHER is the *New York Times* bestselling author of *Star Wars: Shadow of the Sith* and has contributed to the first two *Star Wars: From a Certain Point of View* anthologies and IDW's *Star Wars Adventures* comic. Christopher has also written official tie-in novels for the hit CBS television show *Elementary*, the award-winning *Dishonored* video game franchise and the Netflix phenomenon *Stranger Things*. His debut novel *Empire State* was *SciFiNow*'s Book of the Year and a *Financial Times* Book of the Year, and his other novels include *Made to Kill*, *Seven Wonders* and many more. Born in New Zealand, Christopher now lives in Great Britain. Find out more at adamchristopher.me.

PAUL CRILLEY is an award-winning author and screenwriter. His book *Poison City* is in development with Jerry Bruckheimer Television, and his novel *Department Zero*, about a group of detectives demoted to cleaning up supernatural crime scenes, has been optioned by Boat Rocker Productions. His latest novel, *Breakout* (witten as Paul Herron), a thriller about inmates abandoned in a flooding prison during a Category 5 hurricane, is out now. Paul was also a writer on *Star Wars: The Old Republic*. Other projects include *Star Wars* comics, *Doctor Who*, *X-Files*, Hardy Boys and *Daredevil*. He has also written over 480 episodes of continuing drama and edited 1,220 hours of scripted television.

AMAL EL-MOHTAR is an award-winning author of fiction, poetry and criticism. She is a columnist for the *New York Times Book Review* and the co-author, with Max Gladstone, of *This Is How You Lose the Time War*, which has been translated into over ten languages and received several honours including the Hugo, Nebula and Locus awards. She lives in Ottawa. You can find more of her work at amalelmohtar.com.

M. K. ENGLAND grew up on the Space Coast of Florida watching shuttle launches from the backyard. These days, they call rural Virginia home, where there are many excellent sheep but a tragic lack of rockets. Between marathon writing sessions, MK can be found rolling critical hits at the gaming table, digging in the garden or feeding their video game addiction. MK is the author of seven novels for kids, teens and adults, including *The One True Me and You*, *Player vs. Player* and *Firefly: What Makes Us Mighty*. Follow them at mkengland.com.

JASON FRY is the *New York Times* bestselling author of the young adult space-fantasy series The Jupiter Pirates, as well as *Star Wars: The Last Jedi*, *Star Wars: The Essential Atlas* and many other books and short stories set in a galaxy far, far away. He is a gigantic dork about *Star Wars* geography, the New York Mets, genealogy, custom baseball cards and pursuits even more niche than those just mentioned. He lives in Brooklyn with his wife, kid and an excessive number of ill-advised collections.

ADAM LANCE GARCIA is an award-winning writer featured in the Eisner-winning *Puerto Rico Strong*, the *New York Times* Editor's Choice *The Faking of the President* and the bestselling *The Obama Inheritance*. He is currently completing his Green Lama Legacy series and is a writer/producer for the audio drama podcast *Radio Room*. Adam worked as a television producer for over a decade and is currently a creative producer at Condé Nast. Adam has collected *Star Wars* books his entire life and is excited to add this anthology to his collection.

LAMAR GILES writes for children and adults across multiple genres. He is the author of the critically acclaimed novels *Fake ID, Spin, The Last Last-Day-of-Summer, Not So Pure and Simple* and *The Getaway*. He lives in Virginia with his family.

Hugo-, Nebula- and Locus-winning author MAX GLADSTONE has been thrown from a horse in Mongolia and once wrecked a bicycle in Angkor Wat. He is the author of many books, including *Dead Country, Last Exit, Empress of Forever* and, with Amal El-Mohtar, the internationally bestselling *This Is How You Lose the Time War*.

THEA GUANZON was born and raised in the Philippines as the eldest of three siblings. One of her earliest memories involves watching the original *Star Wars* trilogy on VHS over and over again, and she has been a *Star Wars* fan ever since. Aside from being a writer, she is an avid traveller, a Dungeon Master, an iced coffee junkie and a horror podcast aficionado. She currently resides in Metro Manila with two turtles named Dumpling and Potato Chip, an evil cat named Darth Pancakes and an alarming number of houseplants. Her debut novel, *The Hurricane Wars*, the first book in a fantasy romance trilogy set in a world inspired by Southeast Asia, was released in October 2023 under the Voyager imprint of HarperCollins.

ALI HAZELWOOD is the *New York Times* bestselling author of *The Love Hypothesis, Love on the Brain* and *Loathe to Love You*. Originally from Italy, she lived in Germany and Japan before moving to the US to pursue a PhD in neuroscience. In December 2017, Ali was dragged by her husband to a crowded movie theater to watch *The Last Jedi* (directed by Rian Johnson). She began writing Reylo fanfiction that very night.

PATRICIA A. JACKSON is a high school teacher in Pennsylvania. Her debut novel is *Forging a Nightmare*, a delightfully heretical tale of fallen angels, infernal warhorses and the Four Horsemen of the Apocalypse. She is no stranger to writing in the *Star Wars* universe. Her best-known works are *Black Sands of Socorro*, a smugglers' sourcebook, and 'The Final Exit,' a short story about a Dark Jedi's redemption. When not writing, she's gaming or watching her favourite Japanese anime. In her spare time, she rides horses, the ever-patient Jedi Master Maya and the Sith Lord Indy.

ALEX JENNINGS is a lifelong fan and creator of SFF who lives in New Orleans. His writing has appeared in *The Magazine of Fantasy and Science Fiction, Africa Risen* and *New Suns 2*. He is a graduate of the University of New Orleans. He was born in Wiesbaden (Germany) and raised in Gaborone (Botswana), Paramaribo (Surinam), and Tunis (Tunisia) as well as Columbia, Maryland. He is also an instructor of popular fiction at the University of Southern Maine's Stone-coast MFA programme. He has been shortlisted for numerous awards, and his debut novel, *The Ballad of Perilous Graves*, is available wherever books are sold.

MARY KENNEY writes critically acclaimed video games, books, and comics. She works at Insomniac Games, where she was on the writing team for *Marvel's Spider-Man: Miles Morales* and *Ratchet & Clank: Rift Apart*, and she was a lead writer on Telltale's The Walking Dead series. Her first book, *Gamer Girls: 25 Women Who Built the Video Game Industry*, was released in July 2022 to glowing reviews from *Kirkus* and *Booklist*. Before making games, she studied in the game design master's programme at New York University, and she teaches narrative design at Indiana University. She was an award-winning journalist with bylines in the *New York Times*, *Salon* and *Kotaku*. When not writing or gaming, she can be found buried in a book, running a tabletop RPG or trying to keep her forest of indoor plants alive.

JARRETT J. KROSOCZKA, known since boyhood as JJK, is the *New York Times* bestselling author/illustrator behind forty-five books for young readers, including his wildly popular Lunch Lady graphic novels, select volumes of the *Star Wars Jedi Academy* series and *Hey, Kiddo*, which was a National Book Award finalist. Krosoczka creates books with humour, heart and deep respect for his young readers – qualities that have made his titles perennial favorites on the bookshelves of homes, libraries and bookstores over the past twenty-two years.

SARAH KUHN is the author of the popular Heroine Complex novels – a series starring Asian American superheroines. She also penned the beloved YA romcoms *I Love You So Mochi* and *From Little Tokyo, With Love*, and a variety of short fiction and comics, including the

DC Comics graphic novels *Shadow of the Batgirl* and *Girl Taking Over: A Lois Lane Story* and the *Star Wars* audiobook original *Doctor Aphra*. Additionally, she was a finalist for both the CAPE (Coalition of Asian Pacifics in Entertainment) New Writers Award and the Astounding Award for Best New Writer. A third-generation Japanese American, she lives in Los Angeles with her husband and an overflowing closet of vintage treasures.

DANNY LORE (they/them) is a queer black writer/editor raised in Harlem and currently based in the Bronx. They've worked in comic and gaming shops since the beginning of time. Most of their writing is contemporary speculative fiction, with the occasional foray into science fiction. Their comic work includes *Queen of Bad Dreams, Bloodline Daughter of Blade, Champions, Multiversity: Teen Justice, Quarter Killer* and more. Their prose fiction has been included in *A Phoenix First Must Burn*, Janelle Monae's *Memory Librarian, Fiyah Lit Mag* and *Unfettered Hexes*, to name a few. They're trying to make 'swaggerpunk' a thing, and Lando seems like a prime example of the term.

SARAH GLENN MARSH is the author of several books for kids and teens including the Reign of the Fallen series and *The Girls Are Never Gone*. When she's not writing fantastical and horrific things, she's usually making art in the pottery studio. She lives in Virginia with her husband, daughter and a small zoo of creatures from some galaxy or another.

KWAME MBALIA is a husband, father, writer, *New York Times* bestselling author, former pharmaceutical metrologist and publisher with Freedom Fire Books, an imprint of Disney-Hyperion. His debut middle-grade novel, *Tristan Strong Punches a Hole in the Sky*, was awarded a Coretta Scott King Author Honor, and it – along with the sequels, *Tristan Strong Destroys the World* and *Tristan Strong Keeps Punching* – is published by Rick Riordan Presents/Disney-Hyperion. He is the co-author of *Last Gate of the Emperor* with Prince Joel Makonnen, from Scholastic Books, and the editor of the No. 1 *New York Times* bestselling anthology *Black Boy Joy*, published by Delacorte Press. A Howard University graduate and a Midwesterner now in North Carolina, he survives on Dad jokes and Cheez-Its.

MARIEKE NIJKAMP is a No. 1 *New York Times* bestselling author of novels, graphic novels and comics, including *This Is Where It Ends, Even If We Break, Critical Role: Vox Machina – Kith & Kin, Hawkeye: Kate Bishop* and *Ink Girls*. Before pursuing her lifelong passion for writing, Marieke majored in philosophy and medieval history. She loves to go on adventures, grow strange fruits and vegetables in her garden, roll dice and daydream.

DANIELLE PAIGE is the *New York Times* bestselling author of the Dorothy Must Die series, the Stealing Snow series and the Wish of the Wicked series. She has also written for DC Comics and Archie Comics. In addition to writing young adult books, she works in the television industry, where she's received a Writers Guild of America Award and was nominated for several Daytime Emmys. She is a graduate of Columbia University and currently lives in New York City. You can find her on X and Instagram.

LAURA POHL is the *New York Times* bestselling author of *The Grimrose Girls* and *The Wicked Remain*. Her debut novel, *The Last 8*, won an International Latino Book Award. She likes writing messages in all caps, never using autocorrect and obsessing (and now writing!) about *Star Wars*. A Brazilian at heart and soul, she lives in São Paulo –

where she graduated in literature from the University of São Paulo and now works as a freelance translator – with a copious amount of Kylo Ren merch and a dog that looks like Baby Yoda.

DANA SCHWARTZ is a television writer and the author of the No. 1 *New York Times* bestselling novel *Anatomy: A Love Story*, and its sequel *Immortality: A Love Story*. She is the host and creator of the history podcast *Noble Blood*. Dana lives in Los Angeles with her husband and their two cats.

TARA SIM is the author of *The City of Dusk*, the Scavenge the Stars duology and the Timekeeper trilogy and can typically be found wandering the wilds of the Bay Area, California. When she's not chasing cats or lurking in bookstores, she writes books about magic, murder and mayhem.

Creative art manager within the Lucasfilm Story Group, PHIL SZOSTAK has worked in conjunction with *Star Wars* art departments since 2008. A graduate of the School of Visual Arts in New York, Szostak ran the JAK Films Art Department on Skywalker Ranch for more than three years before joining the narrative design team on LucasArts's *Star Wars 1313*. He is also the author of *The Art of Star Wars: The Force Awakens* (Abrams, 2015), *The Art of Star Wars: The Last Jedi* (Abrams, 2017), *The Art of Solo: A Star Wars Story* (Abrams, 2018), *The Art of Star Wars: The Rise of Skywalker* (Abrams, 2020), *The Art of Star Wars: The Mandalorian* (Season 1) (Abrams, 2020) and *The Art of Star Wars: The Mandalorian* (Season 2) (Abrams, 2022). He lives in Marin County, California.

SUZANNE WALKER is a Chicago-based writer and editor. She is cocreator of the critically acclaimed and award-nominated graphic novel *Mooncakes*, and her short fiction has been published in *Clarkesworld* and *Uncanny Magazine*. Her non-fiction works have appeared in a diverse array of publications including StarTrek.com and academic anthologies. She is a scholar of medieval Italian longsword; enjoys aerial silks, figure skating and baseball; and aspires to be a real-life Jedi.

HANNAH WHITTEN has been writing to amuse herself since she could hold a pen and, sometime in high school, figured out that what amused her might also amuse others. Her first novel, *For the Wolf*, was an instant *New York Times* bestseller and her subsequent books have gone on to top bestseller lists worldwide. When she's not writing, she's reading, making music or attempting to bake. She lives in an old farmhouse in Tennessee with her husband, children, two cats, a dog, and probably some ghosts.

FRAN WILDE won a 2015 Nebula Award for her first novel, *Updraft*; she completed the trilogy with *Cloudbound* and *Horizon* in 2017. Her debut middle-grade novel *Riverland* won a 2019 Nebula Award and was named an NPR Best Book of 2019. The middle-grade novel *The Ship of Stolen Words* appeared in 2021 and books in her Gemworld series with tordotcom have been nominated for Nebula, Hugo and Locus awards. Wilde's short fiction has appeared in *Asimov's, Tor.com, Beneath Ceaseless Skies, Uncanny Magazine* and multiple year's best collections. Her non-fiction has appeared in the *Washington Post*, the *New York Times*, NPR, *Tor.com* and elsewhere. The managing editor of *The Sunday Morning Transport*, Wilde holds an MFA in poetry and an MA in information architecture and interaction design. She has taught for Vermont College of Fine Arts and has been waiting her whole life to write a Mon Mothma story.

SEAN WILLIAMS is a multi-award-winning author of over sixty books and one hundred and twenty shorter publications for readers of all ages. His original works include series, novels, stories and poems, which have been translated into multiple languages for readers around the world. He has collaborated with other authors, including Garth Nix, makes music as a side hustle, and is Discipline Lead of Creative Writing at Flinders University, South Australia. His novelisation of *Star Wars: The Force Unleashed* was the first computer game tie-in in history to debut at number one on the *New York Times* bestseller list.

ALYSSA WONG writes award-winning fiction, comics and games. Their stories have won the Nebula, World Fantasy and Locus awards and were shortlisted for the Hugo, Bram Stoker and Shirley Jackson awards. Alyssa also writes comics for *Star Wars* (*Star Wars: Doctor Aphra, War of the Bounty Hunters: Boushh #1, Star Wars: Return of the Jedi – Ewoks #1*), Marvel (*Deadpool, Alligator Loki, Iron Fist, Extreme Carnage*) and DC (*Spirit World, Batman: Urban Legends*). They have received multiple GLAAD and Eisner award nominations. Previously, Alyssa worked at Blizzard Entertainment on Overwatch and Overwatch 2. They live in North Carolina.

ABOUT THE TYPE

This book was set in Minion, a 1990 Adobe Originals typeface by Robert Slimbach (b. 1956). Minion is inspired by classical, old-style typefaces of the late Renaissance, a period of elegant, beautiful, and highly readable type designs. Created primarily for text setting, Minion combines the aesthetic and functional qualities that make text type highly readable with the versatility of digital technology.